# Sons of Tundyel: The Prophecy

By A.J. Kilbourn

D1714437

## Prologue

When the yells started, Tanneth knew they had reached the Hall. The shouts quickly grew louder as their attackers drew nearer, and the circle of guards around the Rilso family instinctively moved closer together, their shields slightly overlapping. Swords, already drawn, were gripped more tightly and mouths were set in grim lines.

Tanneth looked over at his wife, and her eyes found his for a brief moment. She smiled sadly at him, then pulled their daughter and granddaughter more tightly against her side. Despite the sadness he could see in her eyes, Tanneth still drew strength from her quiet pride. Straightening his shoulders, he took a deep breath to calm his rattled nerves.

He spoke quietly, but somehow his voice still drowned out the yells and cries ringing out from the city surrounding the Hall. "You have been faithful through unbelievable hardships. When given the chance to run, to save your families and yourselves, you chose to stay. Here you are, standing proudly as a hedge around my family. I thank you for your loyalty to my family, but more importantly to all Tundyel. I pray the Fates hold you close, and may your families receive the blessings you deserve."

Suddenly, the cries outside stopped and everything fell silent. In the stillness a small voice

rang out, its purity a strange contradiction to the
death and destruction surrounding the Hall.

> *"The Fates are holding you close,*
> *though the road is in shadows and the*
> *night seems long,*
> *The Fates are holding you close,*
> *and there in the darkness you can*
> *hear their sweet song-*
> *They tell of your homeland and where*
> *you belong,*
> *The Fates are holding you close."*

Tanneth put his hand on his
granddaughter's shoulder, tears making his eyes
glisten.

The doors slammed open.
Wizard's fire shot into the room,
consuming everything in its path.

Chapter 1

The moment everyone had been waiting for with baited breath had finally arrived. The crowd turned as one when Gavin and Roedan, two of the King's Guard, entered the Hall, following Nedra. They held between them the man chosen to receive the healing. He was a farmer, a man many of the city dwellers had seen occasionally coming to market, but few, if any, could name. He carried himself proudly, knowing that he was being judged by the many eyes watching his progress across the Hall to the platform. He stood unflinching as the Master of the Guard pulled his sword from its scabbard. These people already looked down on him, though being chosen for the healing would earn him some respect. He would give them no more reason to see themselves as better than he. The farmer straightened his shoulders and looked the Guardsman in the eye.

The Master of the Guard wasted no time. In a flash his sword was slicing through the man's stomach. As the farmer fell, a gasp spread through the crowd. Nedra turned to face the Guard standing at the door.

"Bring the girls."

One by one, the young girls entered the Hall. Many cried as they knelt beside the dying man, their tears mingling with his blood as his life spilled to the ground. None lingered long, for none knew what to do for the man. Halfway through the line of girls, a small commotion began near the door.

Nedra stepped onto the platform, trying to see the cause of the interruption. The man on the floor before her had little time left, though his will to live was stronger than most. If the other girls were delayed she would have to heal the man and then have the blood of another spilt in order to continue, and that was something she did not want to do. Not because she didn't want to heal the man, but rather because a life of healing had left her with distaste for violence of any kind, and she had no desire to cause another man pain. Though she had seen this ceremony many times, it never grew easier for her to cause even brief suffering.

The shuffling in the crowd was closer to the platform now, and Nedra moved toward the dying man. On occasion a wife, mother, or sister would not be able to stand by and watch the man dying in front of her. The Ancient Healer feared the same was happening here.

Suddenly a small cry was heard. A tiny girl, dirty and rumpled, had pushed through the crowd. She had been playing with friends outside the Hall, oblivious to the ceremony being played out inside. She had run back to the doorway to find her father as the sun had set and discovered that he was gone. She had then begun pushing her way through the crowd in search of him, eventually making her way to the front, close to the platform. That was when she had seen the dying man and had let out the small cry.

"Popa!"

She rushed forward, dodging the hands of all the people who tried to shield her from the almost lifeless body. Nedra started to kneel beside the child's father, started to give him back the life he was losing, but something stopped her.

There was something different in how the child approached her dying father. Though she could be no more than six or seven, she was not hysterical. She had tears in her eyes, but none fell. Instead she knelt beside her father, kissed his pale cheek, and placed her tiny hands against his wound.

Nedra stopped, shock evident on her face. Taking that as a sign, one of the Guardsmen, Gavin of Kauris, moved forward to pull the child away. He stood frozen in his tracks when Nedra spoke her next three words.

"It is she," the Ancient said quietly, yet somehow her statement was heard throughout the Hall. A murmur of disbelief moved in a wave across all present. This tiny child? She was not old enough for the gift to be revealed in her. Surely she could not be as beautiful as the Healers. She was dirty, her charity dress rumpled. Above all else, she was the daughter of a farmer. Healers were always from good families, not of lowly farmers. This simply wasn't possible.

As they watched the child, however, none present could deny the young girl's power. First the man's lifeblood stopped flowing from the wound. The color that had drained from his face now rushed to refill it, seemingly flowing from the child. Soon, heat radiated from his wound as the skin began to knit back together. Life moved from the girl's dirty hands into her father. His eyes began to open, the dull glaze of death chased away by the light of life. Finally the young girl stopped. Her father sat up, relief apparent on his face for having to no longer struggle with death. His expression quickly gave way to one of confusion and anger as his gaze fell upon his daughter. Why was she here? Why had she been allowed to see him dying? The child was only seven years old. A sight such as this would surely give her nightmares… Then, understanding dawned on him. *She* had done this, his daughter, his baby girl. She was the next Healer. He pulled her into his arms, too shocked to do anything else.

After what seemed like an eternity to the astonished crowd filling the Hall, Nedra spoke again.

"Leave us," she commanded, looking only at the child.

Once people started to leave, they could not seem to pour out into the streets fast enough. Though many had expected the next Healer to hail from Lurn, none had expected this. The streets were filled with silent wonder as men and women quickly made their ways home.

Inside the Hall, Nedra approached father and daughter. The Hall was completely empty, and though they were no longer sitting on the platform where he had lain dying, the man still clung to his child. He had moved away from the slick crimson puddle, more for the sake of his child than himself.

*Can it be?* Nedra thought to herself. *Is it possible that this child is the one?* She paused a few feet from the pair to gather her thoughts. This little one would have to be trained for many years. She was not ready to see the pain and devastation required of a Healer. However, she had just faced the looming promise of her own father's death without any hysterics. Yet she was so young, so fragile. How had one with so little life of her own been able to give life to a grown man? That thought struck Nedra, and she hurried to see if the child was alright.

Even before she touched the girl's hand, Nedra knew the child had caused herself no harm. The girl's life still shone brightly in eyes that met Nedra's own confidently. She struggled slightly in her father's arms, and he reluctantly lowered her to stand beside him. He could not make himself let go completely, though, and rested his hand on his daughter's shoulder.

In a voice surprisingly mature for one so young, the girl addressed Nedra. "Are you the Ancient?" Nedra nodded, her face serious. She could not hide the amusement in her eyes, though. Nedra knew she was called the Ancient throughout the Kingdom of Tundyel, but none had ever addressed her as such. "I am Syndria," the child continued, "and this is my father Jamis." She stopped then, obviously waiting for Nedra to speak.

"You may call me Nedra. Syndria, do you understand what you just did?" This time it was the child's turn to nod. "And do you know what it means?"

"Yes. I am a Healer." With the obvious stated, so matter of factly that one got the impression the girl had known her whole life that this day would come, Syndria walked to the window to look outside. The streets were empty now and darkness had fallen, leaving the view rather uninspiring, so Syndria turned back toward Nedra and her father.

"I have told Syndria of the Healers all her life," Jamis told Nedra, his pride in his daughter evident. "Before she sleeps, her favorite tales are those of the True Wizards and the Healers of old."

"Where is her mother? I would speak with you both of Syndria's future," Nedra asked Jamis. Before he could answer, his daughter spoke up.

"My mother died soon after I was born," she stated, walking back to the two adults. Standing in front of Nedra, she held out her arm. "She gave me this," she said, touching a dirty bracelet circling her arm. "It protects me."

Nedra's breath caught. "May I see it?"

Syndria smiled, obviously proud of her prized possession. Looking around the Hall she spied a pitcher of water left over from the feast which had taken place before the ceremony. She took off her bracelet, dunked it in the water, and scrubbed away the grime. Shaking off the droplets, Syndria walked back to her father's side and handed the now gleaming silver bracelet to Nedra.

The bracelet was simple: a pattern of two leaves touching tip to tip followed by two with interlocking stems. The silver was strong despite its delicate appearance. Syndria was not a delicate child and she had not been easy on the bracelet. She wore it while playing and while helping her father on the farm, and yet the bracelet had lasted.

Nedra fingered the silver leaves. *Could it be?*

\*\*\*\*\*\*\*\*\*\*\*\*\*\*\*\*\*

He closed his eyes, letting the colors swirl around him and through him. His mind relaxed, opening wide to the wisdom flowing through the night sky. Opening his eyes, he looked to the stars. For the last decade he had been reading the sky, waiting for the sign that that world was about to change. He had never known what it would be or when it would come, but he knew that one day he would see it.

Tonight, the sky was still. The colors he had felt earlier with his eyes closed were gone and all was quiet. He stared at the sky for hours, hoping for something to be revealed. Sighing, he finally turned to go back inside. He had been waiting for this, never giving up hope. Tonight, however, the stillness of the night seemed to be tearing at that hope, threatening to devour it forever.

He had watched the Kingdom of Tundyel slowly fading under the rule of Simann for much too long. With the Healers under his power, none could touch the man. It seemed the King had everyone fooled. No one in the kingdom so much as questioned him. He had no true powers of his own, yet with the help of the Healers and his Wizards the King seemed able to control everything. True, there had been no major discontent since his reign had begun, but that peace had not come without a price. The people of Tundyel, though, knew nothing of the great costs of peace. Most saw only a just, kind King, the man whose reign brought peace and contentment. Those who saw the truth, who dared speak out against Simann, were imprisoned, tortured, and executed.

With one last glance up at the night sky, he started to go inside. *Maybe tomorrow night will bring the sign. Maybe things will still change soon.* As he took the first step down, something in the southern sky caught his eye. It was faint, but it was there: a golden shimmer slowly moved north across the sky, barely visible to the man standing in his doorway. No one but a True Wizard would have been able to see it.

It was all beginning.

Chapter 2

Twelve years later

Syndria knelt beside the man dying on the cold damp floor, placing her hands on his back. His flesh had been torn many times by the whip and now looked like the mangled prey of a hungry mountain lion. He had broken ribs and a broken arm, and Syndria knew she had very little time to bring him back from his struggle with death. For a moment before she began letting her life flow into his still form, Syndria considered waiting just a minute longer. If she waited, the man would die here deep underground, lying on the cold stone. She wished she could grant him that peace, but the King had demanded that he be healed.

Again.

Slowly, the torn flesh began to knit together. The man began to moan as the life flowed back into his body. He was no longer hanging on the brink of death and would soon regain consciousness. Syndria closed her eyes and concentrated on the pain. All Healers could give life, heal wounds, but Syndria was the only one who could *take* pain. At first she had thought it was normal, just part of being a Healer, so she had never mentioned it to Nedra. Syndria had wanted so much to please the Ancient, to make her proud. The other Healers had shown their displeasure with the fact that one so young would require so much of Nedra's time before she was ready to serve the King. Besides that, the child was born of a farmer. Though young, Syndria's pride was strong and her will was even stronger. The child had decided that in order to earn the respect of the women she could not show any weakness. Thankfully, Nedra had started Syndria's training with scrapes and burns, gradually working up to the life-threatening injuries. Over the years, she had learned to withstand even the most excruciating pain, like that of the man before her on the ground. It had been years before she had realized her gift was different.

The man would not die now, so Syndria stopped the flow of life coursing from her body into the man. She opened herself to his pain, felt it start in her fingertips and radiate up her arms. She steeled herself, knowing that if she lost her concentration for even an instant the pain of every whiplash, every slap and kick, would leap from her and re-enter the man. He would feel an entire day's torture hit him at once. The pain shot through Syndria's body, vibrating off her very bones. Every muscle in her body tried to contract at once, paralyzing the Healer. Finally, it ended. Syndria blinked away the tears in her eyes, the only visible sign of what she had experienced. She concentrated again on the man's wounds and saw that the man's body had relaxed after losing the pain that had wracked his frame. Once the flesh on his back was knitted together, Syndria moved her hands along his ribs and arm, quickly mending the broken bones. The man opened his eyes as Syndria finished.

Leaning close to his ear, Syndria murmured, "I am sorry." The man turned his face slowly toward her, his sad eyes meeting hers.

"I do not blame you, Healer," he whispered. "What choice do you have?" With that he stood, determined to face the Guardsmen proudly. His clothes were torn and bloody, but in that moment he seemed more like royalty to Syndria than King Simann ever had. Syndria stood from where she had still been kneeling beside the man's blood. She slowly made her way toward the door, knowing that when she knocked the guards stationed outside would unlock the door and she would leave. Soon after, the man inside the room would be tortured once again.

"Mistress," the man called to her quietly, his voice almost musical despite the knowledge of what he was about to face. She turned back toward him, her eyes lowered. "Might I know your name?"

The first time she tried to speak, her voice failed her. Taking a deep breath she met his gaze. "Syndria, sir."

"Syndria," he repeated, then smiled. He had been tortured to the brink of death for three days now, yet he smiled. "Now I know who to thank for healing me when I leave this place."

Syndria stared at the man in front of her. He was locked in a tiny room guarded at all times. He was beaten and spit on, mocked and ridiculed. Yet somehow he still clung to the faint hope that he would leave someway other than by the crematory. "And you, sir? What is your name, that I might know who to expect?"

The man's gaze drifted away from Syndria, toward the door. "I am Paodin."

*********************

The next morning, Syndria woke early to the sound of someone quietly tapping on her door. Pulling herself out of bed, Syndria reached for her gown and slid it over her head. She opened the door to Magen, a young girl whom Syndria had befriended who worked in the kitchen. The thirteen year old entered quickly, breathless and wide-eyed.

"Oh, you'll never, never believe it! Nobody knows how he did it, but it's all over the castle!" Magen exclaimed quickly, scarcely pausing to take a breath. Syndria knew the girl would keep rattling on like this, never getting to the point. It was how she told every story. Normally she would have enjoyed the girl's endless chatter, but not *this* early in the morning.

"Magen, who did what?" she prodded, guiding her friend to the edge of the bed. Magen sat while Syndria cinched her silk belt around her waist and then tied back her raven hair with a matching blue ribbon.

Magen was nearly bouncing on the small bed, she was so excited. "The man from the…" She started to say dungeon but stopped herself. The King allowed no one to say what it was for fear his loyal subjects would not approve and become less loyal. "…from the *lower west hall* escaped! The Guards have been searching for *hours* but they can't find him anywhere in the castle!"

Syndria was lost in her own thoughts and didn't hear the rest of Magen's story. *Paodin had escaped?* It was impossible! Surely Magen must have heard a rumor. No one had ever escaped Tundyel Castle. Her thoughts were interrupted and Magen's story confirmed when someone else began pounding on Syndria's door.

"Beg your pardon, Mistress Syndria, but we must search your quarters," the Guardsman Yaldren bowed his head slightly when Syndria opened the door. "A man from the lower west hall has gone missing, and we are commanded to search every inch of the castle." The big man was almost apologizing and Syndria did not wish to make him any more uncomfortable.

"Of course, Master Yaldren. Magen and I were just leaving. You are more than welcome to search my quarters." She stepped aside, letting the Guard into her room. Motioning for Magen to follow, Syndria slipped into the hallway. "All that I ask is that you close the door when you leave. I wish you luck in finding whom you seek." With that she turned, Magen right on her heels.

Through the course of the day, Syndria heard more of Paodin's escape. After she had left, the Wizards had been sent in to torture the man further. The King was convinced Paodin knew of some plan to overthrow him, but the physical torture had done nothing to make the man speak. The five Wizards specialized in torture of the mind and spirit, so King Simann was confident they would succeed in making Paodin reveal the plan. If not, this time the Healer would not be called in to bring him back from the brink of death. However, something had gone awry.

The five Wizards entered the stone room, the door slamming shut behind them. They stood facing the prisoner, filling the small room with a menacing presence. The Healer had left only moments before and the Wizards expected to see the man cowering in a corner or begging for mercy like all the others. To see him standing proudly in the center of the room threw the Wizards. Then he spoke.

"If you are brave enough, hear me. I am Paodin, a son of Tundyel. You and your king claim to serve our kingdom, yet you torture and kill its citizens. You fear nothing and no one, convinced you are invincible behind your stone walls and magic spells." The wizards let him speak, convinced this speech would be the last words of a dying man. "You think you are all powerful, that none can stand against you. Stories of the defeat of the True Wizards have been passed down through your Order for centuries and in your ignorance you believe the lies. I swear to you, your self-righteousness will be your downfall." Having finished all he wanted to say, Paodin looked directly at the Wizards and took a deep breath.

With that, he was gone.

The Wizards were seized with panic. Immediately they cast a barrier spell about the castle, intent on trapping the man inside. They then searched the air inside the small underground room. They were not searching for anything physical, but instead looking for evidence of the spell that had been used. The prisoner had disappeared before their very eyes--magic had to be involved. All five Wizards closed their eyes simultaneously, focusing on the colors in the air. An entire kaleidoscope of shapes and colors was present in the room, swirling through the air and tangling together, most remnants of the Healer's gift. Hidden in the midst of the tightest coil was a different kind of magic, one none of the Wizards had expected to find, one that took them a bit longer to identify. There, woven into the deepest part of the Healer's gift, was the unmistakable magic of a True Wizard.

*********************

The True Wizards had never served one man. They chose the side of the just, sometimes with the King and sometimes against him. When Simann became king he had tried to force the True Wizards into his service. When they had refused, King Simann had ordered them all killed. During that time he had captured all the Healers in the kingdom and brought them to the castle. Simann was young when he became king, only thirty. Through the Healers he still looked youthful, as if he had aged only ten years in the past forty. Once he had killed all the True Wizards, King Simann had no trouble finding wizards who would serve him. They were not as powerful as the Wizards of old, but Simann didn't mind their lesser powers because he could control them.

Before King Simann, one family had ruled Tundyel for many generations. The Rilso family had their share of bad kings, but for the biggest part of the family's reign they had been fair. Simann's father had gathered an army loyal to him, planning to wipe out the Rilso family and become king himself. A great war had broken out which lasted for ten long years. Thousands of lives had been lost in the bloody civil war before the Rilso family had been driven from the castle. Simann's father Daimen had been fatally wounded in the war, so once the castle was taken Simann was crowned king.

It hadn't taken long for Simann to become greedy. Unchecked power made him crave even more control, and before long, citizens of Tundyel had started to grumble. Small groups formed in cities and villages across the kingdom, made up of people who wanted to put the Rilso family back on the throne. That was when King Simann had confronted the True Wizards and captured the Healers. He knew that he would never have ultimate control over the kingdom as long as the citizens of Tundyel saw them as authorities, so he killed the Wizards and moved the Healers into the castle.

In the years since the True Wizards had been destroyed the kingdom had remained peaceful. That peace, however, was only on the surface. If King Simann was powerful enough to kill the True Wizards, the citizens of Tundyel did not see any way they could possibly defeat him. There had still been people who opposed Simann but through the service of his Royal Wizards he had always managed to track them down. He would have them brought back to the castle and put in the dungeon where they would be tortured by the Guardsmen, then healed day after day by the Healers only to be tortured again. King Simann promised them life and freedom if his prisoners would swear allegiance to him. In the end, though, they were all killed no matter what they swore. After all, it would not do to have them telling others they had been tortured.

The next ten years after the execution of the True Wizards had passed by uneventfully. There were no uprisings, no real threats. However, occasionally a small contingency would be found that was unhappy with the King's rule. Most of the groups Simann's Wizards discovered were those still loyal to the Rilso family, so King Simann had decided to put an end to the family once and for all, convinced that destroying the family would end all opposition to his rule. Years ago, Simann had secretly razed the city of Dren, the refuge of the Rilso family, killing everyone. However, he later learned of a daughter by marriage who had been gone during the raid visiting friends in Valgrin. It didn't take long for Simann's Wizards to track her down, fully intending to kill the last remaining member of the family and eliminate the threat. The young bride Laidren, however, was with child. King Simann decided the young woman and her child could be used to his advantage.

Instead of killing Laidren, he had her brought to the castle where she remained until the birth of her child. King Simann planned to raise the child as his own, showing the kingdom how merciful their ruler was. After all, who would dare take his enemy's child into his own home? He would tell of how he found Laidren wandering and took her in, how she had died in childbirth, and how he had taken her child for his own.

Simann knew that even through the Healers he could not live forever. Daily he felt the effects of the decades he had seen. One day he would pass the throne on to the child born of the Rilso family yet reared in his own image, living on through the first years of the next ruler's reign. Only when he was certain of his heir's abilities would he command the Healers to stop lengthening his life. Then, his name would be sure to live forever, even if he couldn't do so himself.

The King took every precaution to keep Laidren safe and healthy until the day of the birth. She was guarded at all times and looked after by the Healers. However, fate would not allow his plan to be fulfilled. As was custom in Tundyel, only one woman could attend a birth. To do otherwise would be to draw too much attention from the Fates, undoubtedly bringing about the death of the child. King Simann chose the Ancient Healer to watch over the birth, knowing she would be the best choice to be there if something went awry.

Laidren's labor was long and difficult. Her pain-filled cries could be heard throughout the castle for an entire day. Nedra was a constant presence in the birthing room, doing all she could to comfort the young woman. Finally, near dawn, the cries coming from the small room changed from ones of pain to those of anguish, and then eventually fell silent. Hearing word from the Guardsmen that the birth was over, King Simann was waiting at the door when Nedra emerged carrying two tiny, still bundles. Her tears were not joyful ones, and as she began to speak Laidren's soft sobs could be heard through the open door.

"My King," Nedra spoke softly, "the lady bore twins, yet neither could I save. They were dead inside the womb, and not even I can work those miracles." Quietly she stood facing King Simann's scornful gaze.

Disgustedly, the King pulled aside the blankets and looked at two matching still faces. "Dispose of them immediately!" he commanded, brushing past Nedra into the room. "Guardsmen," he shouted, looking at the small weeping figure lying in the bed, "kill this woman. She has failed her King." With that he left, ignoring Nedra's pleas that the tiny babies be given a proper burial with their mother.

## Chapter 3

"It is impossible!" Euroin shouted, pacing in front of the blazing fire. "*Those* Wizards are all gone and have been for half a century. That…that mere *boy* in there could not be one of…*those.*" He almost spit the words out. A dark light shone fiercely in his eyes as he stormed across the room.

"If he was one of those Wizards," Alek said, absently running his fingers through his long silver hair, "why would he have allowed himself to be tortured by the Guards? He was brought back from death three times--why go through it all?"

Osidius sat staring into the fire, gazing deep into the dancing light. "He was waiting," he said calmly, instantly getting the full attention of the others.

"Waiting for what, Osidius?" Uylti questioned. "If he had disappeared the first time the Guardsmen had touched him we still would have known him to be a Wizard."

"Perhaps he was waiting for us." Ilcren spun his heavy mug on the table. "He wanted us to see for ourselves that he is a True Wizard." Ilcren was the first of the Wizards to speak the title aloud.

The mug shot out of Ilcren's hands, shattering against the stone fireplace. Euroin spun to face the table where the younger man was sitting. "It is impossible," he snarled, almost nose to nose with Ilcren. "Those Wizards are dead!"

"If they are dead," Osidius interrupted, "how do you explain the old magic being present, Euroin?"

"How do *you* know if it was the old magic?" Euroin challenged, stepping in front of Osidius. "How do any of you know? You have never seen the old magic. You were just tricked! He cannot be a Wizard any different than us. If the four of you would stop being such old *fools*, believing in the impossible, and start searching the kingdom, we would find that imposter and put an end to his lies!" Euroin stormed around Osidius's one-room cottage, knocking over anything in his path. His black cloak billowed around him, looking every bit like a thundercloud ready to burst. A dangerous light threatened to shoot from his eyes, ready to destroy anything--or anyone--in his way. Euroin had served King Simann for his entire reign, longer than any of the others, and very seldom did the other four challenge him. Tonight, though, Osidius spoke up. The newest of the Royal Wizards, he had only come to the castle ten years before.

"Enough, old man!" he shouted, jumping to his feet. His dark hair hung loose around his face and shoulders, giving Osidius the look of a vagabond despite his rich crimson cloak. When Euroin turned to face the newcomer, his look incredulous, Osidius continued. "You saw the same thing we saw! The man vanished before our very eyes and left no trace of a Wizard's spell. You saw the magic the same as we did, hidden within that of the young Healer. What are you going to do next, tell us that the girl has use of the old magic? If so, it is you who are the fool, not us!" The dancing flames that had been reflected in his eyes while Osidius had stared into the fire were still visible as he faced Euroin. When Euroin closed his eyes, the three Wizards silently watching the exchange almost expected to see his powers unleashed on the newest member of their Order. A moment later, however, Euroin simply opened his eyes. The dangerous light present just moments before had faded, replaced by a Wizard's ever-present dull gleam. He sighed, looking as if he had just aged ten years.

"What do you suggest, *old man*?" Euroin asked Osidius, his voice as haggard as his looks had suddenly become.

Osidius studied the other Wizards before he spoke. "The prisoner spoke of the walls and magic of Tundyel Castle, so there must be a plan to attack both fronts. We must gather all the kingdom's wizards, no matter how weak their gifts, and bring them to the castle." He trailed off and Alek picked up the train of thought.

"If all the wizards are here, within the walls of the castle, the prisoner's insurgent group will be able to attack only the walls. Our castle is a mighty fortress. None will be able to breach it. The Guardsmen have two thousand men at their disposal to defend our walls who can be ready at a moment's notice. We will go to the King and tell him of the threat." Alek stood, ready to do just as he had said. It was Uylti who stopped him.

"King Simann wishes for the castle to remain peaceful. We will tell him to increase the guard on the walls, but we must find the group with which our prisoner associates himself and destroy the threat. If he does have use of the old magic, we will not be able to find them using only our minds. We must travel the kingdom physically."

"We will each search a different district," Euroin announced, reassuming his role of leadership in the Order. "Since my powers are strongest I will remain in Rues to protect our King. Uylti will travel to Nethien, Ilcren to Sephon, Alek to Finley, and Osidius will search Meinsley. Now," he said, heading toward the door, "let us approach our King."

Chapter 4

Syndria knocked on Nedra's door but did not wait for the Ancient to acknowledge her before stepping inside. The older woman was sitting beside her window, watching the preparations being made for the Wizards' journeys. Her gaze never left the courtyard below as she spoke.

"Come in, child. You are welcome." Syndria, not waiting for an invitation, had already crossed the room and now knelt at the Healer's knees.

"Nedra, something troubles me. Yesterday it was I who healed the man who escaped. Did I do wrong? Should I have left some of his injury? I do not understand--"

"Child, would you pleasure the Ancient with a walk? It is stuffy in here. I would like to be in the sun," Nedra interrupted Syndria. Taking the young Healer's hand she stood.

"Of course, Ancient," Syndria smiled. Ever since their first meeting she had called Nedra the Ancient, and the title soon became as dear to her as "Popa" had always been. As they started to leave the room Syndria glanced out the window and saw the four Wizards leaving. She considered asking Nedra where they were going in such a hurry, but thought better of it. Over the years she had learned that when the Ancient suggested a walk she had something on her mind and would not speak until she was ready.

The two Healers walked slowly through the castle halls, their appearances strikingly different. Nedra was tall and powerfully built despite her age. Her long white hair was tightly braided and hung past her waist. Her skin was tanned, her eyes a deep green. She carried herself proudly, gracefully, and always appeared to be dancing as she moved. Her slender hands hung peacefully at her sides while Syndria's were constantly moving. While she walked, the young Healer brushed at her gown or fidgeted with her hair, and her hands flew when she spoke. Unlike Nedra, Syndria was petite and appeared fragile. Her shining black hair, never in the customary braid of the Healers, made her alabaster skin seem even whiter. Her bright blue eyes stood out in stark contrast to her black hair and fair skin.

The two walked through the castle doors into the courtyard below Nedra's window. It was empty now, the Wizards gone, and the Healers strolled among the beautiful flowers starting to bloom in the early spring sunshine. Finally Nedra spoke.

"Think about the man from yesterday. What can you tell me about him, Syndria?"

Syndria hesitated for a moment. What *had* she noticed? She had been asking herself the same question but with no result. She could not put her finger in the one thing she somehow knew was important. "I don't know, Ancient. He was a prisoner, a man in pain. What would have been any different about him?" *About Paodin*, she added silently.

"I know you, child," Nedra scolded softly. "Do not lie to me."

"He was different," the girl finally admitted. "He seemed almost…royal." She spoke the word no louder than a whisper, afraid King Simann would somehow overhear.

Nedra looked at Syndria for a long time, studying the young Healer. Finally she moved away, making her way to a stone bench in the midst of the flowers. Syndria followed in silence. Nedra sat down, taking Syndria's hand as she did so.

Lightly touching the silver bracelet the girl wore at all times, Nedra spoke. "Your mother said this would protect you. No matter what challenges lie ahead, remember her promise."

\*\*\*\*\*\*\*\*\*\*\*\*\*\*\*\*\*\*\*

Paodin huddled in the dark, wishing for a fire but knowing it would lead his trackers straight to him. He still did not understand what had happened the day before. One moment he had been facing the five Wizards in a small room deep underground, taking a deep breath in preparation for his inevitable death. The next he had been outside the castle walls, the words, "*Remember those who have helped you*" echoing in his mind. He had told the Healer Syndria that he would leave the castle, but at the time it had been more for her sake than his own. He had wanted her to know that it was possible, that one did not have to always be a slave to Simann. She could have a life serving the people of Tundyel as the Healers of old had done instead of bowing to the King's every whim. He had thought his own fate sealed in that tiny room, but one with powers such as hers would be a tremendous asset in the fight against Simann's cruelty.

How had he gotten out of the castle? The question rolled through his mind, blocking out all other thoughts. In his speech he had talked about the True Wizards, but how could it be possible? No one had seen nor heard from a True Wizard since Simann's hunt centuries before. Of course, there had always been stories--Paodin's own father had often told him tales of the True Wizard who had escaped Simann's grasp and hid out somewhere in Tundyel waiting for the time to be right to destroy the King. It was said in prophecy that one day the True Wizard would put the rightful King back on the throne, an heir of Rilso. That seemed impossible to Paodin since the family had been destroyed twenty years ago, but he was not one to doubt prophecy, especially a prophecy his father had deemed so important.

Paodin had been raised by his father Audon in the village of Gelci, on of the smallest cities in Tundyel. Like many children throughout the kingdom, Paodin had never known his mother; she had died in childbirth. In the time before Simann a Healer had always been nearby, close enough to attend to a woman in hard labor. For too long now the Healers had been forced to serve the King, leaving the citizens of Tundyel on their own.

Unlike most men would have done, Paodin's father had never taken another wife and had raised his son alone. Audon was a good man. Though not wealthy, he had not been poor. He was a carpenter and traveled the kingdom selling his goods and services to all of Tundyel. From the very beginning Paodin had traveled with his father and had seen almost every inch of Tundyel. Tonight he silently thanked his father for that childhood spent atop a cart. It would serve him well as he fled from the castle, especially since he could not return home. The men of Gelci had been planning a campaign against Simann for years now. If Paodin went back to Gelci now, the Wizards would surely find the group and kill them all. He could not allow that to happen, so tonight he was headed south into the district of Meinsley.

\*\*\*\*\*\*\*\*\*\*\*\*\*\*\*\*\*\*\*\*

He watched the sky, certain that things had

finally been set into motion. Twelve years earlier the golden sign had moved across the sky, marking the beginning of the prophecy's fulfillment. Soon he would witness Simann being driven off the throne by the true heir, a descendant of Rilso.

The months, or even years, ahead would prove difficult, of that he was certain, but he had waited years for this time to come. The true heir would need help in defeating Simann, help the old wizard knew he could give. First, though, he had to find the true King, a daunting task. For more than a decade now he had spent countless hours studying the prophecy and the sign he had seen in the heavens, hoping for some insight. Many times he had thought he finally understood the prophecy only to watch events take a different turn. This time, though, he was convinced. Watching the sky tonight, he waited for confirmation. Soon he saw it. Glittering brightly in the black sky was the gold light he had seen from his doorstep twelve years before. This time it was visible to all, though few if any would understand its meaning. To the man staring intently into the night sky, however, the meaning was clear. The heir of Rilso would come from the south.

*********************

Syndria lay in her bed, staring into the darkness. It was late, probably only a few hours before dawn, but she had not been to sleep. She had noticed something different about Paodin, but though she had been trying for hours now she could not recall what it would have been. For a while she had considered the possibility that she had met him before but soon brushed aside those thoughts. She had lived in seclusion with Nedra throughout her adolescent years and doubted she could remember him from her childhood. Besides, the more she thought about it the more Syndria realized that a mere familiarity was not what she had noticed about the strange prisoner. It had been something physical, an object of some kind.

Syndria closed her eyes, trying to picture the proud man who had stood to face what Syndria had thought would be his death. His clothes had been tattered and stained with blood but the Healer had still been able to tell that they were the clothes of a tradesman, probably a smithy of some kind. He had probably carried a sword as did many men of Tundyel, but it would have been taken from him when he was first captured by the guards. Beyond his clothes, Syndria could not picture anything else about the man who had asked her name. That was what stood out most in her mind, for no one she had healed had ever asked anything about her. That, and the fact that he had not blamed her for what she had done.

She did not like what she was forced to do to the prisoners, healing them solely for further torture, but it was a price she had to pay since she refused to take part in Simann's daily ritual of healing. Syndria despised the man she was forced to obey, but only Nedra knew of the girl's deep feelings. The wise woman had put Syndria in charge of healing the prisoners, convincing Simann it would be best for only one Healer to see what happened deep below the surface. Though it tore at the girl's heart to know she was allowing the prolonged torture of the men in the dungeon, she could not have lived with herself knowing she was lengthening the reign of such a cruel man. Instead, Syndria told herself she was at least doing what little she could by easing the pain of the suffering men and took some comfort in that.

Syndria was stirred from her thoughts by the light of day at her window and someone at her door. Sighing when she realized she had still not figured out the difference in Paodin, Syndria stood and reached for her white gown. It took a moment of confusion at not finding the dress draped over the chair before Syndria realized she had gone to bed in the garment. Sighing once again, she unhooked the latch and opened the door to see Nedra standing before her. Before she could speak, the older woman had quickly stepped into the room and pulled the door shut behind her. Startled, Syndria lost her balance for a moment when the Ancient brushed by and she stumbled backward into the room. She had never seen Nedra like this, visibly shaken for some reason. Nedra's eyes darted around the small room and she wrung her hands nervously.

"You must leave," she whispered urgently, moving toward the window. Much to Syndria's surprise, Nedra tore the thin blue drape from its hooks and threw it on the bed. She then pulled a gown from Syndria's dresser and tossed it on top of the drape, adding to that a pair of shoes. Syndria had taken supper in her quarters the night before, but in being too distracted to eat she had left most of the food on its tray. Spying the uneaten food, Nedra shook open the cloth napkin lying on the silver tray, placed the biscuit and meat on it, and tied it into a small bundle. Tossing that on the torn drapes as well, Nedra gathered the meager amount and tied the blue drape as she had the napkin. Shoving the pack at a stunned Syndria, Nedra started to push the girl toward the door.

"That will never do," she muttered, taking in the girl's appearance from head to toe. "You will be recognized before you even leave the gates." Looking around once more she saw the knife lying on the silver food tray. "This will be painful, but it must be done," she told the girl, spinning her around and gathering her thick black hair in one hand. She sawed off most of Syndria's silken locks, leaving Syndria with her mouth gaping.

Syndria tried to speak, tried to ask Nedra what was happening, but he was in too much shock to form the words. Instead, she stood dumbly as Nedra pulled the dark green blanket off the bed and, using the knife to start, tore it in half. One half she tied around the bundle she had thrust into Syndria's arms, and the other half she knotted about the girl's tiny waist.

"Go now," she ordered, opening the door and pushing Syndria into the empty hall. "I will meet you at the stables in Caron by this time tomorrow. Until then, do not speak with anyone. I will explain everything when I next see you." When Syndria still stood frozen, Nedra gave her a shove. "Go, child!"

*******************

"Nedra has nothing to worry about," Syndria muttered, wiping her face. "Even she wouldn't recognize me now." The road from Castle Tundyel to Caron was long and dusty, and despite the spring breeze Syndria was sweating. Each time she wiped her brow, the smudge left behind made her skin look less and less like the creamy complexion the girl was know for, and with her hair cut off there was no chance of anyone mistaking her for a Healer. Syndria had been walking for almost half a day now without stopping. She had no idea what she was running from, but judging by Nedra's haste back in Syndria's quarters it was something she couldn't take lightly. So Syndria trudged on, never making eye contact with anyone. She was getting hungry but didn't dare stop to eat. In another hour or two she would reach Caron--her meal could wait until she reached the stables.

As Syndria drew nearer to the city gates of Caron, she noticed a nervousness in the crowd leaving the city. Though she was tempted to ask someone what was happening, she was more concerned about drawing attention to herself. From the snippets of conversation she caught occasionally, there were Guardsmen stationed at the gate checking each person who entered the city. No one seemed to know who they were searching for, but Syndria knew that if Nedra's concern was any indication she was soon going to face the first challenge of her journey.

She approached to gate nervously, clutching her small bundle tightly to her chest. Though no one in the city would recognize her as a Healer, if the Guardsmen posted at the gate were part of the Royal Guard they would know her the moment she spoke. And even if the Guards weren't ones she knew, what name would she give when they questioned her? What would she say was her reason for being in Caron? Syndria's palms began sweating. She had no answers for the questions she knew she would face soon, and there was no other way into Caron. She had to think of something-- fast.

"State your business in Caron."

Syndria swallowed hard, trying to delay the inevitable. She didn't recognize the man's voice, but she still feared being found out. She had never been good at lying even when she had a reason, and now she didn't even know why she needed to lie. What was she going to say?

"Your business?" the guard repeated, his voice betraying his agitation at this girl who was taking up too much of his time.

"My business?" Syndria stammered. "I-- I'm just coming back from--"

"Kierney, what took you so long?" The young girl speaking took Syndria's arm as she stepped in front of the guard. We've been waiting all morning for you to get here. Momma will be so excited to see you at last." She rattled on until the guard interrupted.

"Take your reunion somewhere else. You are blocking the gate." Turning to the person behind Syndria, he almost knocked the two girls out of the street. Before she knew what was happening, Syndria was being pulled down the main street of Caron by a pretty little girl who was calling her Kierney.

"I'm sorry," Syndria murmured quietly,

leaning toward the girl, "but I'm afraid you have the wrong person. My name in not Kierney."

The girl laughed out loud, startling Syndria. "Oh, Kierney! I can't believe you!" She playfully bumped against Syndria, treating her like they were the best of friends. Soon Syndria was being steered toward a small white-washed cottage with a yard full of children. As the two girls stepped through the open gate, a tiny blonde girl caught sight of them.

"Lyddie!" she called, jumping up from the blue flowers she had been picking. She ran toward the two girls at the gate and leapt into Lyddie's arms, squealing with delight. Hearing her, three other children came running. The young girl, Syndria's rescuer at the gate, knelt laughing as the four children all tried to hug her at once, almost knocking her over.

"My goodness! You would think I'd been gone for months by the way you are all treating me." Laughing, she pulled her skirt out of eight tiny hands as she stood. "This is your cousin Kierney. Why don't you all stay out here for a little while so we can go talk to Momma. Afterward I'll come play with you. How does that sound?" Four little voices cheered as Lyddie led Syndria toward the door.

Once inside, Syndria tried once again to tell the young girl she had made a mistake. Lyddie just laughed and called for her mother, telling "cousin Kierney" how excited everyone was to have her there.

A small woman, not much taller that Lyddie, came bustling into the room, wiping her hands on her apron. "My dear, you must be exhausted!" she exclaimed, taking Syndria's hands in her own as she turned to her daughter. "Lydia, dear heart, would you go heat a bath for your cousin? She has been walking for hours and I'm sure she would like to freshen up before supper." When the girl left the room, the smiling woman drew closer to Syndria and bowed her head slightly before speaking.

"Forgive me, Mistress, but I could not endanger my daughter further by telling her your true identity. The Ancient sent word to my husband telling us of the dangers you face. I pray you may rest easily with us for your stay in Caron. You are welcome in our home."

Syndria nodded to the woman, this woman who knew all about a danger the young Healer could not even begin to grasp. Had she angered the King? She started to ask the kind woman what danger she spoke of but Nedra's warning to speak to no one rang in her ears and she changed her mind, asking instead the lady's name.

"I am Tamara and my husband is Sir Lawrence of the Council. We are--" As Lyddie came back into the front room, Tamara's voice instantly changed back into the sunny, cheerful tone she had used when Syndria first came in with her daughter. "--so glad you are finally here to visit us! Your uncle will be so pleased to see his brother's eldest daughter. It has been so long," she smiled, hugging the Healer. "Now hurry along and bathe while I finish preparing supper. Lydia," she called after her daughter, "try to keep the little ones form getting filthy. Supper will be ready by the time your father gets home." With that she turned back to the kitchen, leaving an awe struck Syndria standing alone in the main room of the cottage.

Syndria cleaned up quickly and changed into the clean white gown Nedra had packed for her early that morning. She wanted to have a chance to speak with Tamara before the family ate their evening meal together. She started to look for a hair ribbon before she realized that her hair was now much too short to be tied back, and the thought threatened to bring tears to her eyes.

"Don't be a child!" Syndria admonished herself. "You have seen suffering and death everyday for twenty years--*hair* is nothing to get upset about." Straightening her shoulders, the young Healer quickly pushed the thought aside and made her way through the cozy cottage to the toasty kitchen where Tamara was cleaning off the large plank table.

"Tamara," Syndria began, but the smiling woman interrupted her.

"Call me Aunt, Mistress, and I will call you Kierney while you are here in our home. I will have my children know nothing of your true identity." To Syndria, Tamara's interruption sounded much like a warning, as if she was afraid the Healer would willingly put the children's safety in jeopardy.

"Of course, Aunt," the young Healer smiled, trying to reassure the woman who was apparently risking so much to protect someone she did not know. "I appreciate all you are doing for me. Tomorrow I shall leave, and your life here will return to normal. I would like to ask something more of you, though. Why are you doing this? I do not wish to cause your family harm, and I fear that my presence here could be doing just that."

Tamara sat at the table and motioned for Syndria to do the same. Once the Healer was seated beside her, Tamara leaned in and began speaking quietly.     "The prisoner you healed last escaped from the castle, as I am sure you know. What you do not know, however, is that the Wizard Euroin went before the King with the idea that you had something to do with his escape."

Syndria interrupted, "How can that be?" Her words shocked Syndria--the Ancient had told her none of this! "I left the dungeon before

Paodin's escape. Why, I even passed by the Wizards as I left the dungeon!" She caught herself afterwards, realizing she had not only revealed the prisoner's name but had also said dungeon instead of "the west hall." She started to correct herself but decided against it. If King Simann was already convinced of her involvement with the escape of a prisoner it wouldn't matter what else she added to her list of crimes.

Tamara put her hand softly on the Healer's arm, silently urging her to be calm before she continued, "That is not what has you in danger, Mistress. The King asked the Master Wizard the same question, for he knew you would have left before the Wizards entered the room. Euroin then told the King they had found a different kind of spell hidden deep within your gift--a spell which sent the young man from the castle," she whispered. "Wizard Euroin convinced the King that you tried to hide the prisoner's true identity, and now they want to…" Her words trailed off, but Syndria knew exactly what the Wizard wanted. He wanted to torture her as a traitor to the King. Though she had done nothing, her torture would buy Euroin time to find Paodin while placating the King.

Syndria's eyes threatened to tear again as she spoke. "I am sorry your family has been brought into this. This is my problem to deal with, no one else's. I shall leave early tomorrow. I was told to meet Nedra at the stables. After tonight I shall trouble you no longer."

Tamara shook her head slightly before she replied, "I'm afraid that is not an option. The King is keeping all the other Healers locked inside the castle, so Mistress Nedra cannot meet you." When she saw Syndria's stricken expression she quickly added, "Don't worry--King Simann has no reason to question the loyalty of any of them. He just wants to make sure you are left to your own devices away from the castle. Also, you will need to stay with us for a few days. The Guard will not let anyone leave the city until feast time comes, so until the week's end you will be Kierney." Just then the cottage door opened and Tamara stood. Children's laughter rang out from the main room, mixed with a man's low rumble. "Ah," Tamara smiled, "Lawrence is home. Come and say hello," she prodded, taking the Healer's hand and leading her out of the kitchen.

Syndria was surprised to see Sir Lawrence in his own home. She had seen him often at the castle, but there he was always dressed in the gold cloak of Ruis, the district he represented. He was always serious, and the young Healer could not remember ever hearing the Councilman laugh. For that matter, she didn't remember seeing him smile before. Today, though, with his four small children tugging on his hands and hanging from his arms, the Councilman was beaming from ear to ear. As his wife entered the room he shook out of the grasp of the children and made his way over. Hugging his wife close to his side he smiled broadly at Syndria.

"Kierney, my niece! It is wonderful to see you again. I'm so glad you agreed to come stay with us until the feast," he nodded slightly, silently acknowledging Syndria's position as a Healer before continuing. "I'm sure Lyddie will be happy to have someone closer to her own age to gossip with," he teased his daughter.

"Oh, Popa!" Lyddie laughed, revealing a smile only slightly smaller than her father's. Looking at Syndria she shook her head. "Popa just doesn't think two girls can talk without gossiping. I tell him all the time that just because that is what he does with the rest of the Council at the castle all day doesn't mean that everyone does it." As she walked past Syndria on her way into the kitchen, the girl whispered, "Although it is fun, is it not?" Her eyes sparkled brightly and she winked, making Syndria smile as well.

"Now," Lawrence said, following Lyddie to the table, "I'm famished! What is for supper this evening?"

Supper was loud and boisterous, with four children all trying to talk over one another to get their father's attention. Syndria had never experienced anything like it. Before she had left her father in Lurn, it had always been just the two of them at the table. Then during her training as a healer she had only eaten with Nedra's company. And since her sixteenth birthday, when Syndria had moved to the castle, she had almost always eaten alone in her quarters. Now she found herself truly enjoying the company of Sir Lawrence and his family. *Uncle Lawrence*, she mentally corrected herself. Perhaps staying here a few days would be alright after all.

After supper was finished and the table cleared off, the four little ones scrambled back into the main room and all seated themselves on the braided rug in front of a strong, sturdy chair. They seemed to be anxiously awaiting the next part of the evening and the young Healer found herself drawn to their excitement. She watched as the youngest, the only boy, tried his best to ignore the three sisters squealing around him. His attempt at a dignified expression made Syndria laugh. He had his lips pressed together and his eyebrows almost met in the center, and with that expression he looked just like the sour Wizard Alek. When Tamara spoke from right beside her, Syndria almost jumped out of her skin.

"The youngest is named Lawrence after his father, but much to his distress his sisters have taken to calling him Lawrie. The two carrot tops," she said, pointing to the four-year-old red heads, "Alysse and Constance, are twins. The blonde is Abigail. She is only six but she already knows just how to keep her father wrapped around her little finger." As if emphasizing her mother's point, Abigail climbed onto her father's lap as soon as he sat down in the large chair. She stayed long enough to get a kiss before wiggling out of his arms and back onto the dark green rug.

Lyddie came out of the kitchen to stand beside Syndria. "It's story time for the little ones. They just love listening to Popa's tales of the old age. Why don't we go to the bedroom instead? We can visit and you can tell me all about Valgrin."

"Valgrin?" Syndria asked, confused. What did she know of Valgrin? She had only traveled through the city once, and that was when she was seven on her way from Lurn to the castle.

"Of course!" the girl grinned. "You can tell me all about your friends from the city." When her mother walked away, Lyddie continued, "And I'm sure you have a suitor or two to talk about!"

That last remark caught Syndria off guard. Healers were not allowed suitors, and the only young men Syndria had met were those she was called to the dungeon to heal. "If you don't mind, Lyddie," she said quickly, "I would like to listen to Uncle Lawrence's story tonight. My father told me stories of the old ages when I was a child, but I haven't listened to those tales in years. It would be wonderful to relive those memories tonight for a little while, and then tomorrow I will tell you of Valgrin, friends, and suitors--although, I fear you may be disappointed. I have had few suitors." Smiling, Syndria took a seat on the floor behind the children as Sir Lawrence began his tale.

"Long ago, before the time of King Simann, there were great and mighty people living in Tundyel. These people were fair to everyone, rich or poor, and always did what was right. They protected the innocent and the weak, and they stood proudly before the most powerful. These people were wise in many ways; most importantly they had the wisdom to tell right from wrong. They refused to stand by and watch a tyrant take over their kingdom."

Little Lawrie interrupted his father. "Who, Popa?"

Syndria was as enthralled with the story as the children and didn't realize Tamara was seated beside her until she spoke. "The children have heard this story many times, yet they always get so excited." Syndria nodded, not wanting to miss a word of the tale.

"Who, Lawrie?" Lawrence smiled. "Why, they are probably the best heroes a young lad could have. They were the True Wizards and the

Healers," he answered, briefly catching Syndria's gaze. "They were the protectors of our people, the defenders of truth. The True Wizards would be controlled by no one, but they always stood for what is right. They served as judges, much like I do as part of the Council. However, there is one major difference between how we judge and how they judged. The Council listens to testimony and forms an opinion, but the True Wizards *knew* the truth just by hearing the truth behind someone's words. As soon as the accused spoke, the True Wizards knew if they were guilty or innocent. That was part of their gift.

"The Healers of old, like the King's Healers today, possessed a gift of their own. Just by laying her hands on you a Healer can take away your injury. The old Healers, before King Simann took the throne, would travel the Kingdom healing others. What many don't know is that in order for a Healer to heal you she must give up part of her own life. Without healing others she could live longer than you can imagine. However, because she gives up so much of herself with each healing a Healer seldom lives longer than a hundred years. She unselfishly helps others to live longer by shortening her own life." The children were sitting quietly, awe shining on their faces. Syndria's glance at Tamara revealed a tear sliding down the woman's rosy cheek.

"Why do you cry?" Syndria asked softly. "The Healers would have it no other way." With that she looked at Lyddie who was sitting by the window crocheting by the full moon's bright light. "Lyddie, would you mind showing me to the bedroom?" she asked brightly. Lyddie, who like all children had long ago learned how to tune out her father's voice, jumped when Syndria called her name. Laying her yarn work aside, she stood and smiled at the Healer.

"Of course, cousin. And since it's not too late perhaps we can talk a while of Valgrin." Motioning for the older girl to follow, Lyddie said goodnight and walked out of the main room, taking a glowing candle off the mantle as she passed the fireplace.

Syndria smiled as she stood. "I have truly enjoyed your story, Uncle Lawrence, but I must now leave you to the children." Bowing slightly to Tamara she said, "Thank you for your kindness, Aunt," then she turned and hurried to follow Lyddie.

******************

Paodin ducked behind the blackberry briars, his heart suddenly pounding. He was traveling at night so he could see only what the full moon illuminated as it peeked through the trees deep in the forest. Now he could see nothing, but he had heard something moving behind him. It was probably just a raccoon or possum out searching the night for a meal, but he couldn't be too cautious. He had ducked behind the briars in hopes of seeing his pursuer as it--or he--passed. He waited silently, focusing on keeping his breathing slow and steady so as not to give away his position.

After waiting for what seemed an eternity, but was probably only half an hour, Paodin began to tell himself not to get so worked up about sounds in the forest. Besides, no one traveled through Brintzwood Forest now that the road had been finished that connected Castle Tundyel and Valgrin. He was simply getting spooked by the typical night sounds of the animals moving through the trees. He stood, prepared to keep moving until a hand clasped his shoulder.

*********************

"Now," Lyddie grinned, hopping onto the small bed, "you must tell me all about the suitors you have. I am just dying to hear about all the strapping men of Valgrin!"

Syndria smiled for the girl's excitement was contagious, but she had no idea what to tell the girl. She had never had a suitor and didn't believe she ever would. To buy some time the Healer asked, "What about you? Why don't you first tell me of all your suitors? I'm sure a young girl as pretty as you has 'strapping' young men of her own following her around."

Blushing, Lyddie giggled. "Oh, Kierney! I am much too young for suitors--or at least Popa thinks so. He says I must be at least seventeen before I can entertain suitors. That is practically an old maid!" She was starting to push her bottom lip out and furrow her brow, a pouting expression Syndria knew well from the time she had spent with Magen at the castle. And if Lyddie was anything like Magen, that expression would be followed by an avalanche of complaints and self-pity. Since she really didn't want to listen to that after a day on the road, Syndria tried to move the conversation back to something positive.

"All fathers say their daughters are too young. Why, your popa would probably keep you at home with him forever if he could!" Seeing Lyddie's pout start to turn into a smile, she continued, "Now, even though you can't have a 'suitor' I'm sure there are some young men who have their eyes on you. Am I correct?"

Lyddie nodded shyly. "Well, there is *one* boy. He walks me home from school sometimes and he is wonderful!" she gushed. Syndria smiled absently, only half listening to Lyddie as she chattered on about the boy she liked. Soon, the Healer was lost in her own thoughts.

What was happening at the castle? Had anyone seen Nedra come to her quarters early this morning? If so, the Ancient Syndria had come to love as family would soon be tortured to reveal her location. Anyone who could say they had seen Nedra helping Syndria would be greatly honored by King Simann, and she feared what would happen to her friend. Maybe she could ask Sir Lawrence. He had gotten word from Nedra once before, so perhaps he would know what was happening to her now.

"Don't you think he's just wonderful, Kierney?" Syndria's thoughts were interrupted by Lyddie's giddy question.

"What? Oh--yes, Lyddie. Just wonderful," she stammered.

"Well, goodnight, cousin. Sleep well." Lyddie pulled back the covers from one side of the bed and climbed inside. Following her lead, Syndria pulled back the thin blanket and slid under it.

"Goodnight," she said quietly. Lyddie blew out the candle, leaving Syndria to stare at the ceiling in the dark. *Tomorrow,* she thought, *I will find out about Nedra. Then I will leave and endanger the Councilman's family no longer.*

\*\*\*\*\*\*\*\*\*\*\*\*\*\*\*\*\*\*\*

Paodin spun, wishing his sword and dagger hadn't been taken when he was captured. Instead, he clutched a broken branch in his hand as a club. Raising it above his head, Paodin was ready to defend himself when he saw who had been following him.

"What do you want, old man?" he asked. Though no longer scared that he would be attacked, Paodin still held the thick branch cautiously. "You almost got yourself knocked silly!"

"Quiet, boy! You are the one who should be answering questions," the old man said as he turned away. "Come with me." That said he started walking away, not even looking to see if Paodin was following.

He thought of moving on, but Paodin couldn't resist following the man who had managed to surprise him in the dark woods. After only a brief hesitation he started after the figure quickly fading into the shadows. Catching up to the man, Paodin started to ask his name until he recalled the old man telling him he should answer questions instead of asking them. He decided the wise thing to do would be to wait for the stranger to speak first. The two men moved quietly through the dark night, neither speaking. Paodin could hear only his own footsteps as he followed the man. Much to his surprise, Paodin found himself struggling to keep up with the hunched old man.

After a few minutes of walking deeper and deeper into the forest, the man stopped and knelt. Paodin watched in curiosity as he brushed aside leaves and twigs, revealing what appeared to be a small trap door in the forest floor. As the man lifted the square door, a soft glow from underground revealed a steep, narrow staircase.

"Shut the door behind you," the man commanded, walking down the staircase ahead of Paodin. Since turning away from him in the woods, the stranger had not once looked back at Paodin. "Leave your stick behind," he called back, already halfway down the stairs.

Reluctantly, Paodin tossed his makeshift weapon back into the trees and pulled the small door shut above him as he descended behind the mysterious man. Once he reached the bottom of the stairs he looked around. Surprisingly, Paodin found himself standing in a large comfortable room. There was a fire burning across from the staircase with a large kettle hanging over it. The old man stirred the steaming contents before taking the kettle out of the fire and placing it on the table. That was when Paodin noticed the table was set for two.

Now that Paodin could see the man in the light he took a moment to study him. The stranger was stooped and ragged, dressed in a grimy gray cloak and heavy leather moccasins. His knotted hair hung past his shoulders. As he spooned the thick stew into the two bowls on the table, the long sleeves of his cloak fell back to reveal hands gnarled with age. Seeing him in the light, Paodin was even more surprised that he had had to struggle to keep up as they walked through the woods.

"Sit and eat," the man said as he sat in one of the heavy wooden chairs. As he ate he stared at his bowl, not at all interested in conversation. Paodin sat down across from the man and ate in silence. For once, he didn't mind the silence. It had been almost a week since Paodin had eaten a good meal, and the stew was delicious. The stranger gave Paodin a second bowl of stew before finally speaking.

"What were you doing sneaking around in the dead of night? That is an excellent way to get yourself into trouble," he said, his gravely voice revealing no emotion. Paodin still hadn't seen the man's face, for even as he spoke he didn't look up.

Swallowing, Paodin answered, "I don't believe it is possible for me to be in any more trouble than I already am." He swallowed another spoonful of stew before continuing, "In fact, you are probably in danger just by having me here. If you want, I will leave."

The old man looked up, staring into Paodin's eyes for the first time. "I can take care of myself. Perhaps it is you who are in danger by being here."

Paodin stared into the stranger's deep

midnight blue eyes. Somehow they looked both younger than the man's body and more ancient. After studying the stranger for only a moment, Paodin spoke. "Your eyes betray you. You are no more a danger to me than I am to you." Looking away, for some reason slightly unnerved by the old man's gaze, he asked, "Why did you bring me here?"

At first the old man didn't answer. Instead he filled his own bowl a second time and started to eat. When he finally spoke, the stranger looked directly at Paodin.

"Bound by nature's strength and frailty,

Though two, as one in unity,
Shall true heir of Tundyel make
And by the Truth the throne room take."

He spoke the words quietly, his raspy voice so low that afterward Paodin wasn't certain the old man had said anything at all. The stranger pushed his wooden bowl aside, his gaze never drifting from Paodin's face.

Suddenly uncomfortable, Paodin struggled not to look away. Never before had he allowed anyone to intimidate him and he had no desire for this old man living deep under the forest floor to be the first. Clearing his throat, Paodin asked, "What did you say?"

"What does it mean?" the old man questioned, his deep blue eyes sparkling.

"What?" Paodin was confused. How did this old man expect him to decipher such a riddle?

"What does it mean?" the old man repeated more insistently, leaning forward to lean his elbows on the table.

Shaking his head slightly, Paodin replied, "I'm sorry, stranger, but my mind does not lend itself well to such riddles. Perhaps you should find someone else to ask."

The rumpled man was not deterred. "What is the Truth? Surely you can answer me that," he prodded, his eyebrows rising slightly as he watched Paodin.

Deciding to humor the man, Paodin answered, "The truth? The truth is what is right."

"Who?"

Not sure he could trust the man across from him, Paodin said what most in Tundyel would: "King Simann."

"Not the Truth!" the old man smiled, clearly amused. "You know. Who?"

Paodin was quickly growing tired of this game. He had no time to answer the cryptic questions of a crazy old man, so he decided to speed up the process. The old man would agree with him or send him from the room, but either reaction would be some progress. "The True

Wizards are Truth," he stated, confidently looking at the old man.

The stranger quickly jumped to his feet, sending his heavy chair crashing over backward. "Yes!" he exclaimed, spinning to face the fire with his back to Paodin. "Now, what does it mean?" he questioned once again, his voice suddenly calm. "Think before you speak."

Paodin closed his mouth. He had started to again tell the old man it was useless to question him before the stranger's last command, but now decided it would accomplish nothing. So he closed his eyes for a moment, hearing one line of the riddle about the truth ringing in his mind. "*And by the Truth the throne room take.*" His eyes shot open. It was obvious--"The True Wizards will help to take back the throne of Rilso," he stated, his eyes wide. "That is not a riddle, is it?" When the old man showed no reaction, Paodin continued, "That is the Prophecy."

"I will help you," the old man stated simply, staring into the fire. "What does the rest mean?" he questioned quietly.

When searching his mind didn't turn up the rest of the Prophecy, Paodin left the table to stand beside the Stranger in front of the fire. He stood silently, gazing deeply into the flames in an attempt to find what the old man was watching so intently. As if reading his mind the man spoke.

"If you study something long enough, you can find the truth behind anything."

"Well," Paodin countered, "the first may have been the Prophecy, but that was a riddle. What are you trying to tell me?" Paodin was starting to get frustrated. Maybe this man really was just crazy. If so, Paodin thought, I should just leave right now.

"Dawn comes soon. Perhaps you should wait until night falls again to continue your journey. That will give you time to understand." The old man opened a small door next to the fireplace. "Rest here."

Paodin sighed. If it truly was approaching dawn he could not travel now. He turned away from the fire to look at the man who had seemingly wasted so much of his time, but the old stranger was gone. He must have gone back up into the forest, though Paodin hadn't heard him leave. He ducked his head and stepped through the small door.

Instead of the dark hole he had expected, this room was warm and comfortable. A cot against one wall of the tiny bedroom was piled high with quilts full of rich, beautiful colors. There were no other furnishings in the room, but it was warmed by the fire it shared with the other room. Paodin lay down on the cot which was another first like the soup had been earlier that night. He planned to rest and try to remember the Prophecy, but soon his eyes closed and Paodin drifted into his first deep sleep in a week.

Chapter 4

Syndria woke long before daybreak. She slept very little during the night, tossing and turning. At one point she had gotten up to pace the small room, hoping not to wake Lyddie. She had waited in bed as long as possible but finally felt too restless to stay in the bedroom. She made her way quietly into the main room, trying not to wake the family. To her surprise, Tamara was sitting by the window sipping from a heavy mug, gazing out into the early morning.

As Syndria walked in, Tamara looked up and smiled. "Good morning, child. Would you like some sassafras tea?"

Child. Syndria felt herself relax slightly at the word. Since she was first revealed as a Healer no one but Nedra had called her that. People seemed almost to fear her, a painful reaction Syndria had never been able to shake off. She nodded, and Tamara motioned for her to sit as she went into the kitchen for another mug.

"It's pretty strong," she warned, handing Syndria the warm mug. "There is some honey if you need to sweeten it." Sitting down beside the young Healer, Tamara gave Syndria time to relax before she began to speak.

"I am truly sorry you have been driven from all you know. So much has been stripped from you-- your appearance, your home, your friends. I wish there was more we could do for you, Mistress," she said, bowing her head slightly.

Syndria felt a pang of sadness at the woman's deference. "Please, I liked 'child' so much better," she said, reaching to take Tamara's hand. "There is nothing else you need to do for me. You have already opened your home to me, putting your own family in danger if the Guardsmen discover my presence. I am afraid that if I stay much longer that will happen."

"Oh!" Tamara exclaimed, "That reminds me-- you need a dress to wear while you are here. Though your hair is now short, you will be easily recognized if you move about in your white gown." She stood, pulling Syndria along beside her. "Come with me and we will find you something." Tamara led Syndria through the kitchen to a small room full of fabrics, threads, and garments in various stages of production. She began searching through the dresses stacked on a small table tucked under the room's only window.

"You are older than my Lydia, but I don't believe there is much difference in size." Pulling a dark red dress from the pile, Tamara turned to the Healer. "Try this one. I can adjust it some once you have it on. Call when you are ready," she added, walking back into the kitchen. She left the door open slightly, giving Syndria some light in the tiny room.

Syndria fingered the dress. For the last twelve years she had worn nothing but white. The red was beautiful and the girl's eyes lit up at the thought of wearing such a rich color. She quickly changed out of the simple Healer's gown and pulled the new dress over her head. As soon as she was dressed she called Tamara back into the room.

When the seamstress stepped in she began laughing. "Well, my dear, I do believe I may have some work to do!"

The red dress hit Syndria in all the wrong places. It pulled tightly across her hips and gaped at her chest. The fabric folded at her waist, pulling the hem of the dress three inches above her ankle.

Tamara struggled to tame her laughter. Still chuckling, she pulled shears, a needle, and thread out of a drawer. "Now," she smiled, tapping a stool, "step up here and let's see what I can do."

An hour later, the dress fit Syndria perfectly and the young Healer was learning to cook by helping Tamara prepare breakfast. Sir Lawrence walked in as Syndria set the table.

"Good morning. The two of you must have gotten up early this morning," he said, looking around at all the food. "You've been busy! Are we celebrating something?"

Tamara smiled as her husband kissed her on the forehead. "I was just teaching... Kierney how to cook. We were having so much fun we just couldn't stop," she finished, turning as the twins stumbled drowsily into the kitchen. "Good morning, girls. Are you hungry?" The girls nodded as they climbed into their chairs at the table.

Sir Lawrence knelt between his daughters. "Well, since we can't eat until everyone is here, who wants to go wake up your brother and sisters?" When neither girl answered, the Councilman scooped them out of their chairs, one in each arm. "I guess all three of us will just have to go." He flew them through the doorway, both girls squealing with delight.

Soon they returned, little Lawrie riding of his father's back. Abigail hurried in ahead of the group, her blonde hair wild. The twins still giggled and an obviously sleepy Lyddie followed behind. Looking at Lyddie, Syndria knew she must have woken the girl with her restlessness the night before.

"I am sorry if I woke you last night," Syndria said as she served the young girl a bowl of oatmeal.

Tamara laughed. "Oh, Kierney, Lydia is always this cheerful early in the morning. It has nothing to do with you." Kissing her oldest daughter on the top of her head, Tamara continued, "She wouldn't know if the house fell down around her at night!"

The breakfast continued with lots of

laughter, making Syndria remember all the quiet mornings she had spent in the castle. For a moment Syndria considered staying on until the feast. It would be amazing to experience a family for the rest of the week. The thought didn't last long before Syndria mentally chided herself. How could she even consider keeping this family in danger longer just to satisfy her own desire to have a family? As soon as possible Syndria would talk to Sir Lawrence and see if he knew what was happening at the castle. Then she would leave Caron.

An opportunity presented itself sooner than expected. Right after breakfast Tamara took the four youngest to their bedroom to dress for the day. As the daughter of a Councilman, Lyddie was allowed schooling with the boys of Caron, so she was getting ready for the day as well. Her father was sitting in the main, room, relaxing for a few minutes before the duties of the day called him into the Hall of Caron.

"Sir Lawrence," Syndria said softly, "may I have a moment?"

He stood, motioning toward the door. "Why don't we walk out in the garden? I need to speak with you as well." He led the Healer outside around the small cottage, then opened a tall gate and led Syndria into an amazing spring wonderland.

There was no doubt that the courtyards of the castle had been beautiful, but Syndria had never seen anything comparable to what she was in the midst of now. A stone path wound its way through brilliantly colored flowers. The entire back wall of the cottage was covered with climbing roses, and Lynberry vines spiraled up the garden walls.

At the center of the garden was a large pond everything else seemed to revolve around. Sir Lawrence guided the Healer around the pond to a bench much like the one she had sat on with Nedra the day before fleeing the castle. Sitting, he motioned for Syndria to do the same.

"I would like to thank you, Sir," the Healer began. "Your family has done so much for me, even offering to let me stay with you until the feast. However, I feel I must leave."

The Councilman turned to Syndria. "Mistress, I cannot allow that to happen. Your life is in danger and that danger will only increase if you leave now. I am sorry, but your leaving is something I cannot permit."

Syndria stood. "*Councilman,*" she said, her voice stern, "You are well aware that as a Healer I do not require, nor am I asking for, your permission. What I *am* asking for is your help one last time. I need to leave Caron and I would like to do so without putting your family in any further danger. If you can just get word to the Healer Nedra telling her I am doing well, I will ask nothing more of you."

When Sir Lawrence didn't answer Syndria took it to mean he had decided not to help her. Gathering her courage, the Healer turned her back on the Councilman. "Very well. I shall be on my way. Please tell Madam Tamara I am very grateful for all she has done."

As she walked away, Sir Lawrence called after her. "Please, Mistress, sit." His voice was low and when Syndria looked back at him the Councilman's expression was serious. Slowly she returned to the bench. None of the Councilmen had ever given the young Healer an order, and though he had added "please" Syndria knew the statement was a command. She had not intended to sit, but Sir Lawrence would not speak until she was seated next to him.

Without looking at the young Healer, Lawrence began to speak. "After you fled the castle, King Simann was outraged. He refused to believe you had gotten past the guards without any of them seeing you and questioned all of them. I would imagine Mistress Nedra sent you away during the changing of the Guard, which would explain why you were not seen. However, the king would hear nothing of the sort. When all the Guards denied all knowledge of your escape he ordered all the Guards on duty through the night and morning killed. They were to be beheaded so there would be no chance of a Healer giving them life as they died."

Syndria gasped. Tears once more threatened to fall as the young Healer thought of all the torture and pain so many had been forced to endure because of her.

"The eight Guardsmen who were to be killed were all young," the Councilman continued, "not much older than yourself." When he paused and looked at Syndria for the first time since telling her to sit, she saw a very different expression in his eyes. "Mistress Nedra could not allow that to happen." He stopped, his eyes wet. "I'm sorry," he finally said after a long pause, "but she is gone."

"No!" she cried, shaking her head. Syndria jumped to her feet. "It only just happened. If I can get to her I still may be able to bring her back. The Ancient is strong and she would have fought hard for life. I just have to get back to the castle--" Sir Lawrence grabbed the young Healer's shoulders, shaking her back to the moment.

Spinning her around, the Councilman ordered, "Listen to me, child! Nedra was a good woman, and I will not see her death be for nothing, and the moment you return to the castle you will be killed as well. Do you want that to happen?"

"Unhand me, Councilman," Syndria scolded. "I cannot just sit by and let Nedra die. I *must* help if I can. Now let me go!" The more the young Healer struggled, the tighter Lawrence held her shoulders.

"Listen to me," he said. "Listen to me! There is nothing you can do for her--she is dead! *Now* you need to be strong and learn to be the Healer Mistress Nedra was. You can finish what she started and restore Tundyel to its rightful king. You must fight for truth, and if you do not think you can fight for yourself or your people, you must do it for Nedra."

Syndria stopped struggling. As soon as the strength that came with her desperate desire to get back to Nedra waned, she could barely stand. The young Healer collapsed onto the bench, her face in her hands, leaving Sir Lawrence standing awkwardly nearby. The Healers were strong women. They faced death everyday, yet he had never seen one of them cry. Now the Councilman stood by watching one Healer sob uncontrollably into her hands, her shoulders shaking with grief. As he watched, the Healer's untouchable appearance dissolved and all the father of five could see was a young girl completely alone with the tragic news he had just given her.

Lawrence sat down next to Syndria and hesitantly put his arms around her shoulders.

Though at first she stiffened, soon the girl was clinging to the man who knew her grief. The father held the girl until her sobs had subsided and then gently pulled away.

"I must go, child. I am expected in the Hall. Please do not leave until we can speak. If you are willing to fight for your people, and for Nedra, I know those who could help you." He stood and turned away. Before the Councilman walked through the gate he turned back and called, "You can talk to Tamara. She is good at this sort of thing."

Syndria stood and walked around to the other side of the pond. She knelt and skimmed her fingers across the surface of the water, watching the ripples grow larger as they spread. *Sir Lawrence was right,* she found herself thinking. The Ancient would not have wanted her to wallow in self-pity. The young Healer tossed a pebble into the pond, watching the seemingly endless number of circles that spread from it.

"Perhaps Mistress Nedra was that stone," Tamara said, startling Syndria. She knelt beside the Healer, hoisting her skirt so it wouldn't get dirty. "She has started things in motion. Now it is up to those she has touched to make sure things spread."

Syndria glanced over briefly when Tamara put her hand on the girl's shoulder before looking back to the rings moving across the pond. "If the

Ancient started the ripples, what can I do? The ripples spread on their own."

Before standing, Tamara squeezed Syndria's shoulder. "If the first ripple never moves, the others never get a chance. Come in whenever you are ready," she said, walking away and leaving the Healer at the pond's edge.

\*\*\*\*\*\*\*\*\*\*\*\*\*\*\*\*\*\*\*

Paodin was disoriented when he woke. It took a few minutes for him to remember that he was underground with the old man who had found him in the woods. He walked back out to the main room where he found the rumpled stranger sitting at the table.

"Come sit," he said. "Have lunch."

Nodding his thanks, Paodin took the offered seat. Already filled, a plate sat on the table. It held a hunk of hard bread, two large pieces of salted pork, and a chunk of cheese. Paodin began devouring the food as if he hadn't eaten two bowls of stew the night before.

"You had time to think," the man said, watching Paodin eat. "What does it mean?" he asked, picking up the conversation right where they had left off.

"To be honest," Paodin said between mouthfuls, "I don't even remember the Prophecy. Perhaps you will repeat it for me."

"What is the ring you wear?"

Sighing in exasperation, Paodin shook his head and took off the ring. How could it be so impossible to get a single straight answer from one man? He rolled the silver ring across the table. He had learned the night before that there would be no point in trying to make the strange man talk about anything he did not initiate.

Picking up the ring, the man asked, "Where did you get this?"

Watching the old man study the ring, Paodin answered, "It was given to me by my mother before she died. I was only a baby so my father held it for me until it fit."

"What did she say?"

Paodin reached out to take the ring back. "I was only just born when she died. How am I to know what she said?" Leaning back he slid the ring back on his finger. Despite the casualness with which he had given his ring to the man, Paodin was relieved to have it back in place. Since the day his father had first given it to him, Paodin had only taken the ring off when his growing hands had warranted it being switched to a smaller finger.

"You do not lie--though you do not remember her saying the words, you know what she said." The man's eyes glittered as they had the night before. "Now, what did she say?"

Paodin spun the ring on his finger as he answered. "According to my father, she simply told me to protect it. Father told me it was very important to her family."

In another change of subject, something Paodin had come to expect at any moment, the old man asked, "What is the strongest thing in nature?"

Without thinking for long, he answered, "The mountains."

"Perhaps," the man stated simply. "What is weakest?"

With the second part of the question, Paodin suddenly remembered the first line of the Prophecy: "*Bound by nature's strength and frailty*," he said, pushing away the plate of half-eaten food. "That is what you are asking me, is it not?" The stranger sat silently, letting Paodin talk through the line on his own. Pushing back from the table the young man stood and began to pace. "Nature's frailty could be anything. The strength could be a mountain as I earlier mentioned. Now, if the Prophecy says 'bound by', that probably means surrounded by or trapped by. Trapped, though, has a negative connotation. I should not think the Prophecy which speaks of returning the rightful heir of Tundyel to the throne would be negative. Bound could also mean protected."

The old man interrupted Paodin's flow of words by repeating an earlier question. "What did your mother say when she gave you the ring?"

"Her words were simply to protect it,"

Paodin said, his frustration at being interrupted obvious in his voice.

The old man nodded slowly, never losing eye contact with the young man.

Paodin's eyes widened. "Protected by nature's strength and frailty. Man is both the strongest and weakest thing in nature. The heir will be protected by man."

"That is one meaning," the stranger said as he stood, "but there is another."

Until he had realized that man was both strong and frail, Paodin had been trying to think of two different aspects of nature. Now he focused on one thing that could fit both descriptions. The old man kept asking about his ring, so Paodin now studied it himself. The pattern of interlocking leaves wrapped around his finger, the silver gleaming despite his dirty appearance. The Lynberry vine was easily broken, but once it had established itself somewhere it was nearly impossible to get rid of. Suddenly, everything fit into place.

"The Prophecy," he said, isn't speaking solely of man. *I* am to protect the heir. When my mother said to protect it she was not speaking of the ring. She told me to protect the kingdom."

"*Though two, as one in unity.*" The stranger repeated the second line of the Prophecy.

Paodin's eyes grew even wider. "Though

there will be two when I find the true heir, we will both have the same purpose-- '*Shall true heir of Tundyel make*'. Soon the true King will be on the throne." Paodin gazed into the fire. Now it seemed so simple. Why had he thought the Prophecy was so difficult to understand when he first heard it?

"You are forgetting something."

The old man's voice broke Paodin's train of thought, bringing with it the last line of the Prophecy. *'And by the Truth the throne room take.'* A True Wizard would put the true heir on the throne. "I have to find the last True Wizard," he said, his spirits falling.

*********************

Euroin stood before his fireplace staring deeply into the flames. The fire danced under his gaze, the flames turning blue with the extreme heat. The Wizard's eyes began to glow with a strange light as the room around him seemed to fade. Soon the flames danced and twirled around Euroin as he stood in an otherwise empty space. He focused on the four other Wizards of the Order, clearing his mind of all else. Soon he was joined in the blackness by four voices.

"What have you found?" he asked. "Have the traitors been captured?"

Alek spoke out of the darkness. "Finley is quiet this morning. So far none seem to know of the prisoner's escape."

"Traitors?" Uylti interrupted. "For whom besides the prisoner are we searching? Has something else happened at the castle since we've been gone, Euroin?"

"The young Healer Syndria," Euroin stated. "She has fled the castle. You doubted her involvement, Osidius, yet her sudden departure proves her guilt."

"But how can she be involved?" Ilcren's voice echoed. "A Healer's gift could never be strong enough to hide the Old Magic. What could the child possibly have done?"

The flames swirling around Euroin shot out into the dark space. "You all know that a Healer cannot use her gift on someone and not know he has powers." His voice was harsh, booming out to the others.

Ilcren's quiet voice answered again. "It has always been so for our magic, that is true. However, we are dealing with a magic we know nothing about, a magic much stronger than our own-"

"Enough! There will be no more discussion," Euroin yelled. "The Healer will be found along with the prisoner. Now, how is the District of Nelthien? Has there been any evidence of the traitors fleeing to the north?"

"I have neither seen nor heard of the prisoner," Uylti answered, then quickly followed with, "and I will be watching for the Healer Syndria."

Ilcren spoke up, "Sephon is also quiet thus far."

"The people of Meinsley know of the prisoner's escape, though none seem to have heard of the young Healer leaving as well," Osidius spoke out of the darkness.

Frustration evident in his voice, Uylti huffed, "Our search would be much easier if we could use our powers to aid in our hunt for the traitors."

Always the peace keeper of the Order, Ilcren answered, "We have no way of knowing if one with the Old Magic would be able to sense our magic." His calm voice quieted the others as he continued, "We are better off to rely on our wisdom and only use magic for meetings such as this."

"Have we not spent too long in this meeting?" Osidius asked. "Perhaps we should only meet if and when someone has new information." When everyone agreed, the voices stopped and the darkness departed, leaving Euroin once again standing before his fire watching the deadly flames swirl before him.

******************

Syndria sat by the pond for a while before finally making her way inside to talk to Tamara.

She straightened her shoulders as she stepped through the door, determined not to appear weak. Her entire life, even as a child before becoming a Healer, Syndria had been known for her strength. She had never been one to get upset when the city kids of Lurn had made fun of her charity dresses and grimy appearance. In fact, she had been much more likely to punch said kid in the nose for the insults. She refused to be weak now.

   Tamara stuck her head out of the kitchen when she heard the young Healer enter the cottage. "I'm making bread. Would you like to learn?" she asked as she brushed away a loose strand of hair, leaving a smear of flour across her face. Nodding, Syndria followed her into the kitchen. As Tamara taught the girl about baking bread she talked all about her children. Syndria heard about the many antics of the young Lawrie and his terrorization of his sisters along with the time the girls had put him in Abigail's fanciest ball gown. The children ran in and out of the kitchen, often asking their mother for something sweet. Tamara would shoo them out with the promise of a special treat after lunch, afterward laughing at their pouts. For a while, as the young Healer helped to knead dough and prepare lunch, Tamara managed to keep Syndria's mind off of Nedra's death. Finally, though, once they sat the four children down outside for lunch, Tamara took her into the main room and brought up the subject of which Syndria was hesitant to speak.

"Lawrence tells me you are wanting to leave us before the feast," she said quietly.

Syndria nodded slightly. "I'm afraid it would not be in the best interest of your family if I were to stay."

"I beg to differ." The woman's statement took the Healer by surprise. "There are many in Caron who know of Kierney's plan to stay with us through the feast. They are expecting to see her seated with us at the Councilman's table during the celebration, and if you leave before that many will become suspicious--not only of you, but of Sir Lawrence."

After sitting quietly for a few moments, the Healer asked, "Why did he say nothing of this to me?"

Tamara smiled, "You must remember, my husband has seen you as a Healer since your gift was first revealed. As you well know, there are certain lines which are not to be crossed, and a Councilman putting his own desires before those of a Healer is one of those lines. I, however, see you mostly as a child." Seeing Syndria's surprise, she continued quickly, "Forgive me if I offend you, Mistress, but in my eyes you are in need of protection as much as my own Lydia. Without the Ancient Healer you are now alone in a world that will undoubtedly prove dangerous for you, and I want to help you as long as possible."

"I know very little about how the people of Tundyel see Healers," Syndria began, "but I do know how I see the others. They seem to think of themselves as royalty, better than those outside the castle walls. Growing up I often wondered how they could feel that way after being taught by Nedra. She was so good, so--pure, in every aspect. She told me stories nightly, much as Sir Lawrence does for your children, tales of the Healers and how we are meant to be servants of the people. She told me that one day I would be called upon to serve once again, and now seems to be that time. Though I always thought the Ancient would be here to guide me, I suppose all she did was leading up to now. Somehow she must have known she would not be able to help me." Seeing Tamara's patient yet puzzled expression, Syndria laughed. "I said all of that in an attempt to lead up to this--I serve the people of Tundyel and pledge to do what is best for them. If my leaving before the feast would not be in the best interest of your family and the people of Caron, I will remain. Perhaps you will have time to teach me to mend my own dresses. I'm sure that is a skill for which I have need."

"Of course, Kierney," Tamara winked as she stood. "I would love to."

Syndria got her first lesson in mending that afternoon. Lawrie fell on the stone path while playing out in the garden, skinning his knee and tearing his breeches. When the tiny boy came inside with tears flowing down his dirty cheeks it was hard for the Healer to do nothing about the stinging knee. She watched in amazement as the child's tears and quivering lip stopped the moment his mother kissed the torn skin. Syndria had never seen the magic a mother could work for her children and she smiled when Lawrie, in a clean, un-torn pair of breeches, scampered back outside to his sisters.

"His father doesn't baby the boy as I do," Tamara told Syndria as she showed her how to close the tear in the knee. "When Lawrie cries, Lawrence takes him by the shoulders and stares him straight in the eye. 'Son,' he says, 'soldiers only cry if there is nothing else that can be done. If you are to be a mighty leader of the Sons of Tundyel, you must be strong.' Then he always leans closer and whispers something, but neither will tell me what secret they share," she shrugged. "Whatever it is, the boy sticks out his chin and goes about his business as if nothing has happened."

Syndria smiled, picturing the small boy and his father. She then asked, "Who are the Sons of Tundyel? I have never heard that phrase."

Tamara replied, "It is an old title, one which belonged to the men who once guarded the Rilso family. It has not been used for longer than you've been alive, though. There," she said, finishing the mending job for the Healer, "that is wonderful for your first attempt!"

A moment later, Syndria heard the front door of the cottage open and Lyddie call out, "Kierney! Where are you? Kierney, I must tell you!" Running into the kitchen, the girl stopped when she saw her mother. "Oh, hello Mama. You don't mind if I steal cousin Kierney away for a moment, do you?" Before Tamara could answer, Lyddie was pulling the Healer from her chair. "You will never believe it, Kierney! The Healers are coming here to begin the search for the next girl with the gift! Oh, I am terribly excited. To think, the next Healer could be one of my own friends." The girl chattered on, oblivious to Syndria's shocked expression. "Isn't this wonderful? It is too bad that you have already passed eighteen or you would have a chance to become a Healer as well. You are truly a beauty." Turning to her mother, Lyddie gushed on, "Mama, we have to prepare my gown. We must have it perfect for the feast now that the Royal Court will be here instead of only Popa!" She ran out quickly, and Syndria assumed the girl had gone to fetch her gown.

The Healer's breath caught in her throat. If the King's court were coming to Caron, it was impossible for Syndria to attend the feast without being recognized. Though she had not spent much time with the three Healers still serving at the castle, if she was to be seated with the Councilman and his family Syndria would be sharing a table with the women. She spun and looked at Tamara who was still sitting at the table.

Calmly, Tamara stood and took Syndria's hand as she spoke. "Lawrence will know what to do, and he will be home soon. Until then you must go to Lydia and show the same excitement she does." She gave the Healer a slight push out the doorway and a stunned Syndria slowly walked to Lyddie's bedroom at the back of the cottage. The young girl was standing beside her bed twirling around, a silver silk gown pressed to her. Her smile grew brighter when she saw Syndria standing just inside the room.

"Kierney, I'm so glad you got away from Mama for a moment. You will never believe what happened today!" She hopped onto the tall bed and patted the spot next to her. "Come sit. I don't want Mama to hear or she'll surely tell Popa."

Syndria forced herself to smile brightly, a trick she had long ago perfected for her meetings with King Simann. She perched beside the younger girl and softly fingered the silver gown. "You must tell me everything, Lyddie," she whispered.

"Oh, you needn't whisper. Mother always goes out to play with the children in the afternoon." Seeing Syndria admiring the gown, Lyddie gushed, "Isn't it beautiful? Mama made it special this year because she said that now that I am a young lady I can wear silver as she does. I helped her sew on all the sparkling pearls and you should see it outside in the sunlight! It practically shines like a diamond."

"I'm sure it does. I have never worn such a spectacular gown as this," she admitted truthfully. The white gowns the Healers wore had no adornments other than the dark blue belts with silver buckles, and Syndria had worn nothing else for the last twelve years. "You will be truly stunning at the feast. No man young or old will be able to look upon anyone else!"

Blushing, Lyddie laid the dress aside and hugged Syndria. "Thank you, cousin." Her eyes sparkled when she pulled back. "I don't care about *all* the men of Caron, but I do hope one likes it. Oh, Kierney, do you remember the boy I told you about, the one who walked me home?" The Healer tried hard to remember a name, but thankfully Lyddie continued without waiting for an answer. "Well, after last session today Fitz walked part way home with me again. His father is the leader of Caron's guard, you know. Fitz--we call him that, but his true name is Fitzgerald--he started talking about the feast and asked me if I was excited to be old enough to finally take part in the dance. After a little while, right before he left to go to his guardsman training, Fitz told me not to take a partner for the dance."

She stopped and laughed, leaning over toward Syndria before she continued. "Now you and I both know what that meant, but I wanted to hear it from him." Syndria nodded, but she had no idea what that meant. As a Healer she had never been allowed to take part in the local customs at feasts, and she had never danced. King Simann saw no need for the Healers in his service to take part, for they were not allowed suitors or marriage. "So," Lyddie continued, "I asked him, 'Why would I want to dance alone?' and he told me that wasn't really what he meant. When I asked him what exactly he meant then, Fitz started stammering and wouldn't look at me. He turned to make his way to the training field and as he was walking away he called back, 'I've learned the dance well. I would make a good partner if you would allow me.' Then he just ran off before I could even give him an answer!" Lyddie squealed and jumped up, once again twirling with her silver gown. "Boys are so silly, don't you agree, Kierney?" she asked, laughing.

Syndria just smiled, not knowing what to

say in answer. As she watched the young girl spinning happily around the room, the Healer had an idea. If she wanted to keep Lyddie from asking more questions about suitors as she had the night before, the girl had to be distracted.

"Lyddie, I just had a wonderful idea," she gushed, imitating the girl's enthusiasm. "Can you teach me the dance of Caron? Though I am only a guest, perhaps the Councilman's niece may be allowed to join in at the feast." Smiling, she leaned in and whispered, "And maybe I will meet someone like your Fitz!"

Syndria jumped when Lyddie suddenly grabbed her hand and said, "Now, why didn't I think of that? Fitz has an older brother who could be your partner. He is terribly shy, but very kind. He would be wonderful for you! Now," she said, laying her silver gown on the bed, "let's teach you the dance."

Though smiling outwardly, on the inside Syndria was cringing as she tried to follow the intricate steps and many turns that carried Lyddie lightly around the room. What had she gotten herself into?

∗∗∗∗∗∗∗∗∗∗∗∗∗∗∗∗∗∗∗∗

Hours had passed, and Paodin was no closer to knowing how to find the True Wizard than he had been that morning. The old man had left soon after their earlier conversation, telling

Paodin to find something in the rough wooden shelves for lunch. The lunch hour had come and gone without Paodin noticing--he had been too troubled to eat. According to the Prophecy, Paodin was supposed to protect the kingdom. It was his duty in life to see the heir of Rilso returned to the throne, but based on the Prophecy that would not be possible without the True Wizard. Paodin remembered standing before the Wizards, telling them confidently that they were fools for believing the lies about all the True Wizards being gone. Though it had taken place just days before, it might as well have been a lifetime.

It wasn't that Paodin was no longer confident that not all the True Wizards had been killed. He knew there had to still be at least one somewhere in the kingdom. There was a difference, though, in believing a True Wizard was alive and in being expected to *find* him. It had taken Simann's men years to find the True Wizards when the new king had ordered them all killed. How then would Paodin, one man, be able to find someone who had been hidden for so long and obviously had no desire to be found?

Soon Paodin's frustration had grown to where he could no longer push it aside to focus on the task ahead of him. He considered leaving, getting on with the treacherous journey ahead of him, but soon thought better of it. The old man may be crazy, but so far he had given Paodin no reason not to trust him. If he left now it would be the middle of the afternoon and the young man couldn't risk traveling while there was still light. It made much more sense to stay underground until nightfall than to try and find someplace on the surface to hide out. He decided to rest and went back to the tiny room and the comfortable cot to try and sleep until the stranger returned to the dugout.

Before long, Paodin woke to voices in the main room of the underground cabin. Stirring immediately, Paodin moved silently to the corner between the fire and the wooden door. He could barely make out the voices over the crackling fire, but it didn't take ling for him to figure out that the old man's guests were not friendly ones, at least not toward Paodin.

"We have reason to believe he came this way," one said, his deep voice growing louder. A brittle voice replied, and it took a moment for Paodin to realize it was the stranger who had taken him in who was speaking.

"What would I know about that? If you hadn't noticed, I don't have much of a view from here. I seldom venture out--I have no desire to talk with people. In fact," the feeble voice continued, a bit strained, "I have no desire to talk to you men. You may leave now." Paodin heard one of the heavy wooden chairs slide slowly across the floor and assumed the old man was making his way across to the stairs.

"We will leave," a new voice boomed, "when we are satisfied, *old man*." Paodin heard heavy footsteps that grew louder as they drew near the door. He quickly slid under the cot, thankful for the pile of blankets and the constantly changing shadows cast by the dancing fire. Together they would at least provide cover against a quick search, and hopefully the men moving toward the door would decide that the old hermit's hole in the ground warranted nothing more thorough.

The small door bounced off the corner of the cot when it swung open, shifting the many blankets and giving Paodin a view of heavy black boots and red breeches. Beyond the four legs and through the doorway Paodin could see the hunched old man shuffling across the room, shaking his fist angrily.

"Get out of here, you vermin! Are you satisfied now?" he asked once he had reached the room. "You broke my door!" Laughing, one of the men pulled a quilt off the cot. "You put that back. My Magdeline made that before she died," the old man cried out. Paodin watched as the beautiful quilt was thrown into the fire, his body tensing as he watched the broken old man clutch at it while the guard kicked it farther into the flames.

"Now," the first man snarled, "we are satisfied." With that, both men turned and left the small room, laughing as they stomped up the steep staircase.

Paodin crawled out from under the cot and opened his mouth to speak, but the stranger silenced him with a finger to his lips. The old man then stood and moved around the main room, muttering to himself in that odd broken voice. "Those savages! How dare they come in here and destroy my things. Why would I have anything to do with some traitor who ran away from the castle? What I don't understand is why anyone would need to run away from someplace guarded by the likes of those oafs!" His ranting continued for a few minutes, but he finally stopped and called out to Paodin. "Come out now. They have gone."

Paodin stood and walked out of the bedroom, surprised by the old man's sudden change. His shoulders were still hunched as they had been before, but he no longer shuffled his feet and his voice returned to the gravely sound Paodin knew. "I am sorry you lost the quilt-" he began, but was interrupted by a raspy chuckle.

"Oh, I bought that quilt a week ago. Did you not notice how clean it was?" He smiled a crooked smile, shaking his head. "My boy, you have much to learn." He sat down at the table and motioned for Paodin to join him before speaking again. "It seems you are a hunted man. Those buffoons seem to think you escaped the castle--is that true?"

Looking the man in the eye, Paodin nodded. "Well, perhaps not I, exactly, since it was not something I accomplished on my own, but yes. I am sorry to have deceived you. If you wish me to I will leave now. I will not hold you to your promise to help me," he said slowly.

"You are not as deceptive as perhaps you would wish to be nor as bright as you think!" the old man said, the crooked grin still on his lips. "Those guards will not have gone far. If you were to leave now you would be back at the castle before morning, and I do not believe you would find it so easy to leave the second time. Eat here and leave after dark," he commanded. After pulling some food off a shelf he added, "You would not make much progress on breakfast alone."

When the old man handed Paodin a chuck of bread, he had to bite his tongue to keep from saying he wouldn't make much more progress thanks to just a piece of bread. Shrugging slightly he bit into the bread to find meat, cheese, and potatoes all baked inside.

"I will give you some for your journey," the stranger said. "Now, where do you plan to go from here?"

Swallowing, Paodin told the old man of the resistance group slowly building in Gelci. "I must make my way there, but if I go directly to my father and the other men there, not only will I be captured again but the resistance there will be wiped out. I will move south first and try to gather more who are loyal to Tundyel."

The stranger sat silently for a few minutes, thinking. "Avoid Valgrin, but go down into Lurn. There is a farmer there who is well known in the city. He is loyal to your cause and will be able to help you, but you will first have to prove yourself to him. I cannot give you his name, but he will not be hard to find if you ask the right questions. After leaving Lurn travel by way of Krasteiv, but stay off the road. I will meet you again, but I cannot say when."

Taking it all in, Paodin asked, "How will I find you?"

The raspy chuckle came in answer. "I suppose the same way you found me before."

Chapter 5

After her three hour dance lesson, Syndria was exhausted. She collapsed onto Lyddie's bed, laughing when the younger girl tried to pull her back onto her feet.

"Come on, Kierney! We still have a lot of work to do--*a lot* of hard work," she laughed.

Syndria moaned, "I need a break. I can't help it if my feet refuse to move in the same direction." Pulling Lyddie down beside her, she laughed, "Perhaps my idea was not so wonderful after all."

Soon, Tamara's voice came from the doorway. "What is it that has the two of you giggling like the twins?" she asked, her hands on her hips and a smile on her lips.

Out of breath, Lyddie still laughed as she sat up. "Kierney had the brilliant idea that I teach her the dance of Caron for the feast." Though her voice became serious, a teasing light shone in the girl's eyes as she added solemnly, "I am afraid she is utterly hopeless." Her laughter rang out again as the Healer tugged lightly on her braid.

Tamara stood watching the girls for a moment before speaking again. "I think I see the problem. Follow me, girls." She turned and walked out of the room, not waiting for the girls.

As she followed Lyddie into the main room, Syndria thought back over the day. She couldn't remember ever having as much fun. The two girls stopped oat the edge of the room and watched in surprise as Tamara moved all the furniture in the room against the walls. Next she rolled up the rug, revealing the bare wood floor underneath.

"You cannot learn to dance without an adequate dance floor," she said, motioning the girls closer. "And," she added, the same teasing sparkle in her eyes as had earlier shown in her daughter's, "it helps if you also have an adequate instructor! Now, opening pose," she said, pulling her arms up gracefully in front of her.

The three were having so much fun with their dance they didn't notice the door quietly open and Sir Lawrence step inside with four uncharacteristically silent children. Tamara was demonstrating the eight-step, moving as if dancing on air, when her husband stepped up behind her. He motioned for the girls to keep quiet, then caught Tamara's hand as she twirled. Laughing, Tamara let her husband lead her through the rest of the dance while her children provided the music. At the end of the dance, Tamara curtsied to her husband and then laughed.

"Well, I don't know about the rest of you, but I am famished! Who is ready for dinner?" As everyone echoed their hunger, Tamara led them all into the kitchen. Syndria would never have thought it possible, but the dinner hour was even more boisterous and fun than it had been the night before. The young Healer didn't even have time to think about the danger they would all face when the Healers arrived in Caron at the end of the week.

Like always, the joyful time had to come to an end. After the table had been cleared of the dishes and food, Lyddie went outside to wash the bowls and cups while Tamara took the children to start their baths. Syndria started to follow, wanting to help, but Sir Lawrence motioned for her to stay behind. Once everyone was out of earshot, he spoke.

"I'm sure my daughter told you of the Healers' impending journey to Caron for the feast." When Syndria nodded slightly, he continued. "I am also sure my wife told you that your visit here as my niece is well known and that your presence will be expected at the feast as well. I know it will prove dangerous, but I would like to ask you to stay."

"Sir," the Healer began, "I do not wish your family harm. I understand the suspicion my absence would cause, but I also know the other Healers will recognize me the very moment they see me."

Sir Lawrence rubbed his forehead with his left hand as he thought, his right hand tapping on the table. Finally he spoke. "Perhaps I can convince the Guard that it would be dangerous for the Royal Court to be in the Hall before the revealing ceremony. Then, you can leave after the dance. Women are always claiming headaches and leaving early from the feast. You can do the same." Looking back up at the young Healer he asked, "Will you stay?"

"Of course," she answered without hesitation. "If my staying will do more to ensure the safety of your family, I will attend the feast as cousin Kierney." To herself, Syndria silently added, *And perhaps, like Lyddie said, I will dance with Fitzgerald's brother and have a glorious time for once in my life--as a woman instead of a Healer.*

\*\*\*\*\*\*\*\*\*\*\*\*\*\*\*\*\*\*\*

The next two days leading up to the feast passed uneventfully. Syndria lived happily as Kierney, spending her days helping Tamara create a gown for the young Healer to wear to the feast and her evenings learning the dance and playing with the children. Young Lawrie seemed to have developed quite a crush on the Healer and was often her dance partner. The day of the feast found Syndria and Lyddie busy getting ready very early in the morning. Sir Lawrence had managed to convince the Guards that the Healers should only be present for the revealing ceremony since the whereabouts of the traitors were still unknown, much to Syndria's relief and excitement. He had left just after sunrise to oversee the activity taking place in the Hall in preparation for the feast, and the two girls had risen soon after.

"Mama taught me this trick once after Abigail found the shears and cut my hair while I slept," Lyddie chattered as she tied strips of cloth in Syndria's short hair. "When we take them out and unwind your hair you will have ringlets like the twins." The young girl's own hair was done in many braids, ready to be piled on top of her head in whatever fancy arrangement Tamara came up with. When Lyddie heard her mother calling softly from the main room she practically ran out, telling the Healer to stay put.

Syndria reached up, feeling the tiny knots over half her head. How those knots would turn into curls she couldn't say, but the Healer had no choice but to trust the girl. She had never in her life done anything but tie her hair up or braid it down her back, and now that it was cut short there was no way she could do either of those things.

When Lyddie appeared in the doorway, she was holding the gown Syndria was to wear behind her back. "I hope you don't mind, but last night Mama and I put some extra touches on your gown. Do you like it?" she asked as she pulled it out, her eyes hopeful.

Syndria was speechless as she looked at the finished gown. Tamara had taken the white silk Healer's gown Syndria had carried as she fled the castle and turned it into a gown worthy of the Caron feast. The long sleeves had been cut off at the elbows and the v-neckline had been cut straight across the chest. With Tamara's help, Syndria had made a bustle to attach to the back. Lyddie had found some silver fabric scraps left from her own dress and helped the Healer put trim along the neck, sleeves, and hemline. The last time Syndria had seen the gown, that was the extent of the adornments. Today, however, white jewels lined the hem of the gown and swirled up the skirt. The design was simple, but intricately done.

"Kierney? What do you think?" Lyddie asked worriedly. "You aren't saying anything. You don't like it, do you? I'm sorry--I shouldn't have done anything without first asking you, but I just-"

"Oh, Lyddie," Syndria interrupted, "I'm sorry. It's not that I don't like it--quite the opposite. It is beautiful!" Syndria cried. "I have never worn something so amazing in my life. Thank you so much." Standing, she hugged the girl. "Thank you for everything. It has been so wonderful being here this week. I have had more fun than I can remember ever having in my life."

Pulling back to look at the Healer, Lyddie asked, "Why don't you stay? Surely you don't have to be home so soon. You could extend your visit and next week I could show you around Caron. We never have lessons the week after a feast, and if you stay we could go out instead of you being cooped up here with Mama all day," she said, her expression hopeful.

Smiling slightly, the young Healer answered, "I would love that, but I must be off. We will have to just make the most of our afternoon with the brothers. Now," she said as she sat down, "will you finish my hair, or do I have to go dance with Frederick with hair half straight and half in curls?"

The two girls spent all morning getting ready, yet the brothers still had to wait when they arrived to escort them to the feast. They sat in the main room with Tamara, Fitzgerald chattering away nervously while his older brother sat silently. When the two girls entered the room both brothers stood, anxious to be on their way. The walk to the Hall was quiet--Lyddie was unusually silent in her nervousness, and Syndria was reluctant to speak for fear of revealing something of her past. Though Sir Lawrence had approved of Frederick being the young Healer's dance partner for the feast, she was still afraid of saying too much.

Once the four reached the Hall, Syndria realized all her dance lessons hadn't fully prepared her for the feast. From the moment they all stepped through the doorway the Healer was trying her best to remember all the steps and twirls Tamara had made look so simple. When she tried to watch the women around her for help remembering, all it accomplished was making the Healer dizzy. When Frederick laughed Syndria looked at him in surprise, a quizzical smile on her face.

"Ah!" he chuckled, "So you can smile. You've been focusing on your feet for so long, I haven't seen anything but your furrowed brow since we arrived," Frederick said softly. "I promise I won't lead you astray--if you will just let me lead."

"I'm sorry," Syndria blushed slightly, "My dance partner the last few days had been glad to let me lead, seeing as how he is only three years of age. Perhaps it would be better for me to follow for a while."

For the rest of the dance, Syndria made herself relax and let Frederick lead. By the time the music started fading to an end, the young Healer had forgotten all the danger she faced and was actually enjoying her dance partner. It wasn't until she heard the final lofty strains of music that Syndria realized she had very little time left to bow out of the Hall before the Healers arrived.

When the orchestra finished the song, Frederick led his dance partner to the head of the table and seated her beside Tamara.

"Lady Tamara," he bowed slightly, "I have truly enjoyed having the honor of being your niece's escort. Could you please tell me where your husband has wandered off to? I would like to speak with him."

Smiling, Tamara replied, "I believe he has gone to speak with some of the members of the city council. Perhaps you can speak with him once the ceremony has ended."

After nodding to Tamara, Frederick turned to his date. "I am sorry to abandon you," he apologized softly, "but I must attend to an urgent matter. I hope you enjoy the rest of the feast." Then he simply turned and walked away, making his way out of the Hall. Lyddie and Fitz walked up to the table just as Syndria's escort reached the door.

"Did my brother say why he was leaving?" the young man asked Syndria as he helped Lyddie settle into her chair beside the young Healer.

Syndria shook her head. "Frederick said only that he had an urgent matter to which he must attend. He did not mention exactly what was taking him away from the feast." Turning to Tamara, she continued, "Aunt, I am afraid I must leave before the dinner as well. My head is pounding so that I would make for terrible company."

Tamara nodded her understanding. "Of course, Kierney. Perhaps we will have a chance to bring something home to you. I hope you are alright."

The double meaning clear to the young Healer, she nodded and replied, "I will be alright."

As Syndria stood, Fitzgerald seated Lyddie and then turned to the other girl, offering his arm. "I'm sure my brother would not want you to go home unescorted. I believe I know where he is. Would you allow me to take you to him?"

Syndria started to tell the young man that she could just walk home alone when Tamara spoke up. "Thank you, Fitzgerald. That would be very kind of you. I'm sure Sir Lawrence would see to her himself were he here, but in his absence I would greatly appreciate you and your brother seeing to Kierney's safety."

There was nothing she could do but smile and agree, so Syndria left the Hall on young Fitz's arm. As they walked, Syndria noted just how different the two brothers really were from one another. While Fitz was average size for his age, Frederick was tall and broad shouldered. The younger brother was also instantly comfortable with Syndria, asking all about Lyddie as they walked. Though his older brother had been polite, Frederick had only seemed comfortable when he had teased his dance partner about letting him lead.

Looking around, the young Healer was a bit alarmed to see that no one else could be seen on the empty street leading around the Hall. She tensed slightly, wondering if she truly should have trusted the young man to escort her. Fitzgerald was, after all, training to join the Royal Guard. Perhaps she should have never trusted the Councilman, either. The King's Council was always with him--this could all have been a ploy to return the Healer to Simann's dungeon. As soon as the idea had developed it faded again. Councilman Lawrence had known Nedra had been the one to send Syndria to Caron, and the young Healer knew that the Ancient never would have betrayed her. If she had trusted the Councilman enough to trust the young Healer to his care, Syndria knew she could do nothing but trust him as well. As the two drew nearer the back of the Hall, Syndria could hear low voices. She looked at Fitzgerald who still chattered on, seemingly oblivious to the fact that they were quickly approaching what seemed to be a very private discussion. Rounding the corner, the Healer was surprised to see Councilman Lawrence talking with Frederick.

"Here you are, safe and sound," Fitz smiled. "If you'll excuse me, I believe I'll return to the feast. All this dancing and wandering around has me famished! I hope you feel alright soon, Kierney." He turned around and quickly returned the way the two had just come, leaving Syndria standing awkwardly as she tried to think of what to say.

Before she could say anything, though, Frederick bowed his head slightly and asked, "Are you ready to leave?" The young Healer found it difficult to hide her confusion. Though his question was not unusual, the nod of respect was one reserved for the King's Court. Syndria decided not to acknowledge the sign and instead replied, "I am sorry to trouble you, but I'm afraid I am in need of an escort home. I believe the excitement of the afternoon has been too much for me."

"It is alright," Sir Lawrence spoke up. "Frederick is a friend. He will be helping you leave Caron tonight while most are in the Hall for the feast. You must leave now to avoid prying eyes. Tamara prepared a pack for you and left it on the bench in the garden. Frederick will protect you--of that I am certain. Now go. I cannot stay away from the Hall any longer." Turning toward the young man, Councilman Lawrence continued, "You are being trusted with our future. See her safely on her journey." That said, the Councilman turned and walked away.

Offering his arm, Frederick led the Healer away from the Hall as he spoke softly. "I apologize for my casual familiarity, Mistress, but Sir Lawrence warned me of the serious consequences if your true identity was discovered. I ask your forgiveness." After the young Healer nodded, he continued quickly, "Sir Lawrence told me of a gate hidden somewhere along the walls of his garden, a gate that leads beyond the walls of Caron. It has not been opened for some time, though, so it may prove difficult to find." As the two passed the front doors of the Hall Frederick's tone changed. Instead of the quiet, respectful tone he had been using, his words held a ring of concern.

"I am sorry you are not feeling well, Lady Kierney. I apologize for my absence immediately following the dance, but as I said, an urgent matter had to be attended to. I do hope you will feel better soon and will be able to enjoy the remainder of your stay here in Caron."

"Syndria nodded slightly and kept her voice soft, hoping she would sound weak to anyone within hearing distance. "It is I who should apologize, sir. You were kind enough to escort a stranger to the feast and then I must end the evening before it has even truly begun. Perhaps I will one day have the chance to repay you for your troubles."

"No trouble, my lady. It was my pleasure to escort you and be your dance partner," Frederick smiled.

Though nervous to be walking boldly through the streets of Caron while the other Healers were close by, the young Healer did her best to appear calm. Her heart, though, was pounding so loudly Syndria feared it could be heard above the commotion in the Hall.

When they reached Sir Lawrence's home, Frederick led his charge directly into the back garden and quickly made his way to the wall. He wrapped his hand around a section of the vine that covered the gray stone, preparing to pull it away in his search for the ancient gate, but stopped when Syndria's hand covered his, holding it still.

"Wait, please. If we pull away the vines we endanger Sir Lawrence and his family. Anyone who sees this wall after we leave must not be able to see that I passed through this garden. The Councilman will already be under suspicion for the sudden departure of his niece. Be patient," the Healer said, easing Frederick's hand back down to his side.

"I beg your pardon, Mistress," Frederick began, his impatience evident in his voice and tense posture, "but why are we waiting?"

"So far, no one has had reason to doubt Sir Lawrence's loyalty or my identity, so we are in no hurry." Syndria spoke quietly, suddenly much calmer than she had been in the city streets just moments before. "If I am correct, this gate you and the Councilman speak of is the one used by the last True Wizard in his escape. Searching will accomplish nothing. This gate opens on its own, but only to those deemed pure of heart." The

Healer stood before the wall only a moment more and then turned away. As she walked toward the bench in the center of the garden, Syndria spoke quietly. "Come. Rest a moment and wait." Frederick reluctantly followed. Usually a man of action, the young man couldn't understand waiting for a hidden gate to open on its own. However, he could not bring himself to go against the wishes of a Healer and sat down beside Syndria. Still tense, he was startled when the Healer suddenly got off the bench and knelt beside the pond.

"Are you positive that the gate is located in the wall, or is it just found somewhere in the garden?" she asked, her voice suddenly excited.

Frederick thought for a minute before replying. "I suppose I made the assumption that the gate is located in the wall, since that is the only logical place for a gate to be found. Perhaps it is possible for the gate to be somewhere else, though I do not see how."

"It is not only possible, it is most likely," Syndria said. "A gate in the wall would be visible from the other side, and the walls outside the city are kept clear of foliage. This is the gate," she finished, staring down into the water.

Frederick said nothing. Though he feared the girl before him must be crazy, the last five years Frederick had spent every day in Guardsman training, in part learning the proper etiquette of the

Royal Court. During that time, Frederick had learned that the Guards were never to argue with the Healers, and he assumed that rule still held true when said Healer had apparently lost her mind. So he knelt next to Syndria, hoping she would not waste too much time staring into the water. Something deep in the pond caught his attention just then, a tiny glimmer in the darkest waters. He leaned closer, straining to see the mesmerizing light. As he drew nearer the strange light seemed to grow and change, taking on a yellow glow and dancing in the water. As he watched, the light spread to encompass the entire pool. The water, the plants in the water, the fish--everything disappeared, swallowed up by the light. Beside him, the Healer stood and stepped into the light. Frederick's hand shot out, ready to catch her when she fell into what had been a deep pond just moments ago. However, when she stepped the light vanished as suddenly as it had first appeared, revealing a steep spiral staircase disappearing into darkness.

Syndria never hesitated. She hurried down the stairs into the dark, calling back, "If you wish to accompany me, you had better follow quickly." Glancing around, Frederick sped down the staircase behind the Healer.

Chapter 6

"Now it is time for you to be on your way."

Paodin looked up in surprise as the old man spoke for the first time in hours.

"The sun has set," he continued. "It is safe for you to travel now, and you have a long journey ahead of you. If you wish to stay ahead of the Guardsmen who were here before, you must be on your way." The old hermit moved quickly about the small room, gathering supplies off the many shelves and piling them on the table. Most things had been prepared in advance, like the small packets of food wrapped in a thin brown cloth, so Paodin's departure would be quick and efficient.

"How do you know the time of day?" Paodin asked, finally voicing his curiosity. "The light down here never changes, and you can't hear anything outside..." he trailed off, realizing that once again the stranger had chosen not to answer his question. So instead, he stood and began combining all the small packages into one gray pack he would be able to carry on his back. Once the table was cleared, Paodin was ready to be on his way. The road to Lurn was a long one across open farmland, with very little cover. If he couldn't make the journey under cover of darkness, his capture was almost guaranteed.

After hoisting the heavy pack and hanging the wide strap across his chest and shoulder,

Paodin tied the leather bands of the dark brown cloak the old man laid over his back. "Thank you for all you are doing for me," he said, turning back to face the man when he reached the foot of the staircase. "Perhaps soon the Kingdom of Tundyel will be returned to the people, with the heir of Rilso on the throne." The old man didn't respond-- Paodin hadn't expected him to, though. He headed up the stairs, half expecting the two guards who had been in the dugout earlier to be waiting for him once he reached the surface.

Slowly, Paodin pushed the heavy board up to reveal the quickly darkening forest. Just before he climbed up into the night Paodin felt, rather than heard, the man's presence behind him on the stairs. He turned to see the old hermit holding a sword. During the entire time he had spent in the small underground home, Paodin had never seen the weapon. The old man hadn't been carrying it when he surprised Paodin in the woods and somehow it hadn't been revealed when the Guards had searched. Without a word now, the old man handed the gleaming sword to Paodin and then walked back down into the room below.

Paodin quickly climbed out and hurriedly dove behind a briar bush before looking around. Once he was satisfied that no one waited for him, Paodin took a minute to examine the broadsword. He couldn't see it well in the black forest, but the hilt felt as if it were made for his hand. The sword was perfectly balanced and felt not only natural in his hand but like an extension of his arm. He swung it through the air a couple times before he realized he was wasting time. He headed south, moving as quickly as he could while still in the forest. In just a few minutes he had reached the edge of the trees and stood looking out over a treeless pasture.

The moon was just past full and bathed the land in light, flooding every hill and valley. Paodin could see nowhere he would be able to hide as he crossed the pasture, but at least the moonlight would reveal anyone watching for him. Paodin crouched on the edge of the woods staring up at the sky while he caught his breath and steeled his nerves. The night was beautiful and cloudless, which would have been wonderful on any other night. However, tonight Paodin silently wished for a cloud to settle over the face of the moon and obscure his path. Tonight, though, that would not be happening. There was not a cloud in sight and Paodin had no time to waste waiting here in the shadows if he was going to reach Lurn before daybreak.

Paodin didn't know how he would find the farmer the old man had said was loyal to Tundyel. He had no plan to take him across to the mountains, no idea what would await him when he finally arrived back in Gelci. Right at the moment, he didn't even know if he would be able to move across the plains undetected. The only thing Paodin was truly sure of was the importance of the journey. Taking a deep breath, Paodin tightened his grip on the sword and stepped out into the revealing moonlight.

*******************

Much to her surprise, the staircase that had appeared in the pond wasn't slick or even too dark. Though there were no torches or lamps lighting the path, Syndria had no problem seeing what lay before her. When she looked back, however, she could see nothing but blackness. She knew Frederick had followed--she could hear his footsteps falling behind her--yet she hadn't seen him since she started down. Once the Healer reached what seemed to be three stories underground, the stairs began to lose their steepness. Soon the path was flat, and much wider than the staircase had been on the way down. As Syndria looked around the tunnel around her began to lighten. Soon she could see not just the path before her but also the rock walls on each side of her. The young Healer stopped, her breath taken away by the beauty she was seeing. The stone glittered as if it held some growing light inside, shining through and giving life to the intricate carvings which covered every inch of the tunnel walls. Lines swirled and spiraled from floor to ceiling, all weaving together to form designs Syndria had never seen, even though she had spent her life in the castle. Nothing King Simann's artisans could create even began to rival these walls. The swirls and spirals seemed to be moving, winding their ways up the wall or down the hallway, flowing streams of gold and silver. Any trepidation the Healer had felt when she first stepped into this enchanted underground world melted away. Somehow Syndria could just *feel* that this was a safe place.

"This is amazing," Frederick said in awe, coming up beside Syndria. "It is hard to imagine that I have lived my whole life with this under my feet and never knew." He started toward the wall with his hand stretched out, drawn to the shining streams. As her escort moved closer to the wall Syndria began to feel uneasy. Just when she opened her mouth to tell Frederick she thought it would be a bad idea to touch the wall, he did.

Nothing happened. "It feels like glass, despite the carvings." Frederick gently glided his hand over the ribbons of gold and silver. Syndria silently chided herself for giving her doubts and fears room to grow as Frederick let his hand drop and took a step back toward the Healer. As soon as he set foot back on the path, a strange sound began buzzing through the tunnel. The shining metallic ribbons suddenly grew brighter, filling the underground passageway with blinding light. The buzzing shot up to a deafening roar, crushing the two intruders under its weight. Syndria felt her knees buckling, saw Frederick crumble to the path beside her, but she refused to fall. Though the pain was tremendous and flooded her body from head to toe, the Healer had spent most of her life taking excruciating pain upon herself. She dropped her hands from covering her ears and forced her eyes to stay open despite the light. Before her, forming out of the gold and silver streams, was a figure.

It didn't exactly look like the form of a man, but Syndria couldn't describe it any other way. There was no face, but somehow the young Healer could still see expressions she recognized. The first emotion she saw was surprise, seemingly a reaction to her stand against the pain. That was quickly followed by recognition. Syndria couldn't understand how, but she was sure that the presence not only knew her, it knew everything about her in an instant. The young Healer felt her every fault being revealed in the searing light. The knowledge that someone, or something, could essentially see right through her made Syndria feel weak, a feeling she wasn't used to experiencing as a Healer. That was when a thought occurred to her. This gate was thought to only open to those pure of heart, but perhaps that was not the case. Maybe it opened to anyone who knew it was there and determined worthiness and intentions once the traveler ventured down into the tunnel.

Syndria fought the urge to fall to her knees under the weight of her faults. Instead, she struggled to think about her strengths and the purpose of her journey, hoping the being she faced would deem her worthy of the path she followed. Then as suddenly as the presence appeared it vanished.

The Healer felt a great weight lifting off her shoulders as she blinked rapidly, trying to make her eyes adjust once again to the dim light inside the passageway. Looking around, all seemed to be as it had been. The gold and silver streams wound their way up the walls and down the length of the tunnel, stretching as far as Syndria could see in the soft light. She looked back expecting to see Frederick where he had fallen when the mysterious presence had first appeared. No one was there. She started back, went a few steps, and then realized she had to keep moving forward. She didn't know what had happened to Frederick, but if she was right about the passageway he had been proven untrue to her path. She took a deep breath, picked up the pack her escort had been carrying, and walked on. To where, she didn't know. Once she reached the surface again, Syndria knew it would be almost impossible to know who to trust. If necessary she would avenge Nedra's death herself, though she hoped it would not come to that. Surely she would find others who could see Simann for what he really was.

********************

"What do you mean, 'He lost her'?" Euroin raged, flying to his feet. The men before him flinched but stood their ground. They were used to the Wizard's temper and knew he needed them too much to cause them any harm--at least for now.

"They went into some kind of gate behind Councilman Lawrence's house where Frederick says they met some kind of horrible beast. It knocked him to the ground with one clawed hand and the next thing our guard knew, he was once again standing in the Councilman's garden," Erik answered. The Master of the Guard, Erik had been put in charge of finding someone unknown to the Healer who would be able to get close to her, someone trusted by the Councilman. Frederick had been a perfect choice. His younger brother was already close to the Councilman's daughter Lydia, and her suggestion that Frederick escort the girl she called her "cousin" had made his task easy.

"I had her in my grasp," Euroin hissed, his eyes sparkling, "and you fools let her slip away! You must find her. I will not let the enemy have her and have the ability to be healed to attack more than once." The Guardsmen stood still, not knowing if the temperamental wizard was finished with them yet or not. If he was, waiting a moment more would be nowhere near as bad as leaving too early if he had more to say. "What are you waiting for? Go find her--and bring the Councilman to me!" With a slight hand motion, Erik led his guards out of the room.

\*\*\*\*\*\*\*\*\*\*\*\*\*\*\*\*\*\*\*

Paodin ducked behind a haystack, hoping for a few minutes rest to catch his breath. By his guess, so far he had made it almost halfway to Lurn. Now he had just about two hours left until dawn and he still had a long way to go. Carrying his sword by hand had slowed Paodin down tremendously, so now he decided to find some way to carry it so he could run. After taking off his cloak, Paodin pulled the pack off his shoulders and leaned back against the hay. At first glance, nothing he saw could be used to hold the sword. The leather strap tying his pack shut was strong but thin. If Paodin had to use his sword he would slice through the leather and then once again have no choice but to keep the sword in his hand. Seeing nothing to use on the outside, Paodin quickly opened his pack and began searching through everything the old man had sent with him. There was some silverware, and a small dagger. The knife surprised Paodin. He thought he had seen everything the old stranger had put into his pack, but somehow he had added the dagger without Paodin noticing. He pulled it out, flipping it in his hand to feel its weight. Even in the moonlight the blade glittered. How did an old hermit get his hands on such fine weapons? No one in the resistance had blades that could even begin to match the quality of the two Paodin had just been given. Maybe the old man would be able to find more swords for the members of the resistance.

Paodin shook his head, trying to refocus on the matter at hand. He looked over everything in his pack again, setting aside the dagger. The fork! He picked it up and started bending it, fitting it around the sword blade, then cut off two small lengths of the leather string. He quickly slid out of his heavy shirt and cut four slits in the back of the thick material. By threading the two leather strings through the holes Paodin attached the fork to the back of his shirt before pulling it back over his head. It took a minute for him to find the makeshift scabbard, but once he slid the sword in it sat surprisingly well against his back. Though it made his shirt collar pull uncomfortably at his neck. He tied the pack shut and pulled his cloak over his sword, making sure he could still get to it quickly. Taking one more full breath as he stood, Paodin started running toward Lurn.

He reached the city gates just as the sun began to rise over the hills. Gasping for breath after running almost constantly for two hours, Paodin moved around the corner to the side wall of the city and collapsed against the cool stone to catch his breath. Here he was, just outside of Lurn. Somehow now he had to figure out a way to find the farmer true to the rightful King and the effort to see that heir back on the throne. Paodin dropped his head into his hands, trying to come up with some kind of plan.

"Are you alright?" a small voice asked. When he looked up he was looking directly into the eyes of a young boy.

Smiling in hopes of putting the young boy at ease, Paodin answered, "I'm only tired. I've just been on a long journey to get here."

The boy cocked his head as he studied the strange man sitting slumped against the wall. "You need rest," he observed, "but you won't get that in the city." Stretching out his hand, the boy took Paodin by the arm. "Come with me. Mum'll give you something to eat and then you can sleep. Come on!"

With the boy tugging impatiently at his sleeve, the exhausted traveler could think of no good reason not to go with him, so Paodin struggled to his feet and followed the boy, his leg muscles burning with every step. He didn't know what to tell the boy about his journey, afraid of saying too much. His fears proved unimportant, though, because the boy kept talking during the walk from the city.

"Mum and me live out here away from Lurn. My father died a couple years ago, so I take care of us. I come to town for the things we need. Mum doesn't like me travelin' alone; she says there's too many people in Lurn who would take advantage of a kid. I have to tell her to remember I'm not a kid anymore, I'm practically twelve! She always says she should go with me, but I wake up early and go without her. The trip's too long for her to make it on foot and poor old Red is almost twice as old as me. It would probably kill the old mule if I put a saddle on him. Besides, those people don't like Mum." As the boy continued, Paodin glanced down at his face and saw a familiar protective spark in the boy's eyes.

"When she does go with me they look at her like she's not worth the dirt she's walkin' on. I'm just happy she can't see that." His pace slowing some, he added, "But I know she hears all those dumb kids, even though she don't say so. Sometimes I just want to hit 'em for the mean things they say, but Mum says not to 'cause they just don't know better. She says that they learn it from their parents, that 'you can't expect people to be good and kind if their leaders are bad,' and that those kids just got stuck with bad leaders." His pace began increasing as his anger intensified, and he was almost jogging along the road when he suddenly stopped and spun to face Paodin. "Do you know better, mister?" he demanded, shoulders back and tense. Though he didn't elaborate, Paodin was sure he understood the boy's meaning.

"I didn't have a Mum like yours, but my father has always been a good leader. Perhaps you can tell me about your Mum and then we won't have to worry about-"

"If you really are good," the boy interrupted, "I don't have to worry." He began walking again, telling Paodin all about Red the mule and his escapades. Soon the two were approaching a small cottage tucked into a grove of oak trees. The front door squeaked when the boy opened it, but the home was otherwise in great shape. Paodin was surprised. This boy who was "practically twelve" really was taking care of his mother.

"Hello, Mum!" he called. "I'm home!"

"Adair, I do wish you would stop going to town alone," came a sweet voice from the kitchen. "Now why don't you bring your guest into the kitchen and we can all have some breakfast. I've made hotcakes."

Paodin looked at the boy, Adair, his eyes wide and questioning. "There are lots of things about Mum that'll surprise you," Adair said, then turned and led Paodin through the cozy front room and into the kitchen, where his mother stood at the fire with her back to the doorway.

"Have a seat and start on those hotcakes," she said. "I'm just finishing the tea."

"I would hate to cause you any trouble, madam. You weren't expecting company, and I'm sure you planned breakfast for two," Paodin said, reluctant to sit.

The lady laughed. "Oh, nonsense! You must not have known my Addie very long."

"It's *Adair*, Mum!" The boy rolled his eyes as he sat down, but Paodin could still see a smile tugging at the corners of the boy's mouth.

Her back still to them, Adair's mother continued, "As I was saying, if you had known my son *Adair* for long, you would know that he brings some soul home almost each time he ventures in to Lurn. Sit, eat, please." Though she still hadn't turned around, Paodin could tell his hostess was smiling with pride in her son. "There, I believe it is ready. Would you like a cup, sir?" she asked as she turned, pot in hand.

Paodin swallowed as he looked up. Though he had hesitated to sit and eat at first, as soon as the woman reinforced her son's invitation he had quickly begun chowing down. "Yes," he started to say as the woman turned around, but his voice caught for a brief moment before he could continue when he saw her face. "I would appreciate some tea, madam."

"It is Brigitte, please," she said as she gently patted the table in search of the mug. Finding it, she filled the stoneware mug and then returned the tea pot to its hook over the fire before taking her seat at the table.

As he finished his breakfast, Paodin studied the woman across from him. Her long red hair was pulled back in a tight braid, but the wisps which had escaped betrayed ringlet curls. Her creamy complexion was smooth and without freckles, unlike most redheads. Looking at her tiny frame, Paodin could easily see from where the boy's small stature came. Brigitte had long slender fingers, but her hands appeared far from fragile. Her movements were sure and steady, the smile on her face unwavering, visible even as she ate. Her beauty could have easily compared with that of any of the Healers. However, Paodin could not ignore her only imperfection. It started at Brigitte's left temple, crossed both eyes, her nose and right cheek, and twisted down her neck to disappear under the neckline of her pale green dress. The scarred flesh was an angry red, telling Paodin this terrible injury had occurred relatively recently. By the cloudy appearance of both eyes, Paodin could see that Brigitte had been blinded by whatever tragedy had befallen her. Judging by the size and shape of the scar, that injury had most likely been caused by the end of a sword.

As he finished his hotcakes, Brigitte spoke. "Adair, were you able to get our cornmeal today?" The boy started to answer, but his words were jumbled by the food in his mouth. "Son, please do not speak with your mouth full."

Swallowing, Adair rolled his eyes at Paodin as he answered, "Sort of, Mum. I traded some birds for fifty pounds, but 'cause I left the cart here this mornin' I've gotta go back for our cornmeal. I'll go this afternoon, after lunch."

"Good," Brigitte smiled, a crooked smile because her right cheek was frozen in place from the scar. "I'll go with you. I want to go and find some fabric--you are beginning to outgrow much of your clothing." She stood, clearing her plate off the table and putting it in the dish pail. "Finish your breakfast, Addie, and then we will get to work. Perhaps your guest will be able to help you mend the coop."

"Of course, madam," Paodin began, following Adair's lead and putting his own plate in the pail of water. "I would be happy to help, in appreciation for your hospitality." Turning to Adair he said, "Why don't you go gather our supplies and meet me outside? I would like to speak to your mother for a minute if you don't mind."

The boy hesitated, staring at Paodin as if he

could determine the man's intentions just by studying his face. Sensing her son's reluctance to leave her alone with the man, Brigitte spoke up. "Go ahead, Addie. Our guest will be right out."

"It's Adair," he muttered under his breath, giving Paodin a look of warning as he walked out of the room.

"Please, have a seat," Brigitte said, motioning to the chair across from her as she sat. Once Paodin sat down she continued. "My son is rather... protective. He has been forced to grow up far too much in the years since his father died, and I'm afraid that he now thinks of himself more as my protector than my son. Now," she paused, taking a sip of tea, "what brought you here?"

Leaning forward, Paodin laced his fingers together around his mug as he thought about how much to tell Brigitte. Before he could answer, the woman continued.

"You do not have to tell me everything." At Paodin's surprised silence she laughed. "I'm sure you wonder how I can be so certain of your hesitation when I cannot see you. To be honest, I can't say. It just seems as if my perceptions have changed. Now, like I said, you do not have to tell me everything. You are, however, a guest in my home right now, and I believe I deserve some kind of answer. If you do not wish to share your business with me, I must ask you to leave."

"I do not wish to lie to you," Paodin began, "but my business is dangerous. I will tell you what I can, and then you can decide if I should leave." When Brigitte nodded, Paodin said, "My name is Paodin. I am on the run right now from King Simann's men-"

"Please," she interrupted, "say no more. You are welcome in our home. Right now, however, Addie is outside waiting for your help in mending the chicken coop."

Paodin stood. "Thank you, madam. I appreciate your confidence in me, and I promise I will not betray your trust. Now," he said, his voice brightening, "I assume your coop is behind the house?"

The lady stood, motioning for Paodin to follow her through the small house. "Yes. I would imagine you saw the barn when you first approached with my son. You will find Addie around against the east wall." Paodin nodded and started out the door then stopped, realizing Brigitte couldn't have seen his nod of understanding. Turning back toward the door, he started to verbally acknowledge Brigitte but stopped his words short because she had already shut the door between them.

Turning to his right, Paodin spotted the barn. Like most farming families in the kingdom, Adair and his mother lived in a house that was half the size of their barn. As he made his way toward the towering building Paodin looked around. Though he was certain Brigitte had not let her tragic injury dictate how she lived her life, he knew she was not capable of helping her son much with the repair work, a never-ending chore on any farm. And though determined, Adair who had introduced himself as "practically twelve" was still too young to take care of even this humble farm on his own. As he looked around, however, Paodin could see very little out of place. He had a feeling the chicken coop and the mule, Red, were the only things in disrepair. He peered into the tree line, almost expecting to see a group of pixies or something else just as mythical waiting to swoop in and finish all the chores in the blink of an eye.

"I was startin' to wonder if Mum had sent you on your way." The boy's voice cut into Paodin's musings, startling him for a moment. "Why don't you grab that wire and we can string it up. We've already lost too many birds, but I ain't gonna tell Mum. She's already got too much to worry about, and I'm good at tradin'." As the boy chattered on, Paodin tried not to be too obvious as he corrected the boy's mistakes.

*********************

She had been walking for hours, yet the path had never changed. The gold and silver streams still shimmered on the walls, but Syndria ignored their beauty and mysterious pull. She had survived the earlier test of her intentions but she was not anxious to try and withstand that force once more. "Besides," she said to herself, "in my present sour state of mind I would probably not be allowed to continue on." Squinting, the young Healer tried to peer into the darkness ahead of her for some sign of a way out of the tunnel, but all she could see were the glittering lights winding their way down the walls. Sighing, she resigned herself to the long walk ahead of her.

Knowing somehow that she was unquestioningly safe inside the Wizards' tunnel led Syndria to let her mind wander, stopping first at the thought that Nedra was dead.
She found it hard to believe that her teacher, her confidant, her only true family since childhood was really gone. The Ancient had been serving Tundyel since the time of the True Wizards and Syndria had assumed her old friend would be around long after her own gift had faded. The knowledge of Nedra's death was made worse by the fact that she had been killed by the very man she had served under for decades. Though Syndria had always known King Simann to be capable of terrible things, she never would have thought him capable of killing the old Healer.

Syndria tried to stop her thoughts by shaking her head. She didn't want to dwell on thoughts of the King or imagine the torture that must have been required to drain the gift of life from Nedra. It would only anger her, and the path she had set out on when Nedra had rushed her from the castle was not one she could follow with eyes clouded by thoughts of revenge. Her battle, the one the young Healer now realized her Ancient friend had been trying to make her see since childhood, the one Syndria could now see clearly, was not a battle she could rush into blindly. King Simann was a powerful man, a king followed by men and wizards alike. While it was true that she felt a duty to her teacher, Councilman Lawrence had reminded Syndria that her true duty as a Healer was to the citizens of Tundyel. In the same way that her eyes had not been opened to the King's cruelty until she was forced to heal prisoners time and again, the young Healer knew the citizens of Tundyel had all been blinded to his evil ways. Her task of convincing them otherwise would be a hard one, for all that those outside the castle walls had ever seen of the King was his apparent kindness and generosity. The people were content, and with contentment came complacency. Those happy with the King, happy with their lives, would not want things to change, and Syndria feared that those willing to speak out had been silenced long ago. Others would be like Frederick who had appeared true to her cause until the two had entered the

Wizards' tunnel but who had then been found unfaithful. She feared one of the hardest tasks she was to face would be finding someone she could trust.

Growing up under Nedra's watchful eye had in many ways proven wonderful, but one thing she had never learned to do was read people the way the Ancient could. Sometimes it had seemed Nedra could peer through the masks people around her wore and see the truth of a person, so Syndria had always relied on her opinion of someone's true character. The girl didn't know how she would be able to determine somebody's true intentions, at least not without leading them through the tunnel which had revealed the truth about Frederick. If only there was some way she could still rely on Nedra's insight, her protection.

Syndria stopped in her tracks. She *did* have a way to test people against the Ancient's words. The day the prisoner Paodin had escaped the castle, when Syndria had gone to her old friend with her concerns, Nedra had asked her what she remembered about Paodin, and then she had reminded Syndria of her mother's promise that her bracelet would be the girl's protection. If Nedra had asked what she remembered of the prisoner, it must be important. Closing her eyes, the Healer blocked out everything else and focused on Paodin's appearance that day in the dungeon. At first the picture was blurred. All she could see was the dark, damp room she had seen almost every day, the blood stained floor, and a man huddled in the center. He slowly came into focus--first, his tattered clothes turned crimson by his own blood. Next, his black hair and broad shoulders. She saw him stand to his feet, could see him clenching and unclenching his fists as he awaited another round of torture.

The young Healer's shoulders dropped and she opened her eyes. Other than his confident stand against imminent death, Syndria couldn't see anything different about him than any other prisoner. Sighing she again began walking, wishing she knew of someone who could help her. Councilman Lawrence and his family would be quick to help, of that she was sure, but Syndria would not put them in any more danger. She had to find someone on her own, someone trustworthy. Absentmindedly she brushed her fingers over the silver bracelet on her wrist, hoping her mother's promise would prove true.

*******************

He was jarred from his sleep, startled by the sudden realization that someone had entered the tunnel not long before. *No*, he thought, sitting up, *two had entered. Only one remained.* Hurriedly he threw on his cloak as he ran outside. The night was not yet black, but it made no difference.

Though the lesser Wizards could not read the wisdom of the sky until the sun's glow had completely fled the darkness, he could. He closed his eyes and threw his head back, letting the vibrant colors flow around him. Soon the rich hues all changed to sparkling gold and silver, the markings of the true magic. He followed as they spun their way through time and space, these shimmering specters. Some began to resemble the True Wizards of old while others seemed content just to dance and twirl through the tunnel, bouncing off the walls and filling the small space with an unnatural light. Suddenly, there in front of him stood the young Healer. She steeled herself, straightening her shoulders against what she must surely think would be a recurrence of the test she faced before.

This time, however, the crippling pain was not present and the deafening roar had been replaced by a hauntingly beautiful melody. The young girl made no move to approach, nor did she falter and shift backward. Instead she stood proudly, accepting of whatever fate awaited her. He watched as the gold and silver beings swirled around the Healer, amazed at her ability to stand unflinchingly in the midst of them. Her only movement was an unconscious fluttering of her right hand to touch the small silver bracelet given to her at birth.

He smiled as he opened his eyes, once again seeing only the night sky. The young Healer would prove to be a tremendous asset to the true king of Tundyel.

Chapter 7

Syndria stood still, half expecting to disappear as had her escort in their earlier encounter with the shining lights. When nothing happened she began to relax, the tension draining from her neck and shoulders as she silently watched the beings twirl around her. Unlike before, this time she could see three faces within the light, all peculiar mixes of gold and silver. Though she felt certain she already knew the answer, the young Healer asked softly, "Who are you?" Though no sound came from the beings, Syndria heard their answers ringing deep in her heart and mind.

*"We are truth."*
*"We are righteousness."*
*"We are just."*

"The True Wizards," she said softly. "You are the ones who determine worthiness, the ones who say who may pass through the tunnel."

*"Wrong!"* she heard.
*"The heart determines one's worth."*
*"We merely reveal the heart."*

The luminous beings pulled back and Syndria began to fear they would leave her soon. Hoping to keep them near, though she did not know why, the young Healer began walking toward them as she spoke.

"Masters," she began, her voice smooth and

calm, "may I ask for your guidance? I am on a strange path to which I see no end, but to you it must be clear."

*"Each must follow his own path,"* the Wizards answered, now speaking as one voice. *"It is not our place to change the young Healer's steps."* As the True Wizards began to fade before her, Syndria hurried her steps.

"I do not ask for your magic to end my journey," she said, "merely for your presence to illuminate the trail."

*"The eyes of your heart are unclouded. Follow them, for they need no illumination."*

With that, the Wizards were gone and Syndria was left standing in the dark. It took a moment for the girl to realize she was standing in the midst of a forest, no longer in the tunnel. Spinning around Syndria searched for the opening, the gate that had let her out of that enchanted place. She saw nothing but trees and the faint glow to the northeast which told her the feast in Caron was lasting well into the night. Not sure where to go, not knowing which direction would provide some measure of safety, Syndria took a deep breath and turned west, deciding her best decision would be the one which put as much distance between herself and the castle as was possible in one night. Perhaps tomorrow she could make it to Saun.

\*\*\*\*\*\*\*\*\*\*\*\*\*\*\*\*\*\*

Paodin propped the pitchfork up against the stall door and then reached for the blanket Adair offered. Shaking it out, he spread the heavy wool over the hay he had just piled in the center of the stall.

"That's the last one Mum's made," the boy said. "When you go I'll take it in to sell in Lurn. Those folks may not like Mum none, but they sure like tradin' for her afghans."

Ignoring the boy's obvious resentment of the townspeople, Paodin agreed, "It is most definitely a fine piece of work. Here, let me show you a trick for when you find yourself out at night." Kneeling at the head of his makeshift bed, Paodin waited for the boy to come up beside him before he continued. Folding the top of the blanket down, he showed Adair how to stuff it with hay and tie the two corners together. "There, a pillow fit for the King."

Though Paodin couldn't see the boy's face in the little bit of moonlight coming in through the window, there was no mistaking the anger in his voice when he spoke. "If you were the King kneelin' here in our stables, I woulda run you through with that pitchfork!" He nearly spit the words in his disgust.

Though inwardly he smiled, Paodin admonished the boy. "It is not fitting for a man to speak of his king in such a manner," he said, hoping he sounded persuasive.

Swinging the lamp up beside Paodin's face, Adair smirked as he said, "You don't fool me! Besides, I heard you tell Mum you'd escaped Simann and his men and that you're on the run. You'd use the pitchfork on 'im, too, if you got the chance!"

Paodin didn't answer. Instead he took the second lighter blanket from the boy and then gave Adair a gentle push out of the stall. "Go on inside now and tell your Mum I greatly appreciate the two of you housing me for the night. Since we were too busy for you to go back to Lurn today, if you will wake me in the morning I will help you load the wagon for you trip into town."

"Night!" Adair called, scrambling out of the barn into the night.

"And you should learn not to eavesdrop!" he called after the boy, smiling.

As Paodin pulled off his boots and laid his pack aside, he thought about the boy's reaction when he had mentioned the King. Though Audon had raised his son with the knowledge that Simann was not the true King, Paodin had rarely seen the hatred this young boy's heart held for Simann even among the resistance fighters of Gelci. What had happened to cause the boy to be filled with such rage for a man by whom most were fooled?

Shrugging, Paodin knew he would not find the answer to his question in the dark barn, so he settled back into his makeshift bed and pulled the lighter blanket over himself. Just as he closed his eyes, Paodin heard something moving around outside. Jumping quickly to a crouched position he grabbed his boots and pulled them back on as he peered out the small stall window. In the moonlight he could clearly see a shadowy man making his way toward the chicken coop from the tree line behind the widow's house. Remembering Adair's earlier statement about having lost too many birds already, Paodin pulled his sword and silently made his way to the barn door, ready to face the man who was apparently the cause of that loss.

Sneaking across the yard behind the man, Paodin approached cautiously. He had encountered a limited number of thieves in his life, and not one of them had been ill prepared for a confrontation. Though this coward stole from a blind widow and her son under the cover of darkness, Paodin thought it better to err on the side of caution than to run full speed into the point of the robber's blade. A few steps behind the man, Paodin extended his sword and placed the tip against the base of the thief's neck.

"Stand, coward," he whispered intensely, "and face me." As the man turned, Paodin spotted the tools in his hands.

"Lower, your sword, good fellow," the man said quietly, "and tell me how you have come to be staying with Evan's widow."

Paodin ignored the man's request and kept the sword positioned at the stranger's throat. "The mistress of the house is fully aware of my presence, though I doubt you could say the same. It is you who should explain yourself. Move toward the barn, away from the house. I do not wish to alarm its occupants."

"Nor do I, lad." The man nodded slightly as he slowly stepped forward, Paodin's sword never losing contact with his skin. The two men moved quickly toward the barn, Paodin steady contact with the thief's neck. Though he had no desire to kill the man standing before him, he would not hesitate if the man's actions proved such drastic measures to be necessarily. Once inside the barn Paodin backed his prisoner into one of the many empty stalls before lowering his sword slightly. He studied the man in the pale moonlight as he questioned him.

"Speak now, man," Paodin said, his voice calm. "What are your intentions here toward Lady Brigitte?" Even as he spoke, Paodin was forced to admit to himself that the man looked nothing like a thief. He was well dressed and well groomed, though not clean shaven or in fine clothes.

"Despite my appearance at the chicken coop," the man began, his voice as calm as his accuser's, "you have my word that I intended to do nothing more than mend the fence. The boy- Adair- mentioned in town this morning that he would be working on it today. Judging by the workmanship," he continued, "it would seem he had some help." Raising his eyebrows the man gazed steadily at his captor.

Paodin pondered the man's words silently before he spoke again. "Your words seem honorable, but what reason do I have to believe you?" Unconsciously Paodin had lowered his sword even more and now rested the point of the toe of his boot as he listened to the man's reply.

A smirk tugged lightly at the corners of the man's mouth. "Surely you are not blind! Look around--can you honestly tell yourself that this place has been cared for by a child and his blind mother? While the lady of this house is indeed very capable, I fear she was not one for farm work even before her injury, though not from a lack of trying."

"Perhaps I am a fool," Paodin sighed after a long silence, "but I believe you." Looking around the dim barn he spied a milk bucket in a corner. Whatever cow the widow had once milked had dried up long ago. Paodin wiped cobwebs coated with dirt off the bucket and then tossed it to the man still standing in the empty stall. "Have a seat and we will talk." Stepping over to his makeshift pallet in the next stall, Paodin picked up a small box which appeared to have once housed a farmer's tools and then turned to the man.

"You seem to know Lady Brigitte well," Paodin began. "Why do you come to help under cover of darkness?"
"It seems I have known her my entire life," the man smiled, sitting. "Her husband Evan was my best friend and sole confidant. Before we speak of the lady, though, I would like to know who I am speaking with, if you will do me that courtesy."

"Of course, sir. My name is Paodin, son of Audon of Gelci. Right now I am on a journey of sorts, which has led me far from home and exposed some formidable enemies."

"Ah!" the man exclaimed. "I have done business with your father on occasion, whenever he has found the time to travel down here to Lurn. I suppose you are the young boy who was with him on those trips. He is a good man and I have little reason to doubt he has raised his son to be honorable as well." Leaning back casually against the barn wall, he continued. "My name is Jamis. Because of your father, I believe I am safe in speaking freely with you. Now, you asked why I come under cover of night?" When Paodin nodded, Jamis answered with a question of his own: "Did the boy know you were correcting him?"

Paodin frowned. "How could I tell him so? Adair is proud and believes himself capable of providing for his mother---"

"Exactly," Jamis interrupted. "I owe it to Evan to look after his family since he was killed, but I cannot do that at the expense of his son. The boy has been thrust into manhood much too early, it is true, but despite his youth he is very much a man. Without his pride, his dignity, a man is nothing."

Nodding his understanding, Paodin asked the older man, "You said your friend was killed. Was that attack the same one that left his widow scarred and started the fire of hatred for King Simann burning in his son's heart?"

Studying Paodin, Jamis replied, "So, the boy has told you of his contempt for our King."

"Not in so many words, no. I believe his statement was that he would like to run him through with a pitchfork."

Jamis laughed, a rich, though bitter, laugh that seemed to fill the barn. "Adair has never been one to mince words, much like his father. I fear that one day that trait will earn him the same fate as Evan. My friend was… not happy with the King, and he was one of a few who were very vocal about their opinions. They came in the night, the guards, and attacked Evan and Brigitte as they slept. Evan never had a chance to even defend himself. He and his bride were both left for dead, but not before the King himself had a chance to steal everything of worth from them both. Evan was forced to watch, bleeding and helpless, as Simann raped his wife and then slashed her face, leaving the scars you see today. Brigitte then heard her husband die at the hands of Tundyel's *beloved King*." Jamis' words were full of hatred and pain as he continued. "I don't know why the boy was left alone. Maybe Simann saw how much more cruel it would be to leave the child with his dead parents. Or it could be that he just didn't care what happened to the boy. Perhaps Adair was attacked but in a way that left no visual scars. We will probably never know. Yet somehow the nine year old boy was able to nurse his mother back to health. He has been taking care of her for close to three years now, with only a few nightly repairs around the farm from me."

Paodin's eyes were dark and stormy, his anger rising as Jamis revealed the story of the attack. Though he had been tortured by the King's Royal Guard almost continuously for three days, his own pain seemed as nothing compared to what the woman now granting him shelter lived through and now lived with daily. Seeing how Jamis' loyalties lay with Tundyel and not Simann, he told the older man of his capture and escape from the castle and also of the old stranger who had told him of the Prophecy.

"He also told me there would be someone in Lurn who would be willing to help me in my search for the True Wizard and the heir of Rilso. I have come to believe you are that someone," he finished, looking at Jamis. The man didn't answer. In fact, Paodin didn't think Jamis had even heard what he said. He was staring past Paodin, and the younger man almost turned to see what held his attention when Jamis spoke.

"The Healer in the castle," he said, his gaze finally jumping back to Paodin, "what did she look like?"

"The Healer? Why do you ask?"

"Please," Jamis leaned forward, "just tell me, if you remember. It is important to me."

His brow furrowed as he tried to remember what seemed to be such a pointless fact at the moment, Paodin described her as well as he could remember. "She was small, with dark hair--either brown or black, I can't be sure now. She was young, I suppose, and kind. She was also very powerful. Not only did she heal my wounds, she removed the pain." As he spoke, Paodin watched Jamis. His eyes grew wide in anticipation as he listened to Paodin's description. "I don't really remember much else about her appearance, though I'm sure you can picture a Healer in her gown with her long hair. The one thing I can see clearly is the color of her eyes. They were a striking blue, unlike any I have ever seen."

Jamis' breath seemed caught. He moved his lips, but no sound escaped.

"She told me her name---"

"Syndria," the man whispered. Then, "Syndria," he repeated louder. "She is my daughter. I have not seen her for twelve years now." Smiling, he shook his head as if to bring himself back to the moment at hand. "Thank you for indulging a father's hope. My wish is that one day I will see her serving her people instead of that man she is forced to obey. Now, I believe you said you need some help? I can take you as far as Krasteiv. We will leave two days from now. I do some selling there once a month at the market. Once there I know a man who will be able to provide you with whatever you need for your journey, even a mount. Though he is not necessarily against the King, he will not ask questions and will give aid to anyone, for a price," he said, standing.

Thank you, Jamis. Until then, I will try and help Adair as much as possible. Sir," he said, stopping Jamis as he walked out of the barn, "Your daughter? I believe she was raised to be honorable as well, and that one day soon you will see her serving her people. She has powers beyond those of a Healer, strengths that come from somewhere deeper than just an ordinary gift."

Nodding, his eyes glistening, Jamis turned and moved quickly across the field and back into the trees.

******************

Smothering the curse under her breath that threatened to escape even through clenched teeth, Syndria pushed herself up out of the unladylike heap in which she had landed. Though the moon shone brightly high above the trees, the ground underneath was dark. This was not the first time the Healer had tripped over some hidden root in her haste, and Syndria could feel the throb of a sprained ankle. The pain didn't bother her--she had dealt with much worse in her years of healing--but the limp caused by her injury frustrated her. Though a Healer had the ability to heal any injury in others she could not use her gift on herself, so Syndria just kept moving. She knew the sprain wouldn't be able to heal naturally unless she gave her ankle a chance to rest yet there was no choice but to keep moving. If she stopped this close to Caron it would be only a matter of hours before King Simann's Royal Guard was upon her.

"Yeah!" she scoffed, "As if I have much more than hours anyway. I'm certain the King has his Wizards following my every move, biding their time. After all, King Simann wouldn't want to waste any energy having his guards follow me if they can just wait until I stop somewhere." Straightening her shoulders and lifting her chin, Syndria brushed aside all her negative thoughts. "So, I just keep moving until I find someone, anyone, to help in my cause. Men are taken to the castle weekly for questioning and torture--surely I am not so blind to the intentions of others that I cannot find the men who oppose Simann's cruelty. If any of the Ancient's gift for reading people rubbed off on me through the years, now is when I need it."

Dusting off her beautiful gown, hoisting the pack to her shoulder, and taking a deep breath, the young Healer picked up her pace. Looking around in the moonlight she took in the trees, the bushes, the flowers just starting to peak out. Somewhere above her an owl hooted, and a brook babbled in the distance. At the base of a tall oak Syndria spotted sticks and twigs leaned up against the trunk, undoubtedly the workings of some child erecting what his mind's eye saw as a mighty fortress. It was for this land that she must fight, and its people were her master. If they could not see Simann for the tyrant he truly was, it was the young Healer's duty to open their eyes to the truth. She would fight to free her people, even if the battle seemed futile. If needed, Syndria was willing to sacrifice her own life to see the good people of

Tundyel freed form Simann's oppression.

\*\*\*\*\*\*\*\*\*\*\*\*\*\*\*\*\*\*\*\*

Euroin's black cloak swirled in the still room, whipped around by an invisible force. The Wizard stood in the north tower of the castle, a tower seldom visited. This tower had imprisoned the True Wizards prior to their executions, binding them in a web of powerful spells none of them had been able to untangle fast enough. Only when all of them died had the web suddenly snapped, leaving in its ruins the remnants of dark and dangerous magic. Though the Royal Wizards were quick to use any powers available to them in their service to the King, through the years none had called upon the dark magic created out of the murder of the True Wizards. Tonight, though, Euroin planned to do just that.

The room he stood in was small but ornate. It had once served as the meeting place for the King and the Wizards, and marble statues stood against each wall. What once had been beautiful likenesses of the creatures which roamed Tundyel had taken on menacing appearances the moment the True Wizards died. Regal cougars now looked like ravaged, starving hunters intent on the kill; mother bears that had been protecting their cubs were now ready to devour them. The room was filled with an evil you could feel even before stepping over the marble threshold.

Since the Healer had first escaped the castle, Euroin had been focusing on finding her. He had been searching across the kingdom but had not been able to detect the girl's presence anywhere, something he was not about to let King Simann know. The only explanation was that she had been hidden by magic, so Euroin had begun searching through every trace of spells in Tundyel, sifting through the layers to find what had been hidden underneath. Despite all his best efforts, Euroin had found nothing more than the simple spells cast by his fellow Wizards to cover memories of King Simann's atrocities or the complex webs made to hide the ruins of some village or farm the Royal Guard had destroyed. Nowhere could he find a spell covering the young Healer. Before now, anytime Euroin wasn't able to find someone he concentrated on was because that person was dead. This time, though, Euroin knew this was not the case. He had not been able to find either the Healer or the prisoner since they had left the castle. As much as Euroin despised the idea, the Wizard had been forced to admit that some more powerful form of magic was hiding both traitors. To Euroin, this meant there was only one thing left to do. That was what had brought him to the North Tower.

His eyes closed, Euroin watched as strange remnants of magic swirled around him. Many of the spells were utterly foreign to the Wizard, spinning in colors and patterns he had never seen and couldn't name. Throwing his arms out wide, Euroin called the spells to him and felt the dangerous magic coursing through his body. It took all his strength to keep the magic from overpowering him and destroying him where he stood. The dark magic battered the Wizard, tossing him about the room and crashing him into the many statues. The strange new power sent shock waves through his body as Euroin struggled to regain control. His mind was completely empty of all else--the only thing he could see was the swirling magic. As he was being thrown around the tower, Euroin blocked the pain out and tried to concentrate on finding the right spell. He couldn't find the Healer, but the Wizard was determined to stop the girl. Suddenly he fell to the floor, the malevolent magic leaving him in a heap on the cold stone.

For a moment Euroin didn't remember what had happened. He looked around in a daze for the marble statues, most of which had been knocked to the ground while the Wizard was being thrown around. Confusion spread across his face when he saw that some of the animals were gone. The confusion changed to satisfaction as understanding dawned on him. The young Healer would soon face an unimaginable challenge, one she had no chance of surmounting on her own.

## Chapter 8

"There has been no sign of either the Healer or the prisoner in Sephon," Ilcren said, taking a seat across from Euroin in the older Wizard's sitting room. "I have left Ridan, the lesser Wizard of the district, in charge of the search. I thought perhaps my services would be of more use here at the castle."

"Ridan? Why has he remained in Sephon when all the wizards of Tundyel have been summoned to the castle?" Euroin raged, fixing his harsh glare on the younger man.

Ignoring the Wizard's quickly mounting temper, Ilcren answered, "The others have all left the district and come to the castle at your bidding. However, I left Wizard Ridan with orders to keep searching for the young Healer and the prisoner. If the less powerful Wizards who are here are to be able to protect King Simann they will require training. My gift of teaching would be useless had I remained in Sephon, and you need my abilities to make up for your own… shortcomings." Ilcren's piercing blue eyes never faltered as he held Euroin's gaze.

Crossing his arms, the old Wizard leaned back as he replied, "Call your young sorcerer away from Sephon. He is no longer needed to search, for I have taken care of the girl myself. And though I do not require your help in the training of these other sorcerers," he spat out, "I will allow you to aid me. You are, after all, much closer to their level. Perhaps you will be easier for the fledglings to understand." Euroin glared at Ilcren for a moment before continuing. "You may, in fact, begin their training now. Leave me."

Ilcren leaned forward, casually laying his arms on the table which separated him from the old Wizard. Ignoring Euroin's command, Ilcren asked, "What of the prisoner? Is he not much more dangerous than a simple Healer? If he is truly from the Order of the Four, should you not focus your energies on him?"

Euroin exploded from his seat, slamming his hands on the small table. "*Those Wizards* were executed decades ago. And even if you were right," he snarled, "a search for him would prove useless!"

"As it well has," Ilcren smirked. He was suddenly thrown back in his chair and the small table crashed against the Wizard's chest, pinning him to the wall.

Euroin flew forward, his green eyes sparkling with a strange light. "You have mocked me too often, Sorcerer. Perhaps the fates are in your favor, though, for today you have a task to begin." As the elder spoke, Ilcren could feel his windpipe being crushed by some invisible force. He struggled to breathe, sucking in tiny gasps of air as Euroin went on. "If you keep your mouth shut and do as I command, perhaps I will spare you." With that, the choking ended as suddenly as it had begun. The table fell to the floor, clattering at Ilcren's feet. Before this, the young Wizard had never felt intimidated by Euroin, despite his explosive temper and often violent outbursts. This time, something was different. The light that sparked in Euroin's eyes was dangerous, a power Ilcren did not know. Silently he stood, head bowed, and walked out of the room.

*********************

Syndria sighed. The sun was beginning to peek brightly through the trees, yet as the Healer looked around it seemed she had made little progress in the hours she had been walking. Until now, she had seldom been required to walk farther than from her room to the dungeon. Even when she had taken walks with the Ancient, the two had never done more than stroll around the outer walls of the castle. Never had she imagined how vast Tundyel must be. The young Healer felt exhaustion such as she had never experienced before, much different than the drain she felt after a healing. She seemed able to feel the blood pounding through every inch of her body, threatening to explode from its ever weakening casing. The dress that had been so beautiful the night before, the wonderful icy creation which had been so painstakingly perfected by the ever adoring Lyddie, was torn and stained, the bouncy rag curls she had worn to the feast limp and stringy. Laughing aloud--a bitter laugh, but still a chuckle--Syndria thought to herself that it would surely be impossible for anyone to recognize her for a Healer now. Maybe it would be alright to stop for a while after all.

Hearing water rippling close by, Syndria pushed her way through briars and thorn bushes to collapse on the bank of the small stream. She dropped the pack Tamara had prepared for her next to her lap, then leaned forward and dipped her hands into the clear water. The stream flowed from a spring to the north, so it was surprisingly cold. Splashing some on her face, Syndria gasped as the icy water quickly snapped her out of the trance-like state in which she had walked for the last few hours. Wiping her hands on the cleanest spot she could find on her gown, the girl untied the pack in anticipation of a chunk of Tamara's sweetbread. Her eyes widened in delight as she took in the pack's contents. Besides the sweetbread, Tamara had packed a hunk of salted pork and fresh cheese. There was also a small bundle tied in red trim, and Syndria's mouth watered as she realized the pretty little bundle held molasses candies she had helped Lyddie make. Once the food was out of the pack, she couldn't believe her eyes. Syndria tore off the soiled gown she had been wearing and tossed it aside. There in the bottom of the pack lay the deep red dress Tamara had first altered for the girl. She splashed the cold water from the stream over her body, more concerned about not getting the dress dirty than with the sting she got from the icy stream in the morning breeze. She pulled the red gown on over her head, smiling with delight at the thought of Tamara's loving gesture. Feeling refreshed in the new gown, Syndria sat down to eat. She tucked the candies into her pocket for later, knowing that if she ate even one now she would devour them all. Just as she took a big bite out of the pork, she heard a twig snap in the forest behind her.

Lowering the pork to her lap, the young Healer cautiously peered over her shoulder into the trees. There, crouching low and almost invisible under the thick brush, waited a large tan cougar, its golden eyes intent on the girl by the water. Its haunches quivered as the cougar prepared to leap, and Syndria felt a chill run up her spine as she watched the beast lick its lips.

She rose slowly to her feet and turned to face the beast, hoping it would not be brazen enough--or starving enough--to pounce while she matched its gaze. Much to her relief, the cat didn't leap. However, that relief soon changed to a different kind of terror as the tawny mountain lion began to inch forward.

Syndria stood frozen, her wide eyes never leaving the cougar. Never before had she seen a wild animal so boldly approach a human. There had been a man in Lurn when she was a child who had tamed a wolf, but he had raised it from a pup. As the cougar crawled out of the bushes into the light, the Healer could see what had made the beast desperate enough to risk coming near. Its right hind leg was bloody and badly mangled. Patches of hair were missing and in one place low on its leg Syndria could see the white of a bone showing through.

Immediately all fears flew out of her mind as the compassion of a Healer pushed aside all other feelings. Stooping slowly so as not to frighten the injured animal approaching her, she picked up the salt pork from where it had fallen onto the ground. The cat stopped in its tracks, unsure of what to do next. Its eyes darted back and forth, looking from the meat in the Healer's hand to the woods behind. Tossing the large chunk a few feet closer to the cougar, Syndria moved back toward the water's edge and sat still. Cautiously the cougar hobbled forward, a wary eye constantly on the human just a few yards away. Once it reached the meat all thoughts of Syndria seemed to vanish as the big cat devoured the pork, seeing as how it never once looked at the girl.

Syndria's heart broke as she watched the

poor animal. Judging by the ravenous way the cougar attacked the pork, it had not eaten since the injury. Since she was so young when her gift had been revealed, Syndria had often snuck away from Nedra during her training and used her gift on injured animals. She had healed birds with broken wings and kittens with thorns in their paws. She knew that she could help the mountain lion if only she could place her hands on the terrible injury. However, Syndria had no idea how she would be able to get close to the devastating injury without coming into contact with the teeth that were tearing into the salt pork or the terrible claws that would so easily tear into her.

Syndria settled in by the brook, watching the starving animal. The meat vanished quickly and the cougar began sniffing the air. It soon spotted the fresh cheese and sweetbread still lying on the untied pack halfway between it and the Healer, but was too wary of the human to approach. Syndria looked away from the cat and sat silently watching the brook trickle over smooth stones. Though she knew staying in one place for too long while she was running from the castle was dangerous, the Healer's empathy won out over the girl's fear, and Syndria waited for three hours before the injured animal drew close enough to eat the bread and cheese. Another long wait found the large cougar limping up to the small brook, now starting to ignore the girl just a few yards upstream.

      After drinking its fill, the big cat lay down beside the water and began licking its hind leg to clean the terrible wound. Soon though, the cougar seemed to finally give in to what must have been excruciating pain and lay still, its golden eyes watching Syndria with only mild curiosity. Slowly the young Healer began inching toward the big cat, careful not to look at it. The cougar didn't move or tense up; it just lay watching the girl. As Syndria moved into the mountain lion's reach she made herself stay calm. Her breathing was slow and steady, her movements smooth as she reached out toward the cat. The Healer had no idea what would happen next, but she knew she had to be ready for the worst. What happened as her hand got closer to the animal, though, was like nothing Syndria had imagined.

      The cougar looked away from Syndria, seemingly unconcerned with her presence. The Healer didn't hesitate, afraid even the slightest hesitation would unnerve her or make the cougar reconsider its trust in her. As she placed her hands gently on the wounded leg and let the healing life flow through to the cat, nothing else mattered to Syndria. She no longer worried about her own safety from either the cougar or King Simann because everything she was, was now focused on healing. She drew the big cat's pain into herself, a little shocked at the intensity. Finally, she could sense that the animal was whole again.

Immediately the cougar's muscles tensed under Syndria's touch and he jumped up, knocking the Healer off balance in his haste. In a flash he was back in the trees, no sign of his presence left beside the stream. Looking around her, Syndria almost wondered if the injured cougar had been part of a dream, that maybe she had fallen asleep beside the stream and just imagined the whole thing. She soon pushed that thought aside, though, for she could feel the drain healing the cougar had put on her gift. She sat still for a moment to gather herself before moving on. Standing a few minutes later, she picked up the pack Tamara had sent with her. Not a crumb was left of the food and now Syndria's stomach began to rumble as she remembered how hungry she was. The Healer shrugged her shoulders, for she knew there wasn't anything she could do at the moment. Turning back to the water, Syndria decided to follow the brook southwest. Maybe she would come upon someone living along the water before reaching Saun who would be willing to spare some food. It would be safer if she could find someone outside of the city, since they would be less likely to know her as the Healer running from King Simann. A smile crossed her face when she remembered the small bundle in her pocket. Pulling it out by its red ribbon, Syndria took out a candy and popped it into her mouth, savoring the sweetness and hoping the sugar would give her enough energy to hold her over until she could find someplace to get some food.

*******************

He closed his eyes, searching through the colors swirling around him. Hidden deep within the most secret of spells was the young Healer, moving along beside the stream. Her tiny frame made her seem fragile, but he could see a strength and resolve that seemed to be growing more and more as each hour passed. Simann could not be allowed to kill the girl or he would be snuffing out the flame of hope for Tundyel that glowed brightest in all the kingdom. Though his powers were strong, he would not be able to hide the girl for long. For there, circling through the bright colors of his ancient magic, was a darkness, an evil magic almost as ancient as his own. Though that evil had not yet found the Healer it drew ever closer, its darkness devouring any light in its path in its relentless pursuit of the girl. He feared Tundyel's chance for freedom from Simann's tyranny would end before it really even began, yet there was nothing more he could do for the young Healer except refuse to give up hope.

*******************

"Good mornin', mister," Adair called from the barn door. "You're not still asleep, are you?"

Sitting up to pull on his boots, Paodin stifled a yawn as he answered, "I suppose I'm being lazy this morning, Adair. I didn't even know the sun was up." He walked out of the stall to see the boy struggling with the wagon. Moving quickly toward him, Paodin spoke up, "If you'll go start gathering the eggs I'll bring the wagon out and meet you at the coop."

Still tugging at the wagon to pull it out of the small cluttered stall, Adair said, "I did that already, before I came in here to wake you up. Mum said you must be tired after your long trip here yesterday and I should wait to get you up so as you could get more rest."

"Well in that case," Paodin said, stepping in between the boy and the stall, "I've missed out on a lot of the work already this morning. Let me get this." He lifted the wagon out of the stall and sat it down in the barn where he could pull it outside.

Walking out behind Paodin, Adair picked up a bucket from beside the barn door and put it in a corner of the wagon. The metal pail was full of eggs, cushioned by hay. Paodin tossed a large bundle of Brigitte's afghans into the wagon next to the pail, tucking it down into a corner to give the eggs more protection. The wagon was small but heavy, even though filled with blankets, and Paodin didn't know how Adair had managed to haul it up and down the hill by himself for the last three years--or at least not when it was loaded.

Adair interrupted Paodin's thoughts. "I need to take some of the birds in to the market today. Mum wants me to get another rooster 'cause she says we don't have enough chicks being hatched. There's a little pen in the barn, so I'll go get that while you take the wagon over to the coop. Then, Mum says we have to go in and eat breakfast before we can leave for town." The boy turned and headed into the barn, not waiting for a response from Paodin. Smiling and shaking his head, Paodin hauled the wagon over to the coop and sat down on the corner of it to wait.

"Let Addie get the chickens. I would like to speak with you."

Paodin jumped up when he heard Brigitte speak. He hadn't heard her walk up behind him from the house. "Of course, Lady Brigitte." Brigitte was already walking back toward the house, so Paodin quickly followed. As the two walked, Brigitte began to speak.

"I understand you plan to go into Lurn with my son this morning. I feel I must discourage that, for you would likely be putting yourself in danger. Though I know little of your past, the fact that you are running from King Simann and his men means that you will not be welcome in the town."

"Is that why you are not welcome there?" Immediately after asking the question Paodin regretted doing so. Brigitte's posture changed completely. Her shoulders tensed and her ever-present smile vanished.

"My son seldom speaks of that night, even to me," she said, quickening her pace. "How is it you have earned his trust so quickly that he would confide in you?"

Paodin winced, glad Brigitte could not see the expression on his face. He knew he had to answer but he was hesitant to reveal Jamis and his nightly visits to the farm. Instead, he replied, "Adair told me nothing of a specific night, but since his... displeasure with the King is so evident I assumed he must have had something to do with the scars that mar your face." Reaching the house, Paodin opened the door and stepped aside to allow Brigitte to enter ahead of him. "After you, my lady." Once inside he continued, "Please forgive me for prying. I am but your guest and have no right to question you."

Brigitte smiled as she seated herself at the table, a smile genuine though small. "Never mind apologizing. Yes, my opinion of Simann is the reason the adults of Lurn do not welcome my presence. Thankfully their dislike does not carry over to my goods, for so far Adair has been able to sell every afghan I have made. Now," she said, no longer wishing to speak of herself, "like I said outside, you will not be welcome in town if any recognizes you for who you are--a traitor, in their eyes. Though you seem capable of taking care of yourself, I do not wish for the townspeople to have yet another reason to tell their children to shun my son. He may be young, but Addie has proven himself very capable in the last three years since my husband was killed. If you will just help him to prepare the wagon, I will ask you to stay behind and do some chore when he leaves." Standing as she heard the door open, Brigitte's demeanor quickly changed and she was once again smiling brightly when her son entered the house.

"So, you slipped inside early!" Adair teased, sitting down in the seat his mother had just left. "I see how you work. You hoped Mum would let you eat my share."

"Adair," Brigitte admonished playfully, "if you keep speaking to our guest like that, *I* just might eat your share! Did you get the wagon loaded?" she asked as she sat a bowl of corn grits on the table in front of Paodin and then turned to dish some up for Adair.

"Yes, Mum. We'll go to town as soon as we eat," the boy answered, digging in to the thick grits.

"I wish you could put this off until later,"

Brigitte said casually as she sat down with her own small breakfast. "There are so many things that I would like to accomplish today, but I need your help to do so."

"Mum," Adair started, his voice garbled by the food in his mouth. He stopped when he saw his mother's raised eyebrows and swallowed before going on. "I can't go later or we won't get a good price. Today's the openin' of market, so all sorts will be in Lurn. I can just help you tomorrow."

"I had hoped we could have a day off tomorrow, perhaps to take a walk out to the bluffs. Oh well. I suppose that will have to wait."

Sensing his cue, Paodin spoke up. "Adair, why don't you stay and help your Mum? I can take your goods in to town to sell," he said, hoping he was reading the boy correctly. His tactic proved effective when the boy answered.

"Nobody in town knows you, so they won't trust you. Why don't you help Mum, and I'll go? I could get a better price on all of it. Can I, Mum? Paodin can help you here, and then we can go tomorrow out to the bluffs, if you still want."

His mother paused as if considering before she answered. "Alright, Addie, but you can't be spending all day at the market. I don't want you staying in to eat at the tavern. I don't like you going in that place."

"Of course not, Mum," Adair said, then

gave Paodin a conspiratorial wink.

\*\*\*\*\*\*\*\*\*\*\*\*\*\*\*\*\*\*\*

"How is it you have failed me for so long?" The question was presented calmly, but Euroin knew his answer could be the difference between life and death.

"My King," he began, bowing low before the stone throne, "forgive your servant. I have failed you until now, it is true, yet soon the Healer will no longer be a problem. She cannot escape my powers any longer."

Simann stared at the Wizard, his blue eyes cold and lifeless. "Perhaps not. Or perhaps it is as I have heard whispered around my castle as of late-- there exists still a True Wizard with powers which greatly exceed your own." Euroin tensed, but he did not speak. In King Simann's court, one did not speak unless given permission. "It is only by my mercy that you and those other four fools were not executed the moment you let that mere boy escape." Crossing his arms over his broad chest, the King leaned back in his ornate throne. "Your magic has proven worthless thus far. This Healer-- from where does she hail?"

"The girl is from Lurn, my King," the Wizard answered, still bowing, for Simann had not granted him permission to stand in his presence.

"Bring me the Master of the Guard," the King called out. Standing, Simann walked across the throne room to look out over the courtyard. He was a handsome man, and when the sun touched his blond hair it shone like the purest gold. His muscular frame moved gracefully, almost like a dancer, as he walked across the room. Within minutes the tall guardsman, Erik, was entering the room.

"You called for me, my King?" he asked as he bowed, slightly breathless from running to the throne room.

Without turning from the window Simann spoke. "You will go to Lurn with my army. Find all the traitors and execute them. When the Healer shows herself in her hometown, bring her to me. Leave me now," he said, not once looking at either man. "It is tiring to have to do everything on my own. Send the Healers to my chambers."

"Yes, my King," Euroin said, quickly leaving the throne room. Once in the hall he stood straight, his eyes burning with indignation at being forced to cower before Simann. After passing the King's demands on to a servant standing outside the door, the angry Wizard stormed out of the main tower of the castle and back to his small cottage in one of the many courtyards. He threw the door open without touching it and sent chairs, tables, and dishes clattering against walls. His black cloak billowed around him as the Wizard stormed through the room, though there was no breeze.

With only a glance from the irate Wizard, a fire roared to life in the hearth.

"You seem upset."

Euroin spun at the words, for the first time seeing the wizard seated in the corner. "Wizard Uylti, why are you here in my quarters?"

Uylti quickly walked across the room to stand in front of the older Wizard. "Please forgive me for intruding, Master Euroin. I have some urgent news, but I was told you had an audience with the King when I arrived back at the castle so I came to wait for you here. I'm sorry for not waiting outside, but I was weary from---"

"Stop blubbering, you fool," Euroin interrupted. "I do not wish to hear how your jumps around the kingdom put a drain on your limited powers. Tell me your news."

"Of course," Uylti said quietly. "As you are well aware, I have been in Nelthien searching for the traitors."

Once again the older Wizard interrupted. "Do not tell me what I already know, Uylti. What is so important that you did not simply send word?"

"I- I thought I should, well," he stammered, his head slightly bowed, "I thought it best to come aid in the training of the lesser Wizards, so I decided to tell you in person. On the border of Finley, in Wykel, there are rumors of a rebellion forming."

Euroin stared silently at the other Wizard, waiting for him to continue. When it became clear that he had no more to say, the Wizard Euroin asked, "Is that all? Your 'urgent news' is that a rebellion is forming? We have known that since Simann first took the throne."

"But Master Euroin," Uylti added quickly, "this is different. There have been wagon loads of swords intercepted in Wykel as they were being sent across the border into Finley. This uprising appears to be more than just a few unhappy farmers as in the past. I believe they are forming an army."

Euroin's laugh surprised Uylti. "Once again, is that all? King Simann commands the greatest, most highly trained force in Tundyel's history. They wield the finest weapons in the kingdom, weapons forged in sorcerers' fires. Do you truly fear field men with inferior blades?" He sat down before the fire, calmer now, before continuing. "And even now all the Wizards in Tundyel are within the castle walls, learning wards and spells as we speak. Since you did not ride back from Nelthien, I suppose you did not encounter the walls Ilcren has been teaching them to weave, walls no ordinary man will be able to breech. Despite their belief in themselves, these rebels will not be able to strike so much as a stone of Castle

Tundyel. Our own soldiers would not even have to lift a finger were it not for King Simann's insane order that they go to Lurn!" Uylti said nothing, unsure of how to react to Euroin's sudden mood change. Instead he stood quietly as the old Wizard continued.

"I have taken care of the girl myself--soon she will not be giving aid to anyone. Yet Simann is so sure of his own plan that he will have all the people of Lurn killed off before admitting that his order was not needed. Once this... annoyance is taken care of, how does that man expect us to be able to cover his reckless deeds? It proves difficult enough to weave a web to cover the ruins of a swift defeat, yet he expects us to keep the people of his kingdom from knowing that he has wiped out a city one by one!"

"I suppose," Uylti said, "it must be almost impossible for someone without our powers to understand the complexities of a web of secrecy. Sometimes it seems as if we could better serve a King who possesses the gift--at least to some degree." Uylti's eyes widened as he realized the danger of speaking such words aloud and he began rapidly trying to qualify what he said. "Though it would be easier, I would want no other King, even should an heir of Rilso be found. Not that I believe an heir of that family still exists---" A knock on the door saved Uylti from digging what was quickly becoming a deep hole, much to his relief. The younger Wizard knew Euroin would not hesitate to reveal his peer's uncertainty to Simann, should doing so raise his own status in the King's Court and give the Wizard more power.

Without even flinching, Euroin opened the door from where he sat across the room. Uylti's brow furrowed slightly in confusion, for he had never seen the older Wizard move objects without so much as a hand gesture. However, he soon shrugged the thought aside when Alek entered the room, Ilcren close behind. While they were giving reports about the training of the lesser Wizards, Osidius appeared in the doorway. Unlike the younger Wizard Uylti, the other four Wizards had long ago mastered the art of shifting and could easily move around the Kingdom of Tundyel in an instant. Osidius was more precise than the other Wizards and could shift into buildings, something none of the others practiced for fear of shifting into a wall or some other stationary object.

"Master Euroin," Osidius began, "the prisoner has been sighted moving south through the district of Meinsley. A farmer who arrived in Lurn for the spring market was heard speaking of a man who he spotted running across his land two, perhaps three, nights ago. I ordered the farmer brought to me and questioned him myself, and I believe this man is the traitor we seek."

Euroin stood facing the other four Wizards of his order. "Perhaps the King's plan will not prove so worthless. Though he will not be able to draw the Healer out, if this traitor is of any importance to the rebellion forming we may be able to wipe out their force sooner than expected," he said, the strange light sparking up in his eyes once again.

*******************

Early in the afternoon, Paodin was replacing some warped boards on the barn when he spotted Adair running up the hill. He pulled the heavy wagon behind him, bouncing its contents wildly.

"Paodin!" he yelled breathlessly as he reached the top of the hill. "Paodin!"

Dropping the hammer and picking up his sword, Paodin ran to the boy. "What is it? Is someone following you?"

"No," the boy panted, "it's not me. They-they-"

"Take a breath, Adair. There's no rush," Paodin laughed, figuring Adair was overreacting to whatever he deemed the problem. Taking the handle of the wagon away from Adair, Paodin started walking toward the house.

"No!" The boy reached out and grabbed Paodin's arm, stopping him. "It's you! They are looking for you in the city. Some man even told me to be careful because you'd be dangerous. You have to leave. They were talkin' about goin' out to search people's farms today and tomorrow, and they already don't like me and Mum. If they find you here..." He let his words trail off, but Paodin understood what the boy left unsaid.

"Let's go inside," Paodin said, pulling the wagon along behind him, "and you can tell me more of what was said in Lurn." Adair followed him in, still trying to catch his breath from running up the hill.

"Is that you, Addie?" Brigitte called when she heard the door open.

"Yes, Mum."

"Why, I must say that I am pleasantly surprised to have you home so early. Was the Tavern going to be serving liver and onions today?" she joked, drying her hands on her apron as she walked out of the kitchen. When Adair didn't answer right away, Brigitte grew concerned. "What is wrong, son? Did something happen in at the market?" Dropping her apron, Brigitte held her hands out to her son, drawing him to her when he reached out and took her hand.

"Mum, they are searching for Paodin," he began.

"Yes, Adair, I am aware of that. I suppose I should have told you last night that our guest is hiding from King Simann and his Guard, but I did not think---"

"No, that's not it," the boy interrupted. "I heard all that while he was tellin' you." Adair continued, either unconcerned or unaware that he had just admitted to eavesdropping. "Some farmer out to the north said he saw Paodin, and now the men in town are searching all the farms. Somebody even said they thought the King would reward them for bringing him the traitor."

Speaking for the first time since entering the cottage, Paodin questioned, "Adair, did anybody see you running home like you were running up the hill?" Moving toward where Brigitte stood, her arms around her son, Paodin knelt before the boy.

Adair nodded and answered, "Yes, but I didn't run until the smithy told me to watch out or the traitor might kill me on my way home." As the boy spoke, all three heard the staccato of hoof beats galloping up the dirt road.

Brigitte stood and quickly stepped toward the front door. "Master Paodin, move into the kitchen. If the men come to search the house you may be able to slip out the back. Adair, go out and begin unloading the wagon. Hurry now," she said, shooing him out the door. Just as the boy stepped outside a rider appeared topping the hill. He rode straight to the front door and stopped without dismounting, pulling a second horse by its reins.

"My lady," the man said, pushing back the hood that shadowed his face, "there is no time to waste."

Brigitte tilted her head to the side as she tried to place the man's voice, quickly coming up with his identity. "Jamis? Why have you come here?" As soon as she spoke the man's name, Paodin hurried through the front room and stood beside Brigitte, sword in hand.

"Please pardon my rudeness, Brigitte, but I have no time for pleasantries." Then looking at Paodin he added, "You must leave here at once. Richard the smithy has gathered a search party and is headed up the hill this way." Nodding, Paodin ran out to the barn to get rid of all signs of his presence and to tie up his pack.

"Jamis," Brigitte began, "how is it you knew Master Paodin had been a guest in my home?"

The man hesitated before saying, "I'm afraid that is a conversation we do not have enough time for at the moment." Knowing that answer would not satisfy her, Jamis added, "However, I promise you an answer once I have seen your guest safely on his way." He nodded then spurred his horse quickly to the barn, arriving at the door just as Paodin stepped out. The younger man mounted the horse being led along, taking the reins from Jamis as he called out to Adair.

"Shake out that blanket to remove the hay before you take it inside, Adair, and take good care of your mother. She is truly a remarkable woman." Then riding close to the house in front of the door where she stood, Paodin added quietly, "Thank you for your kindness, Brigitte. Perhaps we will meet again under better circumstances, when the true heir has taken the throne." With a swift kick, Paodin took off with Jamis and the two vanished into the woods.

"Addie," Brigitte called out, "bring that blanket inside. We don't need it out in the barn when those men get here. Then I want you to come help me finish unloading the wagon."

"Yes, Mum," the boy called back, hurrying to the barn. Then, seeing that his mother was searching for the wagon, he hollered, "It's out next to the hitchin' post." Brigitte counted out six steps from the door to the post and then pulled out the fabric Adair had chosen at the market. It was heavier weight than she would have chosen for Addie's summer shirts, but it didn't matter. Since he had picked out the fabric on his own the boy would never complain. Smiling, she turned back to the house and had just stepped inside when she began to hear the voices of men approaching. She waited a few moments before calling out, "Adair, come inside! I don't want you out there playing around while I try to carry in that big bag of cornmeal by myself. Hurry up now!" She closed the door behind her and took a few deep breaths as she waited for the men to arrive.

Soon, Brigitte could hear the men outside talking to her son. Swinging the door open and stepping outside, Brigitte called out, "If you have business here, sirs, it is with *me*, not my son," then stood waiting, her hands on her hips.

"Of course, woman!" one of them laughed, the man Brigitte assumed to be Richard, the leader. Without moving any closer to the house he yelled out, "We have orders to search your place, seeing as how you and your boy would be sympathetic to traitors," he growled, then motioned for the men with him to spread out. When one of the men approached the door to search through the house, Brigitte did not budge. The man was forced to physically move the woman aside to get through the door, a second man following close behind.

"While there is no question of my alliance," Brigitte snarled back, "there has been no *traitor* in my home. Had I known such a man was in need of someplace to stay, however, I would have gladly given him shelter."

Richard laughed. "I see your temper flames up as red as your hair, woman," he said, once again addressing her as one would a low-class woman instead of the customary title of "lady." "And had you not already been put in your place I would be tempted to do so myself. As you are now, it's not worth the time." At his words Brigitte's face turned red, but not from shame. Her fists and jaw clenched in anger.

Though Adair did not understand all the man's words insinuated, he could read the signs of her anger unmistakably. Quietly he took a few steps away from the man and picked up one of the smaller boards Paodin had been using to fix the barn. While the man spoke, saying something Adair didn't understand about Brigitte's virtue, the boy moved up behind him and swung the board with all his strength, connecting with the man's lower back and cracking the board. The man moaned as he fell to his knees, one hand going to his back and the other catching himself so he didn't sprawl flat on the ground.

Standing over the man and still holding the board, Adair spoke through gritted teeth, "My Mum's better than you'll ever be!" As he spoke, the two men who had been searching the barn came running out. Seeing their ringleader on the ground, one snatched the board out of Adair's hands as the other grabbed the boy tightly by both arms.

"Let me go!" he yelled, struggling to get away from the man who held him.

"Take your hands off my son," Brigitte ordered, moving quickly toward the commotion. "I do not know what he did, but he was defending my honor. Turn him loose!" As she moved toward Adair, Brigitte ran into Richard, who was still hunched over on the ground. A tiny smirk spread across her lips when Brigitte realized her son had knocked the big man to his knees. Addressing the smithy she mocked, "What now? Are you going to teach the boy a lesson? I'm sure your friends will be terribly impressed to hear you won a fight with a child, especially one who was defending his blind mother." At her words the man holding Adair let him go, and the boy quickly moved to his mother's side. Brigitte laid a steady hand on his shoulder to calm the still raging boy.

Slowly, and still clutching his back, Richard stood. "Get Thaddeus. The traitor is not here with this wench." Turning, he slowly began to move toward the downhill path, his men soon following. Brigitte stood still as they left, waiting until she could no longer hear their footsteps. Then she silently hugged her son and the two walked inside together.

*******************

Syndria stood frozen, her eyes wide as she stared at the wolf blocking the path ahead of her. Here by the stream's edge there were just a few feet of clear land between the water and the forest, and the large grey beast stood growling right in the middle.

"First the cat, now this," Syndria whispered. Though she knew little about beasts of prey in the woods, the young Healer knew it was unusual that she was having her second close encounter with one in a matter of hours. Unlike the cougar, though, the wolf didn't appear injured in any way, nor was he made nervous by the human before him. Judging by the tongue that darted out every few seconds to lick the snarling lips, to him Syndria was nothing more than a meal, and an easy one at that. When the wolf crouched and then sprung, the girl closed her eyes, knowing there was little more she could do. A split second later there came a whimper and Syndria opened her eyes in time to see the wolf crash to the ground with the shaft of an arrow sticking out of its ribs.

"You're awful lucky, girl." Turning toward the trees, Syndria saw a man step out into the small clearing by the stream, bow in hand and a second arrow notched and ready. He approached the wolf cautiously, not releasing his bow until he was sure the animal was dead. When he prodded the beast with the toe of his boot, a strange expression came across his face. Dropping his bow to the ground still strung and sliding the arrow back into the quiver on his back, the man knelt beside the dead wolf.

Syndria studied the man as he studied the wolf. Dressed in leather breeches and a leather tunic, the man had a thick mustache and beard which covered his mouth. His wiry black hair was flecked with silver and he wore it tightly pulled back at the nape of his neck. His hands were gnarled, most likely from years of manual labor since the man did not seem old.

"That's one strange creature," the man muttered, speaking more to himself than to the girl just three feet away. "I just felled him and the bugger's already stiff. Oh well, I s'pose a scrawny beast like that's not goin' to make good meat anyhow." As the man spoke, Syndria let her gaze drift from the man to the "strange creature" he had examined. Something about the animal seemed odd, but at first she couldn't place what that might be. The man reached out and with one hand grasped the arrow to remove it from the dead wolf, placing his left hand against the animal's rib cage. As soon as he touched the wolf the man jumped back, almost falling in his haste to get away. His eyes wide, the man seemed more frightened by the dead wolf than Syndria had been of the live one just minutes earlier.

"That ain't natural," the man whispered. "That creature was alive, but…" he trailed off.

Stepping forward, the Healer knelt beside the wolf's head for a closer look. *That is not possible*, she thought, but at the same time she could not deny what she saw. Stretching out her hand to confirm what she already knew, the Healer gently lay her hand against the wolf's fur. Instead of coarse hair, Syndria was touching something hard and unyielding. In fact, the wolf's entire body had turned to stone. When she pulled at the arrow it didn't budge--the head was encased in the marble wolf. What magic was at work here? Syndria hade never seen such a spell worked by any of the King's Wizards, yet who else could have done such a thing? And why had this beast been sent after her, for there would be no other reason for such a creature to be in these woods. Why hadn't Simann just sent a guard?

"Come away from that," the man said gruffly, pulling Syndria's mind away from her questions. "It ain't safe to mess with magic--it's unnat'ral." Syndria obliged him and took a step away from the marble wolf, but she hesitated to move toward the man. If he was so against magic, what would happen if he recognized who she was? Looking him over from head to toe again, Syndria decided she had nothing to fear. Judging by his appearance the man who had just saved her life had little interest in the happenings of the castle. It seemed likely that he would not even know of the search for the Healer who had betrayed her King.

The man had started back through the woods, but stopped when he realized the girl was not following. "Well, come on, girl," he said, his tone impatient. "You're wastin' my hunt. If I get you to the missus quick enough, then maybe I can get back out here 'fore it gets too dark. That woman's likely to tan my hide if I don't get her no meat today."

Syndria smiled when the man turned back to her, holding back a laugh she was sure would irritate and offend her rescuer. Never before had she heard such colorful speech, or at least not that she could remember. She hurried along behind the man, anxious to meet his "missus." The man moved quickly, and soon Syndria was standing in front of a small cabin nestled in the trees. Smoke rolled from the chimney and since a fire wouldn't be needed for warmth today the Healer assumed the woodsman's wife must be cooking. Her stomach rumbled at the prospect, earning Syndria an odd look from her guide.

"I suppose you're gonna be wantin' some grub," be grumbled, stepping through the open doorway. "That's the missus, over by the fire. I don't have time to mess with you if I'm gonna get some meat." Turning, the man left Syndria standing in the middle of the one room cabin. It seemed the woman at the fire hadn't heard her husband talking, for when she turned she jumped at the sight of the girl.

"Why, child, you just about scared the life outta me! Here I was expectin' to see some injured critter dropped off in my doorway and I turn to find a pretty little girl. By all that's good, what's a tiny little thing like you doing out in these woods alone anyway?" The round woman quickly crossed the small room, wrapped her arm around the Healer's shoulders, and ushered her in to sit at a small table. If she felt the girl stiffen at the foreign feeling of having someone's arm around her, the cheery woman didn't let on. "Just sit right down and let me get you something to nibble on. I just started the fire for some stew tonight, so I'll toast you up some of the bread I made yesterday and you can slather on some sweet cream butter. I told Simon I would move out here to the middle of nothin' only if he let me keep Maybelle and that calf of hers, and am I ever glad I did. Sweet cream butter is just one of those things that's hard for a girl to give up!" As she spoke, the woman tore off a chunk of bread and sat it on the rack over her fire, just above the flames.

"Well, where is my head?" she chuckled. "I imagine you'd like to know who's feedin' you. Like I mentioned, that grump you met in the woods would be my man Simon, though he's not as gruff as he would like you to believe. My name is Josephina, but I've not been called that for a long while now. Simon calls me Ina, and I suppose it would work for you to just as well. What would your name be, dear?" she asked, handing Syndria the warm bread smothered with butter.

Unsure how to answer, the Healer took a bite of the bread in order to have time to think. Swallowing, she said, "Forgive me be for being so rude and not answering before I sampled your bread, but it looked delicious and I hadn't realized how hungry I was until you handed this to me. My name is Kierney," she finally said, deciding to use the name Councilman Lawrence had given her. "Your husband happened upon me at the most fortuitous time and saved me from the jaws of a ferocious wolf. I am ever in his debt." She bowed her head slightly in thanks, a gesture with which Ina seemed unfamiliar. "Perhaps one day I may repay you."

"Oh, don't you worry about that, child. I'm just happy you're here because it gives me another woman to talk to. Now, don't say one more thing about 'debts' and 'repayment.' None of that has too much meaning out here anyhow. Now tell me, where were you headed to before my Simon came upon you?" she asked, leaning toward Syndria and propping her arms on the table between them.

"Honestly, madam, I don't know where I was headed. There were those at home who no longer welcomed me, so I sat out to find those who will."

"Why, you're not much more than a child! How old are you?"

Syndria smiled. All her life people had mistaken her for younger, although most realized their mistake when she spoke. "I am nineteen, though I may not look it. And despite my appearance I am quite able to take care of myself."

"Well, I've lived your life thrice over now, and Simon has close to four, so to me you're still hardly more than a child," she said, almost pouting, before cheerfully adding, "However, I suppose you're old enough to look after yourself, seeing as how I was looking after me and Simon both when I was your age." Just then the burly man came through the door carrying a rabbit, and Ina turned her attention to her husband.

"Take that dirty critter out of my house. I don't want you trailin' blood all over my floor again. But take care to keep that hide in good condition this time. I couldn't even use it last time you brought a rabbit home!" Muttering something under his breath that Syndria imagined she wouldn't want to hear, Simon turned and stepped back outside, his wife following close behind in order to oversee his work.

*******************

"This is as far as I can take you," Jamis said, bringing his horse to a stop. "Krasteiv is still an hour's ride to the west. I'm sorry I cannot take you all the way into the city, but I must return to Lurn to aid in the search for you. Perhaps I can delay Richard and his men a while, searching through local barns and such. However, I fear you will have very little time to get out of Krasteiv before news of the 'traitor' spreads. Within a few days' time your journey may prove very difficult."

"I will not stay long in Krasteiv. This stallion is a fine mount--I believe he will easily carry me back to Gelci. Once there I hope to persuade the resistance that it is time to openly increase our numbers. No matter how few join our cause and begin searching for the heir, it will prove better than I alone." Paodin offered his hand and Jamis grasped it. "Thank you for your help, both for myself and on behalf of Lady Brigitte."

Jamis laughed, shaking his head. "I'm afraid she may not be so ready to thank me. Brigitte has always been independent, even when Evan was living. I fear she may not welcome my secrecy."

Dropping the older man's hand, Paodin chuckled, "You may be in more danger than I, friend." Nodding their farewell, the two men had started to part company when Jamis called out for Paodin to stop. Reining in his spirited mount, Paodin turned back toward Jamis.

"Take this," Jamis called, tossing Paodin a small leather sachet. "It is not much, but it will get you provisions for your trip to the mountains. When you get to the Amber Stream Tavern, ask for a man called Red and tell him I sent you." With that he turned and rode back toward Lurn, leaving Paodin with the coin purse. Paodin turned as well, heading west and toward whatever lay in store.

Chapter 9

Paodin walked into the Amber Stream Inn and Tavern just as the sun began to set. The tavern was dark, lit by only a few candles placed sporadically around the room, and the place was empty except for the bartender and two grizzled old men seated at opposite ends of the mahogany bar.

The man tending the bar seemed out of place in the dusty tavern. He wore rich fabrics most often seen on members of the Royal Court and even in the dim light Paodin could see they were spotless. His long coat hung open, which Paodin imagined was a result of his ample stomach outgrowing the buttons. Unlike most of the common men in Meinsley, the man behind the bar wore his thick red hair cut short. As Paodin sat down on one of the rickety bar stools the man turned toward him.

"What do you want?" he asked, bored.

"Are you Red?"

"That's what people call me," was his reply.

Ignoring the man's seeming indifference, Paodin continued, "Jamis told me to ask for you once I got to town. He said you may be able to help me." At Jamis' name Red's interest grew, and when Paodin placed the leather coin purse on the bar his demeanor changed altogether.

"Ah! Welcome to the Amber. Any friend of Jamis is a welcome distraction." Stepping out from behind the bar, Red motioned for Paodin to follow. "Come. Let's see what I can do for you." He scooped the coin purse off the bar and led Paodin through a small door hidden in the shadows.

The room the two men walked into was a complete opposite to the dark and dirty tavern. A large desk sat in the center of the room, polished until it shone. The chair behind the desk was massive and covered with rich burgundy fabric, looking fit to be one of the king's thrones. Red sat down behind the ornately carved desk and motioned for Paodin to sit down across from him. Leaning back in his personal throne, Red laced his fingers together across his prominent belly.

"Tell me, what can I do for you?"

Paodin got straight to the point. "I have a horse, but I need provisions, enough for a three day journey. I also need a heavy cloak, warm enough for nights in the mountains. I am traveling to---"

"Your business," Red cut in, "is your own. My business is to provide a service, and to do so I have no need of knowing your destination. By the looks of you, you could use a scabbard and some boots. Yours appear to be well worn."

Glancing down at his feet, Paodin realized the man was right. His boots were all he had still been able to wear when the old hermit had given him clothes, but they were by no means in good condition. Looking back up at the big redhead, he said, "There are many things I could use, but all I have to give you are the coins in the purse--and even those have been given to me. I have nothing more to offer."

Red dumped the coins onto his desk, talking to himself as he counted them. "This will buy enough food and perhaps a cloak, but it will never spread thin enough for boots or a scabbard. If I get a cloak from the old woman it will be warm enough and cheaper, though it will not last as long. Then there would be enough for a scabbard as well. I still couldn't procure the boots for any less than two days' worth of food, though."

"My boots will serve me well enough," Paodin interjected.

Looking up from the coins, Red ignored Paodin's statement. "How are you with a bow? Are you a decent hunter?"

"It has been a while since I hunted, but I was once fair," was his answer.

"Good. I'll give you a room for the night and I won't even charge you, and then you'll have your supplies at first light," Red said, grinning with pride in himself. "Follow me," he said as he stood. "I'll even give you one of my clean rooms. They're usually reserved for my, um, ladies' guests, but visitors have been few lately!"

Paodin stood, reluctantly following Red from the room back into the dingy bar room and up a rickety staircase. "You are certain my provisions will all be ready at first light? I will need to leave in quite a hurry."

"Yes, yes," the man said casually, pulling at his long coat as the two walked down a grimy hall. "Your horse will be loaded up, watered, and waiting for you to drag yourself from bed, and your supplies will be waiting in my records room, which you saw earlier. Don't you worry--Red is working even now." He opened a heavy door that squeaked on its hinges then stepped in ahead of Paodin. "Lottie, move on down the hall. This guest doesn't require your services tonight."

As Paodin stepped into the room, a blonde woman in only a skimpy dressing gown brushed past on her way out the door. Paodin averted his eyes, not wanting to make the girl nervous. "She can dress first. I don't wish to inconvenience her."

Lottie giggled and patted Paodin's cheek. "Too bad, Reddie. He's a real gem!" With that she blew the two men a kiss and swayed down the hall.

Red laughed, a big hearty laugh that shook his belly. "You must be exhausted, son! Good night." He shut the door as he stepped out of the room, his laughter echoing down the hall.

Paodin moaned with pleasure once he lay down. The large bed was the first he had slept on since Simann's men first captured him, at least if he didn't count the old hermit's cot as a true bed, and it felt wonderful. Though he knew it might not be smart, Paodin let everything relax and fell sound asleep for the first time in more than a week.

Just before dawn, right as the last of the stars was being chased from the sky, Paodin was jarred awake by a knock at the door. Before he could say anything or climb out of bed, Red burst through the door carrying a pile of supplies.

"See, what did I tell you? While you slept in the lap of luxury, Red fixed everything up for you. I even brought everything to you; how's that for service?" He tossed the pile onto the foot of the bed before continuing, "That little stallion of yours is ready. You can leave as soon as you get out of bed, but you may want to go down the staircase behind the building. If you find somebody who needs my business, send him right over. Red will take care of him." Bowing his head slightly, the big man backed into the hall and closed the door, leaving Paodin still sitting in bed.

Yawning, Paodin rubbed his eyes and reached for the things at the end of the bed. A pair of boots lay on top of the pile, and Paodin was surprised to see they were the right size. Red really was good at his business. Next to the boots lay a belt with a scabbard attached, and Paodin immediately pulled his sword out from under the blanket beside him and slid it into the sheath. It wasn't a perfect fit, but it would work. Red had also brought him a rough but heavy and warm cloak, clean leather breeches, and an ankle sheath for his dagger. Stretching to get rid of the kinks in his back and to wake up his sore muscles, Paodin slid out of bed and prepared to leave.

Behind the inn, a young boy was waiting with the young stallion Jamis had provided. He turned to greet Paodin, revealing the same red hair and round cheeks as his father. "Are you leaving, mister?" he asked quietly.

Nodding, Paodin took the reins from the boy and hauled himself up into the saddle.

"You have hard breads in one pack and a little cheese in the other. The canteen is full, but it won't last for a hard ride for you and your mount. Papa said to give you this," he said, pulling a quiver off his back, "for hunting. They're good arrows--I made them myself."

Taking the quiver from the boy, Paodin pulled out one of the arrows and inspected it for a moment. "Well done. This is fine work. Your father must be proud to offer your work." A wide smile spread across the boy's face, then he turned and ran inside.

As the boy left, Paodin looked down at the quiver and bow and muttered under his breath. "I hope I can still use this thing." Shrugging his shoulders he rode off, staying in the outskirts of the town. On the other side of Krasteiv, behind the blacksmith's shop where the fires were already blazing brightly in the minutes before sunrise, Paodin turned northwest. In the distance he could see the silhouette of the Velion Range standing proud and imposing. On the other side lay Gelci, Paodin's home, and his brothers in the resistance.

\*\*\*\*\*\*\*\*\*\*\*\*\*\*\*\*\*\*\*

Syndria stayed with Simon and his wife for two days, enjoying her time spent as an ordinary girl instead of a Healer. Ina never stopped talking, taking full advantage of every moment she had Kierney there to listen. As she listened to the woodsman's wife jump from one story to the next, the young Healer was reminded of young Magen left back at the castle. She hoped nothing had happened to the girl, for their friendship was well known and King Simann and his Wizards would stop at nothing since they had labeled Syndria a traitor. Ina spoke then, bringing the young Healer out of her thoughts.

"I packed you some food for your trip, Kierney, though I can't understand why you won't stay with Simon and me a bit longer," she said, handing Syndria a large bundle heavy with food.

"I wouldn't want to be any trouble," Syndria smiled, adding silently, *or put you in any danger.* "You and Simon have been so gracious to me already; I don't know how I can ever repay you." Setting the large pack on the ground beside her, Syndria leaned forward into Ina's outstretched arms. "Goodbye, Lady Josephina. May your home be always blessed," the girl said quietly, uttering the customary farewell of the Healers of old.

Sniffling, Ina hugged the young girl tightly. "You are welcome in my home any time, child. One day I expect to see you traipsin' in here with a husband and children in tow." Pulling away, the woman wiped away a few tears to reveal her usual bubbling smile. "Now, you take care of yourself, Kierney. Go on now!" The lady shoved the young Healer on her way and then stepped back inside, leaving Syndria with the woodsman. The two walked quietly through the trees for a while, Syndria struggling to keep up with the pack of food on her back.

"She's right, you know," Simon said gruffly. "You can visit whenever you want. With you 'round, the Missus don't talk my ear off. She's got a woman to blabber to."

"Thank you," Syndria managed to squeeze out, huffing as she tried to keep up her quick pace. Simon must have noticed the girl's shortness of breath, for though he never said anything he slowed down. Once again the two walked silently through the trees, and eventually Syndria began to notice that the forest was thinning.

"How much farther, Master Simon?" she asked finally, hurrying up to walk beside him now that there was more room.

"Not too much now, girl, but I'm no 'Master', I've told you. Fancy titles don't mean nothin' out here," he grumbled, but the Healer could see a small smile tugging at the side of his mouth. "I'll have you in Saun before you know it."

"Oh no, I can't go through the city," she said. Most likely, Simann would have guards posted at each city gate in Tundyel. Thinking quickly, she added, "There are people from home looking for me and I will be forced to return. Is there some other way I could travel?"

Simon stopped, turning to face the girl. "You're not just some girl runnin' away from home, are you?" he said, the question sounding more like a statement. When Syndria didn't say anything, he continued, "I don't want to know who you are or who you're runnin' from, but at least tell me--do you know where you're goin'?"

Her spirits sinking for fear that Simon was going to refuse to help further, Syndria shook her head slightly. "I have never traveled Tundyel, never been beyond the confining walls of my home until recently. I have no destination in mind, and my journey's sole purpose is to find others loyal to my rather…dangerous views." Straightening her shoulders and standing to her full height of just over five feet, she put all the authority she could muster into her voice. "Though I will accept the fact that you may no longer wish to help me, I must insist that you do not betray my presence to anyone." She stood still, never letting her gaze drift from Simon's. A full minute passed before Simon turned away and began to walk away, leaving Syndria standing alone beneath the trees.

"Well, come on, girl," he growled impatiently. "You're wastin' daylight."

Smiling in relief, the girl hurried on behind her guide.

*******************

Syndria walked on all day, the mountains her guide once Simon turned back to the edge of the forest. It was quickly growing dark, and though the Healer was afraid of what magical terrors would be able to find her in the open grasslands she was traveling through, the girl didn't think she could make it to the mountains before night covered the land. Simon had told her there were many small caves in the mountain base--she was certain to find shelter in one. To Syndria, though, despite walking for hours, the peaks never seemed any closer.

In the pale moonlight, Syndria saw something begin to take shape in the distance. As she drew closer, the Healer could see what at first appeared to be a hill standing alone in the grassland. Thinking perhaps she could find some sort of shelter there, at least enough to feel more secure, she hurried her pace and quickly reached the strange hill. Once she stood at the base of the hill, Syndria wondered how she had not seen it earlier. Perhaps in the twilight it had blended in to the mountains in the distance.

"Whatever the case," Syndria said aloud, "I am here now and I should look for a place to sleep." Dropping the heavy pack from her back, the young Healer decided to sit and rest a moment. When she put her hand against the hill to steady herself, Syndria jumped back in pain. She felt a tremendous jolt of some kind, a feeling she had felt only once before, and it took the girl a moment to place from where that first feeling had come.

When Syndria had been with Nedra for eight years, the Ancient had explained what the presence of magic in others meant to a Healer. She sliced her palm and asked the girl to heal it, but not without a warning first.

"Before you touch my wound, prepare yourself. You will feel what will seem to be an explosion in your own hand, a feeling unlike anything else. While you touch me it will be as if your palm is burning. Hold the connection only long enough to begin the mending and I then will let the cut heal on its own." When she had touched the Healer, Syndria had felt a pain unrivaled by anything she had felt since, even the excruciating pain of the prisoners on the edge of death. It took every ounce of strength the fifteen year old had to keep contact for the few seconds it took to begin healing the Ancient's hand. After the young Healer had composed herself, Nedra spoke again. "If you are ever required to heal someone who has been injured by a Wizard, you will feel the same feeling. And while it is possible, to do so may drain far too much of a Healer's own gift. Choose carefully how much you do for someone with such an injury."

Kneeling at the base of the hill, Syndria knew there was no question as to the origin of the pain. Though it seemed impossible, this hill had been touched with some kind of magic. But why? What reason would the Wizards have for touching a single hill standing in the midst of a grassland with magic? Though she searched her mind, Syndria could come up with nothing. That was when an idea crept slowly in, the Healer's rational mind trying all the while to push it away. She could take the pain from those she healed. Would it be possible to take the magic from the hill? Perhaps then she would see the reason for a spell's presence.

"You really are a fool, Syndria!" she told herself. The pain of merely beginning the healing process on Nedra had been more than excruciating. What would happen if she tried to take the magic into herself? Besides the immediate consequences, it was possible that the Wizards had contained something within this hill, something that should not be released. But while her rational mind was arguing all the reasons Syndria should just go on her way and leave things alone, one thing changed her mind. It seemed a simple argument had ridden in on the back of the idea to try and take the magic into herself. The Wizards who had cast some kind of spell on the hill she was looking at were undoubtedly the same who tortured and killed good men as traitors. Syndria could not imagine them doing anything for the good of Tundyel. Everything they did was an order from King Simann.

Her mind made up, Syndria took a deep breath as she tried to prepare herself for whatever would happen. Still kneeling, the Healer braced herself and touched the hill, her eyes closed. Immediately, Syndria felt the same excruciating pain she had experienced healing the Ancient. It was as if she were feeling the pain of hundreds all at once. An explosion started in her fingertips and shot up her arm, quickly spreading throughout her body. She felt as if she were kneeling in the center of a potter's furnace instead of the cool meadow. Struggling against common sense telling her to simply pull away, Syndria willed her left hand to join her right against the hill. Her entire body

trembling from the pain, Syndria pushed the
feeling from her mind and focused all her energy
on trying to take the magic as she took the pain
from people. She held it as long as possible, but
after only a few seconds the pain was too much for
her to bear. She started to drop her hands and
realized in horror that she couldn't move, couldn't
stop the pain. Opening her eyes wide with terror,
Syndria began to pull back wildly. No matter how
hard she tried, the Healer's hands would not move.
When she happened to glance up at the top of the
hill, Syndria stopped struggling. The hill seemed to
be disappearing, revealing stone underneath.
Though the pain was no less intense, Syndria again
focused on taking the magic into herself, closing
her eyes once again as unimaginable pain racked
her small body. Suddenly she fell back, no longer
unable to take her hands off the hill. Every inch of
her body shaking from the pain, Syndria curled
into a ball as her mind faded and everything went
black.

*******************

As night fell, Paodin was approaching the
coast. He could hear the waves crashing against the
rocky cliffs along the southern edge of the Velion
Range and the air smelled of salt. As he rode
slowly along, letting the horse set his own pace,
Paodin relaxed under the night sky. From
childhood he had always loved watching the sky,

especially after his father had told him that the True Wizards had written the Prophecies in the stars upon their deaths. For years he had studied the heavens at night, hoping for some glimpse of the Wizards' work, their legacy. Once he had reached his teen years and had begun working with his father daily, Paodin had given up on his nightly study. This night, however, Paodin found himself again watching the stars in their steady progression, wondering which ones held the secrets of the Prophecy the old stranger had helped him understand. As he sat staring up, his horse suddenly reared and threw Paodin, who tumbled to the ground in a painful heap. Before he could clamber to his feet the horse had bolted, heading for home.

Paodin punched the ground, disgusted with himself for getting so carried away with his thoughts that he had lost his mount. Shaking his head, Paodin stood and brushed himself off. The food Red had packed was gone, but at least Paodin had his bow and arrows. He laughed at the irony, for it had been close to two years since he had last shot a bow. As he stood, Paodin saw that he was not the only thing flung unceremoniously from the saddle. The canteen which had been draped over the saddle horn was laying not five feet away. After retrieving the water and taking a sip, he turned toward the mountains to push on on foot.

He stopped in his tracks when he saw what had frightened the horse into bolting.

There before him a giant sand dune seemed to be shrinking, revealing ruins in its place. At first Paodin thought his mind was playing tricks on him--perhaps he had hit his head when he fell. As he approached the ruins, though, Paodin knew he was looking at something real. He stood by until all the sand was gone then stood in awe of the sight before him. He could make little out in the dark, but from what Paodin could see the ruins were what was left of a great city. Its walls were in shambles and the buildings within were little more than foundations in most areas, but the wall before him stretched along the coast, lost in the night. Making his way along the crumbled wall, Paodin found a place he thought had probably been a gate and climbed carefully over the large stones to walk among the ruins. What he saw in the pale moonlight shocked him, for strewn over the ground before him were the skeletons of the entire city.

Some held arrows between their ribs, some were crushed, and still others were scorched by an enemy's flames. The ruined city still held the stench of death, and Paodin realized that it had to have been covered by the sand dune immediately after the battle. Despite that fact, there was very little sand within the walls of the city. Paodin began moving around carefully, not wanting to disturb the slain with a careless step in the darkness. When he found a corner free of the destruction, the traveler sat down to rest. His body was already weary, but now so were his mind and heart. He decided to wait until daylight to travel on to the mountains, hoping the morning would reveal some story behind the slaughter.

*******************

Euroin was walking back to his quarters in the early night, having just come from testing the skills of the sorcerers and lesser Wizards in training. Though he would never tell the younger Wizard so, Ilcren was teaching them well. Already they had woven a ward around the castle, stretching its effects out as far as Caron's walls. Euroin almost wished the rebellion would hurry their fight and march on the castle, for then this nonsense would be quickly ended. He and the other Wizards would then simply have to change a few memories and things would be back to normal.

Suddenly the night around him exploded into colors, spinning around Euroin in a fury. The Wizard was confused as he tried to find the disruption in the spells before him, for this had not happened since the True Wizards had been killed. He quickly examined each minor spell and brushed it aside, his uneasiness growing as he drew closer to the complex webs cast years before. He stopped in shock when he realized which webs had not only been disrupted, but completely destroyed. Clenching his fists in anger, Euroin stormed out of the Wizard's cloud and into his small sitting room, where he was soon joined by the other four of his order, all in varying states of anger and fear.

"Does this not prove the prisoner's words?" Ilcren asked. "Who but a True Wizard of old would have the power to destroy such strong webs?"

Uylti's voice trembled slightly as he spoke. "It took four of us months, almost an entire year, to cover those cities. How strong must *one* be to untangle those webs alone? How do we hope to stand against such an opponent?"

Euroin spun around, his black cloak billowing and bright white hair flying wildly. "How dare you!" he snarled, his face inches from Uylti's. "How dare you question *my* power." As he spoke, the eerie light sparked in his green eyes, making them glow. Uylti rose off the ground, his eyes wide with terror as Euroin sent him hurtling backward toward the wall, all the while ranting. "Even if one of *those* Wizards lives, even if they *all* live, I will not be defeated!" he growled, his voice taking on a strange quality. Uylti slammed against the wall, powerless to stop Euroin's assault. From that wall, Euroin sent Uylti tumbling across the room where he crashed into the table with such force that it broke in half. Next Uylti was flying head first toward the fire but was stopped just inches away when Osidius spoke.

"Enough! Now is not the time for such displays, *Master Euroin*," the newest member of the Order said, flames dancing in his own dark eyes. "What are we going to do about this new development?"

Slowly, Euroin lowered Uylti to the ground. The young Wizard scrambled to his feet, hurrying across the room to stand behind Osidius. Alek and Ilcren were silent, shocked by the display they had just witnessed, but Osidius seemed remarkably calm. "There were only three cities revealed, to my knowledge. Perhaps it will not take long to hide them once more."

When no one else answered, Alek finally spoke up. "The three revealed--Dren, Otarius, and Bronte--were all hidden twenty years past, when King Simann had the Rilso family searched out. They were hidden by our Order, but if we were to weave the barriers again it would take longer," he said, absently running his fingers through his long silver hair.

"It seems, then," Osidius began calmly, "that perhaps we should focus on the other matters at hand, should we not?" He turned to Euroin, waiting for an answer.

The strange light was not gone from his eyes, but Euroin's voice had returned to normal when he answered, "Perhaps. Alek, you will go to Lurn and oversee the army. King Simann sent them south earlier today. If we are to keep the rest of the kingdom from learning of this city we must permit no one to leave its walls once the Royal Army has arrived."

"How then will the Healer find out? Is that not the purpose of the attack, Master Euroin?" Uylti asked quietly, his head lowered.

Euroin laughed a strange laugh as he replied, "I have taken care of the girl. Since the traitor was seen approaching Lurn, we will make this attack work to our benefit. We must draw the rebel forces out of the Finley district in the west and wipe them out all at once in Lurn. You," he said, pointing at Uylti, "will go, seeing as how your meager skills can be easily spared."

"Yes, Master Euroin," Uylti said quietly, his voice thick with shame. "I will not fail you." Bowing as he would before King Simann, Uylti backed out the door to be on his way.

"You should hope not," Euroin called out, his own voice menacingly clear in the still night.

*******************

Syndria moaned softly, opening her eyes as she carefully straightened out her aching body. Though still present, the pain now was bearable and the Healer slowly began to remember what had happened. It took longer for her to recognize her surroundings, however, for in place of the hill stood a razed city, its broken walls towering over her in the dark. Syndria pulled herself together and stood, hardly believing what she saw. Just a few yards away a gaping hole in the wall provided a way in and Syndria walked toward it.

"Perhaps this place will provide shelter tonight," she thought aloud. When she reached the hole and passed through the badly damaged wall, Syndria stopped. Though the moon didn't provide much light, it was enough for the girl to see the terrible destruction which had taken the city. She had seen Wizard's fire enough in the dungeon of Simann's castle to recognize its effects, and almost every surface within the great walls was scarred by the supernatural flames. Skeletons lay scattered along the ground, and just to her left lay an adult clutching a child in what had proven a useless attempt to protect it. Stumbling backward over the fallen stones behind her, Syndria moved as quickly as she could out of the city. She tripped on one stone and fell, and as she hurried to stand her hand rubbed over something odd.

Rubbing her fingers over the stone, Syndria traced the letters carved in the rock. OTARIUS. The name sounded familiar, but it was one she had not heard in many years. She searched her memories and was eventually able to recall the one time she had heard the name. A year or two before she had gone with Nedra to begin her training as a Healer, Syndria's father had been telling her of his childhood. In one story he had mentioned living in Otarius, but when Syndria asked him more of the place Jamis hadn't seemed able to remember even mentioning the name. The girl had soon after forgotten the incident, remembering nothing of it until now. If this was truly Otarius, these ruins held her father's home--and her family.

The thought brought tears to her eyes. As a Healer, Syndria had often seen the devastation caused by Wizard's fire in their torture of Simann's prisoners. Thinking of her father's family, of her family, suffering in such a way strengthened Syndria's resolve. She didn't know what had happened in this city to catch the deadly attention of the Wizards, but nothing could make such a complete destruction necessary. She knew without a doubt that she had a duty to the people of Tundyel. She had seen Simann's cruelty at work, and Syndria knew she was one of the only ones who could show these people the truth.

Though anxious to be on her way, the Healer knew she would make more progress the next day if she were well rested. Still exhausted from the pain of revealing the city, her body was telling her just to lay down where she was. Syndria, however, had never been around death, for she only saw the prisoners to heal them. She couldn't bring herself to sleep so close to the ruins and the remains of her people who had been so brutally murdered. Hoisting the large pack from Ina onto her back, Syndria headed west toward the dark mountains. She knew it would be a long walk still, but the Healer was intent on sleeping safely in a cave tonight.

Chapter 10

Paodin woke with the sun, anxious to see the razed city in the daylight. The devastation before him was more ghastly in the light than he would have ever dreamed the night before. More than a hundred skeletons lay right at the gate. He moved carefully further into the city, careful not to disturb the bones. Once he got past the first wave of remains Paodin was met with an odd sight. A hundred men had been slain at the gate but the streets behind them were clear of bones. As he moved down the deserted street in the early morning light, Paodin passed house after house that had been burned nearly to the ground. In the back corner of one house, framed by a hole in the front wall, Paodin saw what could only be a family huddled together. He averted his eyes, the thought of that family being slaughtered while hiding in their home making Paodin feel sick. Once he passed the small houses and drew near the city's center, Paodin began to see more who had fallen in the streets.

The great hall of the city, a building which usually stood for joy, was surrounded by death. More men had fallen here than at the city's gate, leading Paodin to believe they had been fighting to protect something within the hall. He carefully picked his way through the men who still lay where they had fallen and made his way inside.

Unlike the other buildings in the city, the great hall still stood intact. The tables inside were set for a feast and decorations hung on three walls. The far wall, however, was bare of all its tapestries and candles--they had all been devoured by whatever ferocious fire had left the wall scorched black. In front of that wall, men had fallen in a circle around a small family.

At first, Paodin saw nothing special about the family. There were five adults and three small children together who had been shielded by close to twenty men. *Perhaps this was a Councilman and his family*, Paodin thought, but then changed his mind when he noticed one of the shields lying on the ground. Around the edge of the shield, of all the shields, was the same leaf pattern that wrapped around his ring. Paodin's breath caught as he stared in disbelief. These men were the last of the Sons of Tundyel, the Royal Guard of old.

The family they protected until death could only have been the Rilso family, the true leaders of Tundyel.

This great city had been razed in order to kill the last of the True King's family. Judging by the total destruction Simann's Wizards had used magic, meaning the people never even had a chance to defend themselves. Paodin felt his jaw clench as his anger grew. Though he had known Simann tortured individuals such as himself as traitors, never had he heard of the man ordering such a massive, evil attack on the people of his kingdom.

"It is not his kingdom," Paodin whispered, the sound almost like a shout in the silent city. "Tundyel belongs to its people, and they deserve to see the true heir seated on his rightful throne." Kneeling, he gently picked up a shield which had been dropped by its former bearer. Glancing down at the silver ring on his hand, Paodin noticed that it seemed to shine brighter here, in the presence of these men. "Brothers, I do not know how I came to wear the symbol of your service, nor do I pretend to be worthy of such, but I swear to you that you have not died in vain. I will carry on your mission and you will be able to rest in peace, for the true heir will once again sit on the throne of Tundyel. Your actions here, your devotion to your King, will be known throughout the land." Bowing his head in respect, Paodin stood and made his way out of the city. He would travel on to Gelci and lead the new Sons of Tundyel in the most important quest of their time. The Sons of Tundyel would find the true heir.

*******************

As the sun rose, Erik of Saun, Master of the Guard, met with the other seven commanders of the Royal Guard in his tent, the banner of King Simann snapping overhead. The army was moving south toward Lurn, but Erik was not satisfied with their progress. King Simann had personally given him the order for this mission, and Erik knew he expected immediate results.

"We have been marching for two days now, yet we have hardly made it past Roliek," he said, pacing in front of the commanders. "We must pick up the pace. King Simann expects results, and these men are delaying those results!"

"What can we do to move faster, Sir? We have five hundred men," Commander Lamtek said, "all on foot. We cannot expect then to *run* to Lurn." The others chuckled at this, but Erik did not find it amusing. He knew that if King Simann was not satisfied with the Guard, it would mean death for Erik as their leader.

Gavin, of the mountain city of Kauris, was Erik's closest friend and most trusted advisor. Standing, he said, "We should break camp and be on our way, seeing as how we have no time to waste." By his expression, Erik knew his friend wanted to say more but would wait until the others had left. After dismissing his commanders and giving the order to break camp and forego the morning meal, the Master of the Guard sat down next to his friend.

Gavin didn't hesitate. "I understand your fears, my friend, but you cannot expect the impossible of your men. Though the Wizards are able to jump from place to place---"

"Shift."

"What?"

"They call it shifting, not jumping," Erik muttered.

Frowning, Gavin continued, "Though they can *shift*, we cannot. Five hundred men cannot travel across two districts of this kingdom in a matter of hours."

"But why is it not possible to move faster? We should have entered Meinsley by now, yet here we are camped within sight of the walls of Roliek," Erik said, his frustration evident.

"Erik, you well know that these men have hardly been outside the castle walls. They drill in shaded courtyards and spend their evenings with the cooks and maids! Most of them were exhausted before we even marched an hour the first day. When your men have never had to be soldiers and instead have merely been boys playing at it for a few hours each day, what more do you expect from them?" Gavin shook his head and stood, walking toward the flaps of the tent. Looking back at Erik, he muttered bitterly, "Just be thankful we will never have to fight anyone other than farmers, women, and children."

\*\*\*\*\*\*\*\*\*\*\*\*\*\*\*\*\*\*\*

Standing in the middle of the room, the Wizard closed his eyes and stretched out his arms.

The darkness filled with light, new patterns swirling with ancient symbols. He watched the girl, saw her actions of the night before, and even he was impressed. He knew the strength of her gift but had feared she would never realize it for herself. The Healer was more powerful than any he had ever known.

Yet still the darkness of the other ancient magic crept closer. It was not as large now--part had been thwarted unknowingly by the woodsman--but it was relentless in its quest. He felt fear trying to smother the flame of hope which resided deep in his breast as he watched, aching to do more for the girl but knowing he had to let fate take its course. The darkness was almost upon her now, even as the sun rose and shed its light on the Healer.

\* \* \* \* \* \* \* \* \* \* \* \* \* \* \* \* \* \* \*

Syndria woke suddenly, her heart racing. Bolting to her feet, the Healer looked around, hoping to find the source of her sudden fear yet at the same time hoping it was just in her mind. She had not found a cave in the night, but the girl had been able to find two large boulders against the rocky mountain base which had proven enough shelter to provide some measure of safety. When she didn't immediately see anything, Syndria hurriedly pulled a small piece of bread out of her heavy pack and ate a quick breakfast. Looking at the sheer cliffs and jagged peaks high above her,

Syndria decided to only carry enough food for three days with her. Her heart still pounding in her chest, beating a warning of some unknown danger, Syndria pulled out enough dried rabbit, hard bread, and new cheese to keep her for the next three days and left the rest of the heavy pack for the animals to find. She looked around nervously as she headed south, unable to shake her uneasiness.

Syndria wasn't sure of exactly where she was headed, but Simon had told her of a pass through the Velion Mountains that would lead her to Gelci. He said he had once met a man in that city who had told him they welcomed "differing ideas," but that was all the woodsman would say. Syndria had decided to take the chance, hoping that perhaps she would find others willing to help her. Besides that, she had no other ideas.

The Healer moved quickly along the base of the mountains, amazed by how much easier traveling seemed now compared to the day she had walked to Caron. That day seemed like a lifetime ago, and in a way the Healer knew it was. That day had ended a life of complacency, a life of ignoring the horrors she prolonged each day by allowing the torture of innocent men. She had always tried to convince herself that King Simann had reasons for "questioning" the men in the dungeon, and that she was merely following orders, but after seeing Otarius the evening before Syndria could no longer excuse her own part in Simann's cruelty. Not only was it her duty to help the people of Tundyel, but it was the only way she could even attempt to pay her debt to the kingdom after all the suffering and agony she had allowed.

Something high above her in the rocks caught her eye just then, jerking her attention back to the danger she somehow knew was lurking nearby. She got no more than a glimpse, but that glimpse was enough to let her know she was being stalked by some beast. She could hear it lumbering across the mountain and her heart beat so loud she feared the creature could hear it. Syndria walked faster, keeping her attention on the rocky mountain above her. She walked like this until the sun was high, needing a rest from her fast pace but afraid to rest, when she saw a small road ahead that disappeared into the mountains. It seemed she had found the pass, the road to Gelci. Despite her ever-present fear of whatever creature was lurking in the rocks above her, Syndria felt a small flicker of joy when she realized she was moving towards people. She knew there was always the chance that Simann's Wizards were waiting for her, or perhaps some of the Royal Guard, but that didn't seem to matter. Right then, people meant safety from her stalker.

Syndria stopped in her tracks and her heart skipped a beat. On the mountainside above, standing guard on the south side of the pass, was a mountain lion. It looked like the cougar Syndria had healed in the woods, but the Healer quickly pushed that though aside. That cougar hadn't followed her all this time, or surely she would have noticed. She didn't know what to do. She couldn't turn back or the cat would be behind her. If she tried to use the pass she would have to walk right under the cougar, and Syndria knew she would never be able to climb the steep mountainside like the tawny lion could. However, she hadn't come this far to merely stop. The big cat was watching her, but it didn't seem too interested. Instead it kept looking further down the path, its tail twitching.

"What do you see?" Syndria whispered, then her eyes filled with hope and a smile crept across her face. The pass was the best way to travel from Gelci. Perhaps someone was headed her way through the mountains. Deciding once again she had no choice but to take a chance, Syndria stayed close to the rocks on the north side of the pass and tried to seem confident as she passed the cougar. She watched the big cat, slightly relieved when it didn't move, didn't even look at her. Her relief quickly changed to horror when she looked ahead and saw what held the cat's attention. There in the middle of the path stood a bear, not ten yards away and looking right at Syndria.

The Healer fought the urge to run. The bear before her and the cougar on her left, Syndria knew she had no chance of escape. As the bear stared at her, Syndria noticed something strange. Its eyes looked cold, almost glassy. The bear never blinked and its dead stare never left the girl. Syndria got the feeling that this bear was waiting for her. Perhaps it was the beast that had been stalking along above her in the mountains all morning. As she looked at its glassy eyes, Syndria remembered the wolf Simon had saved her from in the woods. In life, as flesh, the wolf had stared at its prey with the same cold intensity as the bear did now. Even once it had died and suddenly turned to stone, the eyes hadn't changed. Like the wolf, the Healer realized, this bear must have been sent by Simann's Wizards. She had no chance.

The bear moved slowly and deliberately closer, never hurrying. As she watched it, Syndria thought that perhaps she could take the spell from the beast as she had the hill. "Fool!" she reprimanded herself. She would be dead long before she completed the process, and she was already weak from her day's journey. Even if the bear didn't kill her directly, somehow Syndria knew the combination of her weakness, the injuries, and the magic would kill her just the same. The bear rose up on its hind legs, letting out a ferocious growl as it lumbered toward her with its deadly claws flashing in the noon sun. Syndria yelled in a hopeless attempt to frighten the beast away, but the bear just kept moving forward. With the beast only a few feet away, the girl knelt and hugged her knees to her chest. Though the beast had been sent for her, Syndria realized that once she was dead the bear would be left to terrorize others. She knew then what she had to do. Looking up at the bear now towering over her, Syndria took a deep breath and prepared herself. Though she would die, if the Healer could take the enchantment off the bear he would return to stone. At least then Syndria knew her own death could save someone else.

Suddenly the cougar screamed and lunged off its ledge striking the bear full in the chest, claws and teeth digging into the thick fur and skin around the bear's neck. With a roar and one swipe of its mighty paw, the beast sent the cat flailing through the air. As soon as the cougar hit the rocks, the bear turned its attention back toward Syndria. However, the big cat was every bit as intent on the bear as that beast was on its prey. Jumping back to its feet and crouching low as soon as it hit the ground, the cat once again threw itself at the bear, digging its claws into the big bear's back and holding tight. Though frozen with shock the first time the cat pounced, this time she used the distraction to scramble away from the bear. She couldn't get far, though, for the raging beast had soon shaken off its attacker and moved toward Syndria. Behind the bear, the cougar struggled to its feet and once again threw itself at the bear. It tore into the side of the bear's neck, this time apparently managing to get past the hair because the bear howled in pain and outrage. Syndria moved away again, but the cougar soon proved no match for the bear. The big cat was flung to the ground once more, but this time it did not move. The bear, ignoring its injury, charged toward its prey.

\*\*\*\*\*\*\*\*\*\*\*\*\*\*\*\*\*\*\*

Making his way north along the base of the Velions, Paodin's thoughts of what he had seen on the ruined city were shattered by the sound of a woman's terrified yells. Paodin started running, his feet flying and his sword drawn. When the woman's voice was followed closely by a wild cat's bloodthirsty scream and then a mighty roar, Paodin moved faster. At the pass, he stepped into the clearing in time to see the big cat fall motionless and the bear charge toward a girl curled into a ball on the ground. Quickly he dropped his sword and pulled out the bow, placing an arrow against the string and pulling pack with all his might. As soon as that one was released Paodin drew another arrow, barely waiting to make sure the first had flown true. The first arrow struck the beast in the shoulder, glancing off and barely phasing the animal. The second, however, flew straight and wedged itself deep in the back of the bear's neck. As the bear turned toward its new challenger, Paodin let fly a third, and then a fourth arrow. With only three left in the quiver, Paodin tossed aside the bow and picked up his sword.

The last two arrows had struck the beast in the chest, and Paodin was amazed when the wounded animal didn't run off. Instead the bear swiped at the two arrows as it moved toward Paodin. As the beast reached him, Paodin remembered the shield he had picked up in the city that morning. It was hanging on his back, under the cloak. Quickly he spun it to the front, just in time to block the bear's massive paw as it swiped at its attacker. The shield took the blunt of the blow, saving Paodin from the claws, but he was still thrown backward and crashed to the ground. Before he fell, though, he had managed to make a small jab at the bear with his sword, opening a small gash across the animal's stomach. Before Paodin hit the ground the beast had already turned its deadly attention back to the girl. Paodin jumped to his feet and ran at the bear, coming up behind the beast as it towered over the girl. Tossing the shield back over his shoulder, Paodin took his sword in both hands and stepped to his right before lunging at the beast. He drove the blade into the bear's side with all his might, thrusting it up deep into the brute's chest. The bear roared and spun toward Paodin, blood trickling from its mouth. Tugging the sword out of the wound, Paodin readied himself for a final blow. As the bear dropped to all fours, Paodin lifted the blade high above his head and struck down at the bear's neck. As the blade sliced through the air the beast managed one more swipe with its giant paw, catching Paodin across the stomach. Then it fell and lay still.

Paodin collapsed to the ground panting, one hand clutched to his injured stomach, the other still clutching his sword. He leaned his forehead against one knee as he tried to catch his breath. Gently, he probed the gashes on his stomach. They were long, stretching from side to side, but they weren't deep. He would live. Sighing, he struggled to his feet and moved toward the bear to retrieve the one arrow still sticking out of the bear's neck. The two in front had been broken off when the beast swiped at them, but this one looked like it could be salvaged.

"It is no use," the girl said calmly, surprising Paodin.

"What is?" he asked, stopping as he bent over the bear.

"Your arrow. It is no use trying to pull it out of that creature. It will not budge." Syndria walked over toward her rescuer as she brushed off her red dress, a futile action since the dress was filthy.

Ignoring her, Paodin grabbed the arrow and pulled anyway, breaking the shaft off in his hand.

"It has returned to stone," the girl said, lightly tapping the hulking figure with a rock she had picked up.

"Marble, actually," Paodin said, inspecting the bear more closely. Then, "Are you hurt, my lady?" he asked, looking up. Though she was dressed in red, her hair cut short, Paodin immediately recognized Syndria's striking blue eyes and bowed deeply. "Mistress! Forgive me; I did not know it was you."

The Healer gently reached out and placed her hand on the man's shoulder, urging him to stand as she spoke. "Please, sir, do not bow before me; I owe you my life. And even had you not saved me, I am no longer a member of the Royal-" She stopped mid-sentence, recognition dawning across her face. "Are you Paodin? The man from the castle?" When he nodded, Syndria smiled. "By all that is good, I thank you, sir. You have saved my life." Noticing Paodin's wound for the first time, the Healer motioned for him to sit down. "You have been injured! Perhaps in some small way I can repay you." Pushing aside the torn fabric of his shirt, Syndria laid her hands on Paodin's wound and closed her eyes. She let her gift flow out through her fingers, first stopping the blood flow and then beginning to mend the torn flesh. Before she could finish, she felt Paodin's hand take hold of her wrist.

"Please, Mistress," he said, "I will heal. My wound is not grievous." Syndria looked up in surprise, her hands falling away from the wound.

"But I can heal it now, and you will not even have a scar."

"Thank you, but I don't mind a scar. Besides, how would I ever convince my father I fought a bear without so much as a scratch to show for it?" he smiled. "You have done enough, Mistress Syndria." Standing, he wiped the blade of his sword on his leg and then slid it back into its sheath at his hip. Picking up his bow and the one arrow that had merely glanced off the beast he slid them into the quiver on his back. "Tell me, Mistress, why is it you are traveling alone so far from the castle, without even your Healer's gown to serve as protection?"

"Like you," Syndria said, "I am not welcome by many. Simann has labeled me a traitor, and the creature you have slain was sent by his Wizards to kill me. You are the second who has saved me from the latter, though I must say your battle was much more difficult than the last. As for my Healer's gown," she continued, "I had hoped I would not be recognized without it, especially with my hair short." As she spoke, Syndria's eyes drifted to the cougar lying still across the pass. Excusing herself from Paodin, she moved to kneel beside the cat. Even before placing her hands on the cougar, Syndria knew she could do nothing for her protector. The spark of life was gone. Leaning over close to the cat, she whispered, "Thank you, my friend. You have more than repaid me."

Standing again, the Healer faced Paodin. "I am looking for others, men who are willing to stand against Simann," she said. "I have stood by and supported his cruelty by my silence for too long, and now I owe it to the citizens of Tundyel to show them the truth about their ruler. If you did not feel the same way, I do not believe we would have met in the dungeon. Am I mistaken?"

"No," Paodin said, "you are not mistaken. I travel even now to persuade my brothers it is time to take action. With you on our side, I believe they will agree."

"Good, though I am not sure one Healer can do much." Straightening her shoulders, Syndria continued, "Though that may be the case, I am willing to do what I can."

"Our numbers will not be so important, Mistress, for we fight on the side of Truth. And once we find the heir, the Sons of Tundyel will once again protect the throne."

*******************

Paodin and Syndria traveled through the pass for two days, their journey longer than usual because the Healer still hadn't completely recovered from revealing the ruined cities. They arrived in Gelci on the third day, where Paodin was given a warm welcome by everyone in his hometown. After they had received word of his capture, most of the people in Gelci had expected never to see him again. Then, two days before, the Wizard Uylti had appeared in their streets with a warning. He told them, as he had the people of Kauris, that a rebellion had risen up in Lurn. The Royal Army was marching to the city, and Uylti claimed he had come so none of them would travel to the city. After all, King Simann would not want his loyal subjects to be mixed up with traitors.

That evening Audon called a meeting of his brothers in arms. When everyone had arrived, Paodin stood and told them of his journey after being captured. He spoke of the hermit and the Prophecy, showing them his ring and the shield he had taken from the ruins. Syndria's eyes grew wide when she recognized the pattern adorning both, for it was the same pattern that circled her wrist. Surely she could not be part of the Prophecy, but at the same time how could it just be a coincidence that she wore the same pattern? She tucked the thought away, making a mental note to show Paodin her bracelet later, then listened as he told of his time with the widow in Lurn. When he spoke of her scars and of her young son nursing the woman back to health, Syndria felt tears filling her eyes. She blinked them away determined to keep her composure, for Paodin would soon speak of her. He told them of the ruins, of finding the last of the Rilso family slaughtered by what he had learned was Wizard's fire. He then motioned for Syndria to join him, telling the men assembled that he would now let her speak.

The girl stood, swallowing the lump in her throat so she could speak. More than one hundred men filled the hall before her and Syndria took a deep breath before saying quietly, "I am the Healer Syndria." A murmur filled the room, moving in a wave as the people in the front turned to tell those behind them what had been said. Some bowed in respect, others demanded to know why Paodin had brought one of Simann's own into their city. Syndria stood quietly while Paodin tried to quiet the men, but when some still refused to listen the Healer raised her voice above the din.

"Enough! I will speak, and it will do you well to listen. I have lived in the castle, it is true," she stated, focusing all the authority she possessed into her voice, "but I have *never* been one of Simann's own. The Healers belong to the people of Tundyel, not to its King--whether he be good or evil. Though I have not approved of Simann's cruelty, I have stood silently by and allowed his atrocities--even enabled some by healing his prisoners only to let them be tortured again. My part in Simann's rule cannot be excused, but I do ask your forgiveness. If this man," she said, indicating Paodin, "one whom I let be tortured for three days, can forgive me and even save my life, surely you can forgive my actions and move past them. If you will have me," she stated, lowering her head in a slight bow, "I will aid you in your fight against the tyranny of Simann. I know the castle well. There are more than four, maybe five times your number in the Royal Army, but they are not trained for battle. They parade around in the courtyards each day, brandishing weapons few if any have ever used." As she continued to speak, the Healer could tell she was starting to get through the barrier her identity caused.

"Master Paodin tells me you drill daily, as often as possible. With your skill you will be able to take the castle, but not if your numbers dwindle when men fall in battle. I can heal your wounded, give them another chance to hoist a sword. The Sons of Tundyel will succeed, but you need my help." Syndria looked around at the faces before her, faces of proud men who were intent on seeing Simann's rule end. "Please," she finished, "let me have the chance to pay restitution for my silence. Let me help you defeat Simann and return the true

King to the throne."

At first the hall was silent as men carefully weighed the stranger's words, then one man spoke up. "How do we know you are who you say you are? Why don't you prove that you're a Healer?" His questions started a wave of voices rising, many repeating his question and demanding Syndria prove herself.

"I will gladly prove--"

"Berek," Paodin interrupted her, standing as he addressed the man who had asked the first questions, "do you trust me?"

"Of course, friend, but what does that have to do with the girl's claims?" he answered. There were murmurs of agreement from many in the hall.

"If you trust me, take me at my word. Syndria is a Healer, and she could easily prove it to all of you, but in doing so she will weaken herself. No Healer can give life without lessening her own, right father?" Audon nodded, but let his son speak for the Healer on his own. "If you ask her to heal someone now, even if just a small cut, that may mean there will be one man who falls in battle that she cannot save. You have all known me my entire life. You knew my father before me. If you have ever trusted me, please do so again now. Your own life may depend on this Healer as my own has three times." Once again the crowd was silent as they all considered Paodin's words, and once again it was Berek who was first to speak.

Standing, he bowed his head in acknowledgement. "Mistress, I welcome you."

"Thank you, Master Berek. Your confidence in Paodin is well placed. I will give you no reason to regret your trust in him, and I hope one day to earn it myself." Nodding to Paodin and his father, Syndria said quietly, "I will leave you to your men. Thank you," she whispered to Paodin as she left the platform.

A young girl met Syndria at the door. "Excuse me, Mistress, but is that true, what they said about you being a Healer?" she asked, her eyes hopeful. At Syndria's nod she continued, "My mother's real bad. She's having a baby, but it's taking too long and she's real weak. The baby woman sent me after Popa 'cause she's saying Mommy won't make it much longer. I was just thinking that if you're a Healer, and if it's not too much trouble---"

"Of course, child," Syndria said. "Hurry in and get your father and then take me to where your mother is." The girl nodded and ran inside, hurrying back with a worried man in tow. The three took off down the road, leading Syndria to a small house at the end of the road.

Inside, Syndria saw a woman laying on the bed, her face as white as the sheet draped over her. At first the Healer thought she was too late, but then she saw the woman weakly turn her face toward the door to offer her husband and daughter a weak smile. Hurrying to the woman, Syndria instinctively placed one hand over the woman's heart and the other on her pregnant stomach. She told the midwife to be ready and then closed her eyes, not bothering to answer the woman's questions of who she was. The laboring mother soon regained color in her face, and her heart beat grew stronger. The Healer's hand on her stomach felt warm, and for the first time in more than three hours she felt the child within her move again. Mother and child fought together for life, Syndria strengthening both. Soon, with father and sister looking on, the new baby boy arrived, kicking and screaming his way into the world. Syndria dropped her hands and stepped back, marveling at the scene before her. As far as she knew, this boy was the first to enter the world with a Healer's help since Simann had taken the throne. She smiled, realizing a new era had just begun, one in which a Healer again belonged to the people.

News of the birth quickly spread, and by the next morning the men of Gelci were all bowing when they saw her.

"Master Audon," she said, greeting Paodin's father with a nod and smile. When he started to bow to her, Syndria hurried on, "Please do not bow. I serve the people of Tundyel; it is not they who serve me."

"Mistress," he said kindly, "forgive us, but we mean only to show you our respect. In the same way that you address each of us as 'Master,' a title far above our standing, we wish to honor you with our greeting."

"I address you as 'Master' because it is a title you and the other Sons of Tundyel deserve far more than many who bear the title," Syndria said. "Could you tell me where your son is this morning? I had hoped to speak with him before we set out."

"I believe he is in the stables helping to ready the horses," Audon said, quickly turning as someone else approached to talk to him. Watching Audon with the men, Syndria could see where Paodin got his bearing. She slipped away, hoping to talk to Paodin about the pattern he had shown the man and to ask him about the Prophecy.

She found him in the stables, helping to saddle all the horses in preparation for their journey to Lurn. If the Wizard Uylti had been speaking the truth, Simann's army was now marching on a city true to their cause. The Sons of Tundyel would not leave their brothers to face the Royal Army alone. And if Uylti had been lying, as Syndria seemed to believe, Paodin had no doubt there would still be innocent people murdered. He hated to think of Lady Brigitte and Adair dying at the hands of the men who had already taken so much from them. The men of Gelci had quickly decided to ride to Lurn.

"Mistress Syndria," Paodin said when he saw her walk past the stall he was in, "what brings you here?"

She stopped, turning to Paodin and smiling. "Your father told me you would be here. May I speak with you--in private?"

"Of course. Why don't we go to my father's workshop? It is not far from here." He led her out of the stable and past the blacksmith's shop to his father's building. Once inside, he asked, "What is it?"

"You mentioned the pattern on your ring last night in the hall, when you talked about the Prophecy. What did it mean?" she asked, fingering her bracelet.

"The Prophecy was like a riddle, but the hermit I stayed with helped explain it to me. The Prophecy says,

'Bound by nature's strength and frailty,

Though two, as one in unity,
Shall true heir of Tundyel make
And by the Truth the throne room take.'
The old man told me how this pattern," he said, taking off his ring and holding it out for the Healer,

"represents those who protect the King of Tundyel. At first I thought that would only be me, but then I found the slain Sons of Tundyel in that city and saw that my ring merely matches the pattern on their shields. I suppose my ring is a symbol of the men who guarded the King."

Nodding, Syndria urged him on. "And the next line--what does it mean, 'as one in unity'?"

Looking out the door, Paodin could see the activity going on in the streets as the men of Gelci prepared to ride to Lurn. Visibly distracted, he said, "Mistress, I apologize for not telling you of the Prophecy before, but at the moment I should be helping my brothers with the preparations for our journey. Perhaps you can ride next to me once we leave and I can explain to you what the old hermit told me." Bowing slightly as he excused himself, Paodin took a step out the door.

"Please," she said, reaching out and placing her hand on his arm, "I will wait to learn more of the Prophecy, but I would like for you to answer one more question for me before we rejoin the others."

"Of course, Mistress."

"Where did you get your ring?"

Paodin was trying to be respectful of the Healer but he was anxious to return to the stables. "My ring was from my mother, and though the circumstances surrounding her gift to me are not

the best, it is not something I would be unwilling
to discuss with you later. Please, Mistress---"

"I only ask," Syndria interrupted, "because
of this." Holding out her left hand, she pointed out
the bracelet she wore. "Like your ring, my bracelet
came from my mother. I do not know her for she
died when I was born." She watched Paodin's eyes
grow wide as she spoke. "When I was older, my
father gave me the bracelet and told me to always
keep it near. He often spoke of my mother's words,
so much, in fact, that sometimes it is as if I heard
them myself. When she gave me the bracelet, my
mother told me that it would protect me. Nedra, the
Ancient Healer, repeated my mother's words just
before I left the castle, only hours before her own
death."

Paodin looked at the Healer in silence for a
moment, and when he finally spoke his voice was
low. "I do not pretend to know what it means, but
my ring was given to me in exactly the same
manner. The only thing that differs is that my
mother's words were for me to protect it. Though I
wish there was time to talk more, Mistress, I need
to return to the stables. Much must be done if we
are to ride today. Please, find me on the pass
through the mountains. Perhaps we can speak to
my father together and he can help us to
understand these odd findings. I must take my
leave now." He bowed slightly once again and then

hurried back to the stables, leaving Syndria to ponder the coincidence on her own.

\*\*\*\*\*\*\*\*\*\*\*\*\*\*\*\*\*\*\*\*

The Royal Army did not stop for their afternoon meal. Instead, Erik ordered them to eat the dried meat and hard breads they carried with them as they marched. The men had been grumbling all morning since they had been forced to break camp without eating breakfast, and now the whispered grumbles were growing into loud complaints. The ranks were disorderly and the men were slowing.

"Erik," Gavin said, riding up alongside the Master of the Guard, "if you do not say something soon to these soldiers, we will undoubtedly be facing dwindling numbers soon. My lieutenants are already telling me there is talk among the men of deserting."

Pulling his horse up and turning to face his commander, Erik snapped, "It would do you well to remember your place when addressing me before the men, Commander Gavin. As for talk of deserting, have your lieutenants bring me any who are so inclined. I will see to them myself." Spurring his horse to move once again, Erik called back over his shoulder, "Perhaps you will do your job now and pass my orders on to your fellow Commanders."

Gavin of Kauris sighed as he rode through

the men, making his way to each of the other commanders. When he reached his own men at the back of the column, Gavin called his three lieutenants together and dismounted to walk with them as he spoke. "The Master of the Guard is under direct orders of the King, so he will not tolerate any who appear weak or cowardly. Tell your men that they will receive rest tonight, along with a full meal, but only once we have made it to within sight of the city of Valgrin." The lieutenants nodded their understanding and moved back through the ranks to pass on his words.

Though there were still grumbles throughout the rest of the day, Erik's warning was enough to convince the soldiers to keep their complaints quiet. They followed behind the Master of the Guard until they began to see the walls of Valgrin in the early evening, but then the ranks fell apart as men began to find friends and ignore the officers. Erik rode among the men shouting orders to keep moving, but the soldiers didn't listen. Spotting Gavin, the Master of the Guard spurred his mount into a gallop and quickly rode back to where the Commander rode talking to the man driving the cook's wagon.

"What is the meaning of this?" he snarled. "Did you not pass on my orders?"

Gavin turned casually to face his friend. "Of course, *Master Erik*. But since you seemed to have forgotten to mention when we would stop, I took the liberty of doing so for you. The men were very heartened by your generosity, I must say," Gavin smirked, earning him a glare from Erik. As the Master of the Guard rode off, Gavin turned his attention back to the driver. "You may stop anywhere. We will be camping here for the night."

Later that evening, while the men were laughing and carrying on, Gavin found himself waiting outside Erik's tent. A lieutenant stepped out, motioning for the Commander to enter.

Erik stood with his back to the entrance, his arms crossed and shoulders tense. "You have deliberately gone against my orders, Gavin. What use is an army if those in it are weak, if they cannot even manage a simple march?" he said through a clenched jaw.

"What use is an army," Gavin countered, "if those in it have no respect for the man who leads them? Erik, we have known each other for years and have been friends for almost as long. I do not wish to see this mission fail, for like you I know what the consequences of failure would be. As a Commander under your leadership, I know it is my duty to follow any order you issue. However, as your friend I feel it is also my duty to make you see when you have erred in issuing an order." When the Master of the Guard offered no response, Gavin took that as a good sign and continued. "If you alienate your men on this march, how can you expect them to listen when you give them the order to begin slaughtering innocent people, even women and children?"

"How do you know of that order?" Erik demanded to know, spinning to face the other man. "No one but myself and the Wizard Euroin were present when King Simann gave his order."

"No, friend, but word travels quickly among the servants," Gavin said, his voice sympathetic. "I understand your urgency. You must, however, remember that those young men know nothing of what lies before us. To them, this march is just one of the King's whims. You must take their training into consideration when you plan the day's march. If the men see no reason to follow you now, if you show them no leniency, they will never follow you once we reach the gates of Lurn. Inside that city's walls you will be met only with chaos."

Erik sighed and some of the tension drained from his face. "Thank you, my friend. Your words are true, as always," he said, smiling slightly. "Let the men enjoy themselves tonight, but tomorrow we must reach the city. Tell them the morning meal will come early."

"Yes, Master Erik," Gavin said as he left.

******************

"It seems," said Uylti, "you are correct

about the rebellion, Master Euroin. Even tonight a group of men rode through the pass from Gelci. The first of their company reached the plains of Finley just minutes ago."

Euroin stood staring into the flames dancing in his fireplace, watching the men of Gelci move as Uylti spoke. Their number was not great, but there were more riders than any at the castle had imagined. As he watched the fire flickering around the forms of the men and horses, Euroin was confused. Always before, he had been able to identify the faces he saw in Uylti's projections. Perhaps the younger Wizard's powers just could not stretch well enough across the kingdom to show the men clearly. Closing his eyes, Euroin let his mind's eye travel to the plains as he looked at the rebellion himself. Even then, the faces were blurred at first. Euroin easily brushed aside a few spells of hiding that had been woven around the men, though he was unable to determine who had formed them. Any Wizard left a trace of his own essence in the magic he used, like a signature other Wizards could decipher, but the signature tagged onto the tail-end of this spell was not one Euroin had ever seen.

As the last of the spell twirled away from the men, Euroin could see their faces clearly. Some he knew by name, for they were men who had often accompanied Finley's counselor Hestin to the castle as representatives of Gelci. They were men who were well known and respected throughout Tundyel. Others, the majority of the men riding through the pass, Euroin deemed as being of no importance. He scanned the group in search of their leaders, quickly finding two men seated together off to the side of where the other men were preparing camp. Since they were quite a way from the campfires, shadows disguised both men's faces, making it slightly difficult to identify them in the night. The first, an older man, was the carpenter Audon, a man known to people in every city of Tundyel and whose carvings were seen in many great halls. For the first time Euroin admitted to himself that for once Kind Simann's foolish idea was bound to work well, for the Wizard feared Audon would be able to gain quite a following-- were he not about to be killed in Lurn. A smirk crawled across his face as Euroin turned his attention to the other man. The Wizard was thrust back to the reality of his quarters, the vision quickly jerked away, when he identified the second man.

"The traitor is not in Lurn," he said aloud, though he was speaking more to himself than to Uylti who stood nearby. "He somehow made it to Gelci and now leads the rebellion toward the city and the Royal Army."

*********************

Paodin and his father had moved away from the men, for Paodin hoped to speak to his father about the Healer. So far, though, Audon had been busy discussing tactics for fighting Simann's army. Paodin tried to follow everything his father said, but he was too distracted.

"Father, can we not speak of this as we ride tomorrow? There is something I must ask you."

"Of course, son," Audon answered, "but perhaps you should wait, if this is a private matter. The Healer approaches." Standing, Audon quickly bowed to Syndria. "Mistress."

"Good evening, Master Audon," she said quietly. "I hope I am not intruding, but I had hoped to find the two of you together."

"Not at all, Mistress Syndria," Paodin smiled, then motioning toward a large stone he added, "Please, join us. I cannot offer the most comfortable of seats, but at least it will keep you off the damp grass." As Syndria seated herself he continued, "Besides, I was just about to tell my father of our earlier conversation." When the Healer nodded her agreement, Paodin told Audon of the curious similarities in he and Syndria's lives, the Healer holding out her hand to show the older man her bracelet.

When Paodin finished talking, he and Syndria both turned toward Audon. He sat silently for a few minutes, not looking at either of them.

When he finally spoke, Audon's voice was slightly broken instead of strong as usual. He studied the ground as he spoke. "I cannot say anything about your past with certainty, Mistress, but if I said I thought this was all a coincidence I would be lying." He took a deep breath before continuing. "Paodin, for years I have struggled with the knowledge that I have lied to you. There were many times I tried to tell you the truth but I always stopped, telling myself it would be easier for you to understand when you were older. As the years passed, though, it only grew harder. Eventually I thought that perhaps you would never need to know, that perhaps this time would never come." He looked up at his son, his eyes sad and his face full of emotions Paodin couldn't identify with certainty.

"Father," he said, hoping to encourage Audon, "I'm certain you had a reason to keep this from me, whatever the information may be. How can I hold anything against you?"

Audon smiled sadly. "Oh, yes, there were many reasons, but I fear that will not lessen the weight of what I must say."

"Perhaps," Syndria said, standing, "it would ease matters were I not here. I will let you speak alone."

"No, Mistress," Audon said quickly, "stay, for you may understand your own past more with my words. My son, your ring was given to you by your mother, and, 'Protect it,' truly were her words. However, it was not I who heard those words uttered, for I was not present at your birth. In truth, I knew nothing of the event. You were brought to me when you were almost a month old, and together we moved to Gelci.

"I never knew your mother, Paodin. I still do not know her name or why she could not raise you. I know only that I was told to raise you as my own and protect you, for without you the hope of ever returning the heir of Rilso to the throne would die."

"What are you saying?" Paodin asked, though by his voice it was evident he already knew the answer.

"Paodin, I am not truly your father." Tears slid down his cheeks as he choked the words out.

Jumping to his feet, Paodin stormed off into the night without a word. Audon watched him go, knowing there was nothing he could do to ease the feelings of hurt and betrayal he knew the young man must be experiencing. He shifted his gaze to the Healer, realizing he had just been the one to tell her that the man she knew as her father had most likely been chosen as her protector just as he had been for Paodin. Surprisingly, Syndria's expression was one of sympathy, not self pity.

She laid her hand on the old man's

shoulder, wishing she could take Audon's emotional pain as she would if the pain were merely physical. Standing, she said quietly, "Do not worry. You have raised hims well--Paodin is strong, and he will come through this as he has many challenges in the past weeks." Turning, she followed Paodin into the dark. It didn't take long for Syndria to find him, for Paodin had not ventured far. He didn't look up as she approached, but the Healer was certain he was aware of her presence. She stood behind him and waited patiently for him to speak.

After a few minutes Paodin began talking, his words full of anger. "How dare that man keep something so important from me! He had no right to lie to me all these years, telling me he was my father. My entire life he told me that my mother was dead, but now he says he does not even know who my mother is! For all he knows my mother may still live. Who is he to decide what I know about my own life? What gives him that right? How could he keep the truth from me for so long?" Turning to Syndria, he asked, "How could someone do this to one they claim to love?"

"Love is a strange thing, and sometimes it makes a person *do* strange things," she said calmly. "If your father did not love you, it would not matter if you were hurt by his words."

"He is not my father."

"What is a father?" the Healer countered. "It is not someone who protects you, who teaches you, a man who is willing to give up his own hopes and dreams to see your future come to light? You cannot tell me Audon has not done this for you." Paodin said nothing, so Syndria continued. "He was told to protect you, and told that in doing so he would also be protecting the throne. Had someone found out that all hope of the true heir returning would die with you, how long do you believe you would have had before Simann had you killed? Audon protected you the best way he knew to, even though it meant lying to you."

"What about you?" Paodin asked. "Does it not anger you to find out that your own past may be a lie?"

Syndria thought for a moment before answering, "I will not lie--I am greatly saddened by the thought. My father Jamis is a good man, and even if he is not my father by *blood* he is in spirit. What matters now, however, is not the past. There is no way to change what has already happened, but the future is yet to be determined. You are leading these men toward a battle where they will be greatly outnumbered, and in order to do so you must not be distracted by these thoughts of the past. You must focus on the Truth, on knowing what you do is right. Though you do not think the truth matters to Audon, and though you believe he was wrong to hide something from you for so long, your father's timing has in one way been a good thing. When the hermit told you of the Prophecy, finding that your ring meant you were to protect the true heir strengthened your resolve. Now, Audon's words come on the brink of this first battle against Simann's tyranny. They too should give you strength, for his words reinforce the hermit's."

"His words will not interfere with my ability to lead these men," Paodin said. "If anything, him ignoring the truth for so long has shown me how imperative it is that I do everything in my power to see that the people of this kingdom learn the truth about their king. Not only will we ride on to Lurn, we will travel throughout Tundyel gathering those who want the Truth. If we can defeat Simann's army at Lurn, the people of Tundyel will no longer have to fear the consequences of standing against that tyrant who lies to them and claims to be their king." Paodin began pacing as he spoke, his words punctuated by abrupt stops and turns.

Syndria watched him for a moment before speaking, then said, "All actions have consequences, Paodin. For most, this crusade will bring good to their lives. To some, those oblivious to Simann's cruelty and to the unrighteous reign under which they live, to those nothing will seem to change. There will be many from both sides, however, who will lose their lives to your cause. I am a Healer, but there are limits to what I can do." Paodin, having stopped pacing, turned to face Syndria as she continued, "You will see friends die, men I could not get to fast enough. You, as the leader of these men, will be faced with the terrible task of telling their wives or children or parents that those fallen will not return home.

"Even the men you face in the Royal Army will leave people behind, Paodin. Many soldiers who die will be no different from the other innocent people of Tundyel, for there are a great number of soldiers who know nothing of Simann's atrocities. They will be fighting a battle they do not understand for a leader they do not truly know, but they will die just the same.

"And what of the people of Lurn?" Paodin asked. "Are we to stand by as they face Simann's army alone, just to avoid killing the men who don't know who they fight for?"

Shaking her head slightly, the Healer said, "There is little wonder as to why Audon could not tell you of your past before now--you do not listen! I said nothing of standing by and letting innocents be slaughtered, especially since you lead men who have been training daily to be able to defeat the butchers. I was saying, however, that the men serving in the Royal Army deserve to hear the truth no less than does the rest of Tundyel. Do not let your men defeat Simann's soldiers only to become the butchers themselves, cutting down any whose opinions differ. Give as many as possible the chance to hear the truth. Just remember that people do not always welcome those who speak the truth, especially when it differs from what they have always believed." Having said all that was on her mind, Syndria turned away from Paodin and walked back toward the camp.

Paodin stood alone in the dark for the better part of an hour, pondering the Healer's words. He knew her last statement had been aimed toward him and his reaction to Audon's earlier revelation, but Paodin was not ready to just let go and move past his feelings of hurt and betrayal. Pushing that to the back of his mind for the time, Paodin thought about the rest of what she had said. With a smirk, he thought to himself that there was a lot of strength and wisdom in the fragile looking girl. Finally, when his body was too tired and his mind too weary for anything else, Paodin made his way back to camp and slept.

Chapter 11

Paodin had not been asleep for long when something startled him awake. He lay still for a minute as he tried to figure out what had gotten him up long before sunrise. Everything seemed normal--fires were now just glowing embers and the only sound he heard was the singing of crickets. Deciding it must have just been something in a forgotten dream that woke him, Paodin closed his eyes and started to return to sleep. Before he drifted off, though, Paodin felt something hit the side of his head. Opening his eyes once again, he saw a small rock on the cloak he had rolled up and used for a pillow. As he started to look around, another hit him in the forehead.

"Ow!" Paodin hissed under his breath, jumping to his feet. He scanned the darkness for Berek, thinking his childhood friend must be playing a trick on him. Just outside the circle of sleeping men, Paodin spotted two leather clad feet sticking out from behind a boulder. Picking up a good sized rock of his own, Paodin threw it over the boulder and hurried toward it himself.

"Ouch! What was that for?" came a gravely voice, stopping Paodin in his tracks for a moment.

"Impossible!" he whispered. "It cannot be him."

"Well, I believe I am me," the old voice

answered.

Paodin moved quickly around the boulder to see the old hermit rubbing one gnarled hand against the top of his head. "How did you find me here, old man?" he asked.

Ignoring Paodin's question, the hermit instead asked one of his own. "Why would you thump an old man's head with a rock? I'll now have a lump the size of a goose egg! That's no way to treat a friend. Perhaps you could bring the Healer over here to fix what you've done---"

"You'll live," Paodin muttered. "Besides, you hit me first. Why not just wake me?"

"Oh, but I did wake you! Are you not awake right now? Perhaps instead of the Healer you would like to get a school marm so you can tattle!" he smirked, amusement evident in his voice.

"Alright, old man, you've got me. Now why don't you tell me why you are here?"

Standing, the hermit said, "Get the Healer and return. Then we will speak."

Paodin rolled his eyes. "Your thick skull is not injured enough to warrant a Healer's attention. If I apologize will it be good enough?" The old man did not reply, and judging from past experiences Paodin figured that he would not hear another word from the hermit until he had done as he was told. Sighing, he walked silently back through the camp until he found Syndria sleeping next to a dying fire.

"Mistress," he whispered, kneeling next to her. Immediately the Healer's eyes opened and she sat up, surprising Paodin.

"What is it, Master Paodin?" she asked, her voice and eyes clear despite being awakened in the middle of the night.

"Your…services as a Healer have been requested. Please come with me." Syndria stood quickly and followed Paodin through the camp, surprised when they moved past all the sleeping men. Paodin led her to the boulder, motioning for Syndria to step up beside him as he moved around the rock.

"Mistress Syndria," he said, "meet the old man I spoke of before."

The old hermit bowed, revealing manners Paodin hadn't imagined he would have. "It is an honor, Mistress."

"Thank you, sir," she said, bowing her head in return. "Are you in need of my assistance?"

"Now, what did that boy tell you? He gave me a good bump on the head, true, but this old skull is thick enough. He didn't manage to do much damage!" At the old man's words, Syndria turned a disappointed look toward Paodin.

"He hit me first," Paodin muttered, frowning back at the Healer.

"Are you certain you do not require my help?" she asked sympathetically, taking the old man's hand.

"Yes, yes, quite certain," he replied, patting the girl's hand. "You need not worry about this old man--I've survived worse in my time! Now, perhaps you would like to hear why I am here."

"If you are certain you will be alright, then I would love to hear," Syndria smiled. "But first, may I ask why you have requested my presence?"

"It won't do you any good," Paodin smirked, "asking questions. He never answers. Instead he likes to speak in riddles and make you figure things out on your own." Leaning back against the boulder, Paodin crossed his arms over his chest and waited, certain they would be there a while. Syndria shot a quick frown at Paodin before turning her attention back to the old man.

"The Prophecy," the hermit said, "does not speak only of one."

"You told me that already," Paodin said.

"Perhaps," Syndria said, turning to face Paodin, "if you would close your mouth you would find you are more able to listen. Go on please, sir."

"Yes, as I said before the Prophecy speaks of two-- '*Though two, as one in unity*'-- only the two it speaks of are not the two you thought. Mistress, do you wear a piece of silver?"

A strange expression crossed her face as

Syndria held her bracelet up for the old man to see. "Only this, given to me by my mother," she said quietly.

"And what were her words?" the hermit prodded.

Glancing at Paodin and seeing an expression matching her own, the Healer replied, "She said it would protect me."

"That is it exactly!" the old man exclaimed, a look of triumph in his eyes. The two younger people watched him blankly, not yet understanding his excitement, so he continued. "The Prophecy speaks of two, bound together as one. You are the two, bound together by the pattern circling your wrist," he said, pointing to Syndria, "and your finger," he motioned to Paodin.

"So that means that together we will see the true heir returned to the throne," Paodin said slowly as understanding dawned on him. "Our meeting that day at the eastern mouth of the pass means the Prophecy is being fulfilled. Soon the true heir will be found and Simann will be driven from Tundyel's castle."

"But why are we bound together? Why is it that the two of us are the bearers of this pattern from long ago?" Syndria spoke up. "Why were we both given jewelry by our mothers?"

The old man kept silent, but Paodin answered, "The Prophecy does not give a reason for the two of us being bound, it simply states that it is so. Who are we to question it?" Turning to the old hermit he asked, "Is there any more you can tell us, old man? Can you find any mention of where the true heir will be found?"

"You have heard the Prophecy--it speaks for itself," the man stated. "I must leave now, and you must sleep. I will meet you again later."

As he turned to walk away, Syndria called out, "Once we reach Lurn it will be dangerous. Take care not to be seen approaching us by any of King Simann's army." The old man lifted his hand in a brief wave and then walked out into the night, vanishing into the pre-dawn darkness.

When the old man was out of sight, Syndria turned to Paodin. "How did he know where to find you--and that I would be here as well?"

"How he knows anything is beyond me," Paodin shrugged, "but I do not doubt his knowledge. There is something about him that I cannot even begin to understand, something that makes him different from anyone I have ever known."

"And yet, there is something familiar about him, perhaps something I glimpsed in his eyes," Syndria added softly, a faraway look on her face.

"Come, we need to sleep like the old man said." Taking the Healer's arm, Paodin led her back to the camp. "Morning will come early, and I hope to ride into Krasteiv by tomorrow night. First, though, we will travel south to the ruins. The shields there will once again be used to protect the true heir, wherever he may be found. Good night, Mistress. Sleep well."

*******************

The Royal Army rose with the sun and made their way groggily toward the cooks' wagons. Many had headaches from guzzling the contents obtained in secret runs to Valgrin, and most were exhausted from a long night of fireside jokes. Erik watched in disgust as a few soldiers tried in vain to sneak back to camp, having spent their night in the company of Valgrin's low women. Sighing, he knew there was little he could do. Perhaps by the end of the day, once the men marched on to Lurn, their minds would be clear. He hoped Gavin had been right in saying that this small reprieve would make the men more willing to follow his orders in Lurn. Erik knew he could not disobey King Simann's command, though he did not like to think about killing the people of Lurn unprovoked. He hoped the Healer would show herself soon, for she was the only one who could save the city from total destruction.

That thought took Erik back to twenty years before, the last time Simann had issued such an order. Erik had been young then, newly appointed to the King's Army and one of a small group selected for what they were told was a special mission. They had followed the Wizards through the kingdom, moving quickly from one city to the next in search of someone, but only the Wizards seemed to know for whom they searched. They had reached the first city in the hour before dawn, the southern coastal city of Bronte. Its streets were empty, for in the fishing town most woke before the sun. The Wizards led the men through the city gates before giving them their orders.

Erik hadn't known what to expect on that mission, and as he listened to the Wizard Euroin speak his eyes had grown wide and sweat had begun pouring from his brow.

"These people," the Wizard had said, "are traitors. They have been harboring enemies of the King, and now they must pay for what they have done. Go to all the houses--bring everyone into the streets, for none are innocent. We will handle matters from that point." As the fifteen soldiers turned to leave, Euroin had added, "If any refuse, do not waste your time arguing. You have swords-- put them to use!"

The fifteen young men had moved through the city, throwing open doors and tossing entire families into the street. Some had refused, especially as they began to hear the cries of those who faced the Wizards, and those who would not leave their homes were struck down by the soldiers. Erik had moved as quickly as he could from house to house, trying not to look at the people suffering at the hands of the Master Wizard, but try as he might the soldier could not avoid getting glimpses.

Flaming orbs had shot out toward the people, growing to three times their original size before crashing down. The Wizard's fire had grown even more as it hit the ground, exploding with such intensity that it threw people against the walls some ten feet away. Erik had ducked his head and moved on, his senses reeling. Before long it had ended, and everything was still. The fifteen soldiers had made their way back to the gates, all silent as they faced the Wizards.

"What you have seen today," Euroin had said, "no one will know. These people were traitors to your King and deserved no less than they received. However, most in Tundyel are loyal to King Simann. They realize what their king has done for them, what he has provided, and they will be kept safe. Your King is kind--he does not wish for his loyal followers to live in fear. For that reason, once you leave this place you will never speak of it again. The city will be swallowed up, and no man will ever again set foot in these streets.

"Those we search for," he had continued, "are no longer here. They moved north three nights ago, willing to stand against the King in secret but unwilling to fight you. We go now to Otarius, the city of the plains where they now harbor the enemy. If any of you wish to return to the castle and to your training, if you do not want to take part in this important mission for the protection of your King, you will not be forced to march on to Otarius. Step forward, and you will be sent on your way." The fifteen soldiers had all stood silently, considering the Master Wizard's words. Slowly, one had taken a small step forward. "Ah, here is one brave enough to step up--are there others? Or is it that this one is the only who wishes to return to his training? Come now, do not be afraid. Surely you saw that we do not need you in order to defeat these cowering traitors!" More had nervously stepped forward then, breathing a sigh of relief at the thought of returning to the castle. There were seven standing before the master Wizard when Erik had considered stepping forward, but before he could bring himself to move Euroin's hand had shot out and the seven men collapsed to the ground.

"These men were fools!" Euroin had hissed then. "You fifteen were chosen because you were thought to be the best, and now there are eight. You will be honored, for today you have earned your King's trust. You have stood for him when those before you could not. Once our mission is complete and the enemy has been defeated, you will return to the castle and train to become the leaders of King Simann's Royal Guard." With that said, the Wizards had all turned and left the city, eight shocked young men following behind. As they had begun their march north, Erik had looked back at the city, his stomach churning as he realized he could have easily been one of the dead who would be forgotten at its gates.

When the four Wizards and eight soldiers had reached Otarius, the men had been given the same order. The difference was, the people of Otarius had been ready for them and waited at the gates, weapons in hand. Without a word, the Wizards had struck them down with the strange fire they had used in Bronte. Once the initial resistance force had fallen, the eight soldiers had entered the city unopposed and that city had been quickly defeated. As before, Master Euroin had then said the enemy they were seeking had escaped, and they had headed off to yet another city.

"Sir? The men are prepared to march and awaiting your order."

Erik shook his head to clear the memories that had seemed to rush in, the man's voice bringing him back to the present.

"Thank you, Commander Roedan. Please assemble the troops, for I wish to address them together before we leave."

"Yes sir," the man nodded, then hurried off to relay the Master of the Guard's order to the other Commanders. Soon the entire Royal Army stood before Erik, waiting for him to speak.

Erik stood on the back of one of the cooks' wagons, looking out over the five hundred men under his command. Most were barely twenty, half his age now and the age he had been when he had set out on that mission with the Wizards. They had done nothing in the Royal Army so far besides drills in the castle courtyards, and Erik despised the fact that he was about to take their innocence by having them march on Lurn.

He couldn't dwell on that thought, though, and pushed it aside so he could focus on what he must say. Calling to mind once again the words the Wizard Euroin had spoken when they had first stepped through the gates of Bronte with the fifteen soldiers, Erik began to speak.

"Men of Tundyel, tonight we will reach Lurn. I know there are those among us who hail from this city, or who know some of its citizens, but in the morning you will have to push those thoughts aside. You serve the King of Tundyel, and he has given you an order. You see, the people now in Lurn are traitors." At that, Erik had to wait for voices to fade before he could continue. "As you know, our King has very few enemies, and one of these is the traitorous Healer. King Simann has reason to believe the citizens of Lurn know where she is, and we march on Lurn today to find her. This Healer has turned against her King, and any enemy of the King is an enemy of Tundyel. And you, men, *are* Tundyel! Therefore, you march today to defend yourselves, your kingdom, and your King. Any in Lurn who will not give up the Healer must receive punishment as a traitor.

"There will be those who will try to escape the city. They will beg you to spare them, even claiming loyalty to the King in hope of gaining your trust, but you cannot let them pass. The innocent, those truly loyal to our King, will not run--they have no reason to do so! It is the traitors, those guilty of turning against their King, who will be running, for they will fear for their lives. They know you serve the King, and they know you will fight for him.

"Prepare yourselves, men of Tundyel, soldiers of the King's Royal Army, for tomorrow will challenge you and your commitment to your King. Now, we march!" he yelled.

"We march!" echoed the men before him, along with shouts of, "For the King!" and, "Punish the traitors!" Erik jumped down from the wagon and mounted his horse, riding out in front of the men. When he turned away from everyone, Erik let out a breath he hadn't realized he had been holding. For now, the army would follow him, and most would follow his orders in Lurn without question--at least for a while. All Erik could do now was hope the Healer showed herself sooner rather than later.

********************

The men of Gelci reached to ruins in good time, despite getting a late start from waiting on a slow moving Paodin. Once they arrived at the broken walls, Paodin led a small group of men carefully past those slain to retrieve the shields of the Sons of Tundyel while Syndria led others in a search for some sign of the city's name. Eventually, after a quiet, thorough search of the rubble, it was Audon who came up to the Healer, tears welling up in his eyes and a small wooden sign in his hands.

The wood was burnt, and at first Syndria could not understand why the man was showing it to her. At Audon's instruction, though, she ran her fingers over the wood and could feel the slight indentation of letters.

"Dren," Audon said quietly, his voice choked. "I carved that sign long ago, when my father was first teaching me the craft." Looking up at Syndria he said, "This, Mistress, was my home, yet I had forgotten it entirely. I had a young wife, the most beautiful and kind girl I have ever met. Her name was Ariana, daughter of Byrum, of

Krasteiv. I had left the city just days after we were married, for I had been chosen to work on the great hall of Saun. My beautiful Ariana was slain here, and I did not even remember she had lived until this moment. How can such a thing be?" he asked, clearly tortured by his revelation.

Syndria took Audon's arm. "Simann's wizards are powerful. You did not simply forget your life here and your new bride--the memories were stolen from you as if they never existed. But now, as hard as it is, you have been given the chance to remember. Remember Ariana, remember your life here, and use those memories in your fight. If we succeed in driving Simann from the throne, never again will the Wizards be allowed to steal memories from the people of Tundyel. Let Ariana be your strength as you face those who took her from you."

Audon opened his mouth to say something more, but he was interrupted by Paodin and the other men returning through the city gates carrying the shields. "There are not enough shields for everyone," Paodin called out, "but there are enough for our front row to hold and present to Simann's soldiers. We will show them who they face, and they will see that the Sons of Tundyel once again fight for their King!" A cheer went up from the men, who were now gathered around their young leader. Paodin let their cheers die down before speaking again, this time his voice lower.

"As you all know, we have long been training for the battle ahead of us. Tomorrow we will face an army much larger than our own, an army which has the support of Simann and the castle behind it, yet they do not have the one thing that matters--the Truth. We fight in the name of Tundyel's true King, and we fight protected by the Truth. When you ace the Royal Army tomorrow in Lurn, guard yourselves with that thought. Remember that you fight to protect the innocent, to keep as many as possible from being slaughtered.

"However," Paodin said, holding up a hand to ask for the men to listen a little longer, "as I was reminded last night, many of the men you face, many of the men you will be fighting against for survival do not know Simann or who he truly is. They see only what he wants them to see, just as do the people throughout this kingdom. We have been given the chance to hear the Truth, and we cannot let innocent men die without that same chance.

"Do not endanger yourself by hesitating, but if you have an opportunity to reveal the truth about Simann to his men after the fight, seize it. Imagine how much stronger our assault on the castle, our attack on Simann himself, will be if we can turn his own army against him!"

As the men cheered again, Paodin gave the

order to mount up and then rode over to Syndria and Audon.

"If you will ride with me," he said to the weary man, "we will plan our strategy." Audon nodded, a faint glimmer of hope in his eyes at the prospect of a renewed relationship. The two men then nodded to the Healer as they rode off to join a select few at the front of the column. Syndria mounted her own horse and moved into the crowd of men, heartened by their cheering. As the company moved off, Syndria glanced up at the sky and noticed a large black cloud moving from the northwest which seemed to be meeting up with their path to Lurn. It seemed an ominous sign, and despite the cheering men around her Syndria could not shake the chill that began creeping up her spine.

*******************

Euroin once again stood in the forgotten tower, his black cloak and white hair swirling around him. Closing his eyes as he took a deep breath, the Wizard stretched his arms out and focused on the dark, ancient power, feeling it coursing through his body. This time he was able to stand, though he still could not separate and control the different strands of the magic. The Wizard concentrated on the traitor, the prisoner who had escaped and who now rode toward Lurn. Through the darkness that enveloped him, Euroin could see the men cheering, their spirits high. He knew he needed to dampen those spirits in order to give the King's army every advantage, so he concentrated all his strength on that thought. Suddenly he was thrown to the floor, disoriented and with his heart pounding. He felt an almost painful tingle in his chest, but it vanished as soon as it began. Standing, Euroin left the tower and moved quickly down the stairs, anxious to leave that place.

********************

Soon after the Healer first noticed the looming black cloud the rain started pouring down. It was not an ordinary spring shower, though. The rain seemed to be coming from every direction at once, whipped around by a biting wind that drove raindrops like nails into the men and horses. From where the Healer rode in the center of the men it was impossible to see Paodin and Audon at the front of the company. The men of the resistance pressed on, but their progress was greatly slowed by the freak storm.

Syndria could still feel the chill, but now it had spread through her whole body. Though the rain was cold, the Healer knew the chill she felt was not merely something physical. There was something strange about this storm, something unnatural, and it led Syndria to believe this storm had been sent after her in the same way the

Wizards had sent the marble animals.

Like the Healer, the horses seemed to sense something strange in the storm. They fought their riders, tugging at their bits and tossing their heads. Most had to be urged to take each step, either by a quick kick in the flanks or a word spoken near an ear. Syndria's own mount was no different, but she urged the mare on, making her way forward through the ranks until she reached the front and found Paodin.

"This storm is not normal," she yelled, her voice carrying as barely more than a whisper over the howling wind.

"I know," Paodin yelled back. "Never in my life have I seen one that began so quickly and yet with such force!"

The Healer shook her head emphatically. "No! I mean, this storm is not natural--like the bear you fought on the pass! I fear it will follow our path all the way to Lurn. Unless, that is, I am not with you. I will stop and you can ride on---"

"Nonsense!" Paodin interrupted, moving closer to the Healer and leaning closer to be sure he would be heard. "If I were to let something happen to you our battle in Lurn would be in vain, for the true heir would not be returned to the throne. I have been told to protect the kingdom by protecting you, and that is what I am going to do. We can survive a little rain. Now, you can either agree to ride on with us on your own or you can ride along mounted behind me--that is your choice."

Nodding, Syndria fell back into the midst of the men, her head lowered against the storm raging around her. At least here her mare was a bit more sheltered from the strange storm and each step was no longer a battle.

The wind howled and the rain poured all day and into the night, so the men of Gelci were still a two or three hours' ride from Krasteiv when they were forced to stop for the night. The men were reluctant to dismount for fear their nervous horses would scatter, but the animals needed a rest. After fighting the bit all day, the horses were all covered in the sticky foam of sweat, despite the cold rain. None of the men slept that night, choosing instead to stay awake and try to comfort their frightened animals. Few of the men would have been able to sleep even had the wanted to though, for the storm made conditions miserable. All through the night they sat in the rain--unable to make fires, unable to rest, and unwilling to speak to one another. None said the words aloud but some were beginning to regret following Paodin on what now seemed to be a hopeless journey.

In the morning, tired men mounted equally exhausted horses and the drowned party moved on toward Krasteiv. The only thing keeping most moving was the hope of shelter once they reached the city.

\*\*\*\*\*\*\*\*\*\*\*\*\*\*\*\*\*\*\*\*

The Royal Army had camped outside the city the night before and now rose with the sun to enter Lurn's gates. People greeted them cheerfully, none knowing what would soon take place. After calling a meeting of all the citizens of Lurn, to take place in two hours' time in the great hall, Erik ordered his army to stand guard just inside the city walls. The Master of the Guard met with his Commanders and together they chose fifty men who had no ties to the people of Lurn and who would follow Erik's orders without question. These men formed the guard inside the great hall.

Soon the citizens of Lurn began to assemble, some dressed in finery as they would for a feast. They filed into the great hall, chatting and laughing and generally ignoring the five hundred soldiers who stood guard around their city.

Two and a half hours after Erik had given the order the hall was filled. Erik looked around at the people before him, deep down hoping to see the familiar face of the Healer looking back at him. When he did not spot her, he began to speak.

"You, people of Lurn, have those among you who would try to turn you against your King." The crowd fell silent, all chatter stopping abruptly as the Master of the Guard spoke. "We have come today to find those traitors, to weed out those who are not thankful for all their great King had provided. You know who these people are, good citizens of Tundyel. You have heard them speak negatively against their King, and now is the time for their sins to be made known. This is not a time for you to protect those around you--if you are loyal to your King, speak!

People began drawing away from one another, no one wanting to be associated with someone who could be seen as a traitor. Soon accusations were flying-- "You know you said it! We all heard!" "You are always hiding something, why not this?" and "I saw you with him that night, whispering back and forth like you had some big secret!" Soon the room was divided into groups, everyone sure that his group was the only one truly loyal to King Simann.

Seeing how little progress was being made, Gavin approached Erik and said quietly, "The people here are quick to accuse those around them. Perhaps if we question them individually we will hear one or two names being repeated. Then we will not be forced to execute those who are most likely innocent."

Nodding, Erik called out, "Enough! No one will be allowed to leave here until I give permission, for you will all be questioned to find out who is telling the truth. And be warned--if you lie, we will know that you are a traitor to your King!"

The Royal Guard began moving through the hall, pulling random people aside for questioning as they moved from group to group. Some indicated an entire group, but their testimonies were thrown aside as others began to give individual names. One name was repeated time and again, so Erik ordered the Commanders to find the traitor being singled out.

Roedan of Takride soon approached Erik, his tightly gripping a small boy's shoulder. "This, Sir, is the traitor being named."

Erik studied the boy, disbelief in his eyes. "Boy, are you Adair, son of Evan?" The boy only glared at the Master of the Guard, his jaw and fists clenched tightly. To Roedan, Erik said, "Leave him. I would like to question him myself." Once Roedan nodded and walked away, Erik again asked, "Are you Adair?"

"You should know," the boy growled out. "You was one of the men that killed my Pa! You and that cursed king of yours thought you got Mum, too, but you didn't!" He spat at Erik, hatred burning in his eyes.

Suddenly, recognition dawned on Erik and he realized what the boy was talking about. A few years ago King Simann himself had decided to take care of a matter he said the Wizards had brought to his attention, so he and a few members of the Royal Guard had traveled to a small farm just west of Lurn. The King had said the man who lived there was planning to try and overthrow him, and Simann had personally wanted to see him stopped. When they had reached the farm in the dead of night and Erik had realized what King Simann was about to do, the Master of the Guard had waited outside the small house, claiming he needed to stand guard in case they had been seen.

Though he had not seen what was happening inside the house, Erik had not been able to block out the sounds, the anguished cries of a man, woman, and child. At one point the door had opened and a small scared boy had run out only to be grabbed and pulled roughly back inside by a laughing guard. Erik had not seen the freckle-faced boy for long, but it had been enough for him to realize that same boy now stood before him, the terror present in his eyes then now replaced by pure hatred.

Erik called Gavin over, for he was one of the Royal Guard who had stayed at the castle for that journey and the boy would not know him. After telling his friend and most trusted Commander to watch the boy and not let anyone else speak to him, the Master of the Guard once again stood to address the people of Lurn.

"Are you all nothing more than cowards? I

have asked that you reveal the traitors in your midst and you have handed over a boy! What danger is a child? Can he lead a rebellion against our King? Why, I do not believe he could even lift a sword," Erik's voice boomed out, echoing slightly as it bounced off the walls of the great hall. "You will be given another chance to speak out against the traitors among you, for King Simann is merciful. However, his mercy will not last forever. Speak out now, or face the consequences."

His speech was followed by more accusations, but Erik was no longer listening. He walked back to Gavin and the boy, nodded his thanks to his friend, and led the boy outside. As soon as they stepped through the door the boy tried to dart away, but Erik was expecting it and quickly snagged the boy's arm. Kneeling, he looked into Adair's narrowed eyes as he spoke. "Boy, the city is surrounded by soldiers who have been given the order to kill any who try to escape. If you run, you will be killed without question, do you understand?" The boy didn't answer, but he no longer struggled to get away from the Master of the Guard so Erik dropped his hand. "Who do you live with?"

Adair stared at the man before him for a long moment before answering. "My mum. I told you that you didn't get her like you thought!" he said, speaking through clenched teeth.

Ignoring the boy's anger, Erik stood and began walking toward the main gate, his hand guiding the boy along beside him. "This is no place for you to be. Go straight home and lead your mother away from here--you have both seen enough death. But first, you must tell the soldiers at the gate exactly what I tell you--and you have to look like you mean it!"

He spoke quietly as they walked so none of his soldiers would hear. Before they reached the gate, Erik turned back to the hall and sent the boy on alone. Adair reached the gate and stopped, looking nervously around at the soldiers blocking the road.

"I was told to speak with Lieutenant Quinlan," he said. "The Master of the Guard sent me."

One of the soldiers stepped forward, motioning for the men to lower their swords. "I am the Lieutenant. What is it you have been sent for?"

Adair swallowed, using that brief moment to try and remember the exact words he had been given. "You are to grant me passage so I can take word to Castle Tundyel of the progress already being made. The Master of the Guard is sending me as a messenger to our King."

"Why would he send a boy when he has five hundred men? Go on with you--back to the hall!" Quinlan said, slapping the broadside of his sword against Adair's backside.

"The Master of the Guard said that if you do not follow orders and let me pass, you will be demoted. He knows you spent the night in Valgrin with those women--I think he called them short, or---"

"Let him pass!" Lieutenant Quinlan called out, motioning for the men to stand back as Adair moved quickly away from the city. The boy moved north until he was out of sight behind a rundown barn and then turned west and ran with all his strength towards home.

*******************

The half drowned party of men arrived in Krasteiv early in the afternoon. The rain still poured down, now turning the streets of the city into muddy rivers which were churned up even more by the hooves of one hundred horses.

"You must admit," Berek said, leaning toward Paodin as they rode into the city, "this storm has accomplished one thing which works in our favor. It has driven the people of Krasteiv indoors, so we will not have to face many."

Though Paodin had to agree with his friend's observation, the thought gave him little consolation. The closer to Lurn that he led the men and the longer the storm raged on, the more Paodin questioned his own abilities. He had yet to see his twentieth birthday; how in the name of all that is good would he be able to lead one hundred men against an army of five hundred? Perhaps he couldn't do this.

As if she had read his thoughts, Syndria rode up next to Paodin and hollered out over the howling wind, "Do not be discouraged by this storm. It is merely the Wizards' attempt to slow us. It does not mean anything. We must keep on, for Simann's men must be stopped."

Dismounting to walk beside his skittish horse, Paodin waited for the Healer to do the same before speaking. Though he for some reason didn't mind telling the Healer of his doubts, Paodin didn't want any of the men to overhear their conversation.

"What if we--what if I--made the wrong decision?" he asked, able to lower his voice now that the two were walking side by side. "The Prophecy said that the throne would be returned to the true heir but only with the help of the True Wizard. What if I have gone about things wrong? Perhaps it is foolish to attempt to face Simann's army at all without the True Wizard," he finished, his shoulders dropping as did his voice.

Syndria didn't turn her head to look at Paodin as she spoke, instead focusing of pushing forward through the rain. "Do you wish to turn back?" she asked. "Go ahead, and then you can explain to the brave men of Gelci that you led them through the storm for nothing. Tell them that now, because of your own discomfort, you have decided to leave the people of Lurn, your fellow citizens, to be slaughtered at the hands of the enemy. I am sure they will understand--perhaps they will eventually be able to laugh this journey off as the whim of a child." That said, Syndria quickly mounted and rode away from Paodin, leaving him to consider her harsh words.

Paodin was walking along, his head lowered, when a heavy hand fell on his shoulder. Jumping slightly as his thoughts were interrupted, Paodin turned to see that Berek was now walking alongside him.

Berek pushed wet, long strands of hair out of his face as he spoke, though they were soon whipped around again by the wind. "Perhaps we should rest here for the evening. If we push on to Lurn in this storm, we will not reach the city until long after dark. I do not believe King Simann's army would be understanding enough to allow one hundred men a few hours' rest come daylight."

"You are right, my friend," Paodin said, shaking himself out of his brooding. "We can set out before dawn tomorrow and reach the city in the day. We must tell the men not to be discouraged by the storm, for even if it is to follow us to Lurn the Royal Army will be drenched the same as we are." Straining to see through the sheets of rain falling around them, Paodin continued, "There is a large stable on the east end of Krasteiv. Though I doubt there will be enough stalls for all our horses, there should at least be space enough to take them all in out of the rain. There is a man here who I believe will help us find shelter and hot meals for the night--if the price is right."

Syndria, who had been watching Paodin's body language change as he spoke to Berek, had handed her horse's reins to Jaret, the young man riding beside her. Jumping down she had quickly made her way up the lines and began walking unnoticed behind the two men. When Paodin mentioned the price that would be expected, Syndria slipped in between the men and said, "If you will need money, you will need me. Master Audon gave me the purse of coins you collected in Gelci, and it is my responsibility to see that it is well managed."

"No offense, Mistress, but do you not think matters such as these are best handled by men?"

"I have found, Master Paodin," Syndria answered, "that any statement first qualified by 'no offense' is bound to offer just what it claims not to. Perhaps you will take 'no offense' when I tell you that you possess very little, if any, of the charm necessary to procure food and shelter for one hundred drowned, dirty men and their horses with the funds we have collected. Come along and introduce me to this man you know, and I will let you learn that these matters are best left to the one who holds the purse." Smiling politely to Berek, Syndria stepped past him and waited for Paodin to join her.

"Were she not a Healer and therefore playing an integral role in our quest," Paodin said, his voice low, "I would be tempted to turn that girl over my knee!"

Berek laughed, the first cheerful sound Paodin had heard since the storm began. "I believe, my friend, that nothing but her position as such keeps her from doing the same to you!" Laughing still, the big blond man took the reins from Paodin and sent him on his way.

With the wall of rain before him, it took Paodin quite a while to find the Amber Stream Tavern. At the doors he once again tried to convince the Healer to let him go in alone to deal, but Syndria just pushed him aside and walked into the dark bar ahead of Paodin.

When Paodin quickly stepped up to her side, Syndria whispered, "Who am I looking for?" To answer, Paodin simply nodded towards the man pouring drinks behind the counter and told Syndria that he was called Red.

Straightening her shoulders, Syndria marched up to the counter and stated, "Master Red, I would like a minute of your time."

"I'd like a minute of *your* time, girly," slurred one of the men seated at the bar, but his next remark was quickly silenced when Paodin glared at him and pushed back his dripping cloak to reveal the hilt of his sword, glittering even in the scant light of the tavern.

Red said nothing, just simply stared at the two before him for a while. They made quite a picture, these two half-drowned and dirty visitors who were making puddles on the floor of his tavern. The man stood firmly planted between the girl and Edwin, one of the Amber Stream's most regular patrons. His hand rested on the hilt of his sword as a warning to Edwin or anyone else who might attempt to besmirch the girl's honor. His appearance plainly revealed the young man's humble background, though due to his drowned rat appearance it took Red a moment to place him as the young man he had outfitted a short time before..

The girl, though dressed in the riding skirt and cloak of the common woman, seemed somehow not to fit the plain clothes she wore. Something about how she held herself and how she completely ignored the remarks flying at her from all sides made Red think that the tiny girl with the striking blue eyes was better suited to the great halls of Tundyel's finest cities than to his dark tavern.

"When I saw your horse tear back through town the day you left, I assumed your past had caught up with you," he said to the young man. "What is it I can help you with, missy?" he asked then, wiping at the dirty mahogany bar with an equally dirty rag.

"If you do not mind, sir, I would appreciate the chance to state my business in private." Ignoring the whistles and remarks that followed, Syndria motioned for Red to join her at a small table tucked away in a deserted corner of the room. The big man took his time, but ultimately he made his way to join Syndria. Paodin followed close behind but before he could take a seat the Healer sent him away, saying that "Master Red" had kindly agreed to a private audience and that she must honor her offer. So Paodin, aggravated as he often found himself when dealing with the strong-willed Healer, moved away and stood guard lest one of the drunken men decided to do more than talk of their intentions toward Syndria. And though he strained to listen to the conversation behind him, all Paodin could hear were Red's low tones followed by the Healer's softer yet determined ones.

"We would not require too many rooms," Syndria was saying. "Our men have spent the past two days in an unrelenting downpour and will be grateful to simply have a dry place to rest. If your guest rooms are full we will gladly sleep here on the floor of your tavern," she finished, leaning back and giving Red the impression that she simply waited for him to tell her which accommodations they would be given.

Red sat with his fingers interlaced, tapping his thumbs together atop his round stomach. He waited a few minutes, thinking the long silence would make the girl bring up the one thing she still had not mentioned--payment. Finally, realizing that the girl would not be intimidated like so many others, he asked, "Are these men of yours, the ones undoubtedly crowding and making a mess of our stables as we speak, are these the men riding from Gelci?"

"Yes."

Sighing mightily, as if greatly inconvenienced by the entire matter, Red replied, "The arrangements have already been made. Bring your sodden group here and I will have these good men go home to their wives. A dinner will be provided within the hour, but I won't be having my cooks filling any requests--your men can eat what they get." Frowning, he continued, "I don't suppose you feel too much like making up for the business I'll be losing tonight, now do you missy?"

Standing, Syndria smiled genuinely and said, "If arrangements have already been made, I imagine the matter of your lost business has been settled as well. And though I do not feel guilty for sending those men home to their wives early tonight," she said as she pulled out the small purse, "I will give you a token of our thanks for your hospitality." Pulling out a handful of coins, Syndria offered another smile and placed the coins in Red's large hand. "I thank you, sir, as do the men of Gelci." After calling Paodin over to her, Syndria sent him after the men without telling him anything of her conversation with the barkeep, deciding that the man who was so convinced that her attempt would fail need know nothing more than the fact that the men would be dry and comfortable for the night.

After much prodding on Red's part and much charming by Syndria, the men who were all set to drink away the storm left the Amber for their respective homes. As Red had promised, within an hour every table in the tavern had men around it and bowls of a hearty stew sitting on top. Just being in out of the rain had raised the men's spirits tremendously and they laughed and sang as they warmed themselves with the dinner. The party-like atmosphere soon had even Red laughing and joining in on the joyful though off-key songs. Syndria sat off to the side, enjoying the happiness and carefree expressions on the faces before her. It was hard to believe that a day from now she would be all that stood between some of these men and death.

One of the men, a boy actually, no older than sixteen, danced by and grabbed Syndria by the hand, pulling her out of her seat and out of her darkening thoughts. As he led her around the room in an awkward, impromptu dance to the boisterous songs, Syndria let herself get carried away in the simplicity of the night, and for only the third time in her life since her gift was first revealed she forgot about being a Healer.

Chapter 12

The singing and laughing in the tavern had died down a bit, so Syndria decided to slip away and take a minute to refresh herself. Stepping out a backdoor, the Healer found herself beneath a small balcony of one of the rooms above the tavern. It was only about four feet square, but it was enough to keep her reasonably dry since the rain poured straight down now instead of in horizontal sheets. She shut her eyes and leaned against the building, but was then startled out of her thoughts by a crackly old voice.

"I see you found the place--that is good," the old man said. His scraggly hair and tattered cloak were dry, so Syndria decided he must be staying at the tavern himself. Though her heart was pounding rapidly thanks to the old man's sudden presence beside her, Syndria smiled warmly as she faced the old man.

"I had not expected to see you again so soon, my friend," she said, squeezing the old hermit's gnarled hand in greeting. "I'm glad to see you have been staying out of this storm."

"A bit of water never hurt anyone, Mistress, and I have survived much worse in my years." Tilting his head toward the door and the voices within the old man added, "Your men seem to be in high spirits."

"I am glad they are, sir, for I fear the rising

sun will reveal a day quite unpleasant tomorrow. I just hope that this will not be the last joyful night of their lives."

His sharp eyes narrowing and his gravely voice dropping, the old man asked, "Do you doubt your purpose, Mistress? Does the impending battle seem less noble as you draw nearer?"

Syndria's answer came quickly. "It is not the nobility of the battle or the purpose of our crusade I doubt, but rather my own ability to give life back to those who are willing to give everything they have to save people they will never know."

"But if, as you said, they give their lives willingly, who are you to worry about their choices?" he said kindly.

"It is just that--I myself have always been seen as young, especially by the other Healers of the castle who to this day think of me as the child who first arrived on the heels of the Ancient." Syndria paused for a moment, her voice threatening to break when she mentioned Nedra. Composing herself as she had been expected to do for the past twelve years, the Healer continued, "However, I am old compared to many of the men inside the tavern. I have seen more in twelve years than most of them have in forty! They do not know what to expect once we reach Lurn, but the picture of what will happen if we fail is horribly clear to me. Should these men find themselves in Simann's dungeons they will be tortured for months or even years on end."

"If all your men approach battled with the same confidence as you," the old hermit interrupted, "their defeat will be swift and certain. Perhaps you should remember what it is you fight for and leave the outcome to the Fates."

Ashamed of herself, Syndria turned away and stared out into the rain. The strange old man was right. Paodin led the men of Gelci toward Lurn under the banner of Truth, and that was the important thing. Though it might not happen as soon as tomorrow, Syndria knew that eventually Truth would prevail. It was foolish to think that one solitary battle would decide the fate of the kingdom, and even more so to selfishly think that her ability or inability would decide the fate of that battle. She turned to thank the old man for setting her mind on the right path again, but he was gone. Stepping back inside the tavern, Syndria quickly made her way across the room to where Red stood at the front door. "Have you seen the old hermit? I wish to thank him for---"

"How did you figure it out, missy? Did one of my cook staff let it slip?" Red boomed. "He didn't want none of you to know it was him that made these arrangements. Who told you? I'll bet it was that good for nothing---"

Placing a small calming hand on the big man's arm, Syndria reassured him that none of his staff had told her of the old man's kindness, she had merely figured it out on her own. Quietly, hoping none of the men had heard the exchange, Syndria asked Red to tell her in which room the old man was staying.

"He's not here, missy. He came in two days ago and carried out his business and then moved on through. Strangest man I've ever met, and I've met a lot, too," he said, but Syndria had already left and made her way quickly to the small back porch. As she searched the dark night for a glimpse of the old man, it took a minute for the Healer to realize that just as her strange friend had disappeared so had the unnatural storm.

\*\*\*\*\*\*\*\*\*\*\*\*\*\*\*\*\*\*\*

"What would you have us do with the bodies, sir?"

The Master of the Guard stared unseeingly at the young Lieutenant before him. Resting his forehead in one hand, Erik answered, "Move them outside the gates tonight, and in the morning have a group of your men dig a pit. We will bury them all together."

"Very well, sir," the young man said, turning quickly on his heel and moving out of the house. One of the smithies of the city had been quick to offer his small home as quarters for the

Master of the Guard, undoubtedly hoping to prove his loyalty to the King. Just hours later he had been named a traitor by a competing smithy and executed.

"How long do you think the men will last, my friend?" Erik addressed Gavin when it was just the two of them left in the small house. "It has only been one day, and already the bodies of so-called 'traitors' litter the main street. Some of the men are already sick from the sight of so much death."

Gavin sank onto a wooden chair across from Gavin and pondered the question before answering. "If you move some of the weaker men to guard duty outside the city walls and bring in a fresh group tomorrow, I believe the men will live up to their training and obey your every order for two weeks or more," he said quietly. Like it had everyone, the day of make-shift trials and swift executions had taken its toll on the Commander.

"The weaker men?" Erik laughed bitterly at the thought. "Do you not mean those who cannot bear to thrust their swords through the heart of a man named a traitor by a jealous lover or a competing merchant? Those whose hands and clothes are stained by the very lifeblood of men who did not have so much as a stick with which to fight back? What happens when all the men are dead," Erik said, standing now, "and because the *real* traitors have still not shown their faces those boys are ordered to kill women? So far we have been able to avoid make believe trials of any of the women named as traitors, but that will not last for long. What then? Do we and the other Commanders carry out those executions in order to spare those children who are out in the street carrying dead bodies?"

Gavin's voice was tired and low when he spoke, and as he began Erik knew his friend could not answer the impossible questions either. "We were the same age as those young soldiers when we faced the first true test of our loyalty to the King, and the eight of us came through. Perhaps you should have some faith in the soldiers we have trained. After all, they face one city as opposed to three."

"My friend, your memory must be failing you in your old age, for you seem to have forgotten that half our number could not deal with the destruction of the first city." Erik sat once again as he spoke, then leaned back and closed his eyes in a pitiful attempt to close out the thoughts and sights of the day. Though he managed to push aside the pictures of the deaths he had ordered in this city, closing his eyes merely served as an invitation for the memories of death and destruction in another city years before to come flooding back.

*The eight soldiers were standing outside another city along the coast, the city of Dren, when the Wizard Euroin began to speak.*

*"The traitors are here, planning their
attack on your King with the help of the people in
this city. None must be allowed to escape, lest they
go about spreading their poisonous lies throughout
the kingdom. These people have betrayed the King.
Go on--fight for King Simann and his kingdom!"
he had yelled, and then Erik had felt himself being
somehow driven forward despite his fear and
confusion.*

*The young soldiers, none over twenty-five,
charged through the gate where they met one
hundred armed men. The men of Dren all held
their weapons, yet none moved against the eight
royal soldiers. While the others charged forward,
cutting down the men who stood at the gate, Erik
hesitated and glanced back at the Wizard Euroin.
Had the Master Wizard seen young Erik's
hesitation, he would have surely fallen alongside
the men of Dren. However, Euroin's eyes were
closed, his head thrown back and his arms spread
wide, the three others standing behind him in
identical poses. Erik soon realized that the
Wizards were holding the men of the city standing
as statues. His eyes wide with shock and horror,
Erik realized the strength of the Wizards' powers
for the first time. Then, despite his heart urging
him to do the right thing, Erik began to
methodically cut down any man before him.*

*Though his heart and soul were both crying out against his actions, Erik's mind won out, falling victim to the fear of what would happen to him should he appear weak before the Wizards. Soon the one hundred men guarding the gate had all fallen, their useless weapons still clutched tightly even in death.*

*The Master Wizard stepped casually into the city, his only recognition of the dead men a look of disgust such as one would have when walking past a pile of dead rats. He said nothing to the soldiers, yet they all fell in behind the Wizards as they started through the city. Unlike in the two other cities, Euroin seemed to know exactly where he was going in Dren. There were no orders to bring its citizens into the streets or even to go in and kill them in their homes. Instead, the strange fire used in the first two cities was shot out to devour entire houses. Death came so suddenly to those within that they didn't even have a chance to cry out.*

*Soon, the small group of twelve reached the center of the city. More men stood guard here, almost two hundred, standing almost twenty deep in front of the great hall. Instantly most were frozen by the Wizards, many stopping in mid-step with swords raised. Close to fifty, however, were free of the Wizards' spell and charged forward, though visibly shaken by their friends standing still as statues all around them.*

*The fight was a hard one, but in the end the eight soldiers stood over the bodies of the men of Dren. Not one of the eight had avoided injury, but all would survive once they saw the Healers. For the time being, they simply wrapped their wounds tightly and followed the Wizards into the Hall.*

*Almost as soon as they stepped through the heavy door the Wizards sent a shockwave of flame rolling across the room, but not before Erik got a glimpse of the scene before him. Twenty men stood proudly, shields held more as prized possessions than as protection. They were standing guard around a family; men, women, and children who all stood to boldly face their executioners. Together they all stood, and together they all fell. Turning to the men, the Master Wizard said simply, "The traitors are gone now," and left the hall. Erik glanced once more at the guards, this time noticing the pattern that seemed to glow on the red hot metal. He had seen that pattern on some of the old carvings in the back of the soldiers' quarters, on the walls that had been torn down when he had first begun his training. Why would traitors to the King bear shields with markings from the castle?*

\*\*\*\*\*\*\*\*\*\*\*\*\*\*\*\*\*\*\*

Syndria woke to an impatient knock on her door. Sighing, she stretched in the luxurious bed and sat up in the dark. It seemed she had just fallen asleep--couldn't the guards have at least waited until daylight to begin their torture?

"Just a minute," the Healer sighed. When she reached back to straighten her long hair, Syndria's eyes flew wide open in surprise to find the short crop. It took a moment for her groggy mind to remember where she was and the events of the past weeks. The knock came again, louder this time, and Syndria jumped out of bed and hurried to open the door.

"Mistress," Berek said, bowing his head slightly, "Paodin sent me up to fetch you. The horses are all saddled and the men preparing to leave. I've brought you some breakfast," he said, holding out a small sack, "but I think Paodin may have both our heads if you take the time to eat it now."

"Thank you, sir." The Healer offered a calming smile to the obviously nervous man. "I think I can manage to eat on the road. Now," she said, glancing back toward the inviting bed, "if you will give me a moment I will gather my belongings and then not be far behind you." Taking the sack of food, Syndria sent Berek on his way down the hall and then quickly prepared to leave. Looking at the warm, soft bed one last time, Syndria sighed and shut the door behind her before quickly going down to join the men.

Someone led a horse over to the Healer and gave her a boost, but otherwise no one paid any attention to the small woman. Looking around she could see that she had been the last to join the company and mount up. She made eye contact with Berek who said something to Paodin, and the men of Tundyel were once again on their way to Lurn. Though she usually rode at the front next to Paodin, something told her that on this foggy morning she would not be wanted there, so Syndria fell to the back of the column and was content to ride along quietly.

At the front of the company, Berek asked his friend, "What do you expect to face once we reach the city?"

Paodin thought for a while before answering, "The Healer said that the Royal Army is close to five hundred strong. I believe we will find all of them there in Lurn, and they will be stationed all around the city."

"Tell me truthfully, Paodin," the other man said quietly, "are we any match for soldiers of King Simann's Royal Army?"

"The men we face will be good soldiers. They will be strong, quick, and intelligent. However, we must remember that for years now they have been purely ceremonial. The Healer said that though they trained daily in the courtyards their drills seemed more like parade marches than combat." Paodin turned to look back over his shoulder at the men following him to battle. "We have been preparing for this day for years, knowing our training was leading up to battle. That will work to our advantage. And since the Royal Army is not expecting opposition we have the element of surprise. But perhaps most importantly, as has been pointed out to me numerous times, we fight for the Truth. We have a cause that is not only worth dying for, but also worth living for. I cannot tell you the outcome of this battle, but I know that the Prophecy says we will ultimately win the war. No matter the cost, we must take our place in this story."

********************

Erik was awakened by the sudden feeling of a presence in the room. He expected to see another citizen of Lurn standing before him, someone else who would be there to assure the Master of the Guard that, unlike the butcher or perhaps the cobbler, he was a loyal citizen of Tundyel. Instead, he looked around at an empty room. He could not shake the feeling, however, that someone was in the room with him and called out, "What do you want?"

The crackling of the fire gave way to a familiar voice, a voice that had been haunting his thoughts lately. "You have failed to bring the traitors out of hiding, and now because of your inability to act quickly," the Wizard Euroin said, "an army of men rides on the city. Your walls will be breached by the end of the day."

"Are you certain? Could they not be headed somewhere beside Lurn?"

As soon as the questions were out of his mouth, Erik knew he had made a mistake. The small fire shot up to five times its previous size, filling the room with a light as bright as the afternoon sun. The Master Wizard's voice roared out, "Do you truly dare to question me? You have already failed King Simann far too long--he would not even flinch were I to tell him of your death."

Drawing back instinctively from the unnaturally hot flames, Erik did his best to slide back into the Wizard's good graces. "Please forgive me, Master Euroin. I had only been asleep for a little while when you came to give me this warning and I can only say that I was disoriented when I spoke so carelessly. Perhaps, if I have not angered you too much, you will tell me more of this army?" he asked, his voice low and calm.

After a brief hesitation, one in which the Wizard was undoubtedly contemplating whether or not the Master of the Guard was worthy of any further aid, Euroin spoke again.

"There are near one hundred men, all mounted on horseback. They are not soldiers, merely farmers and tradesmen, so they should be of little consequence to you and the Royal Army of Tundyel. They have had no formal training and their spirits have been greatly… dampened in the last days. In all truthfulness, they should not even have been worthy of my attention. However, despite what you may think, I like you. You have failed your King already in your failure to find the traitors and I do not believe he would let a second failure slip by. I have given you this warning solely so that in your weakness you will not be surprised by a group of backward, ill-bred mountain men."

"For your consideration I am grateful, Master," Erik said, biting back the words threatening to spill off his tongue in response to the Wizard's insults. Then, as quickly as it had flared up the fire died down again, leaving the Master of the Guard alone in the pre-dawn darkness. "If he is as powerful as he seems to think himself," he muttered in the silence, "why doesn't he just wipe those men out on his own?" Immediately the fire flared, a dancing flame coming dangerously close to licking Erik's face, and then shrank back to glowing embers once more. Erik could feel the heat on his face long after the flames receded, but that did not unnerve him nearly so much as did the realization that the old Wizard could be listening to him at anytime.

The soldiers would be waking soon, so Erik straightened his uniform, pulled on his boots, and made his way out to the Great Hall. The women of Lurn were busy preparing breakfast for the Royal Army, each hoping that by doing so she would somehow prove her loyalty to King Simann.

"Master Erik, you must be an early riser."

Erik looked up to see a young woman standing before him, holding a large platter full of steaming hotcakes. He had taken a seat in a secluded corner of the hall in hopes of avoiding conversation for as long as possible. Apparently it hadn't worked. He smiled politely in acknowledgement of the woman's observation, but otherwise made no response.

The woman appeared unaffected by Erik's reluctance to speak, or perhaps unaware. Smiling warmly, she continued, "I believe the breakfast has all been prepared. Perhaps you would like to fill a dish for yourself?" When the man gave no answer, she went on, "Actually, I suppose there's no reason for you to get up. I'm headed that way with these," she said, nodding down at the hotcakes, "so I can just fill a dish for you. You do like breakfast, do you not? I've found that many outsiders who come to Lurn are amazed by the spread we provide in the morning. It seems they are accustomed to toast. Can you imagine, starting the day off half starved like that?" She hadn't waited for an answer to any of her questions and headed off toward the center of the hall before Erik could so much as catch up with all she had said. He thought about simply walking out while the lady was gone but his stomach protested loudly against the idea. Besides, the woman would probably track him down outside and force feed him. Shaking his head, Erik turned away from the women bustling about the tables in the center of the Hall and did his best to block out the sounds, hoping for a few minutes of peace.

Soon, a dish heaped with food was placed on the table before him with a flourish. "I didn't know what you might find appetizing at this hour, so I just brought you a bit of everything."

"Thank you, madam," the Master of the Guard said politely. After all, she had taken time out of her already busy morning to bring him food. Looking down at the enormous amount in front of him, Erik corrected himself mentally. This wasn't just food, it was a feast. Erik had expected the woman to leave as quickly as she had come, but much to his surprise a second, much smaller dish was placed to his right and the young woman sat down beside him.

"I realized that I hadn't introduced myself while I was filling our plates. You, of course, are Erik, the Master of the Guard. Everyone in Lurn, probably everyone in Tundyel for that matter, knows who you are!" she smiled. "My name is Andelle. I may not be known throughout the kingdom, but I am famous in my own right, I suppose." She waited, apparently hoping to be asked the reason for her fame.

Erik ate in silence a few moments, thinking that perhaps the lady would tire of her one-sided conversation and leave him to finish his breakfast alone. Soon, though, he started feeling guilty for ignoring someone who was merely trying to make polite conversation. Smiling at Andelle, a genuine, though small, smile as opposed to the forced politeness of a few minutes before, he gave in.

"Just what is it, Madam Andelle, that has make you famous here in Lurn?"

Andelle beamed, her brown eyes sparkling with the satisfaction of finally getting the soldier to put together more than three words at a time. "Why, my hotcakes, of course! Anyone would tell you that I make the best hotcakes in the city. Go on and try them and I know you will think the same thing." She stared anxiously at Erik, her own fork poised halfway between her plate and mouth.

Despite his best effort to contain it, Erik could feel a small smirk tugging at the corners of his mouth. There was something about the young woman seated next to him, something different that he couldn't quite put his finger on. Mentally shrugging off his thoughts, Erik took a big bite of the hotcakes. He wasn't a very good judge of the quality of breakfast foods, considering that he was one of many who, according to Andelle, started the day off "half-starved" with toast and tea. However, he had to admit that he had never tasted anything like the light and fluffy cakes.

"Ah ha!" Andelle clapped her hands together in delight. In doing so the bite of pork sausage that was waiting suspended on her fork flew off and landed in the middle of Erik's food. The Master of the Guard expected the profuse apology which usually followed any mishap, no matter how small, in which he was the injured party. To his surprise, the brunette started laughing heartily, reached over and stabbed the offending piece of meat, and quickly popped it into her mouth.

"What did I tell you?" she grinned. "They speak for themselves."

Soon, Erik found himself lost in conversation with the engaging woman. They didn't talk about anything important--just food, mostly, and a little about family. Andelle had come to live in Lurn with an elderly aunt when she was ten. The old woman had died five years later, though, and Andelle had been on her own for the entire second half of her life. Erik had been sent to train for the Royal Army at fourteen and the last twenty-five years of his life had been spent in unquestioned dedication to duty. Due to their unique circumstances, neither knew much about their families.

The time moved quickly, and Erik was a little disoriented when he glanced behind him and realized that the soldiers were all finishing their meals and leaving the Hall.

Jumping to his feet, the Master of the Guard turned hastily toward Andelle. "Please excuse me, madam. I'm afraid I allowed myself to lose track of time. I must go out and address the men. Perhaps we will get the chance to speak again later?" Erik didn't know why he added the question, but he found himself waiting in anticipation for the answer.

Andelle smiled as she stood and took the empty plate from his hand, adding it to her own. "I would like that, Master Erik. I'll look for you at the midday meal. Now go on--I have a job to do as well, you know," she said, looking around at the messy hall.

As he hurried to meet all the Commanders back in the smithy's quarters where he had spent the night, Erik thought about his breakfast companion. During their meal he still hadn't been able to determine just what it was that made her different. It wasn't her looks--her brown eyes, brown hair, and average build were just like so many others in the city, and though she wasn't ugly she wasn't extraordinarily beautiful, either. Her voice was cheerful but not musical, and her smile was a bit uneven. Just as he reached the small building that was serving as headquarters he realized what it was that made Andelle so much different from everyone else in the city. While they had sat together, never once had she mentioned her loyalty to the King or acted intimidated by his position in the kingdom. She was the first in years, besides Gavin, to speak to him as a normal person.

Once he stepped through the doorway, Erik immediately pushed aside all thoughts of the young woman famous for her hotcakes and slid naturally into his role as head of the Royal Army. Ignoring all pleasantries offered by the Commanders, the Master of the Guard got directly to the point.

"This morning, the Master Wizard gave me a warning. Even as we speak there are one hundred men riding toward Lurn. They are not soldiers as we are, but had we not been warned they would have had the element of surprise and been able to most likely put a sizable dent in out lines on the perimeter of the city. Now that we know of their approach we have two options," he continued, sitting down on a dusty stool across from the Commanders. "First, we can simply warn the troops stationed outside the walls, perhaps backing them with platoons from within the city. If these men the Wizard Euroin sent word of do not turn away and they truly reach the city today, the people of Lurn may have one day's reprieve." Erik paused, looking over the faces in front of him for signs of their reactions. Much as he had suspected, most did not seem pleased with the idea of simply waiting for the enemy to approach. "Our second option is to march out and meet these traitors, a move they would undoubtedly not be expecting." At that, the Commanders began voicing their approval.

"Commander, what should our approach be?" Erik asked, turning to Lamtek of Foreen. Lamtek had a mind for all things tactical, and the Master of the Guard knew he would have been planning a strategy from the moment Erik had revealed the small threat they faced.

"If we take two hundred men we will have them outnumbered two to one and still have enough soldiers here that we have no reason to fear the people of the city getting out of hand. We can simply march out to meet the men who are riding toward Lurn, and then the element of surprise will be on our side."

The other Commanders were all agreeing and already coming up with the platoons who should be sent when Gavin spoke up. "All of our planning is well and good," he said, "but it is of little consequence if we do not know where these men are coming from. What good will it do for us to march west if our attackers approach from the north?"

For a while Erik began to think they would have no choice but to wait. The idea made him nervous, for he feared that when the citizens of Lurn saw the battle they would quickly join in, in hopes of driving the Royal Army from the city. He and his men had not made themselves particularly easy guests. While he did not fear the townspeople, Erik hoped to spare the lives of as many of them as possible and he feared the day would turn into a bloody massacre if the men were to find themselves stuck in the middle. Then, something the Wizard Euroin had said came back to him.

"I believe we do know from what direction they will approach," he said. "When the Wizard spoke, he called the men riding to Lurn 'mountain men.' Kauris and Gelci are the only towns in the Velion Range, are they not?" At the others' agreement, he went on. "If they are traitors traveling from the mountains, they would be afraid to travel through the other cities and will most likely be approaching from between Krasteiv and Valgrin."

Commander Yaldren of Krasteiv stood, waiting for Erik to acknowledge him before speaking. "One of the soldiers in my command hails from Krasteiv like myself, and he came to the castle just three years ago so the layout of the land between here and his family's home will still be fresh in his mind. I will send him and another to watch for these men." When the Master of the Guard nodded his approval, Yaldren left to do as he had said.

"The rest of you gather the troops who will go to battle these men. They must be prepared to leave the instant Commander Yaldren's scouts return with word of the approaching traitors." As the Commanders left, all seemed confident of a swift and sure victory. Erik, however, could not help but wonder if their confidence was somehow misguided.

The morning passed without incident. Given the threat of attack Erik had decided to postpone all trials for the day and the citizens of Lurn were methodically trying to go about their everyday business amidst the grieving of families who had lost fathers, husbands, and brothers to the executioner's sword. However, they made the best of what they had. As midday approached, Andelle and many of the other women of the city began preparing a spread of food for the five hundred soldiers.

As he made his way to the Great Hall for lunch, his mind stuck on the thought of how great it would be to sit and talk with Andelle again, Erik noticed a commotion near the front gate. He quickly made his way through the two hundred men who had been ordered to stay close to the gate, the men who were preparing to go fight. There, panting from his sprint back to Lurn, stood one of the scouts, an eighteen year old named Godwin. Between breaths he told Commander Yaldren that the enemy had been spotted on the edge of the Brintzwood Forest, directly east of Krasteiv and following the road. The two hundred soldiers snapped to attention as the Master of the Guard mounted his horse before them, followed by Commanders Lamtek, Roedan, and Hiasin. Soon Erik gave the command and the troops began marching out of the city.

\*\*\*\*\*\*\*\*\*\*\*\*\*\*\*\*\*\*\*

Paodin led the men of Gelci forward. It seemed that the closer they came to Lurn the more the men talked and joked with one another. Their spirits seemed high, but Paodin couldn't help but think they were all simply trying to cover their nervousness. Berek and Paodin had been doing the same, making meaningless conversation as they rode along. At Audon's suggestion, Paodin had ordered the men to ride in ten columns of the same number. The front row of men, as well as five down each outside flank, each carried a shield recovered from the ruins of Dren, a shining silver shield bearing the Lynberry leaf pattern which Paodin and the Healer each wore. They had ridden out of Krasteiv in this formation, but once the men had entered Brintzwood Forest the road had narrowed to nothing more than a thin path which forced the men to ride two by two. Now, however, they were nearing the eastern edge of the woods and would soon pass into the clearing just a few minutes' ride this side of Lurn.

Paodin, lost in his thoughts, didn't notice Berek had been speaking until he stopped. Paodin began to apologize to his friend, but Berek said urgently, "Stop the men." Immediately Paodin lifted his closed fist, and just as quickly the signal was passed to the back and one hundred men stopped in their tracks and waited in silence.

Berek said nothing, just dismounted and rapidly moved out of sight through the trees. Paodin was anxious to know what had so suddenly grabbed his friend and Second in Command's attention, but he could do nothing but wait. Berek was a hunter who had spent the majority of his life in the forests, so Paodin knew he himself would only prove a hindrance if he tried to follow. So instead he sat still, holding the reins of Berek's dapple grey stallion. The wait was not a long one, for Berek soon reappeared soundlessly on the edge of the path beside his mount.

"It seems that our approach is not as much a surprise as we had thought," he said, taking the reins from Paodin as he mounted the powerful horse. "The Royal Army waits at the end of our road through Brintzwood, though not with their full strength. They appear to have approximately twice our number, all on foot. I believe it is only their commanders who are on horseback," he finished quietly.

Audon, who had been riding directly behind the two young men, had edged his horse up alongside Paodin when Berek had returned. "How are they armed?" he now asked. "Do they carry bows, or swords alone?"

"I did not see any archers, but then I got only a quick look. However, I believe they carry only swords," Berek said.

Paodin turned to the man who had raised him. "What do you suggest we do? Ride forward as we are now?"

Audon thought for a moment, gazing blankly ahead as his mind searched for a new strategy. "We have little choice. Either we ride meekly forward and hope our mounts will give us enough of an advantage to hold off the Royal Army long enough to get our full number clear of the forest or we charge in and try to use speed, as well."

"It would seem we have no choice," Paodin said. "Spread the word that at my signal we will charge forward with everything we have. The battle is about to begin."

Chapter 13

The crashing of hooves was the first thing to alert the front lines of the Royal Army that their opponents were close at hand, followed soon by the shouts of one hundred men as they charged out of the forest into the midst of the waiting soldiers. Immediately sounds of battle rang out--swords crashing, men yelling, horses snorting and stomping. Blood spilt to the ground, staining the once innocent field where men young and old now fell in agony. The Royal Army, though twice as strong in numbers at the beginning of the battle, was being cut down.

The Healer dismounted and ran into the thick of the battle. Like in the dungeons at the castle the twenty-six year-old girl vanished and was replaced by a woman who seemed ageless, a Healer whose only purpose was to restore life to those out of whom it poured like water from a spring. She knelt beside a man here whose bone showed through a leg ripped open, mending flesh and spirit with a touch. Turning, there she saw another whose insides were threatening to spill out as he lay writhing on the ground. Everywhere she looked, someone was reaching out to her for help and comfort.

Each time she touched a wound, pain tore through the Healer's body. Long ago she had learned to ignore the excruciating pain of near fatal injury, but never before had she taken so much upon herself in such a short time. Syndria's mind and body cried out, begging her to stop, but her heart won the battle of wills. The young Healer knew it was her sole duty to heal these men and to her that meant completely, pain and suffering included.

It was not long before the Healer knelt beside a man whose flame of life had already been extinguished. Judging by the appearance of the injury, death had come almost immediately. Syndria sat in stunned stillness beside the man, her entire body numb. She had always known that the torture King Simann ordered ended inevitably in death, but she had never seen the prisoners who had met their end. Never in her life had she come upon someone she couldn't help, and the sight paralyzed her. For a long moment even the sounds of battle faded away as she sat staring at the young man. Her heart ached as it occurred to her that she did not even know his name. Tears began pooling in the girl's eyes, but as quickly as they had come the unwelcome visitors vanished when Syndria heard the groans of a man who had just fallen behind her. The Healer once again took over and Syndria pushed aside her own fears and weaknesses in order to take on more pain.

As soon as she turned, the Healer knew the man she was looking at was a soldier of the Royal

Army. His uniform was quickly turning to scarlet, the lifeblood flowing out of his chest creating a rapidly growing circle. Conflicting thoughts poured through the girl's mind in an instant: *This man is the enemy. We came to save the people of Lurn from dying at his hand, and his death would mean one less sword with which to contend. Yet, he is only a boy, younger than I am. How can I just sit back and watch him die?* The moment of hesitation over, the Healer knew what she must do and placed her hands over the wound. The young soldier opened his eyes as the pain quickly left his body and was replaced by an odd warmth.

"Am I dead?" he asked, finding the Healer's eyes.

"I should hope not," she smiled warmly, "for if you are that means I am as well. No, I fear you are still on the battlefield."

The boy's eyes widened suddenly as recognition dawned on him. "You are Mistress Syndria, the traitor we are searching for!" he said, sitting up and pulling away from her.

"Then I believe you have found me. Now what are you going to do?"

"If you are a traitor to our King," the young man asked, now gripping the sword that had fallen from his hand as he lay dying, "why is it that you healed his soldier?"

The Healer was anxious to move on,

knowing that while she sat speaking with this young man more were falling all around her. However, she had vowed to open the eyes of her fellowmen, to enable them to see the truth about the man they called "King." What meaning would that pledge have if she abandoned it now?

"You are correct in saying that I have betrayed your king," Syndria said calmly, "but it is something I do not regret, not even for an instant. Even were my decision to cost me my life, I would die knowing I have done the right thing." The young soldier said nothing, so Syndria continued, "You say the Royal Army is searching for me, and most likely the other traitor, the prisoner who escaped, as well. Tell me, if you knew the identity of who you were searching for, why have others been slain as well?" The Healer did not know for sure the fate of the citizens within Lurn's walls, but the young man's reaction confirmed her fears. "Why would a fair, kind King order an entire city slain?"

"Not the whole city," he said, defensively, though his voice betrayed his wavering belief. "The King gave us orders to execute the traitors, those not loyal to him."

"Traitors very much like those who are kept hidden away in the depths of the castle, those so called 'guests of the west hall.' If they are traitors, what are their crimes? Have they been unfaithful in paying their tributes? Have they moved against you, the Royal Army sent to kill them? Have they so much as said a wrong word?" The young soldier seemed to be considering her words, but the Healer could wait no longer. "I'm sorry, but I cannot spend any more time here with you. There are many others who need my touch. I hope you will recognize the truth, and if so know you will be welcomed to our cause." With that she moved on to the nearest wounded man, hoping the soldier would come to his senses but knowing she had to push all thought of him aside in order to do her best for everyone else.

In terms of battles, the one the men of Gelci fought that day against the Royal Army was a short one. The sun set on a quiet field, stained with the blood of soldier and rebel alike. The groans of men grew fainter by the minute, some forever silenced in death but most quieted by the Healer's gentle yet powerful touch. Soldiers of the Royal Army were gathered and guarded. And though some members of the rebellion opposed, all the soldiers were told of Paodin's torture at the hands of King Simann and were given the chance to hear the truth about the man's cruelty. At Paodin's command, any who claimed to have had a change of heart were accepted fully into the ranks of the rebellion. A few men of Gelci grumbled, reluctant to trust the men they had been fighting such a short time before. These men Paodin called together.

"What do you want to do, simply kill all those we now hold?" he asked. "Think of our reason for this quest--Simann is an evil and cruel man, but at the same time he is charming and intelligent. These men are no different than those we came to rescue. They have been deceived into fighting for a cause that is not their own. If we deny these men, these boys who could be your sons or brothers, the chance to fight against the oppression they have always lived under, how are we any better than Simann?" Paodin spoke of the truth and of their cause for a while longer, and though some of the men were still not comfortable with their new brothers in arms, they agreed to keep their thoughts to themselves and be content to keep watch from a distance. With a day's battle finished and one conflict held off a while longer, Paodin decided to look around for the Healer. He finally spotted her off by herself, leaning against a tree at the forest's edge. As he drew closer, Paodin could see that Syndria's hands, face, and dress were all covered in blood. His concern for her grew when he saw the pained expression on her face, and he hurried to kneel beside her.

"Mistress," he said, putting his hand on her shoulder. When she didn't open her eyes or even stir, he shook her gently and said, a bit louder, "Syndria!"

"What is it?" she asked quietly, her eyes still closed. "Am I needed?"

Relieved that his fears appeared unfounded, Paodin sat down as he spoke. "I see only one person in need of a Healer right now, and that is you. Are you alright?"

Syndria opened her eyes and slowly turned to look at Paodin. She offered what she hoped would be a reassuring smile but knew she just looked tired. "I will be," she answered. "All I need is some time to recuperate. By morning I'll most likely be my normal, opinionated self."

"If that is the case, and you truly are alright, why don't I escort you back to the stream and let you get cleaned up? You may feel better by merely washing off those reminders of today's battle."

Exhausted from hours of bearing the pain of others, Syndria wanted nothing more than to just lie back against the tree and let her mind fade into the darkness waiting just behind her eyelids. She started to tell Paodin just that but stopped when she saw his expression. The young man was suggesting the one thing he could, anxious to help, so the Healer nodded. "You are probably correct. However, I'm afraid our journey may be slow."

Standing, Paodin offered his hand and helped Syndria to her feet. As she turned toward the woods, Paodin put his hand to her back to steady the weakened Healer. Startled, he pulled back and looked at his hand, now crimson. At first he thought it was blood from one of the men like the dark stain that covered the girl's front. It took only a moment, though, for Paodin to realize that this blood came from the Healer, from a wound still bleeding. He quickly grabbed hold of Syndria's shoulders, stopping her.

"What happened?"

"What do you mean, 'What happened'?" she asked, confused. "Have you blocked out the day already?" She tried to turn to face Paodin but he held fast to her shoulders as he tried to examine her back. Syndria, not knowing what he was doing, continued to try and pull out of his grip until Paodin chastised her.

"Hold still, girl!" he ordered in a tone he had never used while addressing the Healer, though the same could not be said for when he talked *about* her. Shocked, Syndria froze, and Paodin moved one hand back down to the middle of her back. "You've been injured," he said, lightly tracing his fingers along the edge of a wound that began just under her right shoulder blade and ended across under the back of her left ribs. "This is a nasty wound," he said. "Why didn't you tell me before I made you stand?"

Trying unsuccessfully to look back over her shoulder at the cut, she said, "I suppose I didn't notice being hurt. Maybe that's why I can't seem to get any energy back now."

"Didn't notice?" he asked incredulously. Shaking his head, he continued, "Why has it not healed? Have you just not done it yet?"

Finally able to shrug off Paodin's hand, the young lady turned. "It will have to heal on its own. Perhaps it is a way to keep us in check or maybe just a twist of fate, but a Healer's gift will work only on others. None of us can heal herself," she said.

Paodin thought for a second before saying, "Wait here," and then he was gone. It was only a moment before he returned on his horse and reached out to pull Syndria up behind him. "None of the men here know much about cleaning and dressing wounds, and those who do know a little would most likely be far too nervous at the thought of having their hands on the Healer." Though he was thinking it, Paodin chose not to add that he didn't like the idea of some man putting his hands on her bare skin. "I know a woman who does not live far from here. She helped me the last time I passed through here and I am sure she would be willing to help you as well."

"But what if more soldiers come? I have to be here to aid the men who fall. The pain from my back is nothing I can't bear."

"I believe you, Mistress," Paodin said,

urging his horse forward, "but if your wound is not dressed and taken care of I do not think you will be here to help them for much longer. You have lost a lot of blood judging by the amount your gown had soaked up, and you are still bleeding. I promise I will bring you back as soon as Lady Brigitte finishes. Besides, it is quickly growing dark and I cannot see any more of the Royal Army attacking until morning."

Content with his answer, Syndria closed her eyes and just held on to Paodin as the two turned south east and rode along the edge of the woods.

*********************

It had grown dark already when Euroin stepped out of his quarters and made his way across the courtyard. He held his black cloak tightly wrapped around his body and the moonlight made his white hair shine eerily. To those who happened to look out a window as he passed the Wizard almost appeared to be an apparition, a head moving without a body. He hurried into the castle and up a winding staircase to the north tower, moving as if he were being pulled by some powerful being. His green eyes danced with anger and disbelief, for when he had summoned up a picture of the battle outside of Lurn he had seen the Healer Syndria, that mere child, not only alive but kneeling beside one of the traitors to heal him.

Euroin burst into the marble room, his cape now being whipped around as if caught in a whirlwind. He threw wide his arms, opening himself up to the malicious powers coursing through the air. He still could not control the destructive dark magic, but each time he encountered it it became easier to stand under the bombardment. In the dark night, the Master Wizard concentrated on nothing but the girl. He could see her face, the innocent face of a child now aged beyond her years. As he focused on the Healer, dark spells spiraled around her in ever-narrowing circles. The unimaginable colors spun and leapt, moving in like a pack of wild dogs circling their prey. Bright colors shot toward the girl, jumping like flames as they reached for her. Euroin couldn't stop concentrating on Syndria for long--he knew he wouldn't be able to maintain what little control he had over the dark power. He couldn't help himself, though, and stopped focusing on the dark powers long enough to imagine what terrible fate might befall her. That was a mistake.

The Wizard was whipped around and tossed across the room, much like the first time he had ventured up into the tower. This time he was ready for it and managed to stop himself before he was slammed against the wall. He walked back to the center of the room and once again focused all his attention on the girl. As he did so, following her as she moved through the night just outside of Lurn, the Master Wizard couldn't believe his luck. Riding along with the Healer was the prisoner who had escaped his grasp in the dungeon. Without realizing it he had been directing the dark magic toward both his problems. Now he would be able to destroy both together. The sinister spells were closer to them now, drawing in on every side. This was it--soon he would be rid of the traitors, and without them the rebels wouldn't have a chance.

******************

It was darker in the woods than it had been in the clearing, for here all the light from the full moon was blocked out by the dense tree cover. It was almost as if the moon and stars had all been snuffed out. However, it wasn't the darkness that bothered Paodin--it was the even darker shadows that he could see moving through the woods around them. His horse had quickened its pace, and Paodin could feel the growing tension in his mount's muscular body as they rode deeper into the forest.

"Easy, Thrul," he whispered, rubbing the big stallion's neck. The whisper may as well have been a shout, for it rang out in the unnatural silence of the dark night. There were no birds of the night to be heard, no small feet scurrying along the ground. He didn't even hear the night song of any crickets or tree frogs. At first the Healer had kept up a steady stream of conversation, but now even she had fallen silent behind him.

"It won't be long now, Mistress," he said, trying to put a normal tone in his voice. "How are you feeling?"

Out amidst the trees, the shadows drew closer.

"Mistress?" Paodin asked a little louder when she gave no answer, "Are you alright?" He pulled back on the reins, bringing the big red stallion to a stop. Craning his neck, Paodin tried to look back over his shoulder at the Healer.

The shadows were coming even closer.

"Mistress, please answer me. How are you feeling?" he asked again, this time lightly slapping one of the hands she had clasped together around his waist. When he touched her hand, her grip went slack and Paodin could feel her sliding to the right across his back. He turned as she fell, somehow managing to get a hold on her arm as the Healer toppled off Thrul towards the ground. Her legs, now dangling in the air, brushed the stallion's back leg. Under normal circumstances Paodin's steady mount would not have even side-stepped. Tonight, though, with him already nervous, the unexpected touch was too much. He bucked, kicking out behind him and twisting away from the Healer's limp form. Paodin, already off balance from holding the Healer up, was thrown. Thrul whinnied in fear and took off, crashing through the woods and into the darkness.

Paodin hit the ground with a thud, still holding on to the Healer who was crumpled beside him. He sat up slowly, soon realizing that nothing was hurt but his pride. Leaning over the Healer's still body, Paodin was relieved to hear her moan quietly because it meant she was still alive. Shaking her shoulder gently, Paodin was trying to wake the Healer when he noticed something moving from the corner of his eye.

At first glance, Paodin saw nothing more than the dark forms of the trees around him. Thinking that his nerves were getting the best of him he turned his attention back to the unconscious girl beside him on the ground, only to once again notice something moving. This time when he looked up Paodin thought he must have hit his head in the fall, for he would almost swear that the darkness was moving towards them. Narrowing his eyes, Paodin watched in confusion as he realized he wasn't imagining things--a dark shadow was moving forward, growing larger as it approached. Logic told him to look around, for a shadow could only exist if it was being cast by something. In this case, Paodin knew he had to ignore logic. This shadow wasn't an ordinary shadow. It was blacker than anything he had ever seen before. If there had been light shining, Paodin had a feeling it would have been devoured by the utter blackness. As he watched it approach he realized that the dark shadows which had been moving through the trees earlier had all combined to form this one, sinister…nothing. For that's what Paodin was seeing, nothing. Looking at the shadow creature was like looking into a void. He sat still, almost mesmerized by what he was watching as the shadow began to take shape.

It was formed vaguely like a man, but its proportions were different. The body was too long, the shoulders too broad, and the head too small. It had five fingers on each hand, but they looked more like long talons. It had legs but it didn't move forward on them. Instead it appeared to be gliding over the ground. Now it was less than three yards away, raising one long arm as if to strike.

With a start, Paodin was jerked back to reality as the black talons raked the air towards his face. He managed to duck, avoiding that first blow, but it was almost instantly followed by a second, this one aimed at the Healer. Paodin cringed as he threw himself across her unconscious form, not knowing what to expect from the shadow creature's blow. There was no pressure, no feeling of contact, but Paodin did feel a searing pain as the skin on his left shoulder was torn open. Rolling off of the girl and onto his feet, Paodin drew his sword and swung it with all his might. It went through the Shadow as one would expect to see a blade cut through smoke. The blackness separated for a second, curling in the air before joining again. A hiss came from the Shadow, not one of pain but of anger. As Paodin moved a few feet away from the helpless Healer the Shadow followed, as he had hoped. Paodin struck out again, this time aiming higher and cutting down through the neck and shoulders. As before, his blade met no resistance as it passed through his foe.

 While Paodin was still in mid swing, the blade of his sword still in the middle of the darkness, the Shadow struck again. This time he couldn't duck and the black talons slid across his face and neck. The searing pain came again and Paodin cried out as he felt the skin being sliced open across his left cheek and under his chin, ending on the right side of his neck. As soon as he reached the end of his swing, Paodin swung again, crossing down over his previous strike. Perhaps it was just his imagination, or wishful thinking, but Paodin thought he saw a little of the Shadow drift away into the night following the blow. He didn't have long to contemplate, though, because the Shadow struck out at him again. Dropping to his knees, Paodin rolled out of the terrible creature's reach. The Shadow turned away, which gave Paodin a moment to catch his breath until he realized that it had turned toward the Healer.

Jumping to his feet, Paodin reached out and cut through the back of the shadow creature just as its talons raked against Syndria's back. The Shadow turned mid-strike, making the wound a little less severe than it would have been, but Paodin could see that it had still done quite a bit of damage to an already nasty injury. For a minute, panic threatened to set in. Paodin knew he had to protect the Healer, but how could he keep her safe from the Shadow? The faces of friends lost in the day's battle flashed through his mind. If he let this creature win, if the Healer was lost, those men would all have died in vain. Paodin attacked with renewed determination, stepping in to slash at the Shadow and then moving back just enough to keep drawing the creature farther away from where Syndria lay.

They fought for what seemed to Paodin like hours, but in truth was just a few minutes. He was exhausted, his muscles burning with every strike. Occasionally a small tendril of darkness swirled off into the night, but otherwise he saw no evidence of the battle taking a toll on his foe. The few muscles that weren't aching from the effort of swinging his sword through the air were now threatening to give out as well. Every step, every dodge was getting harder, and he was being raked by the black talons much more often than at the beginning of the fight. As Paodin grew weaker, it seemed the Shadow grew stronger. He wasn't sure he could hold out much longer. He wasn't even positive he had the strength--or will--to try.

******************

He stood in the midst of the swirling colors, watching. The girl lay still, holding on to a fading spark of light with all her might. Her only hope was getting help soon. However, the young man could not survive against the Shadow for much longer. The ancient dark spells pushed in on every side, crushing his spirit as well as his body. He held on desperately to the sword, clinging to it with both hands as if that alone would save him. At his ankle, tucked into his boot, was the weapon he should be using, but he would never use it while he held the sword. Fighting this way, both the Healer and her protector would be lost.

Chapter 14

"Just give up. You can't win--it's useless even to try."

The voice came out of the darkness, the first sound Paodin had heard besides his own groans and the angry hisses from the Shadow since their fight began. In his surprise he looked around, which caused him to let his guard down and open himself up for another attack. The talons raked across Paodin's chest and right arm, causing a deeper gash than those before. The sword fell to the ground as Paodin stumbled backward, clutching his arm.

Its foes weapon gone, the Shadow drove in relentlessly. The creature sliced at Paodin with both long hands, forcing him to either keep backing up or be sliced to ribbons. Avoiding those talons was almost like trying to escape the very night surrounding him--all he could do was back away. Maybe that voice was right, whoever he was. Maybe he should just give up. The pain he was in was already unbearable--surely it couldn't be much worse to just lie down and die. Just then he tripped and went crashing to the ground. As he lay sprawled on the forest floor Paodin could see what he had fallen over. It was the Healer, still and silent.

At first the Shadow didn't seem to notice the girl. It sped toward Paodin, a predator closing in on its downed prey. Paodin closed his eyes in defeat and awaited the end. It was a few seconds later when he realized the final blow should have come already that he opened his eyes, fully expecting to see the terrible creature looming over him. It wasn't. Paodin sat up and was horrified to see that the Shadow had turned its attention to the helpless girl.

It swiped at Syndria almost tentatively, as if checking to see if she was alive and worth the effort it would take to kill her. The black talons streaked across the Healer's hip and lower back, drawing an almost inaudible groan from her. At once, Paodin realized that in his resignation to death he was also resigning the Healer to that same fate, something he had no right to do. He had no thoughts of the kingdom, no concern for seeing the true heir on the throne. All he knew was that he had to give Syndria a chance to live, and the only way to do that was to fight as hard as he could with every fiber of his being. In that same instant Paodin rolled to his feet, pulling the dagger from his boot as he stood. He longed for his sword but he had foolishly let it go. Now he would have to move in close to do anything at all to the Shadow creature. He lunged forward, barely even having time to notice that the dagger glittered in reflection of a light nowhere to be found.

Paodin threw himself at the Shadow, fully

expecting to fly straight through to the other side. To his amazement, the dagger's blade disappeared into his foe and a split second later Paodin crashed to the ground atop a solid body. The creature hissed again, this time in pain instead of anger. It thrashed wildly against Paodin, its talons raking his chest as it tried to push him away. Paodin held his ground, pinning the creature down as he pulled the dagger out of its gut and plunged it into the creature's black chest. The Shadow creature gave one final cry then was silent and still. Paodin rolled off to the side, anxious to be away from the being. He pulled the dagger from the creature's heart as he moved, and as soon as the blade left the dark body the Shadow changed back to a black mist, broke apart, and scattered into the night.

He lay there in the silence, staring at the dagger he held in his hand. The blade looked normal now, except for the odd fact that it was completely clean. Perhaps he had only imagined the shine he saw earlier, because now it appeared dark and ordinary. At the same time he knew the dagger was far from ordinary, for it had done what his sword could not--it had slain the Shadow. That though reminded Paodin that he needed to retrieve his sword. It may not have proven useful against the unnatural shadow being of the night, but it had been far from useless throughout the day's battle. After putting the dagger back in its boot sheath he slowly stood, scanned the small clearing, and saw the weapon partially hidden, its hilt sticking out from underneath a small bush right in the tree line.

As he approached, Paodin heard movement in the forest off to his right. He remained calm, trying to slow his breathing back to normal as he readied himself for another battle. Every muscle cried out in protest, desperately needing a rest, but Paodin could still hear someone moving. Grasping the sword tightly with both hands, Paodin took a deep breath and then spun, stepping forward into the trees with the blade held out in ready.

"Boy," came a gravely voice, "I'm starting to believe you hold some grudge against me!" The old man stepped forward into the clearing, pushing the sword aside as he would a small tree branch were it in his way. "Have you lost something?" he asked, and Paodin saw that Thrul walked calmly along behind the old hermit. The reins were draped loosely across the stallion's neck, yet he followed as if he were being led.

Lowering his sword and letting his shoulders sag from exhaustion, Paodin said, "I'm glad it was you, old man, though that is strange to say. I was afraid I was going to be forced to fight again, and I'm not sure I would have survived."

"Yes, you do appear a bit worse for wear," the man said lightly, brushing off Paodin's wounds as mere scratches. "Is the Healer…?" His question

trailed off when he caught sight of her motionless
frame laying a few feet away. Pushing past the
young man, the hermit hurried towards Syndria.

"She still lives," Paodin said, "but barely. If
she were not so strong, she would already be
dead." As he spoke he made his way to where the
old man knelt beside the Healer. Leaning close, he
noticed that her breathing had grown more shallow
and she no longer moaned quietly. Though he tried
to remain positive, Paodin felt hope dying as he
knelt beside the ever weakening Healer. "We are
still quite a distance from Lady Brigitte's home.
I'm afraid she may not make it." As he spoke
Paodin scooped Syndria up, his muscles straining
under the weight however slight it was. He laid her
across Thrul's back and then pulled himself into
the saddle.

"Do not lose hope," the hermit said. "You
may find you are closer than you think." He then
slapped the horse on the rump, sending Thrul off
with a start. Paodin struggled to hold Syndria on at
first, but he soon compensated for his awkward
positioning and settled in to the stallion's gait.
Thrul moved quickly through the woods, faster
than Paodin thought safe. No matter how hard he
pulled on the reins, though, the big stallion refused
to slow, darting around trees and jumping fallen
logs.

Much sooner than Paodin had expected,

they were breaking out of the trees on the western edge of Brigitte's property. Thrul stopped directly in front of the door, the change so abrupt that Paodin felt the Healer almost slip from his grasp. He jumped down from the saddle, sliding Syndria off into his arms. When he turned, Brigitte stood in the open doorway despite the late hour, a thin blanket wrapped around her shoulders against the slight chill. Adair stood beside her, his face still soft from a child's sleep. Brigitte turned to her son, a questioning look on her face as she waited for him to tell her who had arrived on her doorstep at such a late hour. The boy said nothing, however, apparently too shocked by Paodin's appearance and the sight of the lifeless body in his arms.

"It is Paodin, Lady," he called out. "I need your help."

"Come in." She stepped back, holding the door open wide as she motioned Paodin inside. "You sound exhausted. What is the matter?"

"I'll be alright, but I have a friend here who may not be." Paodin had to squeeze past Adair as he stepped through the door. The boy still stood in a mild state of shock, his eyes wide as he stared at Paodin. "She has suffered some serious injuries."

"Lay her there," Brigitte said, motioning toward a small cot tucked against the wall. "Addie," she said, "go and get some water." Adair snapped out of his shock and hurried past them into the kitchen. "First bring some to me, and then stoke the fire and warm some," she called after him. When Paodin laid the Healer down, Brigitte reached out with sure hands and felt for signs of life. "What happened to her?"

"She was cut in a battle," he answered. "The wounds are on her back."

He had lain the Healer on her side facing the wall, her back to Brigitte who now probed gently at the wound, running her fingers lightly over the gashes to determine their sizes. Adair arrived with the bowl of water and a wet rag which he handed to his mother. Brigitte began washing the wound as she spoke again.

"I need the sheers, son. They are next to the shirt I'm sewing, on the table." He hurried off again as she continued, "The cut is deep, and she seems to have lost a lot of blood, but she is not gone yet." When Adair handed his mother the scissors she quickly began cutting the back out of Syndria's dress. "I suppose you were in the same battle," she said to Paodin. "Were you injured?"

Paodin once again began to say that he would be alright, but Adair interrupted him.

"He's hurt, too, Mum, but not so bad as the lady. I can take care of him."

When Paodin protested, saying he would like to help attend to Syndria, Brigitte shook her head. "If you are not taken care of, I may end up with two in serious condition instead of one. Go with Adair. He is quite capable of dressing wounds. When he has finished and you have some time to rest you may return." Paodin did as he was told, too tired and too sore to argue. He followed the boy into the kitchen and sat down in the chair Adair pulled out for him, removing his shirt as he sat. Before turning his attention to Paodin, Adair carried the pot of warm water in to his mother.

When he returned, Adair dipped a rag into his own bowl of water and began cleaning Paodin's wounds. The more he worked on Paodin the more perplexed the boy's face grew.

"What happened to you?" he finally asked. "All your cuts are real deep, but none of 'em is bleedin'."

"I fought…something in the woods on the way here," Paodin answered. "I don't really know what it was." As the boy turned his attention to the cut across Paodin's face and neck, Paodin gritted his teeth. Until Adair started cleaning his wounds, Paodin hadn't noticed how much they really did hurt.

Adair hesitated for a moment, his hand hovering over Paodin's shoulder. Figuring Adair had seen him grimace and was afraid of hurting him, Paodin assured the boy, "Don't worry, you aren't making it any worse."

"Oh, I'm not worried about that," he

answered. Glancing at the kitchen door, Adair asked quickly, "Would you tell me about the battle? I was in town--I saw them soldiers. Are you fightin' them?"

Judging by Adair's glance toward the other room, Paodin assumed Brigitte would not want him telling her son the details of the day's bloody battle. If he told of the Shadow, though, anything Brigitte heard from the front room she would figure to be just a story, and the boy would most likely be fascinated. "Oh, that part was nothing. I would imagine those soldiers still in Lurn will be running home soon, too scared to fight." Paodin reminded himself to ask Adair later about being in town. Any information he could take back would be helpful. "Now, that…creature, in the woods, *that* was something unbelievable," he said. "You probably don't want to hear about it, though, because you wouldn't believe me."

"Tell me!" Adair said excitedly, then composed himself--after all, he was almost twelve--and added, "I mean, if you want. I'll bet I'd believe it, if it's true." So Paodin told him of the Shadow, glad to have something to keep his mind distracted from the not so delicate hands of the boy. Telling about the fight would also give him a chance to think more about the events of the battle.

Paodin was at the end of his story, telling Adair about the old hermit showing up with his horse, when Brigitte stepped into the doorway. He finished quickly then stood as he asked, "How is she, Lady Brigitte?" He started to put his shirt back on self-consciously, realized it was torn and ruined at the same time he realized Brigitte was blind and wouldn't mind him being shirtless, and ended up standing awkwardly for a moment, the bloody garment held halfway between the table and his shoulder.

"Please, sit," she said as she walked by him into the kitchen. "You should rest some while you are here. Addie, please go refill the kettle and I'll make some tea." As the boy went outside to fetch more water, Brigitte answered Paodin's question. "The bleeding has stopped from the main wound on your friend's back, but she has lost a lot of blood. She hasn't wakened yet and her breathing is still shallow. After we have some tea I will make her something for the pain. That should help some- -if we can get her to swallow. Other than making her more comfortable, I'm afraid I've done all I can do for now. The rest is up to her--she must decide she wants to fight."

"She'll fight," Paodin said confidently. "I don't believe she knows how to do anything else."

*********************

*She was safe and warm, wrapped in gold and silver light which danced around her. For what seemed like the first time in ages there was no pain to block out, not even a hint of the pain she somehow knew she should feel. She could see nothing but the light, but she could hear a beautiful melody drifting toward her from somewhere close by. She had heard it before, but Syndria couldn't remember when or where.*

*"You may come to us, if you wish." The words came from the same place as the music, three voices speaking as one. "You will never again feel pain, never see the ugliness which is in the world. Here there is only good."*

*"You have done well, child," said a loving, familiar voice. Though Syndria couldn't see her, she knew it was the Ancient who had just spoken. "However," Nedra continued, "there is more yet to do."*

*"I'm happy here, Ancient," Syndria replied. "I feel wonderful, like never before."*

*"You may come with us now and never return," came the three voices, "or you man go back and come to us, and rest, later. You cannot stay here."*

*"That is a simple decision," Syndria smiled. "Either enter into peace, truth, and rest, or return to a world of hatred, lies, and pain." She started to answer but faces began appearing before her. There was Paodin, standing before the men of Gelci. Next, Simon and Ina, the couple from the woods. There was Councilman Lawrence and*

*his family, followed by a whole stream of faces she
had seen during the feasts through the years. "If I
go with you," she asked, "what will happen to the
people of Tundyel?"*

*"Another will come. The kingdom will be
restored, though none now will see it come to
pass," the Three answered.*

*Syndria still hesitated. The Three spoke
again, separately now.*

*"Come or go."*

*"You must decide."*

*"What is your choice?"*

*Quietly, Nedra's voice came once again.
"Follow your heart, child."*

\*\*\*\*\*\*\*\*\*\*\*\*\*\*\*\*\*\*\*

Erik rode back to Lurn, his spirits all but
crushed. Though they had outnumbered the traitors
two to one, the Royal Army had suffered a quick
and definite defeat. The gate opened as he
approached, and Gavin stood waiting, shock and
fear written on his face and questions waiting on
his lips. Erik dismounted, handed the reins to a
soldier who waited nearby, and then began walking
beside his friend.

"Let's go back to your quarters. You can sit
down as you tell me of the battle," Gavin said
quietly.

"If I go back there, I will undoubtedly face
another meeting with the Master Wizard, and that

is something for which I am not yet prepared," Erik sighed. "How many have returned?"

"A few," Gavin answered, "but no more than a dozen, Commander Lamtek among them. A soldier saw Commander Hiasin fall, but there has been no word of Commander Roedan. I was starting to fear we had lost you as well." When Erik said nothing, Gavin continued, "We will go to the hall. Perhaps we can find some food left over from this evening's meal." The Master of the Guard had no desire to eat, but he was too tired to get into what he knew would be a useless argument with his friend.

The two men had just sat down at a small table tucked away in a corner of the hall when a platter of food was placed between them and a small plate in front of each. Erik glanced up to see Andelle smiling softly.

"I noticed you did not eat, Commander," she said, "so there is enough food for two." Then, as quickly as she had come, she was gone.

Erik took a roll off the platter and picked at it as he spoke. "Both traitors were there, the prisoner leading the rebellion and the Healer in the midst of the fighting, helping any who fell."

"Is her presence what gave them an advantage?" Gavin asked. "She was healing them to fight again?"

"You misunderstood me--she was healing

everyone who fell, their army and ours alike. Why would a traitor do such a thing?" Erik had been deeply troubled by the day's events and now it was obvious in his voice as he spoke to his friend. Gavin didn't have an answer for him, so Erik continued. "Something else troubles me." Glancing up from the roll he had been studying as he spoke, the Master of the Guard made certain no one was close enough to hear before he went on, "Do you remember that day years ago in Dren?"

"I had not thought of it since that day," Gavin answered, though confused by the question. "However, as of late is seems I have been able to think of nothing else. Why?"

"Did you notice the shields those men held, the ones with the pattern from the soldiers' quarters at the castle?" Gavin nodded, so he went on. "Those men today carried those same shields. Or if not those, the ones they had bore the same markings."

"But that is not possible! The city was completely gone, almost like it had never existed to begin with." Gavin shook his head. "I'm sorry my friend, but you must be wrong."

"I'm not wrong!" Erik slammed the uneaten roll back down on the table in anger, drawing the attention of everyone nearby. "If you do not believe me, ask Lamtek. He will tell you the same."

"Commander Lamtek," Gavin said, "did not return under his own power. He was seriously injured and is being tended to by one of the townswomen. The last time I checked on him he was still unconscious. Erik, I want to believe you," he stated calmly, "but how do you expect me to believe something that is so… impossible?"

"I know what I saw," he sighed, "but I don't suppose I can expect you to believe without seeing something that I have trouble grasping after seeing it with my own eyes. No matter--I'm sure you will get the chance before the stars come out tomorrow night." Pushing his chair back without having taken a single bite of the food set before him, Erik stood. "Now, if you will excuse me I suppose I should go to my quarters. There's no use in putting off Master Wizard Euroin any longer. Seeing as how I'm sure he knows the battle has long been over, all I am doing with this delay is angering him even more." With that he turned and made his way through the darkness, trying to avoid anyone still in the streets.

The fire was already blazing inside the small room, making it stifling hot and bright as day. Erik took one last deep breath as he stepped inside out of the cool of the evening and into the furnace.

"You fool!" Euroin's voice boomed. Flames shot out and circled Erik, dancing around him and hissing like snakes. "You were defeated by a bunch of farmers! You, the so-called capable leader of the Royal Army, could not even handle one hundred men. Be careful. Next they may send out their children to face you. You disgust me! What have you to say?"

"Nothing I can say will excuse today's events, Master Wizard," Erik said. "The rebels were stronger and more capable than we gave them credit for, and with the Healer---"

"*She* is no longer a problem!" Euroin interrupted. "You must eliminate the traitors. If you fail again in such a disgraceful manner, you will find that I will no be as patient as I have been of late." The flames twisted around even closer, licking at Erik's clothing and skin. With flames all around him the fire was all Erik could see, and it took all his strength not to panic. Then suddenly, as if nothing had happened, the fire was small and once again crackling invitingly in the hearth.

Erik took a deep breath and then collapsed onto the small chair waiting at the table. Now that they had seen the enemy and knew what they were up against, would it make a difference? How can you defeat an army that stands again to fight after being struck down? If the Master Wizard was right and somehow the Healer was no longer there to worry about, perhaps defeating the traitors was possible. Standing, Erik decided to go speak to

Commander Lamtek about a strategy for the next day's inevitable battle. Two hundred men were gone, but that left another three hundred in the city who were still able--- he stopped mid-thought and mid-step. Gavin had said just minutes before that Lamtek was still unconscious. Now, even if he had regained consciousness, the Commander would be in no shape to discuss tactics. Besides, the thought came suddenly; he didn't even know that the traitors really *were* traitors. Where had they gotten those shields, and what did their having them mean? Who had those people, that family in Dren, been, the ones who had stood together so proudly as they faced death at the Wizards' hands? How could they have been traitors? But they had opposed King Simann, so didn't that in itself make them the enemy? And what of these traitors? The Healer had joined sides with them, the young Healer who had spent most of her life as the King's servant. He had seen her in the dungeons time after time healing many traitors, so that was not new. Before, though, she had been healing men for further torture. Now that had changed, all after she had helped that prisoner who had escaped. What had she seen in him that was so different?

In all the years of torturing King Simann's prisoners in the name of keeping peace, even thinking of them as traitors had not been enough to get him over the guilt of torturing a man for sometimes weeks on end. At first, the faces, the pleading, and the screams had haunted him anytime he had paused. Eventually he had trained himself not to notice. He tried to see every man as the same--faceless, emotionless, and unable to feel. With time, the haunting sights and sounds had tapered off until he only had to face them at night in his dreams. Now, though, he tried to recall that last prisoner.

At first he could remember nothing unusual. In his mind's eye he saw the man being beaten. The same blood poured from his wounds, he wore the same dirty clothes, and he had the same peasant's haircut. Slowly Erik began to remember more, something that he had notice at the time but then must have forgotten. The man had stood. The Master of the Guard had tortured many prisoners in the past twenty years, and no matter what their differences there had always been one thing they all had in common. No matter the size of the man, or with what bravado he had initially faced the guards, when the guards entered the cell to continue the torture each man had cowered in a corner. They would beg, plead, and cry for mercy, their voices breaking and sobs shaking their shoulders. This prisoner--this traitor-- had stood. He had proudly faced the guards, his shoulders square and his expression calm. He had met Erik's gaze unflinchingly, simply waiting for any injuries the guards would inflict. Erik remembered telling himself at the time that the man's acceptance of his fate could only be seen as an admission of guilt. However, if that were the case it would mean that the other men, those who had begged for their lives to be spared and had subsequently sworn allegiance to the King, were innocent by comparison. Erik found that hard to believe. Since the man had been so ready to accept punishment, did that mean he truly believed in his cause? He apparently thought it important enough that he was now risking his life again by attacking those who had tortured him.

Was there anything in his own life for which Erik was willing to risk death? He was fighting for King Simann, true, but he did not truly think his life was at risk. He was the leader of an army still three times stronger than that of his enemy. In the morning they would leave a small guard in the city and the rest would march on the rebellion, less than one hundred men who were tired and scarred from today's battle. The Royal Army may have lost that first battle, having been surprised by the fierce commitment the rebels had shown to their cause, but Erik was confident they would win the war. His own life was hardly on the line. What cause could the former prisoner believe in so much that it would lead him to put his life on the line? Erik told himself that it didn't matter. He was the Master of the Guard of King Simann's Royal Army. His entire life Erik had been trained to follow orders. Since he was a young teenager he had been told what to believe and how to think. Not since he was a child had he been encouraged to think for himself. Erik had never though that was bad, until now.

The traitor did not follow the King, it was true, but he followed a belief with more conviction than Erik felt toward anything. Erik knew that with the Royal Army behind him and a new understanding of his enemy he could wipe out the rebellion. Perhaps it would take a day or two, but sooner or later the rebels and whatever beliefs they held would not be a problem. Then King Simann would thank him, perhaps give him some fancy title, and life would go on as if nothing had ever happened in this city. The memory of the traitor and his small rebellion would disappear--perhaps with time, but most likely with the aid of the Wizards. In time, Erik would not even remember the traitor.

But was that what he wanted?

*******************

He could see her there, standing in the presence of his brethren, the three True Wizards. He knew the choice she faced, but he could do nothing to interfere with her decision. As he watched, unseen by the girl, he saw the expression of joy and peace on her face. How could he expect her to choose to come back to the pain she would have to face when she had the opportunity to experience eternal happiness? Could he really hope for such an unselfish act? Slowly her expression changed as she watched faces flash before her, faces of those the girl knew and those she had merely seen once before.

He smiled. Her decision had been made.

Chapter 15

The sun had not yet begun to rise when Paodin woke to Adair gently shaking his shoulder.

"Your friend is comin' to. Mum said to come get you," he said sleepily.

Immediately awake, Paodin moved through the dark house without running into too many objects, a task made much simpler due to the lack of furnishings in the small home. He could barely make out Brigitte's small figure kneeling next to the cot in the dark room. In his still exhausted state, Paodin wondered how Lady Brigitte could be tending to the Healer without any light. It took him a moment to shake away the cobwebs of sleep and realize it was only he who needed the light. Soon, though, his eyes began adjusting, and Paodin could see that Syndria was beginning to stir.

"She has not come back to us yet," Brigitte said as Paodin knelt beside her, "but I believe she has started the journey. Perhaps it will not be long before she is well enough to open her eyes."

Quietly, as relief finally began to creep in, Paodin told Brigitte, "I cannot thank you enough for your help, Lady. I do not think she would have stood a chance had you not been willing to help. Perhaps one day soon I can repay you."

Brigitte smiled sweetly and then spoke. "I am sure you need more sleep so your own wounds have some time to heal, but I can tell by the restlessness in your voice that I will not be able to convince you to stay." Paodin's eyes widened slightly. He was still surprised by Brigitte's ability to read him without seeing his expressions. "Perhaps, though," she continued, "I might be able to convince you to at least have something to eat before you return to the battlefield?"

Paodin hesitated. He needed to get back to the men and he didn't want to cause Brigitte any more trouble. However, Adair still stood in the doorway and waiting would give him a chance to ask the boy more about the situation in Lurn. "I can't take long, but I would appreciate anything you have to offer. Thank you."

Lady Brigitte stood, laid a reassuring hand on Paodin's shoulder, and then walked to the kitchen. Once she was gone, Paodin motioned to Adair to come over to him.

"You mentioned last night that you were in Lurn. What can you tell me of the military presence there?"

The sun was not yet peering over the horizon, but the sky was beginning to lighten and Paodin could see Adair's eyes narrow. He had seen that expression on the boy's face before, when Adair had spoken of his mother's treatment in the town. Now, though, there was something more in his eyes.

"Them *scum* that say they're soldiers were

there. They're swarmin' all over the place, struttin' 'round like they own it." Looking back and seeing that his mother was out of earshot, Adair leaned closer to Paodin and said, "I ain't told Mum, but I seen one of the ones that made her blind. He's called the Master of the Guard, and he's the one that let me out."

Paodin hated to see the darkness burning in the boy's eyes, replacing the innocence that should have been there, so he tried to get Adair's attention on something else. He asked Adair if he knew how many soldiers had been in the town.

Adair was reluctant to let go of his hatred, but he answered, "Some of the women, they were complainin' 'bout those soldiers needin' so much food. They said it was like havin' to make a feast for the whole town at every meal. I didn't ever hear no one say how many, though--sorry."

"Here you are. I wrapped up something for you to take as you go," Brigitte said, holding out a small white bundle. "It isn't much, but at least it will help you recover some strength as you ride."

"Thank you, Lady."

"Your horse is out in the barn," Adair said, hurrying toward the door. "I'll go get 'im for you."

As the door shut behind her son, Brigitte smiled. "He was so proud to get to help tend to your animal last night. I'm sure he was very careful, but you may want to check your saddle before you mount. It has been some time since he has done anything other than bridle an animal." She handed him the bundle then continued, "Your friend will be alright--do not worry. She is fighting, and I believe she will pull through. Go now--she will be safe here."

"Once again," Paodin said as he walked to the door in the now pale morning light, "I am in your debt. Thank you for everything. I cannot say when I'll be able to return, but I will either come myself or send someone to check on..." he started to say "the Healer" but then thought that perhaps if Brigitte and Adair did not know who was in their house it would somehow be less of a danger. "...Syndria."

"Go, and be careful," she said, hugging Adair to her side after he returned with Thrul.

Paodin considered checking his saddle but didn't want to insult the boy, so instead he just climbed up and prayed the Fates would be kind. He hadn't realized how sore every part of his body was until Thrul started trotting. His muscles cried out for him to slow, but instead Paodin pushed the stallion into a run. Though the smoother gait did help slightly, Paodin still had to grit his teeth against the pain. In an effort to distract himself, Paodin focused on the battlefield to which he was returning.

When he had asked Adair about the

military presence in Lurn, the boy's recollection of the woman's words confirmed his belief that Simann had sent his entire army south to the city. The Healer had said them to be five hundred strong, so even with the tremendous dent the Sons of Tundyel had put in the Royal Army, Paodin and his men were still outnumbered more than three to one. The thought overwhelmed him. The Healer's touch had been all that kept most of his men in yesterday's fight. Now that she was fighting for her own life, how would the men who had counted on their Healer be able to face more men without her?

*******************

Syndria could barely stand to do it, but she turned away from the light of the three True Wizards. All she faced now was darkness, but the Healer did no hesitate to step forward. As she stepped out of the light, the darkness seemed to close around her. Suddenly the pain she had barely remembered feeling came back in full force, pressing in on her from every side. For a brief moment Syndria's logical mind told her to turn back, to return to the True Wizards and that place of security and peace. To return to Nedra.

But as quickly as the thought had come to her it faded away. There were too many counting on the Healer for her to give in now to something as trivial as pain. Pushing forward seemed to take all she had, but the Healer knew she had to do it. She glanced behind her, hoping for one last look at that comforting light as a reminder of to what she would one day return. There was nothing. Had she wanted to turn back, it was not possible now. Her only choices were to remain stuck in darkness or push on through the pain. Syndria pushed harder.

*********************

Erik had not been able to sleep for most of the night. His mind kept a continuous debate going while his body tried to rest, resulting in what seemed to be a wasted night. As dawn approached, the Master of the Guard was still wrestling with his thoughts.

Now, however, there was no time for him to focus on his thoughts about the prisoner and his cause. The rebellion was waiting not far from the city walls, and the Royal Army would soon be forming ranks in the street. As Master of the Guard it was Erik's job to stand before his men without wavering. Today he would lead another two hundred men against the rebels. Perhaps they had underestimated the farmers' abilities to fight the day before, but if so that was one mistake they would not make again. Having slept in his uniform, which bore the blood of friend and foe alike, Erik had but to put his boots on before going to stand before the soldiers.

A small platform had been raised beside the

gates, and it was not long before Erik stood there overlooking two hundred young faces. He could see apprehension written there, and knew that these men were thinking about their brothers-in-arms who had fallen yesterday at the hands of the traitor and his rebellion. They were quiet, the usual gaiety having been replaced by an angry, mournful silence.

"I know," began the Master of the Guard, "that today is a day of mourning. Those brothers, those sons, we lost yesterday deserve nothing less. However, the battle they fought has not ended the war. The enemy awaits, their swords drawn and ready. They have slain your brothers and now hope to run their blood covered blades through you.

"However, I say today is a day for avenging our brothers!" Erik's voice boomed. "Today is the day we show those traitors that we will not fall on their swords. Today, we fight in the shadow of those they have killed."

A few men yelled, "We fight!"

"We fight for revenge!" Erik yelled louder.

This time, a fourth of the men joined in, "We fight!"

The Master of the Guard finished, "We fight for the Kingdom!"

The Royal Army echoed back, "WE FIGHT!"

\*\*\*\*\*\*\*\*\*\*\*\*\*\*\*\*\*\*\*\*

As Paodin raced through the woods atop Thrul, he could already hear the sounds of battle. He urged the stallion to go faster, though his attempts were unnecessary as Thrul seemed to be a war horse at heart and was pulling at the bit with all his might in his thirst for the fight. All thoughts of the Healer vanished as Paodin broke through the tree line and crashed onto the scene. Before him the battle was in full force. Though he knew they were exhausted, the Sons of Tundyel fought with an intensity Paodin could scarcely have even imagined existed. Some of the prisoners from the day before fought alongside the men they had just yesterday been against, going blade to blade and even hand to hand with the men they had called brothers. He also saw some he recognized as having professed to a change of heart turning once again against the rebellion, but that he had expected. Now, though, was not the time to think-- now was a time for action.

As the sun inched higher, the battle raged on. Men on both sides fell with no hope of the Healer's touch. The one Healer they could count on was fighting for her own life, and the others were no more than a hallway from the king. Men fought and died valiantly, but there was no time for their friends to honor them as they fought for their own lives. And that's what the battle had quickly become--not a fight for ideals but instead merely for survival.

The air was full of cries; not only the cries of the dying, but also the battle cries of desperate men. The Royal Army fought for revenge, so most fought with a reckless abandon not usually seen in the fighting of trained soldiers. Occasionally, a soldier would come face to face with a friend he had assumed dead. Then, for a moment, the battle cry would stop as a look of astonishment came over the soldier's face. The moment would not last long, though, for not far from the rebellious soldier would be an original member of the rebellion and the soldier of the Royal Army would turn his attention to the man he saw as his enemy. The battle cry would pick up again then, but with less intensity. Most of the soldiers who had joined the rebellion stood watching the battle. They no longer wanted to fight against Paodin and his men, but neither could they bring themselves to fully turn against the brotherhoods forged by years of living and training together. Their mere presence, however, was enough to serve as a hindrance to the Royal Army and a boost to the Sons of Tundyel, who fought almost frantically with the knowledge that the Healer was not there to save them should the need arise.

*********************

At that moment, Syndria was writhing in agony on the small cot while Brigitte sat next to her, humming an old lullaby in hopes of somehow comforting the girl. Adair had gone back to his bed after Paodin left, but he had not been able to sleep due to the anguished cries of the girl. Now he crept cautiously to his mother and placed a small hand firmly on her shoulder, for even in the midst of his own fear he felt the need to protect her. Brigitte stopped her song long enough to squeeze her son's hand and send him outside to the barn, then went back to comforting Syndria.

Adair hurried outside, anxious to be able to close out the cries. Once in the barn, the boy let himself dissolve into tears. Even after his mum had been attacked, throughout the weeks of nursing her back to health, Adair had never heard such terrible cries, and the lady's wounds seemed to have gotten worse during the night. Maybe it had been a trick of the morning light, but some of the gashes seemed to be turning black. He curled up in a small pile of straw and finally, after he had no more tears, fell asleep.

*******************

The marble room in the north tower was abnormally cold when Euroin stepped across the threshold, and the chill that ran up his spine made the Master Wizard smile slightly. Instead of a raging wind whipping his black cloak around there was a deathly stillness in the room. Euroin barely had to concentrate--he saw the girl immediately and his smile grew wider. He could see her there, thrashing. The dark magic circled her, pressing in on her relentlessly. The swirling colors probed the wounds on her back, seeking entrance to the Healer's soul through the blackening gashes. Euroin laughed, the sound filling the silence around him, as he watched the broken girl.

\*\*\*\*\*\*\*\*\*\*\*\*\*\*\*\*\*\*\*

Paodin had no idea what was happening. It was all he could do to hold his sword, and impossible to swing it. He had no time to think about it, though, for he faced another attacker. Switching the sword to his left hand, Paodin struck out awkwardly. His swings were uncoordinated and sloppy, but he still managed to hold his own against the soldier. Unbelievably, his right arm now hung helplessly at his side. He snuck a glance over but could see no wound that would have caused such a grievous injury. His breathing was becoming more and more labored, and though he knew it was partly from exhaustion, Paodin also knew he should not be this tired. Something was terribly wrong. He knew that he would not be able to fight for much longer and searched the sea of faces for someone who could help him. He soon spotted Berek, and began making his way toward his oldest and dearest friend. Berek had never been one to do anything half-heartedly, and battle proved no different. The big man was right in the thick of the fighting, his blond hair flying wildly as he fought no less than three royal soldiers.

Paodin avoided as many confrontations as he could, but the closer he drew to his friend the more hectic the battle grew. He fought off as many blows as he could, but the weakening young man felt swords slice his skin many times. The battle around him was still raging, but Paodin could no longer hear it. His vision was growing dark. Paodin knew he was dying. Desperately, he lunged forward and called out to Berek. Before he could even know if the big man heard him, Paodin felt himself falling into the blackness that now surrounded him. He barely even felt the sword that ripped across his shoulders, or the ground that rushed to meet him.

Berek spun when he heard his name called by a familiar voice. "So, you've come to join in the fray, have you?" he asked, ducking low as he swung at the stomach of one of his attackers. The man fell, dropping his sword and clutching his opened gut with both hands. He looked for Paodin as he finished the swing, but could not see him. He didn't have long to look, though, for there were still two royal soldiers slashing desperately at him. Berek had little trouble fending off their frightened blows. He froze, though, when he saw his friend and leader out of the corner of his eye. One of his attackers got in a clumsy strike, cutting Berek's thigh and getting a rare curse out of the man. He spun, his strike catching the soldier's arm and making the man drop his sword and scream out. Berek grabbed Paodin's shirt collar with one hand, dragging him out of the thick of things as quickly as he could while battling the men who took full advantage of the situation. Once he got far enough away from the fighting, Berek hoisted his best friend to his shoulders and moved him to the cover of the trees.

Paodin was still clutching his sword, the only obvious sign of life Berek could see at first, but oddly it was in his left hand instead of the right. When the big blond leaned in closer, he was reassured by the discovery that his friend was still breathing, though shallowly. Berek sat back, quickly scanning his friend for the wound that had incapacitated him. He could see blood seeping slowly out from under Paodin's shoulders, so Berek quickly rolled him over and pulled the torn shirt apart to see the damage. The cut was deep, but not serious enough to have knocked the young man out. Berek had seen Paodin withstand worse in their childhood adventures. He rolled Paodin onto his back again, and fell backward in shock.

The unconscious man had a small cut across his jaw and neck, something Berek hadn't looked at before. The cut was not deep or bleeding, but it sent a chill up Berek's spine just to see it. A blackness was spreading out from it, finger-like protrusions that were creeping up the right side of his friend's face and down his neck, disappearing under the neckline of his shirt. Berek reached down and tore open the front of the thin shirt .

"Fates help him," he whispered, shaken by what he had revealed. The blackness on Paodin's face was nothing compared to this. His friend's entire chest was veiled by the sinister blackness, and it was still spreading. It wrapped around his right arm, at least giving Berek an answer as to why Paodin had been carrying his sword in his off hand. Berek looked around frantically, searching for someone who could do something, anything, to help. He knew it was no use, though. Paodin needed the Healer.

\*\*\*\*\*\*\*\*\*\*\*\*\*\*\*\*\*\*\*

He watched the darkness closing in on the girl, helpless to stop it. So much had happened, so much of the Prophecy had been fulfilled. How could it all be ending? He sent his own spells swirling into the dark mists circling her, but they were instantly devoured by the blackness. The dark fingers were tearing at her now, raking and clawing ferociously at the sobbing girl. He could do nothing to help her.

\*\*\*\*\*\*\*\*\*\*\*\*\*\*\*\*\*\*\*

*"The Fates are holding you close,*
*though the road is in shadows and the*

*night seems long,*
*The Fates are holding you close,*
*and there in the darkness you can hear*
*their sweet song-*
*They tell of your homeland and where*
*you belong,*
*The Fates are holding you close."*

Brigitte sang quietly, gently stroking Syndria's short hair, for there was nothing else she could do for the girl. Addie hadn't come back in from the barn, and for that she was grateful. Despite the tragedy she had seen and been through, never in her life had Brigitte known anyone to be in such pain. This tiny girl's entire body was convulsing, her sobs shaking her from head to toe, yet she still hadn't opened her eyes. The whole thing mystified Brigitte. When Paodin had left just a few hours before, the girl seemed to be getting better. She had been quiet and still, and her wounds had quit bleeding. Now, though, the wounds felt feverish and she had been crying for at least the past hour.

Suddenly Syndria stopped crying, though her body still trembled. Brigitte quickly found the girl's hand and squeezed it tightly, hoping to at least show the girl that she was not alone in her struggle, and kept singing.

## Chapter 16

All around her was darkness. Once, Syndria thought she saw a glimmer of light like that she had encountered in the tunnel of the True Wizards, but it did not last. The darkness was so complete she seemed to have forgotten what it was like to be in the light. Syndria had started out walking, but the pain had gotten so intense it knocked her to her knees. She lay there weeping, sobs racking her body. Out of the darkness came the sound of someone else, someone who was crying out and fighting the dark, but she could not see him. Somewhere in the depths of her mind she recognized the cries. She had heard them before, in the dungeon at Simann's castle..

Paodin.

She had thought she was alone here, alone with the darkness and the pain. The realization that someone else was there, someone she had come to realize was probably her only true friend left in the world, made Syndria the girl disappear and the Healer reawaken. Syndria pulled herself together. The pain she felt was tremendous, excruciating, but she knew she had to fight it. The blackness was crushing her, clawing at her, burning her. She pushed back. Paodin was out there somewhere, and he needed the Healer. He needed her, and she would find him. If he could fight, so could she.

Syndria struggled to her knees, then her

feet. Her own tears had stopped, though her body was still shaking. The weight of the shadows was intense, but by itself it did not compare to the weight she had stood under in the tunnel. There had been no pain then, but pain was something with which she knew how to deal. It was her life, her calling. She wanted to search for Paodin, but now that she was able to focus she realized that she couldn't even tell which direction his cries were coming from. They seemed to be all around her, part of the blackness itself. She closed her eyes there in the dark, shutting out everything so she could think.

The Healer knew what to do. She straightened her shoulders and took a shuddering breath, then willed herself to let go. She embraced the pain, embraced the darkness. She opened herself to it, gave herself over to the blackness. Somewhere, past the cries, above the darkness, she heard laughter.

\*\*\*\*\*\*\*\*\*\*\*\*\*\*\*\*\*\*\*

Paodin was thrashing side to side, the darkness spreading quickly. Berek was powerless to help his friend. All he could do was sit by him until the end. He owed his friend that much, at least. Someone had to bear witness to the end of such a man.

Without warning, Paodin stopped. Berek's head dropped, silent tears running down his cheeks, then he stood. Paodin deserved more, but at the moment there was a battle raging and Berek knew he had a part to play in how it turned out. He turned, let out a loud yell, and ran back into the fight like a man possessed. He didn't see the blackness retreating from Paodin's skin as quickly as it had spread.

Paodin gasped, and his eyes opened. For a moment he thought the Healer was beside him, taking his pain as her own. He knew something had happened, for when he tested himself he found his right arm could move once again. He reached across himself and found his sword, then slowly pushed himself to sit. When that attempt worked, Paodin climbed to his feet. He didn't know how, but that girl had saved him. Paodin shook his head, flexed his muscles just to feel them working, and ran back into the battle. He had a lot to do.

The Royal Army they fought today was very different than the one the rebellion had faced the day before. They may not have ever been in battle, but it was obvious they had been well trained. They had started the day with two-and-a-half times the number of soldiers as the Sons of Tundyel had men, and they still outnumbered the rebellion two to one at the day's end. The Royal Soldiers steadily hacked away at the rebellion, whittling down their numbers. By the time both forces drew back for the night, a mere fifty men stood for the Sons of Tundyel. Fifty men, exhausted and disheartened. Paodin found Berek seated under a tree, staring out over a battlefield littered with bodies of rebel and soldier alike. Some moaned or crawled toward the tree line, but most were still. Men of the rebellion who were the most versed in tending wounds moved as quickly as possible through the carnage, searching for those they could help before night fell. Some were carried back to the trees while others were offered a drink and the hand of a brother to hold as they passed from this world to the next.

"I fear tomorrow will see our end."

Berek jerked, his eyes wide as he looked up at his friend. "I swear by the Fates that you were dead when I left you!" he said, astonished.

"Ah, so it was you who moved me off the field. I didn't think I got to that tree under my own power. I owe you my life," Paodin said as he sat down next to the big man.

Berek stared at Paodin in disbelief. "You were dying if not dead. I saw you. Your skin was turning black, as if it were already dead."

"I am sorry to disappoint you, friend," Paodin laughed, the sound out of place in the death of the day. "I still have the blackness, if that makes you doubt yourself less," he said, pushing aside the torn shirt he still wore to reveal the black scar across his chest. "I suppose I have you to thank for the new styling of my garment. I thought it was torn enough to begin with, but I suppose you felt differently."

Berek clasped his friend's shoulder and laughed, "I do not know what happened for the Fates to bring you back to us, but I am glad they did."

"What do you think our fate will be tomorrow? Will any of the men survive?" Paodin asked.

Berek sat quietly for a minute, looking at the men moving slowly in the moonlight. Finally he answered, "If some do survive, I fear they will only wish they had died. What of the Healer? I saw that you did not bring her back with you this morning."

"She was badly wounded in yesterday's battle, then on our trip through the woods she received the same sort of injuries as I," he answered, motioning to the black streaks across his chest and arm. "I left her in the hands of a friend, and she seemed to be doing better. However, that was before the black appeared in my wounds." He hesitated for a moment, trying to decide if he should tell Berek his beliefs about how he was healed. His friend waited patiently. Berek knew Paodin and could always tell when something was on his mind. Figuring there was no point in hiding anything, seeing how the day's fighting had turned out, Paodin finally continued. "I was dying, Berek. I know I was. I was fighting it, but there was nothing I could do--not really. But then, I felt her, just as I felt her each time she came to me in that dungeon. I couldn't see her, but the Healer was there, taking away the pain. I can't explain it, but I know it happened, just as I know that she is now worse because of it." The thought hadn't come to him before, but as he spoke the words he knew they were true. In saving him, Syndria had put herself at an even greater risk.

Berek looked at him thoughtfully. "I think I can ease your mind one way or another," he said. "Turn and let me see your back." Paodin didn't know what Berek wanted, but he turned. "I don't know what powers that girl has," he said, pulling Paodin back around to face him, "but she is more than just a Healer. She did come to you, somehow. You had a wound across your back, and though it was a shallow wound it went from shoulder to shoulder. It is gone now. And if you think the blackness is still there, you have no idea what *was* there. Your entire chest was turning black, along with your neck and face." Paodin's hand went quickly to the wound across his jaw as if he could see it by touch alone. "Most of it is gone now, that is certain. I hate to tell you though, friend, I fear you have lost some of those boyish good looks. You will draw stares of a different kind from most girls now."

Berek had never been one to hold back, and though he appreciated his friend's honesty part of him wished the big man had just kept that information to himself. "No matter," he said, trying to make light of it. "I will probably not draw stares from any besides the beasts after tomorrow."

Berek stood then, offering a hand to pull Paodin to his feet. "Put those thoughts aside, friend. You are the leader of these men--now you must address them. They have to know that there is still a reason to fight, whether you think so or not. You brought them here. Now you must tell them why they must stay. I have already seen a few sneaking into the woods. If you do not speak to them, you and I will face the Royal Army alone tomorrow."

The two men had started walking back to the small group of men when they heard a commotion. Paodin whirled, looking back to the battlefield in disbelief. Had the soldiers returned so soon to finish off the rebellion? Confusion flooded his face, for there was no one but the dead and dying on the field.

*******************

Erik led the men back through the gates of Lurn. From the reports he had gotten, half the force he had taken to the battle was gone. One hundred boys, all dead at the hands of farmers. Erik shook his head in disbelief, then sighed. Tomorrow, everything would be over. There weren't many left to fight for the rebellion, and he hadn't seen the Healer. Those few men would fall quickly. The Master of the Guard dismounted and handed his reins to a stable boy, then made his way through the men.

Five hundred had marched on Lurn, and now only two hundred and fifty remained. How had he let that happen? Erik started toward his quarters but quickly decided against it. A bed was waiting for him there, true, but he knew that the Wizard Euroin would be waiting as well. He had no desire to face that fire, so he walked aimlessly for a while. When he finally noticed where he was, Erik was standing in front of the great hall. Once inside, it didn't take long to find what he had come for.

"Here, sit," she said, pulling out a chair at the end of one of the long tables. "I'll get you something to drink."

Erik did as he was told, watching Andelle move quickly through the hall. The tables were still set up, but half of them were serving as beds for the wounded who had been carried back from the battlefield. *Small wonder no one is eating in the other half,* Erik thought to himself. It was hard to focus on anything but the cries of the young men dying on wooden tables.

Andelle quickly returned with a large mug and handed it to Erik. "If you'll join me, I was just about to go home and find some more cloths to use as bandages. You can help."

Erik nodded, silent. He had ordered too many men to their deaths today--it was a relief to be taking orders for a change. He followed Andelle out the door and down a dark street, listening to her talk. He barely heard the words, but he heard every intonation of her voice as they walked through the darkness. Andelle talked about everything and nothing, avoiding any subject pertaining to the battle that seemed to be on the lips of soldier and citizen alike. She seemed unfazed by the fact that her company never spoke a word. Once they reached a small house, Erik obediently tore the sheets she gave him into strips and piled them on a small table. Neither one spoke, and Erik drew more strength from the silence shared with her than he would have from a full night spent trying to sleep. Finally, on the way back to the great hall, he spoke.

"What do you believe in?"

Andelle didn't ask him what he meant, didn't look at him oddly, she just answered simply, "The truth."

"And what is the truth, my lady? How can you be certain of it?"

Andelle's expression was not visible in the

dim light of night, but Erik could hear the smile on her face when she answered, "I am certain because it is the truth. Nothing is more certain than that." They were at the door then, and she continued without missing a beat, "You can come in and help me bandage boys, or you can go get some rest. Whatever you choose, I have to get to work." She looked at Erik, waiting for an answer.

"Lead the way." Andelle spent the next few hours making her way up and down the rows of tables, Erik following close behind.

*********************

"It is coming from the trees."

Paodin followed Berek's gaze, waiting for some glimpse of what was coming. The small group of men moved together, preparing themselves for one last fight. They didn't have long to wait before men on horseback broke into the clearing, riding from the west. Even in the starless night, Paodin recognized one of the men riding at the front.

"I see your numbers have dwindled since you dirtied up my place the other night," the big man said. "No matter--now there won't be quite so many to feed when we leave this accursed place behind us tomorrow." Red somehow managed to recline even on his mount, the biggest stallion Paodin had ever seen. It would have to be, to be able to carry a man Red's size and not be lathered from the exertion.

"What brings you here?" Paodin asked. "I was under the impression you never took sides in any argument."

The man laughed, "That may be so, my good man, and that being the impression most have, a man such as myself tends to gather a very small set of companions. With so few friends, when one asks a favor there is little I will refuse him." That was when Paodin took notice of the man riding beside the big barkeep.

"Master Jamis? I had not hoped to see you again. What brings you here?"

Jamis didn't answer Paodin, instead turning around and addressing someone behind him. "You might as well come up here, boy. He will see you soon enough." In the dark it took a minute for Paodin to recognize the boy, especially since he had no reason to imagine him being there.

"I didn't know what to do, mister," the young boy said quickly. "I could tell you'd be needin' help, and I knew the only man Mum trusted was Jamis, so I thought I could get him and he could help. And then, when I told him the name of that girl you brought to Mum, he just up and left. It was all I could do to keep up with him, seein' as how I was ridin' ol' Red. I had to leave him at that stable in Krasteiv, the poor thing. I think he's pro'ly dead by now."

Paodin said nothing, just stood listening to the boy. Lady Brigitte would be worried about the boy, there was no doubt, but Paodin could do nothing about that now. He wasn't about to send the boy home through the woods alone. There were deserters from both sides lurking out there, and the horse a twelve year old boy rode would be seen as an easy acquisition. Knowing the boy, Adair wouldn't let the mount go without a fight, either, and would end up getting himself hurt. Red spoke, ending the awkward silence that had fallen as the men listened to the boy.

"I've brought you some men," he told Paodin, then called back loudly over his shoulder, "Cutthroats and thieves, every one, but I suppose that makes them well suited for what you are doing." He motioned for the men to follow him, and they began dismounting and walking among the beaten men they saw before them.

Jamis motioned to Adair, who had quickly followed the men away from Paodin and the older man. "He didn't search me out. I found him in the barn, crying in his sleep. I figured something had happened to his mother, but then he told me…is it really her, son?" Paodin looked at Jamis, confused. "The girl," he explained. "Is it really my Syndria?"

In his exhaustion, it took Paodin a minute to remember the conversation he had had with the older man about the Healer. "It is, sir," he said, "but I'm afraid she has been hurt. There are those who wish only to see her fail."

"Then we shall have to stop them." Jamis said it so simply, so matter-of-factly, that Paodin had no choice but to believe him.

Later that night, Paodin called a meeting to find out just where the rebellion now stood. He was surprised and relieved to see Audon following Berek over to his fire. He hadn't seen him since the fighting had begun, and Paodin had almost taken it for granted that the man had been killed. Taking a deep breath, Paodin cleared his throat and said, "It's good to see you are still here, Father."

"You too, Son." He could see the smile in Audon's eyes, though it did not manage to find its way to his lips. Audon took a seat, and the meeting began.

Jamis had ridden hard to Krasteiv, the only place he knew to go. He had found Red in the bar, just as he knew he would, and had asked for his help. As Red had said earlier, the barkeep didn't call many men friends, and those he did claim, he stuck closer to than a brother. Literally, seeing as how his own brother had disowned him years ago, saying he did not approve of the company his older brother kept. When Jamis came seeking men, Red had been quick to gather them. The men were all outcasts of society, men who took full advantage of any situation in which they found themselves.

They were thieves and liars, conmen who had nothing to lose by standing against the soldiers. The men seemed to come out of the woodwork when Red had opened his purse strings, each giving his word, whatever it was worth, that he would fight. Jamis had not been surprised that Red had been able to gather so many so quickly, nor that they had all agreed so readily (when given the proper motivation), but he was greatly surprised when Red had mounted up to ride beside him.

"Every man needs a little adventure every now and again," he had said as explanation. It wasn't until the men were preparing to ride out of the town that Jamis had spotted Adair. He was furious with the boy, but there wasn't anything he could do about it. The boy sat atop the old mule he had ridden in on, and it was easy to see that the poor animal wouldn't last much longer. Jamis conferred with Red for a minute, then rode to the stables and came back leading a small, gentle yearling mare.

"This does not mean I approve of you following me, young man," he said to the frightened boy, "but I cannot have your mule giving out on you on the way back. The woods are likely to be too dangerous for you to return home alone, so you will follow me. Keep up, and stay close." Adair's eyes had shone, but he had been careful to just nod, mount the new horse, and see the mule to the stables before riding out with the men.

In all, Jamis and Red had managed to bring a hundred men with them to join the battle against the Royal Army. With this addition, the Sons of Tundyel now numbered three times their size of just a few minutes earlier. The fifty men who had been so dejected moments ago now told stories of the battle and their fallen brothers, assuring the new men that the Sons of Tundyel would be victorious in the next day's fight. Their spirits were renewed, confidence brought on by the knowledge that more had joined their cause. Though they knew the rebellion was still outnumbered and would face the Royal Army once again with the dawn of a new day, there was once again laughter in the camp as men who would have never had any reason or desire to speak to one another before quickly became brothers in arms.

Paodin was glad to see the men in such seemingly high spirits, but he couldn't help but wonder what lay ahead of them with the Healer absent.

*******************

Brigitte didn't know what to do for the girl. The fever earlier had scared Brigitte, but the chill that had recently overcome the girl's small frame worried her much more. To make matters worse, Adair still had not come back. She made her way across the yard, counting her steps to the barn. Once there, Brigitte slid her hand along the rough wood and pulled open the heavy door.

"Addie?" she called. There was no answer, and Brigitte could hear no sign of the boy's presence in the barn. Thinking that maybe he had decided to do some more work on the chicken coop, Brigitte made her way out of the barn and around back. When calling for her son proved useless, Brigitte got a horrible feeling in the pit of her stomach. Adair had told Paodin that he knew one of the soldiers in Lurn from the night his father was killed. Surely, though, the boy wouldn't have gone into the town, not with the battle raging nearby. Whatever he had done, though, Brigitte could do nothing for him. She whispered a quick prayer that the Fates would protect her son, then turned to make her way back across the yard to the house. She could not focus on her son, not with the Healer dying in her home.

Though Paodin had been careful to not tell Brigitte who the girl was, she had known the moment he had said that her name was Syndria. Jamis had always been Evan's best friend, seemingly from the day he arrived in Lurn with the tiny baby in tow. Brigitte had watched Syndria grow and had quickly come to love the bright, precocious young girl. It had been hard to watch her ride off with the Ancient Healer all those years ago. Now Brigitte was tasked with keeping the girl alive, something she was beginning to doubt was possible.

Chapter 17

Paodin knew he needed to address the men, to give them some great motivational speech about how they would defeat the Royal Army and soon see the Kingdom of Tundyel returned to its rightful heir and its glory of old. He needed to stand before them and say that the presence of the men who had just joined their ranks was poof that they were fighting for the Truth, and that with the Truth backing them, they were guaranteed success. He needed to assure the men that the Healer's absence would not lead to their downfall, that they had proven their abilities in battle and would come out victorious without the Healer to mend their wounds. He needed to reinforce their beliefs in themselves, their abilities, and their purpose, but he didn't know what to say.

The problem was, Paodin didn't know if he still believed in those things himself.

He sat in the shadows, quietly watching men talking around small campfires. Occasionally laughter would ring out, but mostly all Paodin heard was a low murmur. As he sat, Berek sat down beside him. The two friends didn't speak for quite a while, but eventually Paodin broke the silence.

"What do I say? How can I stand before these men, men who are willing to give everything even though their sacrifices may never be known, and tell them that tomorrow they will defeat the Royal Army? Our numbers have grown dramatically, but we will still be outnumbered and the Healer is dying, if not already dead. How can I stand and tell my brothers something I don't know if I still believe myself?"

Berek didn't answer at first. When he finally spoke, Paodin had to strain to hear him. "I suppose," he said, "that you will have to speak honestly. Now, I am going to gather the men. They deserve to hear something from you." He stood and walked away, leaving Paodin with his thoughts.

A few minutes later, the men were gathered and waiting. As he stepped up in front of them, Paodin still didn't know what he was going to say. However, he had led these men here, had gotten them into this war. As Berek had said, they deserved to hear something, even if Paodin could give no real encouragement. So, looking out over the proud faces of his brothers in arms, he took a deep breath.

"You are all here tonight knowing that tomorrow's battle will prove hard. Many of our ranks may fall, and the Healer is not here to help us—she is battling for her own life as we speak. You have followed me unquestioningly since we left Gelci, through the storms brought on by both nature and man. I do not deserve your faithfulness, but I thank you for it. Perhaps one day the citizens of Tundyel will know of your actions here on this bloody field, and they, too, will thank you. For, no matter what tomorrow's outcome, you have started a revolution, and one day what you have begun will lead to Simann's downfall. I pray the Fates will watch over you tomorrow, and grant you victory." He could think of nothing else, so Paodin nodded to Berek who was standing nearby and returned quietly to his place in the shadows.

********************

Not long after daybreak the Royal Army marched over the hill, their armor glowing red and golden in the morning light. The battle began quickly and raged for most of the morning before it took a decided turn in favor of the trained soldiers. Despite the reinforcements Jamis had brought the night before, the Royal Army's training was beginning to pay off since they had finally stopped underestimating the rebels. Without the Healer, men from both sides fell with no hope of standing again. The number of fatalities on both sides was overwhelming, but the Sons of Tundyel were losing men faster. Just before noon, Erik ordered his Commanders to split the army and surround the rebellion.

Paodin saw what was happening, but he could do nothing to stop it. The men he had led, along with the men who had voluntarily come just the night before, were falling all around him, and there was nothing he could do. Searching the chaos around him, Paodin found Berek just a few feet away. He began making his way toward his friend, planning to ask if he should surrender and save as many of his friends' lives as possible, when he saw the sword swinging behind the big man.

"No!" he yelled, lunging toward the sword, but there were too many men in the way. Paodin saw the sword strike Berek's broad shoulder and slash across his back. The big blond man fell with an anguished cry, and Paodin scanned the battlefield desperately for the Healer before reality sunk in with the help of a broadsword slicing the air in front of him. The Healer was not here—his best friend had fallen with no chance of healing. Though he had wondered just moments before if he should surrender, now all he could think of was getting even in some small way. All other thoughts faded from his mind and the animal side took over as Paodin lunged into the heart of the fray.

\*\*\*\*\*\*\*\*\*\*\*\*\*\*\*\*\*\*\*

Erik fell back from the battle, watching with relief as the tide finally turned in his favor. He had been surprised to see that the rebellion's ranks had grown during the night, but his soldiers were finally proving that their training was superior to the poor organization and equipment of the farmers they were facing. After spending the night helping Andelle bandage boys in his charge, Erik was finally seeing his boys succeeding. It had indeed taken a while, but it appeared the battle would be over soon. The Royal Army was surrounding the rebels, whose numbers had dwindled despite the reinforcements that had come in the night. It would soon be over, and the Master of the Guard would be able to return to the castle where he was comfortable. Just when he thought everything was working just as it should, Erik heard a commotion behind him, just over the hill.

The Master of the Guard couldn't believe what he was seeing. There, coming over the hill, were the people of Lurn. Some carried swords, but most were wielding staffs, pitchforks, and various other common items as weapons. Erik watched helplessly as his tactic backfired and his own army was split in two. Besides that, when the rebels saw the citizens of Lurn rushing toward the battle they seemed to fight with renewed strength. His boys were falling all across the field.

*********************

At first, Paodin didn't understand the sudden change in the men around him. They seemed to be fighting with a new spirit, even in the face of inevitable defeat. When he saw the people coming down from the top of the hill, Paodin was even more surprised. Though it had been his hope from the start that others in Tundyel would see the truth about Simann and join the Sons of Tundyel in their cause, it had been just that—a hope. He hadn't expected to see it happen, especially not so soon. He didn't have time to think about it, though, because as his own men grew more confident, the Royal Army grew more desperate. They became almost savage as they watched their own forces being cut in two. What had already been a bloody battle quickly escalated to a gory, dirty fight. Men who lost weapons were resorting to hand-to-hand combat instead of surrendering, intent on death instead of capture. The citizens of Lurn, who had watched their friends and loved ones kneeling before the swords of Royal Army executioners, were being led by vengeance. They showed no mercy to the soldiers they faced.

As the battle drew to an obvious end, members of the Royal Guard began to retreat. Paodin couldn't help but smile as he thought of them running back to the castle, knowing they had been defeated by a bunch of commoners. The smile quickly faded, however, as he thought about what most likely awaited them. If Simann had been so cruel to him, what might he do to the men returning, men he would see as having let him down?

Paodin couldn't think of that at the moment, though, because he needed to focus his attention on the wounded men around him. He himself had a cut across his left thigh, and although it was by no means minor, it was a scratch compared to what some of the men were suffering. With the threat of battle gone, everyone focused his energy on nursing his brothers back to health. Without the Healer, though, it proved difficult. Men from both sides were dying on the blood soaked field. The women of Lurn were making their way through the men, using gentle, steady hands to stitch the wounds of those who might recover and comfort those who were drawing a final breath. They paid no attention to which side the men had fought for, and it was not uncommon to see a woman comforting a dying man, holding the hand that only days before had wielded the sword which had executed her husband, father, son, or brother. If Paodin had doubted himself and his cause the night before, all those thoughts were gone now as he watched. These women who were so merciful were who he fought for, women who deserved to be ruled by a just and merciful king instead of the tyrant on the throne.

******************

*Tap tap tap.*

The sound was so light that at first Brigitte wasn't certain she hadn't imagined it. When it came a second time, though, she moved quickly to the door. In the years since she had lost her sight,

Brigitte could count on one hand the number of times she had truly wished for its return. Now, when the Healer lay dying on a cot in her small front room, was one of those times. She wished she could peek out a window before opening the door to someone who could quite possibly mean the girl harm. However, Brigitte had always trusted her instincts, and at the moment they were telling her that she could trust whoever was knocking so quietly. She opened the door.

"I'm a friend of the girl's," a gravelly voice stated as soon as the door opened.

"What girl?" Brigitte answered. Though her instincts told her the stranger at her door meant what he said, it never hurt to be cautious.

"The girl," the gravelly voice continued, "who will surely die if you keep blocking the doorway as if to keep out King Simann himself!" Despite her surprise at the stranger's knowledge and boldness, Brigitte kept her voice neutral as she questioned the man again.

"Who are you, if I may be so bold as to ask who is requesting entrance to my home?"

"You may ask," the stranger replied, "but I can tell you no more. I am an old man, my dear, and I am afraid little things such as names have a tendency to escape me in my old age."

Brigitte could hear the smile in his voice, along with some quality she could not identify that somehow assured her that his intentions were true. Though she had every intention of questioning him further, she instead found herself opening the door.

The old man wasted no time with small talk, and Brigitte had not expected him to do so. He knelt next to the girl, his rough hands moving quickly over the girl's wounds. Brigitte sat quietly, holding Syndria's hand. Though she had no reason to, Brigitte trusted the old man. She could not, however, leave the girl who had been entrusted to her care. She had promised Paodin—but even more than that, this Healer was Jamis's daughter. The girl had been alone long enough. She deserved a friend sticking beside her.

The stranger was muttering something under his breath, but even in the stillness of the house as night was falling Brigitte could not make out what he was saying. If she were to trust her ears, she would have to say that the old man was speaking some other language. As she listened, Brigitte began to realize that his voice was losing its gravelly quality.

The three did not move for more than an hour. The old man muttered continuously, his hands moving over the girl's wounds the entire time. Brigitte held the girl's still hand, praying to the Fates to spare the girl's life. Then, realizing that they had been sitting long enough that night would have fallen dark, Brigitte reached to feel for the candle she knew Adair had left beside the cot. Before she could find it, though, Brigitte saw something. For the first time in years, she saw light.

In the first few weeks after the injury to her eyes had begun to heal, Brigitte had been able to see light and shadow. It had given her hope, making her think that eventually her sight would come back. However, as the weeks had turned into months and the months to years, Brigitte had lost he sight entirely. Now, even turning her face directly into the sun did not change the darkness which had become her constant companion.

At that moment, though, Brigitte saw light.

*"What is the reason for which you have called us, brother?"*

Brigitte was startled when a voice spoke out of the midst of the light. The door had not opened, of that she was sure. Also, she had head no footsteps moving across the floor. Brigitte could feel the old man as he stood beside her and turned to face the light. If she could see this light, how could one with sight bear to face it?

*"The Healer has chosen her path. Now she must follow it."*

When the voice spoke this time, Syndria noticed something she had somehow missed before. Instead of one voice, she made out three distinct voices speaking as one being.

"She has proven herself faithful, giving of herself even when there was nothing to give."

At first Brigitte did not recognize the voice. She had heard the gravel slowly leave the old man's voice as he had muttered over the girl, but it was very different to hear him actually speaking aloud. As she listened, though, she could pick out the same quality that had made her trust him when he was standing at her door.

*"Her choice was to give herself."*

*"She has made her own destiny."*

*"Who are we to challenge the Fates?"*

They spoke as three now, and Brigitte sat mesmerized. Could this really be happening? Others would say it was impossible, but Brigitte knew it was true. She was witnessing a meeting of the True Wizards. As amazing as that thought was, though, what struck Brigitte as even more incredible was the fact that they had called the old stranger "brother." That would make him the last True Wizard.

Did this mean that the old prophecy was soon to be fulfilled? Would the true heir return and drive Simann from Castle Tundyel? If so, what role did the Healer have to play in it all, that she would be deemed important enough to merit the presence of the last True Wizard? Brigitte had so many questions, but she knew this was not the time for her to speak.

"Her destiny does not lead her so quickly to death!" he said, his steely voice ringing out in the stillness of the small room. "We all know the truth of the Healer's purpose."

All was quiet for a long moment. If it hadn't been for the light that Brigitte could still see, she would have thought that she and the girl were alone in the room.

*"You have spoken Truth. Still, it is not our place."* The three spoke as one being, and then the light began to dim.

*******************

Paodin stood silently, tears rolling down his face to drip from his jaw. They had won the battle, but at what cost?

Audon walked up behind Paodin and placed a comforting hand on the young man's shoulder. "He was a great man and will be missed," he said.

Paodin glanced at his father and could see tears glistening in the moonlight in his father's eyes as well. "He was a great man, yes, but more than that, he was my dearest friend." He stood staring for a moment at the grave where Berek now lay, then looked around. All across the field that had been stained with blood there were now graves which held those who had fallen. The bloody battlefield had demanded payment from the Royal Army and Sons of Tundyel alike, and now young and old, soldier and rebel, all lay side by side.

"They were all great men, Father. I can only pray to the Fates that their deaths, friend and foe alike, will not be in vain. I can't help but wonder, though, if that is exactly what has happened. The Healer is not here, and without her the Prophecy cannot be fulfilled. Have I led these men to nothing more than a senseless death?"

Audon was quiet for a moment, as Paodin had expected him to be. The older man seldom answered any question hastily. When he did speak, his voice was so low it seemed a part of the night itself.

"Perhaps her role is not the one you have envisioned. In my experience, the thoughts of one seldom encompass the whole vision. Do not limit the Fates to your own understanding, my son."

Once again, as had happened so many times in his life when his father spoke, Paodin felt almost foolish. Who was he to think he had figured out the plan of the Fates? He, in his unending ignorance, was trying to understand a Prophecy that had been spoken in all wisdom by the True Wizards. His father was right, as usual.

"Father, do you think these men will be remembered?"

"We will be certain of it," Audon said with no hesitation. He squeezed his son's shoulder and then walked off, leaving Paodin alone with his thoughts.

He stood beside the grave a moment longer, recalling good times spent with Berek as youth in Gelci. Youth. Paodin almost laughed out loud when the word rolled through his mind. Though he was by no means old, the carefree days of his youth seemed like a lifetime ago. In the past few weeks, those days had seemed like little more than a dream. Lately, he had been named a traitor, been beaten to the very brink of death for days on end, mysteriously escaped Simann's dungeon, taken command of the Sons of Tundyel as they rose to fight Simann's tyranny, been told his father was not his father, and lost his best friend. Along with all of that was the Healer, but he wasn't sure where she fit into the story of his life. Somehow, though, her presence could be found woven into the fabric of each story.

Shaking his head, Paodin brought himself back to the real world. There was too much to be done to think about his own confusing story. Right now, he needed to focus his time and attention on his bothers in arms who would still need his leadership, no matter how inadequate he found himself.

Paodin made his way across the field, helping to fill in graves, comfort the dying, and dress the wounds of the living.

\*\*\*\*\*\*\*\*\*\*\*\*\*\*\*\*\*\*\*

Euroin had long before stopped watching the battle, confident he knew the outcome, when he felt it. Something had gone wrong. His cloak snapping in the night air, the Master Wizard pulled the battlefield back into view, which served only to increase his rage. The Royal Army had been defeated, those not captured or killed sent running like scared dogs. He would have liked to strike them down as they fled, but there was something more than the defeat of well-trained soldiers by ignorant, common people.

He saw the people of Lurn who had joined the fight on the side of the rebellion. Looking deeper into the past, Euroin could see them overpowering the soldiers who had been left to guard the city. Some of the guards had been killed, something the Master Wizard saw as their good fortune. Those who had merely rolled over like some mangy dog would not experience such a swift death, of that Euroin would make certain. However, they could be dealt with later, for there was still something more.

The Master Wizard could see it the instant he pulled the darkness into view. In the center, surrounding the target of his wrath, was a light so intense that he had to avert his eyes. He could feel his very being recoil from its presence. No matter what he did, he could not get the darkness to encroach upon the light. Instead, every effort he made resulted in the darkness being pushed a little father away from the traitorous Healer and his own being convulsing and contracting deeper inside itself. Euroin made one more attempt, calling on every ounce of power available to him. He watched the darkness squeezing in, moving closer to the girl and drowning out the light. His inner being swelled, and the Master Wizard began laughing.

*********************

The light around her was powerful yet comforting, and Syndria realized in an instant that it was the same light which had surrounded her in the Wizard's tunnel. The True Wizards had come again, this time meeting her in the darkness and chasing it away. She could feel their presence, a very welcome change from the cold darkness through which she had been struggling.

Suddenly, though, she could see the darkness closing in again. At first she thought the darkness was overcoming the light, but she quickly realized that was not the case. Instead, the light was leaving her. Syndria's heart began pounding as she thought about being enveloped by the crushing blackness. She couldn't do that again, couldn't keep fighting if she was left alone in the dark. It would be so much easier to just give up, to let go and let the darkness have its way. She was scared, and where just a moment before there had been the light to comfort her, now there was nothing. Her breathing was fast and erratic as the girl felt herself giving in to her terror, until a thought occurred to her.

"Since when," she thought, "have I let fear rule my actions?" She took a deep breath, and then the Healer reached out past the edge of the light and touched the darkness.

\*\*\*\*\*\*\*\*\*\*\*\*\*\*\*\*\*\*\*\*\*\*

The Master Wizard's laughter stopped abruptly when the light surrounding the traitor suddenly flared. Something deep inside of him shrieked, and Euroin was thrown across the room. As he crashed into the wall of the marble tower, Euroin could not shake one strange thought.

The light had seemed to come from the girl.

## Chapter 18

The light flared brighter than before, then Brigitte was left once again in the darkness to which she had grown so accustomed yet which somehow seemed desolate now after experiencing such a light. All was quiet in the small room, and though Brigitte wanted to know if the True Wizards had remained, she did not dare to speak the question aloud. Still holding the girl's hand, Brigitte felt Syndria shudder. Then, she felt something she had not felt from the girl in a long time—warmth.

"It would appear," came the gravelly voice, now tempered with the strong hint of a smile, "that the girl agrees with me about her fate."

Brigitte was beginning to think that surprises might soon become common place when she heard the old man's voice as it had been when he first arrived at her door. He offered no explanation of the night's events, so Brigitte did not ask the questions dancing through her mind. Instead, she simply nodded and squeezed Syndria's hand, glad that she had been allowed to stay beside Jamis's daughter through everything. She knew she had been witness to something incredible, and that was enough.

Once the warmth returned to the Healer's small body, things happened quickly. Soon, Syndria began to stir, and it was only a few minutes later that Brigitte felt the girl squeeze her hand.

"My lady," came a quiet, calm voice, "please tell me your name, that I might know who to thank for my life."

"My name is Brigitte, Mistress, but it was not I who saved you. Perhaps you should ask your friend," she answered, inclining her head to where the old man had stood beside her.

"Where is he?"

Brigitte smiled slightly. She had not heard the stranger move away, but now that the girl was implying that he was gone, Brigitte was not surprised. "I suppose he left," she answered the girl, then squeezed her hand. "How are you feeling?"

Before she answered, Syndria gently tested her body. Though everything hurt, she was relieved to discover that it was all the ordinary pain she had dealt with innumerable times in her life as a Healer. She smiled. "I will live, I believe, and at the moment that is enough. Now, how can I repay you for the kindness you have shown me?" Gingerly, Syndria sat up in the darkness.

"I need nothing from you, Mistress," Brigitte said, steadying the girl before releasing her hand. "Let me get you a drink—I'm sure you could use some water." She moved quickly into the kitchen, thinking to light a small candle on her way back. "Here you are, my dear."

"Thank you, Lady Brigitte." Syndria looked up, and with the help of the small candle saw for the first time the woman who had helped see her through the darkness. "If I may ask, do you have your sight?"

Brigitte smiled, glad to see that the Healer still possessed some of the traits which had so endeared Syndria the girl to her in years past. As a child, Syndria had always been straightforward, and it appeared years spent in the castle had not changed her. "No, my dear. That was taken from me a few years back."

"Perhaps that is how I can repay you—as a Healer, maybe I can restore your sight," the girl said, reaching out her hand to gently touch Brigitte's face.

Brigitte softly covered Syndria's hand with her own and pulled it down. "You have only just now begun to recover, Mistress," she said. "I would not have you expend your energy on me, especially when there are men fighting and dying, in need of the Healer."

Syndria was puzzled. In the years since she had been revealed as a Healer, there had never been someone she met who did not have some ailment to which he or she had wanted the Healer to attend. Now, she had seen one man face a bear and not want her to heal him and a woman who, when given the chance to regain her sight, thought first of men she had never met. If ever she had needed some reassurance that the people of Tundyel were worth fighting for, worth being labeled a traitor for, lately she had been given that reassurance by seeing the overwhelming goodness that people possessed. The peace and comfort offered by the True Wizards had been tempting, but Syndria was glad of her decision. There was pain now, to be sure, something she would have never had to face again if she had stayed in the light when she had the chance, but pain was what she was called to handle, her way of helping the good people of Tundyel like Lady Brigitte who now stood before her.

"One day, my lady, I hope you will allow me to repay your kindness. Now, as you mentioned, there are men who need me. Is there any way for me to return to them, perhaps a horse?" she asked, anxious to get back to Paodin and the men of Gelci.

"There was an old mule, but I'm afraid he went missing when my son disappeared. I fear they are both already at the site of the battle," Brigitte said, and Syndria could see a look of fear quickly flash across the woman's face when she spoke of her son. "He is only eleven," she explained, "but since he became the man of the house at such a young age, he seems to think he is older than his years."

"I will look for him and make sure he is safe," Syndria promised. "If you can tell me which way I should go, I will start making my way to the battlefield. Night is probably the best time to travel, anyway, so I may as well—"

*Tap tap tap.*

Both women froze when the knock interrupted Syndria. It was Brigitte who acted first, quickly calling out for the person at the door to wait a moment while at the same time shooing Syndria toward the kitchen.

Before unlatching the door—which was strange, because she hadn't latched it back after the old stranger had left—Brigitte calmly asked, "Who's there?"

"It's Jamis, Lady Brigitte."

Brigitte quickly opened the door, her heart speeding up at the thought of Syndria's father standing on the other side. It seemed this night was full of surprises.

"Forgive me for the late hour," he started, then hurried on, "but I was told—is it true? Is my Syndria here? How is she? Do you think it would be alright for me to see her?"

Brigitte laughed. "My friend, I believe I can answer all of your questions with this: Go into the kitchen."

Jamis started to move through the small

house to the kitchen, but hesitated. "It has been a long twelve years. Will she even remember me?" He peered into the darkness, his hand absentmindedly rubbing the hilt of the sword in his scabbard.

"There is only one way to find out," Brigitte said quietly, finding Jamis's shoulder and gently pushing him forward. "Mistress," she called, "it is alright—a friend."

The Healer stepped through the doorway, then froze. For a moment no one moved; it seemed no one even breathed.

"Papa?" The question was quiet and unsure, but it was all Jamis needed to hear. His Syndria remembered him after all those years apart. He stepped forward and opened his arms, and the girl rushed into them. Father and daughter were together again, and for the rest of the night everything else faded into the background.

\*\*\*\*\*\*\*\*\*\*\*\*\*\*\*\*\*\*\*\*\*\*

Euroin slowly picked himself up from where he had crumpled against the floor, testing to make sure nothing had been injured too badly in his crash against the wall. He wasn't sure how much time had passed, having been knocked unconscious when he hit the wall, but he could see that the dawn was approaching.

As he approached the center of the room fire flashed in his eyes, the flames threatening to escape their confines in their search for something to consume. Somehow that traitor, that mere girl, had managed to slip from his grasp yet again. Anger boiled inside him, and the dark power coursing through him demanded retribution. He pulled the now quiet battlefield into view, wishing he could send out Wizard's fire to engulf everything and everyone he saw. It didn't work that way, though—he had not come into contact with the people he saw moving about on the battlefield, so he could not directly attack them. The Master Wizard searched the scene, a small smile curving the sides of his mouth upward ever so slightly when he spied one man he could assail. The Master of the Guard was there among the wounded men of the Royal Army, himself guarded by one of the traitorous commoners who had managed to outwit the highly trained soldiers. This outrageous defeat was as much the fault of the Master of the Guard as it was anyone's, perhaps even more. Euroin reached out across the distance and watched as the darkness closed in on the unsuspecting Master of the Guard.

\*\*\*\*\*\*\*\*\*\*\*\*\*\*\*\*\*\*\*\*\*

In the predawn light, Syndria and Jamis mounted the two horses he had brought with him and told Brigitte goodbye.

"I will be forever grateful, Lady Brigitte, for your kindness. One day, I hope you will allow me to repay you," Syndria said, leaning down from atop her mare to kiss Brigitte's cheek. Brigitte smiled and reached out for the girl's hand.

"My dear, you owe me nothing. You have made an old friend happy, and that is repayment enough for what little I did. Now, go, and the Fates grant you safe travel. Master Jamis," she added quickly, "please, watch over my son." Jamis had brought word of Adair's role in the battle, granting Brigitte some peace of mind. However, it was a struggle to keep the tears from choking up her voice now that she no longer had the Healer's struggle for life to compete with a mother's fears for her only son.

"I would have brought him back with me, but the battle has ended and he seemed to revel in the attention of the men. I will bring him back to you soon, my lady." Jamis nodded to Brigitte as he spurred his horse, and father and daughter rode off together to return to the battlefield.

They rode in companionable silence, listening to the birds greet the new morning. Syndria felt a peace which she had not experienced since she had last been with the Ancient, a feeling that she truly belonged. In the back of her mind, though, the conversation Paodin had had with Audon kept playing. Finally, Syndria had to ask.

"Father, I learned something recently, and I need to ask you about it."

"Anything," was Jamis's quick reply.

Taking a deep breath, the girl let the words rush out as quickly as possible. "Paodin, whom you've met, has a ring that matches my bracelet. He and his father were talking, and Audon said that he is not truly Paodin's father. It seems a crazy conclusion to draw, I know, but I was wondering—" The words stopped, and it seemed Syndria was unable to form more. Instead, she trusted her father would know what she was asking and waited quietly for his answer.

Jamis's voice was low and a bit sad when he answered. "I do not know the circumstances surrounding Paodin's infancy, but I suspect from what you have said and from these recent events that his story is in some way much like your own." He paused for a moment, staring straight ahead though he could feel his daughter's eyes searching the side of his face. Once the words started, though, they poured out. "You were brought to me in the night, a tiny thing wrapped in no more than a blanket. I was told to raise you as my own, to leave my home that night and go where I was not known. What I have told you about your bracelet is all I know of your origins. The man who brought you said to teach you the Truth, and to tell you your mother's words, that your bracelet would always protect you. He disappeared into the darkness, and I was left with this child I knew nothing about raising. I packed a few belongings, and the two of us set off to Lurn. I, an unready father, you, a perfect little bundle that did not know any better than to depend on me. I always thought I would tell you someday," he added with a small chuckle. "I never imagined it would happen under circumstances such as these."

"I knew, I think, when I heard Audon's explanation. The coincidence would have been too great otherwise." Syndria's voice was quiet, but Jamis could hear no sadness in her words as she continued. "I thank you, Father, for taking on a responsibility which was not your own. I am glad you were chosen to be my father."

Jamis finally looked over at the girl, relief flooding his body when he saw that Syndria's expression held no contempt. The two rode the rest of the way in silence once again, taking in the morning. The sun was just breaking over the horizon when they reached the battlefield, but the beauty of the new morning was overshadowed by the horrific site which greeted the riders.

Syndria knew the battle she had left had been a bloody one, but she could not have imagined the pain of seeing so many men so close to death. Fresh graves lined the clearing, and often the men doing the digging were not in much better shape than the man who would be lain to rest in the dark earth. Urging her mare forward, Syndria was leaping off before her mount even came to a stop. The Healer stood among the men, quickly scanning the wounded to determine who needed her help the most. She then knelt beside a man who was barely clinging to life, his blood having already stained the ground beneath him a deep crimson. The Healer placed one hand on his fevered brow and one on the gaping wound across his stomach, letting his pain flow into her as she let her life flow into him. Immediately, the blood stopped flowing and his brow began to cool as the agony left his body. As soon as she was convinced the young man would live, and that the pain he faced would not be too horrible, she stopped, turning to find the next man.

The Healer moved among the wounded men, not noticing whether the man she knelt to attend to wore the clothes of a farmer or the armor of the Royal Army. She took on the pain of friend and foe alike, bringing each man to a point where the pain and injury were not more than he could bear and moving on to the next. As she helped the men, Syndria could not help but think that if this had occurred just a few days earlier, she would have thought taking on the intense pain of so many to be more than she could bear. With the events of the past days, however, the Healer barely noticed the pain she was taking upon herself.

"Mistress," a voice called quietly from

behind her. Syndria turned, slightly startled. Since she had begun moving among the men the only ones who had spoken to her had been the men thanking her for their lives or begging for her touch. Now, a lady stood before her.

"Mistress," she repeated, "there is a man in need of your help. Will you come?"

"Of course," the Healer answered. "Where is he?"

The lady led the Healer to the edge of the battlefield, saying as she walked, "His name is Erik. He is the Master of the Guard, though that title does not mean as much now. He refused to be tended to until he saw after his men, saying his own wounds were not serious. Just before dawn he collapsed, and has been mumbling incoherently ever since. I cannot rouse him." The woman's voice was calm, but Syndria could hear that it was tinted with worry.

"Though he may not welcome assistance from me, my lady, I will help him. Please do not worry." The woman's shoulders relaxed a little, and Syndria found herself wondering what this woman was to the Master of the Guard.

When they reached Erik, the Healer quickly knelt beside him. He was deathly pale, covered in a cold sweat and weakly shaking his head back and forth. The Healer scanned his body, searching for the wound that had done the most damage. While there were many small injuries, she could not find anything grievous enough to cause his current condition. Puzzled, the Healer reached out to touch his brow and soothe his pain. When her hand touched his cold skin, Syndria was shocked at the overwhelming, familiar pain. This was the same thing she had felt in the midst of the darkness, pain and despair combining to make something much worse than all the pain she had taken from the other men on the battlefield. For a moment the girl was scared to do what she knew to be the duty of a Healer. What happened if somehow she was pulled once again into that darkness? She quickly pushed the fear and doubt aside, though, taking a steadying breath. She had been through the darkness and survived. She had helped Paodin get through it even though they had been apart. Now, she had to help this man find his way through. The Healer summoned her strength and closed her eyes, focusing on pushing the darkness away from the dying man.

\*\*\*\*\*\*\*\*\*\*\*\*\*\*\*\*\*\*\*\*\*

He couldn't believe it—she was there again, this time helping the Master of the Guard. Euroin pushed the darkness harder, forcing it in on the man. He could feel the fear emanating from Erik, and he willed the darkness to tighten its icy grip. That traitorous girl had stolen so much from his grasp—he was not about to let her deprive him of the satisfaction that would come with watching this incompetent fool die a lonely, painful death.

The darkness wrapped itself around the girl as well, but she didn't seem to notice. There had been a slight shudder when she first encountered the familiar power, but she had quickly moved past her fear. The Master Wizard felt a strange opposition to his power, and the harder he pushed, the stronger that resistance grew. His cloak snapping in the still room, Euroin screamed out in his rage. How could this little girl be able to withstand his assault? Not only that, but she was helping someone else to do the same. Euroin quickly turned his full attention back to the Master of the Guard. He may not be able to crush her, but he could break her, none the less. If he could rip this man from the Healer's grasp, it would shake her confidence, and a lot could be said for that.

\*\*\*\*\*\*\*\*\*\*\*\*\*\*\*\*\*\*\*\*\*\*

Syndria could feel the darkness closing in around her, and fear started building. What if she couldn't get out this time? She was terrified at the thought of being left once again in the darkness; she was afraid she would never get out. The girl wanted to just step back, to simply take her hands off of the Master of the Guard. After all, he was King Simann's sword, in effect. She had seen him many times standing outside the door when she had been called to once again heal a man who had been tortured, waiting for the chance to bring the prisoner once again to the brink of death. What great loss would it be if she just let him die? It would just mean one less threat to the true heir returning to the throne. This man was part of the problem.

If it were that simple, though, why was he being attacked by the darkness?

Syndria was scared, but the Healer knew her duty. Hers was not to judge, but to heal. She had been in the dark with no one there to help and knew the utter despair it caused. As a Healer, she could not leave him there alone.

Pushing all else aside, the Healer focused on the man in front of her. The darkness was closing in, threatening to choke out the light. She ignored it. As she let go of her fears, the Healer noticed something she hadn't paid attention to before. Reaching out to the darkness gave her the same feeling she had experienced when she had touched the hill. For a brief moment Syndria thought back to the first time she had touched the darkness. She felt the same pain now, but it didn't seem as excruciating as it had the first time. What she noticed for the first time, though, was a strange sense of waning power. As Syndria thought about it, the power seemed to strengthen again and the darkness squeezed in more tightly. Shutting everything out again, the Healer thought of nothing but the man in front of her. She felt her life flowing into him, battling the darkness for position.

But then, something changed. Syndria felt the darkness creep in to her and touch the very core of her being, and in that instant she could feel herself changing. The Healer was no longer battling against the darkness--she was embracing it. It had become a part of her, the biggest part, the only part that mattered. She saw the Master of the Guard before her, not as a man, but as a means of increasing her power. Her touch grew cold as the Healer began draining life from the man who now began writhing in agony under her hands. His fear and pain grew exponentially, and as they grew so did the power within her. When he was right on the edge of death, she stopped for a moment, letting him waver and reveling in his desperation.

The hesitation was brief, but it was all the Healer needed. In that moment, she could feel a strong hand on her shoulder and knew without a doubt that it was Paodin beside her, lending her his strength. She could not drive the darkness out of herself--she had let it gain entrance, and it was now destined to stay--but she locked it away in the deepest corner of her soul. The Healer then focused entirely on the man before her, taking his pain as she let her life flow into him. That dark part of her soul tried to fight, desperate to hold on to the power it had tasted, but the Healer pushed it back.

She felt the now familiar pain radiating from her fingertips throughout her body, and knew that she could not pull her hands away now even if she tried. Soon, the man before her stopped moaning and his eyes fluttered open.

Syndria's hands fell away, and the girl fell back. As the day around her faded, she saw for a moment the concern in Paodin's eyes as he caught her, keeping her from crumpling in a heap on the ground.

\*\*\*\*\*\*\*\*\*\*\*\*\*\*\*\*\*\*\*\*\*

She could hear a worried voice calling her name, but Syndria did not want to open her eyes. She wanted to lay there, curled up in the warmth of the old blanket, and sleep for days. She could ignore the voices and was not the least bit bothered by the hard ground and the tree root making a sizable dent in the small of her back. What did bother her, though, was the smell, and it only took a moment for the girl to realize that the warm blanket was the source of the horsy smell that was quickly overwhelming her. Syndria's eyes fluttered open as she pushed the blanket away from her face.

"You're coming back to us finally, I see," Paodin said lightly, though his eyes betrayed his concern.

"Yes, thanks in part to the smell of the riding blanket I seem to be wrapped in," Syndria said wryly, pushing herself to a sitting position beneath the tree and pulling the blanket further away from her face. "I suppose that was your doing? Perhaps you thought it would wake me sooner?"

Paodin shrugged. "It appears to have done it's job, then, has it not?" he smiled. "Here, drink this. You need to regain your strength." He held out a small stone mug. "I'm afraid it has lost it's warmth, but it should still help."

Syndria accepted the cup readily, pulling it quickly to her lips and taking a large gulp to quench her dry throat. It was all she could do to not spew it back out all over Paodin once the taste hit her tongue. Sputtering when she finally managed to choke it down, Syndria stared wide-eyed into the cup. "What is this?" she asked, barely squeaking out the question as she held the cup out for Paodin to take back.

Laughing, Paodin pushed the mug back toward her. "It is something to make you feel more like yourself, compliments of Red. I'm not sure what all is in it, but I can assure you that it works." His expression growing serious, Paodin continued, "Will you be alright here? I need to see to the men, but then I will be back--to talk." When Paodin was satisfied Syndria would stay put, and when he had watched her take another, though much more tentative, drink, he moved quickly back to the men, leaving the Healer to her thoughts.

At the moment, that was the one thing Syndria did not want to face. She was afraid to look inside herself, frightened of seeing the Darkness that she knew still lurked there. She did not want to think about what had almost happened, of what she had been doing to the Master of the Guard. So instead, she pushed those thoughts aside and focused on the revelation that both she and Paodin had been raised by men who were not their fathers, both given a piece of jewelry and a cryptic quote by a mother. It was too much of a coincidence, and Syndria wondered if what she was thinking could possibly be true. Was there more of a connection between she and Paodin than either of them realized? Not wanting to think anymore, Syndria took a deep breath to steel herself then threw back her head and quickly gulped down the rest of Red's concoction. Sputtering, she set the mug aside and lay back against the tree. The battle with the darkness had taken its toll, and now with the horse blanket in her lap instead of wrapped around her shoulders, the Healer quickly dropped off to sleep once again.

Chapter 19

As the daylight began to fade, Syndria stirred. Whether it was the rest or Red's drink, she had to admit that she was feeling better. Just as she was about to make her way back to the men, Paodin came back. She could see the worry on his face as he walked up to her. Syndria smiled and started to stand, but Paodin stopped her.

"Don't stand--I'll sit," he said, bracing himself with a hand against the tree Syndria was leaning against as he sunk down beside her. "Are you alright? Would you like something to eat? There's not much, but there is some bread and cheese being passed around."

"Yes, I am alright. A little weak, but I'll be fine. I don't think I could eat anything, especially with the taste of whatever foul drink Red sent to me still in my mouth. How are you?"

Paodin shook his head, laughing under his breath. "However foul it may have been, you have to admit that it worked. Now, I'm not letting you off so easily. We have time to talk for the first time since our walk to Gelci, so you are going to tell me what you just went through." Paodin crossed his arms across his chest and settled back against the tree, seemingly getting comfortable for a long conversation.

"Aren't the men preparing to move into Lurn? We should help," Syndria said, pulling her feet underneath herself to stand. She was stopped by a heavy hand on her shoulder.

"Sit," Paodin said. "They can manage, I think I can find Lurn on my own should we be left behind, and Thrul can carry us both--he has done so before. Now, what happened to you? I have seen you take pain from life-threatening injuries without so much as a flinch, and yet when you finished helping a man with no visible major wound, you collapsed. You had all of us worried. What was so different this time?"

Syndria was quiet for a moment, staring out over the silent battlefield without really seeing. When she finally spoke, her voice was low. "That's what I have been sitting here considering. I have always known I was different from the other Healers. From the very beginning I could take pain from those I healed, and that has become commonplace. Until recently, I thought that was the extent of things. On my journey, before I met you, I learned of my ability to reveal what was hidden underneath a spell when I uncovered the ruined city, and I was shocked. That, however, was before the darkness."

She was quiet again, but Paodin did not push her to keep talking. He knew what the darkness had done to him, and he knew that somehow she had reached out to him in the midst of that darkness. He couldn't wrap his mind around what had happened, and he could only imagine the difficulty Syndria would have in trying to understand recent events. He hadn't really let himself think about the darkness, in all honesty. The battle had been raging when he had come back from that dark place, and then he had faced the deaths of men he had known his entire life, including his best friend. Now in the stillness, he allowed himself to think back.

He had been alone, the darkness closing in on him. He had wanted to fight, but, unlike when he had faced the Shadow in the woods, there was nothing to fight. He had been helpless, crying out to the Fates to save him, but there had been no answer. He could do nothing for himself. Then, through the darkness, he had felt her touch. He hadn't seen her, but he had known it was the Healer. He had felt her touch before, both in the dungeon of Simann's castle and in the pass through the Velios, and he had recognized it then. In little more than an instant, the darkness had started to give way to light. The pain had stopped soon after, and then Paodin had opened his eyes once again to the battle raging before him.

"I don't know how to explain it," Paodin said, breaking the silence, "but I know you came to me in the darkness, and I somehow know it made you worse. I owe you my life twice over now. Thank you."

"Good to know you can acknowledge help from someone."

Paodin spun around at the sound of the familiar gravelly voice. Syndria turned, too, the smile on her face standing in stark contrast to the frown on Paodin's.

"Hello, my friend," she said. "It is good to see you again." She extended her hand to the old hermit, and the man stepped across Paodin and settled to the ground on the other side of the Healer with surprising grace.

Paodin shook his head in disbelief. How did this man keep turning up?

"My dear," the old man said kindly, "I am glad to see you looking well. You gave us all quite a scare."

"Yes," Syndria said, "I believe I owe you thanks. Lady Brigitte told me of the presence of a strange gentlemen by my bedside who I can only assume was you. You seem to turn up just when you are needed."

"You owe me nothing, Mistress. I am just an old man who could do nothing for you. I hear you have been doing battle again recently?" he said, the question obvious in his voice.

Syndria's face changed dramatically, the smile replaced by an odd sadness. "I don't really understand what happened. I have faced the darkness before, but it was different this time. I felt a power in it, a sense of evil so strong it threatened to overtake me. For a moment, it started to accomplish that very thing. I felt the power enter me, and I started taking life from the Master of the Guard. I could sense his fear, and the darkness inside me was feeding off of it, even reveling in it."

When she stopped talking, Paodin felt as if he should say something, anything, to comfort Syndria and assure her that she had done nothing wrong. A look from the old man stopped him though, and Paodin sat quietly by her side instead. After a moment, she spoke again.

"I wanted to kill him. I wanted to do to him what he had done to so many others like you," she turned to Paodin, "who had done nothing wrong. No, that is not completely true. In all honesty there was no reason, no thought of his torture being punishment for his past wrongs. I wanted to let him hover at the brink of death then restore his life just to take it again, solely to make him suffer. Actually it was more than that. I *needed* to make him suffer. I said the darkness was feeding off of his fear, but that is merely scratching the surface of the truth." Tears suddenly filled her eyes as Syndria continued, "*I* was feeding on his fear and pain because I *was* the darkness." She broke down then, the tears streaming down her face as sobs racked her body.

Paodin was helpless. He had grown up without being truly close to any member of the fairer sex, so he had never learned how to handle a woman's tears. Besides that, this was the Healer in front of him. He had seen her strength time and again, seen her take without the slightest twinge pain which had full grown men writhing in agony. Now here she was, transformed into a fragile girl, shaking as huge sobs racked her tiny body, and he could do nothing for her. Give him the Shadow any day; he would gladly take a fight over this feeling of helplessness.

"Don't just sit there, you fool!" the old man said, reaching across the girl to thump Paodin on the head with his walking stick. "Do something!" Then he quickly stood and walked away, ignoring the look of panic that spread across Paodin's face.

He sat frozen for a moment. The Healer was curled up, her head buried in her arms which rested on top of her drawn up knees. Paodin opened his mouth to speak multiple times, but each time he quickly closed it when no words would come. After a brief hesitation, he put an arm around her shoulders. Syndria collapsed against his chest, and Paodin held her as she cried.

After a while, her tears finally spent, Syndria sat up and smiled slightly as she dried her face on her sleeve. "You must think I have gone mad, carrying on like this over the dark, what some would see as little more than a dream."

"There is no need to apologize, Mistress. Though I might have thought that to be the case a few weeks ago, I do not think so now," he said. "I have been in the darkness, so there is no one who could convince me it was only a dream.

"You were broken by the knowledge that for a short time you were part of that darkness, that it had become part of you," he said, "but I am in awe for the same reason." He saw an argument forming on her lips, so Paodin quickly continued. "You say you were one with the darkness, yet you overcame it. You have a strength others can merely dream of possessing. While I was in the darkness, it did not become part of me because I was not strong enough to contain any part of it. I was simply crushed beneath its presence. You stood against it and overcame it, time and again. And though I stand in amazement at your ability to fight the darkness, I do not envy you that responsibility."

Syndria smiled slowly. "Thank you for your kindness, Paodin. You speak of amazement of me, but what you do not realize is that it is I who was first amazed by you." When Paodin started to speak, Syndria shook her head. "Keep quiet--I listened while you spoke, so now it is your turn to listen," she said, though not unkindly.

"When I was a young girl, my father told

me stories of the old Healers and True Wizards. When I left Lurn with the Ancient, my head was filled with dreams of traveling the kingdom as they did, helping others. Once I arrived at the castle after training with Nedra, those dreams were snuffed out when I learned my sole purpose in life would be to serve King Simann. My refusal to heal him each day led to my placement in the dungeon.

"For a while, I was proud of myself. I convinced myself that I had taken a stand, and that in some small way I was fulfilling my true purpose in life--to help the innocent. I simply shut my eyes to the truth that all I was doing was allowing the torture of innocent men. It wasn't until I saw you that I learned what it meant to actually take a stand. You thanked me for healing you, knowing full well that it was just so that you could be beaten again, and then you stood in the center of a blood covered room to face those who would carry out King Simann's orders. You stood, though there seemed no reason to do so. No one would see you, and no one would have blamed you for cowering in the corner to await the seemingly inevitable. Yet you stood, all the same. That was courage I had never before seen. I left that dungeon knowing you were different, and I am still amazed by your ability to stand in the face of insurmountable odds.

"While it is true that I was able to push the darkness aside, I know I have been changed by it,"

Syndria continued, her voice aged by a grief few could understand. "There is still a part of that darkness in my very core, a part of who I am that will forever be linked to an evil I cannot even begin to name." Her voice trailed off, and for a moment Syndria stared unseeing at the quiet field before her. Shaking her head slightly, she forced a small smile as she brought herself back to the conversation at hand.

"Well, since it seems you do not think I have lost my mind, I have something else to speak with you about," she said. "Do you think we have a few minutes more to spare before we follow the men to Lurn?"

Glancing over his shoulder, Paodin saw that the last of the small band of citizens was moving out of sight over the hill. He did not want to stay too long, since the two of them alone would be an easy target if any of the soldiers of the Royal Army had stayed close. They could take a few more minutes, though, so he nodded as he turned back to face Syndria.

"The conversation you had with your father made me think, and today I had the chance to speak with my own father," she said quietly. "Like you, I was brought to him as an infant--Jamis is not my real father."

A strange look crossed Paodin's face, one Syndria could not interpret. He sat silently for a moment, staring at his ring as he spun it on his finger.

"A strange coincidence in a string of such occurrences, to be sure," he finally said, "and not something I have any hope of explaining. Perhaps one day things will make sense." Shrugging, he stood and offered a hand to Syndria. "To Lurn?"

Shaking her head as she let Paodin pull her to her feet, she said, "I am amazed by your acceptance of whatever comes your way." Then, imitating his shrug, she replied, "To Lurn."

\*\*\*\*\*\*\*\*\*\*\*\*\*\*\*\*\*\*\*\*\*

That night, the men of the rebellion were fed well by the women of Lurn and rested peacefully for the first time since leaving Gelci. Erik, however, was not at peace. He was asking to speak with Paodin, the leader of the rebellion, but no one was willing to ask him to come to the make-shift holding cell in the center of the town. Finally, in the middle of the night, Lady Andelle found the Healer and gave her word of Erik's request.

\*\*\*\*\*\*\*\*\*\*\*\*\*\*\*\*\*\*\*\*\*

The morning brought with it laughter and a semblance of normalcy, with no talk over breakfast of the battles fought in the previous days. Those present in what had the days before been the quarters of the Master of the Guard, however, were nothing but serious.

"We have won the battle," Audon said, "but the war is far from over. I fear King Simann will take drastic measures when word of the events here reach Castle Tundyel. We should give the men time to rest, but we cannot spend too much time sitting still."

Paodin nodded his agreement, then asked, "What should be our next step? Where do we go from here? Do we march on the castle and pray to the Fates that we will surprise them?"

The men discussed the options for a while, but could not seem to agree on what would be the right action to take. No one paid much attention when Syndria quietly slipped out, but her return had quite a different effect. She walked in quietly, the Master of the Guard following close behind.

Paodin stood, his body visibly tensing as the leader of the Royal Army was led into their planning room. In fact, everyone in the room could be seen to tense except for Red. He stayed leaned back in his chair, his hands folded casually across his stomach. Erik stood quietly, not shrinking back under their steady gazes but not really knowing his place. The Healer stood beside him, and something in the way she held herself told the men she was there in her authoritative capacity and commanded their respect. She met the eyes of each man in turn before speaking.

"Though you have all proven yourselves to

be fearless warriors, we are all at a loss as to how to proceed from here. Last night I had the opportunity to speak with the Master of the Guard. He asked for a chance to speak with you, Paodin, but the opportunity has not presented itself. Instead, since you, the leaders of these men, are all gathered together this morning, I asked him if he would like to speak to the whole group. He has agreed, and I believe it will do you well to listen to what he has to say." Nodding to Erik, the Healer took a seat between him and the leaders of the rebellion. No one said anything. They watched Erik, some grudgingly and some curiously, waiting for him to speak.

Erik started quietly, "I know you have no reason to trust me. Were the situation reversed and one of you came to me, I would be quick to dismiss your words. I will not blame you if that is the case now. However, in light of recent events both on the battlefield and some more…unusual, I felt I should speak with you." As he spoke, the Master of the Guard grew more sure of himself and fell into the comfortable position of speaking to soldiers. He told them of the memories he had for so long forgotten, encouraged by the light of understanding he saw dawn on a few faces. "The men surrounding that family, who I know now to be the remainder of the Rilso family, were holding the shields your men carried into battle. I questioned at the time why traitors would be in possession of shields bearing markings found throughout the castle. I knew King Simann's father had overthrown the last Rilso king, but I did not know there were those who had remained loyal to the members of that bloodline. When I saw your men carrying those shields, I was struck by the fact that now, twenty years later, there are those who are still loyal to the Rilso family. I cannot help but think that I know of none who, even as few as five years after King Simann's death, will still be willing to fight and die bearing his crest. If there are any, I know I would not count myself among their numbers.

"I have done terrible things in the name of the king. I have slaughtered men, women, and children. I have tortured men to the edge of death time and time again, though I could see innocence in their eyes. I could say I was following orders, that I had no choice," he said, glancing at the Healer, "but I cannot use that as an excuse. There is always a choice. The consequence would have been death, but the choice was still mine to make."

Looking at Paodin, whose gaze he had been avoiding, Erik said, "You were one of those men, and though I know it does nothing, I give you my apology for what I did. Now, I am asking you for the chance to begin making up for all I have done. I want to fight with the Sons of Tundyel."

The silence of the room was broken by a low laugh and the roar of flames as they shot out of the fireplace, leaping toward the Master of the Guard. The flames surrounded him, and the men sitting before him instinctively drew back. Paodin, though, dove forward, knocking Erik to the ground and rolling him out the door. Their prey gone, the flames immediately returned to the hearth as if nothing had happened. The laugh, though, echoed through the room for a few seconds more before fading.

\*\*\*\*\*\*\*\*\*\*\*\*\*\*\*\*\*\*\*\*\*

The Master Wizard stood in the marble room of the North Tower, his laugh mingling and dancing with the dark currents of magic swirling in the air around him. He knew the burns would not last, that the traitorous Healer would once again make the man whole, but it had still brought satisfaction to see the man's horror and pain as the flames circled his body. Euroin's robe snapped in the stillness of the day, swirling around him.

Somehow, that girl had been able to pull the former Master of the Guard away from the darkness, out of his grasp. That was no matter--the rebellion was talking of attacking the castle. When they came, he would be ready for them.

Closing his eyes for an instant as he stepped out the door of the marble room, Euroin opened them again as he stepped onto the Royal

Army's training field. All the young sorcerers of the kingdom were there, practicing the new spells and wards they had been taught. The Master Wizard quickly spotted Ilcren, who turned when he sensed Euroin coming near.

Bowing his head slightly, Ilcren asked, "What can I do for you, Master Euroin?" The light in his blue eyes had given way to a dull gleam, showing the weariness he felt from teaching the young sorcerers.

"Are they ready?" Euroin snapped, barely slowing his pace. Ilcren quickly matched his step, anxious not to displease the Master Wizard. The memory of their last encounter was still sharp in his mind.

"Some are. There are those among these sorcerers who might eventually become members of our order, given enough training. Others, however, barely have the ability to create the wards. They will never be able to maintain them," he answered.

"Kill them." The order was given without a second thought. "We do not need their lack of ability getting in the way, and I will not have them released to join the rebellion out of spite." Euroin kept walking, and Ilcren followed along, not sure if that was what the Master Wizard wanted him to do or not, but not willing to risk walking away. His decision proved wise, because Master Euroin spoke again when the two wizards reached King Simann's guards. "We will have an audience with the king," he said, once again barely slowing despite the arguments from the two guards. The heavy wood door flew open and the two wizards walked through. When one of the guards moved to stop them, he was thrown back through the door. It slammed shut behind him, the sliding of the lock echoing in the still room.

King Simann was seated on his throne in the center of the ornate room, the four Healers kneeling around him, each with her hands outstretched and eyes closed. As the two wizards entered, Simann stood and pushed their hands away. All four quickly stood and hurried out a back door as the king spoke. "What is the meaning of this intrusion?" His voice was calm, but his eyes gave away the fire raging just beneath the surface.

Ilcren stopped just inside the room, bowing deeply before King Simann, but the Master Wizard strode directly toward the throne. He stopped a mere arm's length from the king. "We have come with word of the preparations," he said, staring the king straight in the eye. Catching a glimpse of movement behind the king, Euroin narrowed his eyes and the back door slammed shut before the guard standing outside could enter, its bolt sliding in place as well.

To his merit, King Simann did not flinch.

He stared at the Master Wizard, his cold calculating eyes taking in the man from head to foot. Finally he smiled slightly. "And how are my sorcerers?" he asked.

Taking the following silence as a cue, Ilcren spoke up. "They are learning, my King. Some more slowly than others."

"Those deemed incompetent, I have ordered executed," the Master Wizard interrupted, his eyes never leaving King Simann's.

After the slightest of hesitations, King Simann glanced over at Ilcren. "I have given him control in these matters. Do as he says, Wizard," he said, his voice quiet and calm. A flick of his wrist dismissed Ilcren, who bowed again and closed his eyes, quickly shifting out of the room.

Their only audience gone, King Simann let his voice grow more threatening. "How dare you! I am your king--you do not come before me unbidden." He was suddenly thrown back, landing hard upon his throne.

"Of course you are king. You are, after all, the one on the throne!" Euroin smirked.

"Know your place, Wizard." The statement was a warning and an insult, but the Master Wizard simply laughed.

"Your fellow Wizards take their orders from me." Simann continued. "You may be the Master Wizard, but I am the Master of this kingdom and *all* within its borders. They will not hesitate if I give the order for you to be bound, your spells useless to you," he said, unable to keep the snarl from his voice.

The Master Wizard laughed again and gestured at the empty room. "Look around you! You would be dead before you could utter such an order, *my King,*" he smirked. "I do not need you," he continued. "However, if I were to kill you, it would take time for the people of Tundyel to see me as their king, and right now time is something I do not have. It would appear, then," he said, spinning to walk towards the door, "that for the moment you have earned a stay of execution." At the door, he stopped with his hand on the bolt and turned back to Simann. "Call off your dogs before I open the door, or I may decide to make the time."

His eyes cold but not fearful, King Simann stared at the Master Wizard. After a short time, he called out to the guards beating on the door, "It is all right." When Euroin opened the door, the young guards rushed in, their swords drawn. "It was simply a private meeting. The wizard is leaving now." The two guards bowed to King Simann and stepped clear of the door, though they did not sheathe their swords.

The Master Wizard brushed by them without even a glance.

## Chapter 20

Erik opened his eyes to the Healer kneeling above him. Though he knew perhaps more than any other man that her power was something that could stir fear in the bravest of souls, he still found comfort in her presence. Though he could still feel some of the pain, Erik pushed himself to sit up and gently shrugged off the Healer's hands.

"Thank you, Mistress, but please do no more. I do not wish to tire you," he said quietly. Nodding, the Healer quickly turned away from him to Paodin. Erik saw her take his hands in her own and watched in amazement as the burns trailing up the young man's arm began to fade back to normal. He had been healed and had seen the effects of the Healer's touch on the men in the dungeon, but he had never watched the Healer work. It was incredible.

"What was that?" The question seemed to come from everyone at once, with no one able to explain what they had just seen. Once Paodin's burns were healed, Erik spoke again.

"If you will permit me just another minute of your time, I believe I can explain. I regret I hadn't thought of it before your meeting. Perhaps we could move the meeting elsewhere, somewhere without a fire?"

It didn't take long for the group to move to a different building, choosing a barn solely because it lacked a fire. Once the men and Healer were settled, Paodin nodded to Erik to continue his explanation.

Standing before them, Erik said, "The room you were meeting in was used as my private quarters during our occupation of Lurn. The laugh we heard was the Master Wizard. He used the fire to communicate his displeasure with me once before, though only in the form of a threat. I fear he is somehow able to listen to everything that goes on in that room. I am sorry I did not think to bring it to your attention sooner." When the men remained silent, Erik took it as permission, though reluctantly given, to continue. "You spoke of taking the castle by surprise, but it is obvious now that the Master Wizard heard your discussion. Even if he hadn't, though, I have been around him long enough to know that surprising him would never be possible. And though there is little left of the Royal Army to fight for King Simann, he does still have the Royal Wizards. I have experienced no power like that they possess, and you can be certain their powers will be put to use.

"He will appoint a new Master of the Guard, as well, and the man I believe he will choose has many friends in the kingdom. They will not be trained, but I guarantee he will bring many to the castle under his leadership."

Some of the men began murmuring to each

other at that, wondering just how quickly the Royal Army would be returned to its full strength in numbers even if not in training. The rebellion hovered around 100 men, a number that would mean swift defeat against a rebuilt Royal Army and the wizards on their own turf.

"Numbers are perhaps the least of our concern." Red was seated on a hay bale in his customary reclined position, his fingers still interlaced atop his ample belly as he spoke. "This new leader is not the only one with…acquaintances he can draw into the fight. I'll send a few of my own men out after we've made plans. I can double our numbers easily, probably more. Just say the word, and tell me when and where to have them."

Jamis nodded at Red then spoke up himself, motioning toward Audon. "Master Audon is well respected among the craftsmen of the kingdom. I can travel with him to gather more troops, as well."

"That just leaves the question of logistics," Paodin said. "Master Erik, do you have any suggestions on how we should approach the castle? You know those grounds better than anyone else." "Gavin will have all entrances sealed, forcing us to the main gate. We could spend time trying to break through a different door, but we would be better served by boldly approaching the front. If our numbers can be increased as drastically as you seem to believe, we may have a chance.

"Like I've said, I know you have no reason to trust me. I believe I could be of some service gathering troops, but I won't ask you to release me on my word. Perhaps, though, you gentlemen will allow me to travel with you?" Erik turned his attention to Jamis and Audon, who looked at one another for a brief moment before nodding.

Paodin had been pleasantly surprised by the soldier's words, even grateful for his expertise in undertaking an attack on the castle, something he was sure he was not prepared for on his own. The thought of sending the former Master of the Guard off with Audon made him stiffen, though. "Are you sure, Father?" he asked, his brow furrowed. Audon simply nodded, and Paodin knew he wouldn't get any more of an answer from him. "You have been granted the trust of two great men," he said to Erik. "The Fates help you if you prove that trust to be misplaced." He added nothing else, but the warning in his words was obvious to all present. "Now," he went on, "how long do we have before we march on the castle?"

Erik considered the question for a moment before answering. "We need time to gather troops, but every day we have is one Gavin is given as well. I am thinking about a fortnight? Since we will be spreading out I believe that may give us the time we need."

"Very well. We will go through Valgrin and Saun and gather men, then we will all meet back together in two weeks," Paodin said. As all the men stood, ready to scatter to prepare to leave, Paodin added, "may the Fates preserve us all."

Audon stayed behind after everyone else left, something for which Paodin was grateful. When they were alone he asked again, "Are you sure about this, Father? We know very little about this man, and what we do know gives us very little reason to trust him. I don't like the idea of you riding off with him."

Audon clasped a hand on Paodin's shoulder. "I know you're worried, son, but I've been taking care of myself a long time. Jamis has, too--the two of us will be fine. We're taking that boy you met with us as well. Adair, I believe it is? Jamis promised the boy's mother that he would watch over him. And from what I've seen and heard of the boy, his eyes will be glued to Master Erik at all times. You focus on what you have been called to do, what you were born to do. I'll see you soon."

*********************

"From the reports coming back," Paodin told the Healer, "we will have close to 400 men when we reach the castle." People seemed to be pouring out of the woodwork to join the fight. News of what had happened in Lurn quickly spread throughout the kingdom, somehow arriving even at the far reaches of Tundyel before those gathering troops. They weren't soldiers, but they were farmers, fishermen, smithys, tradesmen--men strengthened by both their daily work and their love for the land they called home. Some had known men who had been captured by the Royal Guard and then never returned. Others had never even guessed at the atrocities carried out in the name of King Simann, which somehow made it worse. All were united in the desire to avenge the innocent people executed to casually in Lurn and those wiped out in the cities just recently remembered.

The two weeks had passed quickly, and as he led 200 men toward the castle Paodin received word from his scouts that Red had been seen approaching from the northeast with close to 100 men of his own. Jamis, Audon, and Erik came from the west with another 100 men, and they would all meet up by the time they were in sight of the castle. They had stopped for the night so the men could rest, though the thought of the next day's battle kept most from sleeping. They would rise before daybreak to march the last couple of hours, then they would be in sight of the castle.

"I fear what we will face when we reach the castle," Syndria said. "I have experienced the powers of the wizards many times, first when aimed at prisoners in the dungeon and now more recently as the target of their spells. I would feel so much better were the True Wizard with us, but despite all the people joining forces with us he has yet to show himself. The same is true of the heir-- why have they not spoken up, not come out of hiding? Wouldn't the revelation of their identities draw more people to our cause?"

"I won't insult your intelligence by pretending to understand all that has happened recently and all that is yet to come," Paodin said, his eyes never leaving the dagger in his hands or the sword laid across his lap. "Just like I don't understand these blades. No matter what I use them for or how often I try to sharpen them, their edges never change. For some reason, all of this just *is*, and nothing we do seems to change it. I suppose it falls to us simply to keep moving forward and trust that events will unfold as they should." He laughed abruptly the, startling Syndria. Looking up to see a confused expression on the Healer's face he explained, "I'm sorry, it's just that I was thinking just now that I would give almost anything to hear that grating voice of the old hermit spinning his riddles. I don't know how he does it, but somehow that old man manages to clarify things with his muddled words. Too bad he only shows up when it is convenient for him instead of when he is needed."

Syndria just smirked and shook her head ever so slightly. She didn't think she would ever understand why Paodin was so bothered by their odd friend. Something about the old man was oddly comforting to Syndria, maybe even familiar. She did share one opinion of Paodin's, though: she would give almost anything to hear his voice.

Chapter 21

As the Sons of Tundyel drew closer to the castle, walking toward the sunrise, they could feel a change in the air. Soon they were struggling to walk, as if they were wading through thick mud. Before long, the horses refused to go any further. Some threw their riders and spun, running back the way they had come. Others simply stopped, and no amount of prodding could make them move forward. Even Thrul refused Paodin's commands. Still, the men pressed forward.

Paodin found Syndria as she was dismounting her own mare. "What do you make of this, Healer? I can only assume that all our men are experiencing the same thing right now. What is this?" he asked, keeping his voice low. Despite the increase in their numbers, the rebellion still faced odds that would make even the most battle-hardened soldier cringe. Now, they were experiencing their first real taste of the opponent's might, and it was threatening to break their spirits and their ranks.

The Healer shook her head. "I have tried reaching out into the magic as I have done in the past, but I haven't accomplished anything. It is as if this is a new power, something I haven't had to face before today, and I don't know how to touch it. Although I can feel it pushing us back and slowing us down, it is as if there is no real physical presence behind it. The darkness was different--I could touch it somehow, even though I could not feel it's physical side in this world." A mirthless laugh escaped her lips when Syndria noticed the expression on Paodin's face. "I'm sorry. I know I'm making no sense to you, for I make no sense to myself on this matter. Now," she said, "you have men to lead. We are not far from the castle, but I fear things will get worse before we are even in range to be able to fight. King Simann may not have the sizable Royal Army he once had, but he does have the Wizards."

"I just hope the Prophecy holds true, and that we were not mistaken in the hugely conceited assumption that we are the two of which it speaks," Paodin said quietly.

"You cannot think that way. You have an army to lead, and we must be focused on the battle ahead. It does no good to question now." Giving him a small smile, Syndria continued, "I do not know with any certainty what we will face. I cannot tell you that there is no doubt in my mind that the Prophecy speaks of us. I can, however, tell you that what we do today will be worth the sacrifice, beyond a shadow of a doubt. No matter the outcome of today's battle, you have accomplished something great. The people of Tundyel are fighting for themselves once again, something they have not done since the end of the reign of the Rilso family. I believe in the Prophecy, and I know that what has been spoken will come to pass. Perhaps we will see it, or perhaps it is only our role to start events that will one day bring about the return of the true heir. Whatever the case, today it is our duty to fight, knowing nothing more than that we fight on the side of truth. Know that I stand alongside you."

The two were quiet then, pressing forward with the men. Despite the invisible force they struggled against, it was not long before Paodin caught his first glimpse of Castle Tundyel. It would soon begin.

\*\*\*\*\*\*\*\*\*\*\*\*\*\*\*\*\*\*\*\*\*

King Simann stood in the throne room, his sword and shield leaning against the throne in the center of the room. The rebellion had just been spotted as they approached the castle, and the king was alarmed by the number of men being reported. He walked to the window, anxiously awaiting the start of the battle. According to the reports he had been getting from the Wizards, the wards in place around the castle would stop many of the men now approaching. Those who passed through would then face his recently appointed new Master of the Guard. Gavin had quickly proven the wisdom of his appointment, gathering enough men to rival the old Royal Army in strength of numbers, at least. They had little training, but King Simann was satisfied with the progress he had seen in them thus far. Besides, standing beside the men were all the sorcerers in Tundyel. They had been training for this day for a long time, and King Simann expected to see them prove themselves. Perhaps this day would see a new Wizard added to the Order of the King's Wizards--and an old one removed.

\*\*\*\*\*\*\*\*\*\*\*\*\*\*\*\*\*\*\*\*\*\*

As planned, the rebellion stopped once they were within sight of the castle. Without horses the meeting of the leaders took longer than anticipated, but soon Paodin, Jamis, Audon, Erik, and Red were gathered together with the Healer.

Red was the first to speak. "I've lost some men," he said. "They turned back when they felt this strange magic in the air. I suppose that is for the best, though. We would not want companions who would turn away from a fight just because it got hard."

The others spoke up then. In all, the rebellion had lost nearly one hundred men. If the intelligence gathered by Erik's scout was accurate, that made the rebellion outnumbered two to one for the battle ahead, not counting the wizards and sorcerers.

Paodin was silent for a moment, looking at the men who would lead the charge on the castle and King Simann's forces. Before he spoke, he looked at the Healer. "Your words to me were true, and with your permission I would like to share them with these men." When the Healer nodded her consent, Paodin turned back to the leaders of the rebellion. "I do not know what will happen here today. Some say it is our destiny to see the true heir returned to the throne as a result of this battle. Others say the Prophecy can amount to nothing because all the True Wizards were killed. If the Fates will allow, we could be the victors here. We could wipe out Simann's army and his sorcerers and see peace come once again to Tundyel. Whatever happens, I know the Prophecy is true. I was reminded just moments before Castle Tundyel came into view that the only thing we are not sure of is our interpretation of the Prophecy. Perhaps we will see the true Rilso heir crowned at sunrise tomorrow, or perhaps we are just the men who have been given the great opportunity to start the events that will lead to such a morning. No matter which is true, we must remember that we fight on the side of Truth. Return to your men. Prepare them for this battle," he said. "At my cry, we will attack."

\*\*\*\*\*\*\*\*\*\*\*\*\*\*\*\*\*\*\*\*\*

The Master Wizard made himself comfortable in the throne room. Though he had not gone so far as to seat himself on the throne, Euroin had moved a chair of his own into a prominent position beside the marble throne. Now he addressed the Royal Wizards as if King Simann's presence was no more than an annoyance. The rebels were close now, and the battle would be starting soon.

"The wards have held. Our scouts have been bringing work throughout the night of rebel soldiers turning away," Uylti said to the Master Wizard, though his bow was directed toward the king.

King Simann gave a quick nod and opened his mouth to speak, but his jaw forcefully snapped shut before he even had time to form the first word. He turned his icy glare on the Master Wizard seated beside him, but Euroin gave him no notice.

"Were you concerned they would not?" he asked, an odd amusement in his voice. "When the rebels charge forward, have the sorcerers stop. We shall show them the calm before the storm." When Uylti did not hurry out of the throne room, the Master Wizard snapped, "Do you think I am giving you orders for my own benefit? Go!"

Uylti, torn between obeying the head of his Order and honoring the King, still hesitated. It wasn't until King Simann gave an almost imperceptible nod that the younger wizard turned to do as he was bidden. Fury flared in Euroin's eyes, and suddenly Uylti was thrown across the room where he crashed into the wall and fell in an undignified heap on the floor. He quickly scrambled to his feet and hurried out the door as the Royal Guards threw it open, swords drawn. At the calm lift of King Simann's hand and a slight tilt of his head to indicate he was alright, the guards stepped back outside and pulled the heavy door shut behind them.

\*\*\*\*\*\*\*\*\*\*\*\*\*\*\*\*\*\*\*\*\*\*

Having given the other men time to get back into position, Paodin turned to the Healer. "Mistress, are you ready?" At her nod, he gave the signal: hoisting his sword into the air, the leader of the rebellion yelled, "We are the Sons of Tundyel! Forward!"

All around him, other voices took up his call. "Sons of Tundyel!" could be heard clearly as men poured out of the tree line. No sooner had the first call been heard, the first round of arrows were flying from the castle walls. The rebellion pressed forward, though, renewed by the feeling of the oppressive weight they had felt on their approach being lifted. Soon, the clashing of swords rang out to fill the still morning air as the new Royal Army ran to meet the rebels.

One good thing about hand-to-hand combat was that it limited what action the wizards could take. Wizard's fire, though extremely powerful, was not very accurate. Though the Royal Army outnumbered the rebellion, there was not enough of a difference in numbers for even the Master

Wizard to see the benefit of releasing such power into the midst of the battle.

Syndria stood a moment, frozen in place. She had been on the battlefield at Lurn, but somehow this seemed different. The girl was afraid to step into the fray. However, when an arrow pierced the shoulder of a young man as he ran past her, the Healer forgot the fears of the girl. She quickly turned to the young man, bracing one hand against his shoulder and grabbing onto the arrow with the other. At his pained nod, the Healer pulled the arrow through. The man's cry quickly faded as the Healer's touch mended the torn flesh. A second nod, slightly deeper than the first, conveyed the young man's gratitude, then he ran forward once again.

It seemed never ending. When the Healer would finish with one man she barely had to take three steps before running across the next man who needed her help. Syndria had no time to think, let alone consider how the fight was progressing.

Paodin, in the middle of the battle, could not shake the feeling that the silence of the wizards was a bad sign. Whatever his concerns, though, he could not focus on them now. He could not stop anything the Wizards chose to do, so there was no point in worrying.

As the battle raged, it would not have taken long for an observer to see that the rebellion was driving the Royal Army back toward the castle walls. Only a few of the soldiers had been part of the battle for Lurn. The majority had been recently summoned to the castle and therefore had no fighting experience and very little training. Slowly, the Sons of Tundyel began to notice the forward progress. Spirits lifted and the men fought with renewed strength.

As darkness fell, the Sons of Tundyel were forced to fall back and regroup, having not yet breached the castle walls. As the Royal Army found shelter within the gates arrows once again began raining down, pushing the rebellion back farther. Despite the progress made during the day's fighting, they had to retreat almost back to the tree line. However, the men were still in good spirits as they set up camp.

Along with a few members of Red's staff from the Amber Stream, some of the women of Lurn had followed the rebels and had prepared massive kettles of stew. Fires roared in the night, though the Master Wizard's use of fire kept everyone cautious of the flames. The Healer made her way through the camp, healing as many as would allow her. Many men politely refused, telling her they would prefer to keep their battle scars. No matter how quickly she had moved among the men during the fight, though, bodies still littered the battlefield. The Healer moved to the edge of the camp, just past the edge of the fire glow, her ears straining to hear a cry from someone she had missed. Syndria peered into the darkness.

"You have done your part, missy. Come now--eat and rest." The voice surprised her. Syndria turned to see Red holding a small bowl out to her. She began to refuse, to say she still had work to do, but something stopped her. There was a quality in the tavern owner's voice she had never heard before, a quiet kindness she doubted many ever heard. One last look over her shoulder into the darkness made the girl realize there was nothing more for her to do on the battlefield, at least not until morning. She nodded her thanks to Red, took the bowl he offered, and followed the big man back to the warmth of the camp.

Erik sat staring into the fire, not seeing anything going on around him. The men had all taken heart from the day's battle, but Erik was bothered by it. During the fight he had noticed Gavin. The new insignia he wore denoted his status as the new Master of the Guard, a fact that did not surprise Erik. What did surprise him, though, was the apparent cool indifference with which he had approached the battle. He had not joined the fight, which in itself was strange enough. Instead, he had remained mounted on his big stallion at the rear of what was now his army. Erik had watched as his former second in command had slowly moved back with his men. As he sat in the calm of the cool night, his face warmed by the fire into which he stared, Erik was able to think more clearly about what he had seen, and the conclusion he came to put a rock in the pit of his stomach. The Royal Army had not been pushed back. They had been slowly drawing the rebellion in. Why, he couldn't say, but Erik had no doubt that Gavin had been guiding the rebellion into some kind of trap. Though he had nothing but a feeling telling him something was wrong, Erik looked around for Paodin. Even if it didn't amount to anything, he had to tell him the rebels needed to be on guard.

The first person Erik found was the Healer. She was sitting quietly, picking at a bowl of food. As he approached, Erik saw her gaze repeatedly being drawn back toward the castle. At first he thought she must be nervous, being so close again, but then he realized that it wasn't the castle she was looking at. The lights from the castle were not in her line of sight--her gaze fell instead on the dark battlefield. He could see her trying to search the darkness.

"Mistress, if I may?" he asked, motioning to the ground beside her. Though she had startled at the sound of his voice when Erik spoke from beside her, the Healer quickly regained her composure. Sitting her bowl aside, the Healer motioned for Erik to sit.

"Master Erik, I am glad to see you are well," she said. "I am also glad you did not require my assistance in today's battle."

"So am I, though I wish more could say the same thing. The rebellion was hit hard today."

Syndria nodded, then watched as Erik's expression changed. Though his words fit the conversation, it was obvious his thoughts were elsewhere. She did not want to push, though. He had sought her out; he would speak when he was ready. For a while the two listened to the low voices of the men mingling with the night sounds. The peaceful combination almost made it possible to forget the events of the day. Syndria considered making small talk as the silence continued, but only briefly. The Master of the Guard had something on his mind, and the Healer decided that pointless conversation would serve no purpose other than allowing him to put serious conversation off further. Eventually, the sounds of crickets and frogs won out over the voices of men, and that was when Erik finally spoke.

"Mistress, there may be nothing to my thoughts, but I'm not sure. My instincts are telling me to be cautious of Gavin, the man who now serves as Master of the Guard. It may be nothing, but could I ask your opinion on what I think I saw?"

"It is my experience that one should always trust his instincts, Master Erik," the Healer said, "especially when they warn of danger. However, I would be happy to listen, though there are many who are better suited to decisions of warfare." The push was subtle, but Erik heard it. Despite his acceptance by the leaders of the rebellion, though, Erik felt more comfortable sharing his concerns with the Healer he had known before life had taken such a different turn, one that now had him attacking Castle Tundyel and the Royal Army.

"All I ask is your opinion, and then I will speak to Paodin if you do not think I am merely imagining." Erik went on to explain what he had seen and his fears that Gavin was setting a trap, perhaps leading the rebellion into something involving the wizards. He knew all the sorcerers and minor wizards of the kingdom had been summoned to Castel Tundyel, and he shared that with the Healer as well.

When he stopped speaking, Syndria was quiet for a moment. Finally, she asked, "How well do you know Gavin, the man whose actions concern you?"

"We joined the Royal Guard together twenty years ago, and he has been my most trusted friend and advisor since that time."

"Come," Syndria said, standing. "We need to find Paodin."

\*\*\*\*\*\*\*\*\*\*\*\*\*\*\*\*\*\*\*\*\*\*

All was quiet in the castle, except in King Simann's chambers. There, the king was meeting with Uylti and the Master of the Guard. The Master Wizard had set up what appeared to be permanent residence in the throne room, and since he had no desire for Euroin's presence at this meeting, the King had quietly summoned these two to his quarters.

"The rebels do believe in their cause, that much must be said," the King said.

"Yes," answered Gavin, "but so far that is playing to our advantage. Their moral assuredness is giving them a false sense of security. Even with their Healer on the battlefield, they are falling every moment. They see our numbers fall and seem to forget that we have three Healers within our walls. They push forward without realizing they are being drawn."

Nodding, King Simann turned to the young wizard. "And Master Uylti, are your ranks prepared for once the rebels breech our walls?"

"Yes, my King." Uylti's voice was shaky as he addressed King Simann. "They have been well trained and will not disappoint."

"I should hope not, Wizard, since our victory is so dependent on their skills." Then, addressing both men, he asked quietly, "What news is there of the Master Wizard?"

Both were silent, for though each man knew what his king wished to hear, neither could honestly offer an answer he would like. The truth was, Master Euroin seemingly grew stronger and more volatile by the hour. He regularly stole away to the North Tower, and each time he returned with eyes a little more wild and a temper a bit more easily set off. Even together, the Royal Wizards had very little chance of controlling him. Uylti also knew that even were there more of a chance, he would never get another of the Order to turn against Master Euroin--they were all too scared of the new, unknown power he possessed. Master Euroin was untamable, and Uylti feared for the King's life once this rebellion ended.

And after meetings such as this, he feared for his own.

\*\*\*\*\*\*\*\*\*\*\*\*\*\*\*\*\*\*\*\*\*\*

They found Paodin and Audon together. Jamis was organizing the patrols for the night, given the experience, however odd, he had gained while sneaking around Lady Brigitte's farm at night over the years. Red was snoring soundly from a tent pitched next to the grub wagon. The two men stood when they saw the Healer approach, each bowing his head to her in silent acknowledgement of her position.

It didn't take long for Erik to explain his thoughts to the two men, and even less time was needed for them to decide to call together all the leaders of the rebellion. Erik's fears made sense--it had seemed too good to be true when the wards and spells that had pressed against the approaching rebel army had been suddenly removed. If all the wizards of the kingdom were within the walls of Castle Tundyel, the battle would change dramatically once the Sons of Tundyel passed through the gates. At the same time, though, inside the castle was where they would find King Simann. They had to push through. How, though, can an army enter a trap without being trapped?

That was the question they were all asking, yet none could answer. Eventually, the general consensus was that they should delay. If they could somehow hold back in the battle instead of being drawn forward, they could buy some time to think of a plan.

Chapter 22

The Master Wizard did not return to the
throne room early the next morning when everyone
else did. He had gone up to the North Tower
immediately after hearing reports of the day's
battle the night before, and no one had seen him
return. He was not present for the morning meal,
nor did he appear for the briefing. The Wizards all
agreed that someone should go up to the tower
after him, but no one volunteered to be the
someone. Osidius, being the newest member of the
Order and therefore the one with the least
seniority, was chosen.

The marble staircase which climbed up the
tower was naturally cool, but it grew colder as
Osidius approached the door at the top. At the
threshold, he could see his breath. That cold,
however, could not compare with the chill that
went through his body when he silently opened the
door.

Euroin stood in the center of the room, his
arms outstretched and body still as a statue. His
cloak, however, snapped around him, cracking like
a whip amidst the strange lights and colors swirling
through the air. Though it made no logical sense
even when the thought occurred to him, Osidius
could only describe the lights as being full of
darkness. A sound so low that it was felt more than
heard filled the marble room, and Osidius could

feel it shaking his very core. He couldn't move, couldn't take his eyes off the strangely mesmerizing sight before him.

Suddenly, Euroin was right in front of Osidius. It happened in the blink of an eye, and Osidius was so startled it knocked him off balance and he started to fall backward down the long stairway. An icy hand shot forward and caught him by the collar, pulling Osidius back to his feet.

"We couldn't have our closest equal meeting his end in such a manner, now could we?" The voice was emotionless, though the comment itself seemed a thinly veiled threat. The Master Wizard's eyes were completely black and seemed to look at the other Wizard without actually seeing him. In fact, looking into those eyes Osidius believed that the Master Wizard saw nothing.

As quickly as he had appeared before Osidius and then caught him, the Master Wizard sat Osidius aside and glided down the staircase, leaving the other wizard standing in silence at the top. Once Euroin was gone, Osidius once again peered through the doorway.

Most of the marble in the room was cracked, and the walls appeared to have been smashed. Remnants of a dark power still lingered in the air, leaving Osidius with no desire to actually step inside. Whatever evil had been created in this room when the True Wizards had been killed seemed to have found a welcoming host in Euroin. In fact, the Master Wizard did not even appear to be playing host any longer. That evil, that darkness, seemed to have taken over.

As he made his way back to the throne room, Osidius had only one question on his mind. What had Euroin released?

*********************

The next two days' battles went as planned for the rebellion. They were able to fight without significantly closing any distance between the front line and Castle Tundyel, and by dusk each night they would fall back once again to make camp. Jamis organized the night patrols, then made his way to Paodin's tent to join the planning. A few hours into the discussion, it was obvious no one had any new ideas.

They had all agreed that Erik's instincts seemed right. The new Master of the Guard had seemed frustrated that the rebels were not pushing forward, a strange reaction from an enemy under normal circumstances. The Royal Army had seemed hesitant as well, striking and then drawing back instead of pushing the rebels farther from the castle walls. What wasn't obvious, however, was what to do with this knowledge.

"There seems to be very little being said, for all the talking going on."

Hands all around moved quickly to swords,

but before anyone could react further the Healer stood and extended her hand, smiling. "Do not worry--he is a friend," she said, drawing the old man into the light. When Audon looked to his son for confirmation of the Healer's words, he almost laughed aloud. The look he saw on Paodin's face was one he had seen often throughout the young man's teen years, one of exasperation and barely disguised disdain.

"Masters," Syndria said, "I would not be here tonight were it not for this man."

"I owe you much then, friend," Jamis said, clasping the old man's hand. "Although, I must admit I am troubled by your presence, for apparently you passed by our patrols without incident or notice."

The gravelly voice replied, "Young men know a harmless old fool when they see one." His eyes twinkled and he glanced at Paodin. He was greeted with a roll of the eyes, which drew a loud snort of amusement from Audon. The old man turned back to Syndria then and continued, "Your favor does my heart well, Mistress, but I must confess that I had very little to do with your magnificent recovery."

"That is not all I spoke of, friend," she smiled.

"Now," the hermit said, turning quickly back toward the leaders of the rebellion. "As I mentioned, you men are talking a lot about nothing. Is it not time to take action? Or have you led these men here only to have them back down?"

His words made defenses go up all around, yet no one spoke against him. He was, after all, seen as a friend by the Healer.

And, he spoke the truth.

It was Paodin who spoke up. "And I suppose you know what we should do, old man?" At the tone of that comment Audon narrowed his eyes at his son, and Paodin sat back and crossed his arms.

"Of course!" grinned the old man. "You take the castle!"

Though his answer drew laughter from all the men before him, it quickly became obvious he meant what he said. Then, ignoring everyone else, the old hermit stepped in front of Paodin, leaning almost nose to nose with the young man.

"What does the Prophecy say?"

Paodin sighed. "I know the Prophecy, but-"

What does it say, young man? I did not ask if you knew it. If you didn't know it, I wouldn't ask you what it says!" Some of the men chuckled, but Paodin rolled his eyes again.

He didn't know why, but this old man really got to him. He didn't want to answer; he wanted to see if, for once, he could outwait the strange old man. He knew, though, that his father would frown on that. Paodin had been taught to respect his elders, and he supposed that courtesy extended to the crazy ones, too. So, without leaning away from the old man or breaking his gaze, he quoted,

"Bound by nature's strength and frailty,

Though two, as one in unity,
Shall true heir of Tundyel make
And by the Truth the throne room take."

"Exactly!" The old man smiled, clapping his gnarled hands together. "And do you fight for Truth?"

"Well, yes, but-"

"And are you and she still united?"

"Yes, of course."

"Then it is simple," he beamed, spinning nimbly around to face everyone again. "You take the throne room!"

\*\*\*\*\*\*\*\*\*\*\*\*\*\*\*\*\*\*\*\*\*\*

"My King," the Master of the Guard said, "the rebels have not pushed forward as we had planned. Your former Master of the Guard, the traitor Erik, must somehow have figured out they would be walking into a trap if they advanced to within our walls." Gavin glanced at the Master Wizard, unnerved by his silence. The wizard had been that way since his return from the North

Tower. He sat deathly still, not even blinking. Were it not for his steady, slow breathing and the movement of his now black eyes to stare through whoever was speaking, everyone in the throne room would have thought him dead.

"Your friend is a traitor, but he is also a well-trained soldier," King Simann said, ignoring his Master of the Guard's glance toward the Master Wizard. "I am not surprised that he has seen through your strategy. And seeing as how I appointed him over you, I would be disappointed had he not."

"Yes, my King," Gavin said, bowing his head in acknowledgement.

King Simann turned his attention to Uylti. "Wizard, are your sorcerers in possession of enough talent to change to an attack?"

Uylti could feel the Master Wizard's eyes boring into him, yet he did not take his eyes off King Simann. "That would mean the collapse of many of the wards surrounding your throne room, my King, but they are capable of moving on the rebels."

"Good. At dawn we attack. This rebellion ends tomorrow."

Later that night, Simann was pulled from his thoughts by a knock at the door of his chambers. "My King," Gavin said, bowing deeply as he stepped into the room, "the Master Uylti requested an audience with you."

King Simann had retired to his room two hours before and his Healers had already come and gone. Despite the late hour, though, he could not sleep. "Bring him in," he said. As the wizard entered the room, bowing deeply at the waist, King Simann sighed lightly. "No need to stand on formality, Wizard," he said. "Stand and approach."

Uylti bowed deeper still before standing, then moved forward. The King stood by the window where he had been looking out to the fires in the distant tree line. Now he turned fully toward the Wizard, still imposing even in his bed robe.

"My King," Uylti began hesitantly, "I am sure you have noticed the... changes evident in the Master Wizard of late." At King Simann's slight nod, he continued. "His power has evolved somehow, becoming something the Order does not recognize. In fact, we fear it. And now, I fear for your life," he said bluntly.

"The Master Wizard would not dare oppose me," King Simann said, straightening his shoulders. "I am his king." Uylti shrank back slightly at the statement, not wanting to argue with the king.

"Forgive me if I speak out of turn, Sire," the Master of the Guard said, bowing as he stepped forward, "but perhaps the Wizard speaks truly. This is, after all, a matter of magic. May the Fates prevent it, but if there is the slightest chance the Master Wizard wishes you ill, I pray you heed Master Uylti's warning."

King Simann studied the two for a long moment, then said, "Very well. Master Uylti, as the battle draws to an end tomorrow, I will expect you by my side. You as well, Master Gavin."

Uylti just bowed in acknowledgement, then hurried out the door at the flick of the King's hand.

\*\*\*\*\*\*\*\*\*\*\*\*\*\*\*\*\*\*\*\*\*\*\*

King Simann, seated on his throne in the royal robes, studied the men before him in the light from the sconces lining the walls. As they prepared for battle, the Royal Wizards and the Master of the Guard waited for final orders. He noticed that some of the Wizards stole glances at the Master Wizard, but Euroin did not return their gazes. As had been the case lately, his black eyes stared straight ahead, seemingly unseeing until someone spoke. A chill crept up Simann's spine, threatening to make his body betray the uneasy feeling the Master Wizard's very presence caused him, but the King suppressed the shiver by speaking.

"Today, we will put an end to this rebellion. The Royal Army has not been able to draw the rebels into the clutches of the wizards you have been training, so instead you will lead the wizards to the battlefield. Master Gavin, relay final orders to your next in command and then return to my side. Your presence will not be required on the field today." The Master of the Guard nodded, then left when King Simann gave a dismissive flick of his hand. At the order, Uylti was relieved to know the King was at least taking the threat from the Master Wizard seriously, though the Master of the Guard would be no real opposition for the Wizard.

King Simann caught Uylti's eye for a moment, and the Wizard thought he would request he stay behind as well. Instead, the king said, "The rest of you, take your positions with the wizards you have trained. I expect a quick resolution today, and then you will report once again to my side. The Royal Army will deal with the clean up." With that he dismissed them, but the Master Wizard did not move.

"Master Euroin," Uylti began quietly, "will you be joining us?"

The Master Wizard's eyes fixed on Uylti, narrowed, then went back to staring straight ahead. As the Royal Wizards left the throne room, King Simann made his way to the window, putting some distance between he and the Wizard. Once there, though, his unease only grew--he could feel the Wizard's black eyes boring into him.

Chapter 23

In the predawn darkness, the rebellion gathered around Paodin and the Healer. She stood once again in her white gown, a gift brought to her by the old hermit and given to her as he left the camp, though he would not say how it came into his possession. The men were quiet, waiting to hear the plan.

"Today," Paodin said, his voice strong in the stillness, "we do not hold back. I brought you here to take the castle, but for the last two days I have been hesitant and unsure of our next move. For that, I apologize. You are here to fight. Today, we take the castle." His speech was met by cheers that spread in a wave across the men. "It is my honor today to fight alongside you, my brothers. Today, the Sons of Tundyel will once again stand inside the castle. For Tundyel!"

"For Tundyel!" the men echoed, their voices rising with the sun.

Then they crashed through the trees onto the battlefield once again, weapons raised and a war cry on their lips as they ran toward the castle.

\*\*\*\*\*\*\*\*\*\*\*\*\*\*\*\*\*\*\*\*\*

The Royal Army filed out of the gate and fell into line, but they did not rush forward to meet the rebels. Nor did arrows fly to rain down on the approaching force. Instead, an eerie calm lay over the castle. As the rebels drew closer, the ranks split and the Royal Wizards stepped forward, two dozen sorcerers and minor wizards following. The Royal Wizards raised their hands, and the rebellion stopped.

It was as if they had suddenly hit a wall. But not only could they not move forward, they couldn't retreat. Every man was frozen in his tracks, helpless to do anything but watch as the sorcerers standing behind the Royal Wizards began moving their hands, small sparks beginning to form between their palms.

Syndria stopped, too, but not because her steps were halted by the Royal Wizards' spells. She was shaken by the fear that had suddenly replaced the utter determination seen on the face of each man just a moment earlier. She could understand the change--they had come here willing to give their lives in battle, but not to be slaughtered by Wizard's fire--but understanding did not make it easier to take. For a moment, the girl considered turning away. The sorcerers were not very powerful, so it would take some time for them to all summon the Wizard's fire. Syndria took one small step backward, but then her eye caught on Paodin.

He stood at the front of the Sons of Tundyel, staring straight at the Royal Wizards. As she watched, his shoulders straightened a bit more and then his voice rang out. "We are here for all the citizens of this kingdom who were not given a chance to fight for themselves. Stand strong, men, for we are on the side of Truth. We are the Sons of Tundyel!"

As the men roared in answer, Syndria took a deep breath. The first time she had met Paodin, he was making a stand in a dark, damp cell, determined to stand strong until his last breath was breathed. Now, here he stood a second time, at the end of a journey which had led him full circle and once again had him standing before those same captors. The Prophecy spoke of two, and it was very clear to Syndria that she and Paodin were linked together. She could run, but what would that accomplish? She would be pursued relentlessly, the only witness to an event that would undoubtedly be erased as effectively as had the ruined cities. For that matter, those cities would once again be hidden, their occupants again wiped from the memories of those who had loved them years ago. Lurn, the home of her childhood, would likely join them, she realized with a start. There might be nothing she could do, but she would not run. Her place was beside Paodin, and that was where she now made her way to, to stand.

From her place beside the leader of the rebellion, the Healer closed her eyes. She could immediately feel the wall. It wasn't like the darkness--this did not have that same sinister, malevolent feeling. This felt instead like when she had come across the ruins of Otarius. This time, though, the pain was not a shock. That was one thing that could be said for the darkness; it made this sensation little more than an annoyance. The Healer raised her hands to the invisible wall and began drawing the power into herself.

The Royal Wizards were shocked when they felt their spell begin to weaken. Uylti glanced behind him, anxious to see the progress being made by the sorcerers and minor wizards who were preparing Wizard's fire. The glowing orbs in their hands gave him a boost of confidence. The young Healer was somehow managing to draw power away from the holding spell, but she would not be able to withstand the sudden onslaught of fire. This would all be over soon, and things in the kingdom would return to some semblance of normalcy.

\*\*\*\*\*\*\*\*\*\*\*\*\*\*\*\*\*\*\*\*\*

King Simann watched from the window in the throne room. It had been strange to see all the men of the rebellion stop as if frozen in place, stranger still to see the young girl move through the men to stand at the front. Now he watched with a growing sense of wonder as the rebels slowly began moving again, able to press forward to where the girl stood with her eyes closed and hands outstretched. Glancing over his shoulder, King Simann wondered what the Master Wizard's reaction would be to this strange turn of events. The Wizard, though, remained as before--seated in a chair beside the throne, unmoving.

\*\*\*\*\*\*\*\*\*\*\*\*\*\*\*\*\*\*\*\*\*\*

"One of us should stop her," Ilcren said, glancing around quickly at the other Royal Wizards. "Master Osidius, we can hold the wall. You go forward and see what you can do." The others nodded in agreement.

"Should we not just wait on the Wizard's fire?" Osidius asked. "Surely the girl can do nothing to stand against it, and then these rebels will no longer be a threat."

"Go. You would not want Master Euroin to have a reason to believe you did not do all you could to end this if something were to go awry," Uylti said.

Osidius glanced at the others, then dropped his hands and stepped toward the girl. As he moved closer, he began searching the air around her for some hint of the magic she was using. He was also constantly aware of the sorcerers behind him, ready to create a ward around himself when they let loose the fire. Stopping directly in front of the girl, he spoke one word in a voice so low only she could hear.

"Mistress."

\*\*\*\*\*\*\*\*\*\*\*\*\*\*\*\*\*\*\*\*\*\*

Syndria's eyes flew open, and the men

around her once again found themselves suddenly unable to move. She stared at the Wizard in front of her, an odd expression on her face. Paodin glanced from the Healer to the Royal Wizard and back again, trying to determine what was happening, but he was at a loss. As he studied her, though, a small smile began to creep across her face. The he heard her whisper, and the words rang loud as a cymbal in his head.

"We've found the Truth."

He didn't have time to contemplate her words, though. A scream caught in his throat as Paodin looked back toward the castle. Wizard's fire was flying through the air toward them.

Osidius spun as the Healer's hands shot up. With one swift wave of the wizard's hand, the fires fizzled out in midair. Then the Wizard touched one hand to the Healer's, and after only a moment the ?Sons of Tundyel were free to move forward. With a roar, they all crashed toward the wizards.

Seeing that the magic attempt hadn't worked, the Royal Army began running through the gate to meet the rebellion. A wave of Osidius's free hand sent them crashing to the ground and the minor wizards and sorcerers scattered. The Royal Wizards stood their ground, sending whatever spells they could conjure forward, but their attacks were absorbed by the young Healer and Master Osidius.

Suddenly from inside the castle came a sound like nothing anyone had ever heard. Full of rage and a burning hatred, the roar filled the air as if it were a thick fog. The men of the rebellion were knocked back and the Royal Wizards were thrown out of the way as Euroin stormed through the gate, his cloak swirling all around him. As he moved forward, those close by were knocked to the ground. He threw his hand up, the yell still filling the air, changing to a hiss as he spoke.

"So, you have chosen to reveal yourself," he said, his black eyes staring at Osidius. Raising his voice, he somehow spoke loud enough for everyone to hear. "You have given them their 'True Wizard.'" he sneered, "But the throne room belongs to us. We have already cleared it of its last occupant." Master Euroin's laugh somehow echoed in the clearing. Then a flick of his fingers sent the rest of the rebellion to the ground, leaving only Osidius and Syndria standing, their palms pressing one against the other.

To the men looking on, not much was happening. The Royal Wizards, though, watched in fearful amazement as a terrible battle raged before them. Terrible colors swirled around the Master Wizard, colors none of them had ever seen, striking out ferociously at the two standing their ground in front of him. As they watched, it became more and more obvious that Euroin was merely toying with the True Wizard and Healer, who were struggling to defend themselves against the powerful magic. The attacks Osidius was able to make were brushed aside as easily as one would bat away a gnat. Nothing was touching the Master Wizard.

Paodin watched the silent battle before him, desperate for some way to help. He could see that both the Wizard and Syndria were quickly tiring, yet the Master Wizard appeared to be expending no energy. They had come all this way and found the True Wizard in the midst of the enemy, though that fact still confused him. He knew the Prophecy had to be true, especially now, and that meant there had to be some way for him to help. What could he do, though? When the Master Wizard had knocked them all to the ground, Paodin was struck with intense pain. Every inch of his body screamed out for him to just be still, to lay motionless on the ground so he wouldn't hurt so much.

As he watched, Paodin realized with astonishment that he was seeing a familiar foe. It was hard to see at first, but once he saw the Shadow around the Master Wizard it became obvious. Remembering his fight in the woods, Paodin fought through the pain and slowly began creeping toward Euroin. Glancing at Osidius and Syndria, he hoped they could hold their own long enough for him to close the distance between himself and the Master Wizard. When he looked back at Euroin, though, Paodin could see that he was quickly growing bored. There wasn't much time.

"Fates be with us," he whispered, then summoning every ounce of strength he still possessed he stood and sprinted forward.

Master Euroin saw the young traitor running toward him and laughed. What did he expect to be able to do? If the last True Wizard could do nothing, what made this mere boy think he could succeed? His right hand still held out toward the two who were feebly trying to stand against him on a magical level, Master Euroin raised his left hand toward Paodin.

At that moment, a blinding light shone around the young leader of the rebellion. Gold and silver mingled in the white light, dancing through the air around Paodin. The Master Wizard hissed, his hand stopping before it was fully outstretched. He was blinded by the brilliant light moving toward him. Then, with a yell, Paodin burst forward. As he reached the Master Wizard, he swept the small dagger from its sheath.

The Master Wizard spun quickly, both hands flying out toward Paodin. His action didn't stop the young man, though, and he could do nothing more than watch as Paodin dove forward, the dagger reflecting a light to rival the brilliant white light. Master Euroin started to laugh, though, as he saw Paodin fall to the ground behind him. He had missed--the Master Wizard had not felt even a scratch from the dagger.

Before the laugh could escape his lips, a terrible scream filled the air. As in the forest, Paodin's dagger had pierced the Shadow, and now it dissolved like smoke into the air.

As the Shadow dissipated, Syndria saw the darkness retreat. She watched as the True Wizard shot his hand forward, and Master Euroin fell to the ground. Then, as quickly as it had appeared, the light was gone.

The clearing was silent. Though the Sons of Tundyel and the Royal Army had not been able to see the extent of the magical battle raging before them, they had seen the blinding light, heard the blood-curdling scream from the Shadow, and seen the Master Wizard fall. None were anxious to see what might happen next, and all were in near agony after the Master Wizard's entrance onto the battlefield.

It was the Healer who made the first move, slowly walking toward Paodin. She offered her hand and he took it, slowly standing. Every part of his body protested the movement, but Paodin knew every eye was on them. He couldn't let Syndria look to be the strong one, could he?

The two walked slowly through the gates of

Castle Tundyel, the True Wizard following close behind. As they approached the throne room entrance they saw guards lying dead by the door. Paodin drew his sword, though he was sure he would not need it. When the three stepped inside, they saw King Simann crumpled on the floor beneath the window. His body was twisted and broken, as if it had been caught up in a whirlwind. Beside him lay Master Gavin, his hand still on the hilt of his sword which was partially drawn from its scabbard. It was obvious the Master Wizard had disposed of them before storming out to join the battle.

Paodin was relieved. Enough had died at his hand. He was glad Simann was gone, but equally glad he had not been the one to take the man's life.

Seeing there was nothing to be done in the throne room for the moment, the Healer spoke. "I must return to the battlefield. Send for the other Healers--they will be waiting in their chambers. There will be many who need our help," she said, then bowed her head to Paodin and Master Osidius before leaving the room. Once back on the battlefield, Syndria was greeted with a familiar face.

"Mistress!" Magen called, her voice full of awe. "I just knew I would see you again, despite what everyone said!"

Syndria gave the girl a brief smile. "Magen, I am glad to see you are well. It seems as if it has been a lifetime since I last saw you. Forgive me, but I cannot speak with you now. Perhaps we can find one another later?"

"Of course," the girl answered cheerfully, "but I came to help. I was watching from the wall, and as soon as I saw that things had ended I hurried down. I can bind wounds or offer water or something," she said.

Syndria shook her head slightly in amusement. No matter what had changed in the past few weeks, Magen was still the same. Nodding, she motioned for the girl to follow. As the two knelt by the first man, the Healer noticed a change come over the girl. Placing her hands on the man, she began to draw his pain into herself as Magen smoothed his brow. The Healer felt something strange, like a competing power. Curious, she pulled back and looked over at Magen. The girl seemed completely unaware of what was happening, but the man on the ground could definitely tell. The girl was a Healer, and her gift was being revealed right there on the battlefield without a life-threatening injury to initiate it.

Apparently she had been wrong. Not even Magen has stayed the same. The girl grinned at Syndria, her excitement and amazement visible, then moved on to help another injured man with her newly found gift.

After a while, Paodin and Master Osidius returned to the battlefield with the other Healers. Paodin made his way to Syndria, a curious look on his face.

"Have you seen the Master Wizard?" he asked, scanning the battlefield once again.

The Healer finished with the man before her, then stood. "Though I haven't been looking for him, I haven't seen Master Euroin either. Have you checked with the Royal Wizards?"

"Master Osidius is with them now. I'm sorry--I won't bother you. I know there are many who need your assistance. Please let me know if I can do anything," he said, then bowed slightly and moved away, his eyes once again searching the battlefield for the Master Wizard.

It took the entire day for the Healers to help all the men and for them to all be gathered into the barracks under the guard of Master Erik and the newly formed core of the Sons of Tundyel. Throughout it all, though, the Master Wizard was never found.

\*\*\*\*\*\*\*\*\*\*\*\*\*\*\*\*\*\*\*\*\*\*

The Royal Court had been summoned to the castle, and Erik had instructed the Sons of Tundyel to be on guard. The Council would likely not take well to Simann's death, though the True

Wizard's presence would go far in persuading them to assemble peacefully. With the death of King Simann, the throne was left empty. He had no heir, and he personally had seen to the end of the Rilso line. Master Erik's biggest fear now was that the members of the Council would begin vying for the title themselves. Though the defeat of King Simann, Master Euroin, and the former Royal Army by a newly restored rank of the Sons of Tundyel had gone a long way in promoting faith in the Prophecy, power was a strange creature. In the quest for it, men would often do the unthinkable.

Paodin and Syndria were in the throne room with Master Osidius. The True Wizard had called them there, but he refused to answer their many questions. The only answer he would give was to quote the Prophecy.

It was that alone that made Paodin finally realize what Syndria had known on the battlefield.

"You're that crazy old man!"

The Wizard's blue eyes twinkled as a smile lit up his face.

"Did he tell you?" Paodin asked, turning to Syndria. "Is that how you knew that morning on the battlefield? And why am I just now finding out?"

"Some things are more fully understood when one learns them in their own time." The Wizard's voice took on a familiar gravelly tone as he went on, "And why should she have told you if you were too dense and stubborn to find out on your own?"

Syndria, laughing at Paodin's scowl, smiled at Master Osidius. "It was his eyes," she said. "When we were face to face, I recognized the kindness there."

The three fell silent then as the Council began to file in. Syndria was thrilled to see Lady Tamara joining all the Councilmen, but her happiness over seeing a friendly face was quickly replaced by pain at the realization that Tamara was filling her husband's seat. She felt tears filling her eyes, knowing Sir Lawrence had likely died for helping her, but she blinked them away. Today, she faced the Council as a Healer. In such strained circumstances it would not do to show weakness.

Once the Council was seated and the doors were shut, Osidius stood to speak. As he stepped up in front of the throne, gold and silver light began circling him. Alarmed enough at that development, the members of the Council were visibly shaken when voices spoke out of the swirling lights.

"*We are Truth,*" they said, three voices speaking in unison. "*Our brother stands before you. Hear his words and hear us.*"

When Osidius began to speak, his voice was somehow different, almost musical. Despite his feelings toward the old hermit, Paodin was mesmerized by the strange quality. No one on the Council took their eyes away from the True Wizard as he spoke.

"A king was slain in this room just days ago. An unjust and illegitimate king, but a king none the less. His death came at the hand of the man who had been serving as Master Wizard, a man who brought much darkness into the kingdom through the release of a power he did not understand, nor could he control. That man was defeated in battle, but then vanished. The battle against the darkness is only just beginning."

This brought a few murmurs from the Councilmen, but Osidius paused only long enough to let them quiet down before he spoke again. "You have heard from my brothers; you know who I am. Therefore, you know that what I say to you is the Truth. You know the Prophecy, that two will be as one in purpose, and through the Truth they will see the true heir returned to the throne. I am here to tell you that today, that Prophecy is fulfilled." This time, only stunned silence filled the pause. No member of the Council dared speak for fear of missing even the smallest syllable of whatever came next. The True Wizard stepped to the throne and lifted the crown from the seat. When he raised it high above his head, he was suddenly transformed.

For a moment, Paodin saw the old hermit before him, clothes torn and hair dirty. That visage was quickly replaced, however, by a face that had no equal. The gold and silver lights that had been dancing around Osidius converged, making the True Wizard's skin glow an other worldly color. His face was somehow changing constantly, revealing three other faces in turn. When he spoke again, it was a chorus of four voices at once.

*"The Princess Ladriel gave birth to twins, the last of the Rilso line. The Ancient Healer Nedra was witness to their birth. Draining the life from the two tiny babes, the Ancient took them from their mother and revealed the two still bundles to King Simann. He ordered their mother killed and the small bodies disposed of, marking the end of the Rilso family. Though the Ancient could do nothing for the mother, she did not dispose of the infant twins.*

*"When she drained their lives, the Ancient left a spark of life in each babe. These she restored to full fire, then sent the infants to our brother Osidius. He took each child to a different man of Tundyel, good men who would raise the babies to respect the old ways and to love Tundyel's citizens. With each child was a token to prove the infant's identity."*

It was obvious that those in the room were in no way prepared for what they were hearing, but none present could doubt the testimony of the True Wizards. They sat in stunned silence, waiting.

The True Wizards continued. *"Here, before the Council, the heir to the throne is revealed."* The gold and silver lights shot out, swirling around the ring on Paodin's finger and making it glow with the same brilliant light as had his dagger. *"This is your king, the last son of Rilso. And behold the Healer, your queen."* The light spread to Syndria's bracelet as well.

Lady Tamara was the first to react. Standing, she bowed low to Paodin and Syndria before the Council. "Your Majesties." Slowly, one by one, the Councilmen stood and followed suit. Bowing his head in return, Paodin stepped forward at Syndria's slight nod.

Stepping up to the throne, Paodin took a deep breath. The gold and silver spreading to envelope his entire body and the True Wizards guiding him, Paodin took his seat on the throne.

Paodin, the last son of Rilso, was crowned King of Tundyel.

23572458R00266

Made in the USA
Lexington, KY
15 June 2013